$+$ $=2$

$25.95

CUSTER'S CAVALIER

A JOHN WHYTE NOVEL OF THE
AMERICAN WEST

CUSTER'S CAVALIER

THOM NICHOLSON

FIVE STAR
A part of Gale, Cengage Learning

GALE
CENGAGE Learning®

Farmington Hills, Mich • San Francisco • New York • Waterville, Maine
Meriden, Conn • Mason, Ohio • Chicago

LIBRARY OF CONGRESS CATALOGING-IN-PUBLICATION DATA

Nicholson, Thom.
  Custer's cavalier / Thom Nicholson. — First edition.
    pages ; cm. — (A John Whyte novel of the American West)
  ISBN 978-1-4328-3140-0 (hardcover) — ISBN 1-4328-3140-2 (hardcover) — ISBN 978-1-4328-3152-3 (ebook) — ISBN 1-4328-3152-6 (ebook)
    1. United States—History—Civil War, 1861–1865—Fiction. I. Title.
  PS3614.I3535C87 2015
  813'.6—dc23   2015025248

First Edition. First Printing: December 2015
Find us on Facebook– https://www.facebook.com/FiveStarCengage
Visit our website– http://www.gale.cengage.com/fivestar/
Contact Five Star™ Publishing at FiveStar@cengage.com

Printed in the United States of America
1 2 3 4 5 6 7 19 18 17 16 15

CUSTER'S CAVALIER

Chapter 1

"Why am I always the last to get the word?" grumbled Lieutenant Colonel John Whyte, the commander of the Fifth Michigan Cavalry Regiment, US Army of the Potomac, as he hurried to the headquarters tent of the Second Brigade, pulling on his blue blouse while running across the muddy road. He could see from the tethered horses outside the tent that the other three regimental commanders of the brigade, the famed Michigan Brigade, had already arrived at General Kilpatrick's headquarters. John had felt the lash of the mercurial brigade commander's tongue in the past, and certainly did not need another today for arriving late at a staff meeting. He'd been in his tent asleep, exhausted after forty-eight hours of hard riding with his command on a fruitless patrol to find JEB Stuart's Confederate Cavalry, which had disappeared somewhere behind the Blue Ridge Mountains.

Lee's gray-clad veterans were on the march, somewhere to the north, hidden behind the cavalry screen of JEB Stuart's famed Confederate Cavalry Corps. Every Union cavalry command available had been in the saddle for the past week, desperately trying to gather any information, no matter how scant, as to the intentions of the dreaded Army of Northern Virginia and its feared commander, Robert E. Lee.

"Ah, Colonel Whyte. You're the last to arrive, I believe. Now, we can begin." Brigadier General Kilpatrick's tone of voice expressed enough sarcasm to reveal that he was annoyed at

7

John's tardiness. Still, Kilpatrick's face reflected a deep satisfaction about something—what, John did not know.

John bristled at Kilpatrick's rebuke, but he bit his tongue and joined the other commanders facing their jointly disliked commander. Kilpatrick was intensely vain and John knew he did not want to make more of an enemy of him than he already had. Kilpatrick could not forgive John for his personal friendship and patronage of President Lincoln. Somehow, the dapper but mediocre general maintained favor in the higher commands of the Third Cavalry Division despite the loathing the men in the ranks felt for him.

Kilpatrick could not hide the satisfaction from his voice. "Gentlemen, there's been a change in command at HQ, Cavalry Corps. General Pleasonton has assumed command, and I'm going up to take over the Third Division. Your new brigade commander is in route from Fredrick as we speak. In fact, I think that's him coming now." Kilpatrick turned toward a rapidly approaching rider, galloping down the road on a large black stallion, riding like the wind, sitting straight and supple, displaying the skills he had learned as a boy back in Michigan.

John and the other regimental commanders turned as well, wondering who would be their new leader, the man whose decisions might mean their lives, as the officer dramatically slid his panting horse to a stop, and then swung down in one graceful motion. The rider was tall and lithe, with long, blond hair curled to his shoulders and a sparse, drooping, blond mustache growing over his upper lip. He wore a sleek, black-velvet jacket with looped, gold braiding extending past each elbow, over a light-blue naval officer's dress shirt with a single silver star embroidered on each collar tip. A striking scarlet-silk kerchief was tied around his neck. Black, highly polished riding boots rose to above the knees of his light-blue cavalry pants. As he confidently strode toward the waiting men, he swept the broad-brimmed campaign hat off his head, shaking out still more blond ringlets, which cascaded down to his shoulders. John's eyes widened and his mouth dropped as General Kilpatrick made the introduction.

"Gentlemen, your new brigade commander, Brigadier General George Armstrong Custer."

The regimental commanders snapped to attention and saluted the new arrival, wonderment reflected on every face. Momentarily stunned, John blurted out. "George Armstrong Custer? Is that you?"

"The very same, Colonel Whyte," Custer giggled in a child-like manner. He stuck out his hand. "Good to see you again, John."

John took the offered hand, his face neutral but his mind proclaiming to the heavens. *My God, may the Saints preserve us.*

CHAPTER 2

The youthful Custer, ebullient with excitement from his auspicious reception, practically skipped around John, still thunderstruck with surprise. Custer fairly gushed, as he spoke. "Yes, Colonel Whyte, the very same Audie Custer who worked for you last year at Department of the Army HQ, who helped you write the training manual for mounted troops. Me as a lieutenant, and you a captain, as I remember."

"Yes, sir," John gulped. "And look at you now. Congratulations, General."

"God bless the war, Colonel Whyte. Now, excuse me while I meet the other regimental commanders of the brigade." Grinning broadly, he was introduced to the commanding officers of the First, Sixth, and Seventh Michigan Cavalry Regiments, giving each man a hearty handshake, and a sincere greeting. As Custer finished, he slapped his gloves in his other hand, while the three veteran commanders, all lieutenant colonels with hard months of fierce combat experience, stood in stunned silence, gaping at their new brigade commander.

"General," Kilpatrick broke in as Custer finished, offering the boy general his hand. "I must be off to Division HQ. You have a fine brigade here and every commander has proven himself in battle to my satisfaction. We march tomorrow, so get yourself settled and then join me at Division HQ at seven sharp for your instructions." Kilpatrick turned to his regimental commanders. "Farewell, gentlemen. Give your new commander every bit of support you can. Hard fighting is near for all of us."

The officers saluted as General Kilpatrick quickly walked toward his horse, mounted, and trotted away. Custer turned back to his new quartet of regimental commanders, his face serious for the first time. "As General Kilpatrick said, gentlemen, the division and this brigade march at dawn tomorrow. General Meade has replaced General Hooker as commander and is taking the Army of the Potomac into Maryland, to position his troops between Lee's army and the capital. I specifically asked General Pleasonton for the Michigan Brigade and he has graciously allowed me to command you. I'll become better acquainted with all of you as the days pass, but as we start out on our first campaign together, know this one thing. We will be the goddamned best brigade in the division, in the Cavalry Corps, and in the entire Army of the Potomac, or we'll lay dead on the field of battle. The papers say the Reb cavalry is better than us, and that's donkey crap. We're gonna whip Johnny Reb's ass every time we meet him, until no gray back wants anything to do with the Michigan Brigade and that's a promise. I'll lead you to glory, or my name isn't George Armstrong Custer and by God, that's what it is."

Custer smiled at the stunned men listening to him, and dramatically slammed his white gauntlets against his pants leg. "Now, prepare your regiments for the march. I'll send for you as soon as I return from the division briefing tonight, so you can make your final plans." He took the salutes from the four lieutenant colonels and watched as they turned to depart. "Oh, Colonel Whyte. Would you stay a moment, please?"

John stopped and stood silently beside Custer while the other three commanders rode off. Each had many things to accomplish, if their regiment was to be ready to march at sunrise.

Custer stuck out his hand again. "Well, Colonel Whyte, you don't mind if I call you John, when the situation allows?"

John mentally cleared his head, reeling under the shock of Custer's rapid rise from the rambunctious, unreliable, young Custer, who had left him as a lieutenant barely nine months earlier. "Certainly not, sir. Whatever you want. Once again, my congratulations on your promotion."

Custer laughed. "It was a surprise to me, I assure you. I was a brevet captain on General Pleasonton's staff and had no idea it was coming. Me and Elon Farnsworth. You know him, don't you, a staff officer in the Second Division? Both of us from captain to brigadier general, in one step. He got command of the Second Brigade, New York boys, mostly. Pleasonton told Meade he wanted some aggressive commanders in his cavalry commands, so here we are. And that poses the reason I asked you to stay." Custer's face took a more grave expression. "I'm certain you never expected this, John, and I need to know. Can you serve under me or would you rather I request a new assignment for you, perhaps another brigade? General Kilpatrick says you're a damn fine regimental commander, but he doesn't want trouble between us. He'll find another place for you in the division if you prefer. Do you need some time to think it over?"

John gulped. He had not anticipated having to make this kind of decision. But he knew the answer as soon as he heard the question. "No, General. I don't want to leave my regiment, under any circumstances."

Custer nodded, relieved. "Marvelous. You keep your regiment, then. And please, when we're not engaged in official duties, you may call me Audie, I'd like that. I suspect I'll get enough of *General* from everyone else."

I doubt that, John thought. He remembered Custer from before. The boy was fairly bursting with a desire for glory and rank. "As you wish, General, er, . . . Audie. I must be honest with you, sir. You know why I left the British army. I've seen your spirit and rashness. I cannot stand silent, if you should choose to send my regiment into a senseless danger, because your fighting blood is up. If I think it's a wrong decision, I'm going to tell you, straight away."

Custer again slapped his gauntlet against his thigh apparently enjoying the crack of leather, while nodding his head so vigorously that his golden ringlets bounced all around his shoulders. "Damn right, you are. I want you to. I know I'm up to this job but I also know I'm probably the goldamnedest hothead in the whole Union army. When I get my wind up and you think I'm about to make a critical error in judgment, I expect you to speak up. I swear to you, I may not do what you want, but I'll listen to you and evaluate your reasoning. Fair enough? You listened to me when I worked for you at Army HQ. I'll return the favor."

"If you do that, General, I'll follow you with my men into the fires of Hell and back out the other side. And we'll win for you all the glory you'll ever want in the bargain."

"By God, John, that's the spirit," Custer exclaimed, slapping John on the back. "With me leadin' and you advisin' me, we'll make the First Brigade the goldamnedest fighting unit in the Army of the Potomac." He wiped spittle from his lips with the back of his hand. "Now, Colonel, return to your regiment and prepare them for the march. We're off to twist JEB Stuart's tail for him."

John saluted the flamboyant boy general before hurrying toward his HQ tent, still shaking his head at the impossibility of the whole situation. In his year as a Union army officer, he had not been party to a more bizarre occurrence.

Pushing aside the flap, he entered the oversized HQ tent to find his adjutant, Major Wil Horn, and his regimental sergeant major, Khan Singh, his former color sergeant from the Twelfth Bengal Lancers of Her Majesty's British Army of India, sitting on his field trunk, softly talking. They both leaped to attention, ducking their heads as they hit the sloping, canvas wall.

"New marching orders, John?" Major Horn blurted, as soon as John sat down in the only chair in the tent.

John motioned both men back to their seats. "That and more. Command changes in the division. Kilpatrick is going up to head the division. Pleasonton is being bumped up to head of the Cavalry Corps. And even more yet . . ." John paused.

"The new brigade commander . . . ?" Wil asked the obvious question.

"Brigadier George Armstrong Custer. Audie Custer."

Horn's face screwed up in thought. "Custer? Where have I heard that name before?"

John chuckled. "He was the rambunctious cavalry lieutenant that worked for me, when I worked for you last fall, in the Plans Division at Army headquarters."

Horn slapped his palm against his forehead. "Merciful God. You mean the blond-haired kid who kept running around trying to wrangle an assignment to a unit in the field?"

John nodded. "The very same. He's been a captain on General Pleasonton's staff until yesterday and now he's the brigade commander."

Horn groaned. "My God. And to think I complained about Kilpatrick. Great God Almighty, he'll have us charging every breastwork in the Rebel army. We're doomed men, I swear."

John shrugged. "We'll have to keep his head on his shoulders, at least until he runs into a Rebel minié ball. As impetuous as he is, that shouldn't be long." John looked at Khan Singh, sitting impassively. His longtime friend and senior sergeant had seen too many commanders come and go to become too excited about this latest one. "Old friend?"

"Yes, Sahib?"

"The regiment marches at sunrise. Sergeant McQuinn needs to immediately issue rations and ammunition to the troop first sergeants for distribution. Send me Sergeant Vernon and Captain Mansur."

"At once, Sahib." The old Sikh warrior turned to leave. He had ten troop first sergeants to coordinate with and not much time.

"Wait, old friend."

"Yes, Sahib Colonel?"

John quickly rummaged through the trunk under his cot, and pulled out a bolt of silk cloth, dark maroon in color. "I was saving this for a special occasion, Khan Singh. I think now's the time to give it to you and the other Sikh warriors with my compliments, along with my wish for good fortune in the coming battle."

Khan Singh cradled the precious silk. There was enough of the cherished material to make new turbans for himself and the rest of his Sikh family members serving in the regiment. It was indeed a good omen. "Many thanks to you, Sahib. We will wear them with pride when we march tomorrow. Now, you must excuse me."

Once again, John thanked his fate to have so reliable a soldier for his senior enlisted man. He had been overjoyed when Khan Singh and his extended family had agreed to join him in America after his dismissal from the British army in India. Now, Khan, along with his son Rava, who was John's orderly, and older brother, Shah, who was first sergeant of M Troop, John's old command, were soldiers in the Union army. Additionally, Khan's two younger brothers, Basu and Modma, were sergeants serving in the Fifth Michigan Volunteer Cavalry Regiment. All had joined the Union army as soon as they arrived in the United States. Now, all were serving under John, and most ably. Their demonstrated bravery and military deportment was an inspiration to the rest of the regiment.

After completing an inspection visit to General Grant's army fighting out west at President Lincoln's bequest, John had taken command of the Fifth Michigan Cavalry and tirelessly trained his men and transformed them into what he and Khan Singh now felt was a superb fighting unit. He knew the test of all the training and hard work was about to be thrust upon all of them. He prayed he had done a good enough job.

Sergeant Tim Vernon tapped on the front tent pole, only entering upon John's command. "You wanted to see me, sir?"

John nodded at the former pony-express rider, now his regimental scout. "Have the troop livery sergeants check every horse in the regiment. We march tomorrow, and I don't want a single man falling out because his horse needed shoeing or attention. Also, make sure twelve pounds of oats per horse and a complete reissue of ammo for every trooper are carried in the regimental supply wagons."

"Yes, sir. We headed north?" The lanky Vernon scratched the fine, brown mustache he was trying to cultivate over his upper lip.

"Almost certainly."

Vernon nodded. "We'll be in good forage then. We should have plenty of feed for the horses, up thataway."

"I still want oats, all we can carry."

"Yes, sir. I'm on it."

As Vernon turned and departed, Captain Lee Mansur poked his head in. "You sent for me, sir?"

John nodded at his friend, the first he made in America. Now, Lee commanded a battery of four-inch rifled cannon, modified to be mobile enough to stay up with mounted troops. It was an idea John had picked up from Sheridan, when he rode with General Grant's diminutive but fiery cavalry commander back in Arkansas, during his visit to Grant's headquarters. "Yes, Lee. We march tomorrow. Insure your caissons are double loaded with shot and powder. We're after JEB Stuart, and may need all you can carry and more."

"Right away, sir. Oh, by the way, who was that peacock I saw riding up to Brigade HQ?"

"Our new brigade commander. Kilpatrick is taking the division. It's George Custer. Pleasonton made him a brigadier."

"Audie Custer? The lieutenant from Pleasonton's staff? The one who worked for you in Plans, last year?"

"The very same."

"Good Lord! What's this army coming to? See? Didn't I tell you? We're insane to be doing this. We oughta surrender tomorrow and let the idiots back in Washington take our place."

"I'm inclined to agree with you. To be fair, the generals we've had up to now haven't been worth the hair off a cat's back. Maybe someone like Custer is the answer?"

"More like you, if I was to hazard a guess."

John laughed. "If George Custer can make general, there's hope for us all, Lee. Even a Hoosier schoolteacher turned cannoneer, like you."

"Maybe so, Colonel, but I doubt it. That would make too much sense, and the Army don't work that way."

The orders clerk, sitting in the adjoining tent, looked up. His commander was laughing so loud he must have heard a very funny joke.

CHAPTER 3

General Kilpatrick looked up as General Custer poked his head into the division commander's tent. "Hello, Fanny," he greeted Custer, a rather sly smile on his pinched, intense face. "What do you think of your new command? Confident they'll be able to carry their share of the load?"

Custer ignored Kilpatrick's use of his dreaded nickname from his Plute days at West Point. All plebes got some sort of derogatory name from the upperclassmen, or Hazers as they were called by the suffering freshmen, but most had the good manners to drop it as soon as the junior cadet graduated and became an officer.

Obviously, Kilpatrick, who was Custer's senior by two years at the Point, was determined to keep his newest brigadier properly humble by a constant reminder of his junior status. The boy general cocked his head and kept silent, determined not to allow Kilpatrick to get under his skin.

"They're a good bunch from everything I saw, General. I'm gonna get along just fine with them."

"How's Lieutenant Colonel Whyte taking the news that you're his new commander? Is he going to stay with the Fifth Michigan?"

"We hashed it out. He says he's not eager to leave his regiment and will stay in command. I think we'll have no problems. When I worked for him at Army HQ, he was a decent chap. He'll be an asset to the brigade, I'm certain of it. If I'm wrong,

I'll have plenty of opportunity to transfer him later. The brigade has had enough turmoil today."

Kilpatrick nodded his head, his eyes boring into the younger officer before him. "I don't want any trouble, George. We're gonna be busy fightin' Stuart's cavalry and don't need any jealousy among commanders. The high command thinks the coming battle will decide the war. We have to win it and win it decisively. I'll go along with your suggestion for the time being. Don't forget, there's plenty of lieutenant colonels out there who would give their arm for a command in the cavalry."

"Yessir, but not like John Whyte. He's got exceptional credentials. You know his history?"

General Kilpatrick pursed his lips, shaking his head. "All I know is, he's from England and a favorite with President Lincoln and Secretary of War Stanton."

Custer smiled. Nearly every officer in the Union army of any rank at all owed it to some political connection including Kilpatrick, who was supported by the senior senator from New Hampshire. "John is the youngest son of the Duke of Bransworth. When his father died, and his oldest brother became the Duke, John was sent to Sandhurst, the British West Point. From there, he went to India, and his combat record was so outstanding he was made commander of a special unit of cavalry, the Twelfth Bengal Lancers, I believe."

Custer paused, recalling what he had heard, mostly from Lee Mansur, who delighted in telling the story to anyone who would listen. "When his unit was decimated due to an ill-planned attack on a fortified castle, John disobeyed orders and led his remaining soldiers on a surprise attack against the rear of the fortress, winning the day for the British army. Then he proceeded to tell the British general, in great detail, what he thought of his stupidity. For that he was cashiered out of the army and sent back to England in disgrace. His brother refused to help him fight the dismissal and John was at loggerheads as to what to do until he opened his trunk from India. His grateful men had slipped jewels from the outlaw castle in it before he had departed for England."

Custer laughed. "It must have been a fortune, because John certainly has plenty of money now. Anyway, John came to America, planning on joining the Union army. In route he was approached by a Rebel spy and reported it to Mr. Lincoln, whom he had the brass to go and meet his first week in Washington. Lincoln assigned John to act as a counterspy against the people who wanted to use him to spy against the Union. Rose Greenhow. You remember her and the story about female spies using their feminine charms to worm information out of our senior Union officers? Well, John was right in the middle of that, and was responsible for the downfall of the entire ring.

"From there, President Lincoln sent him out to check on the rumors about the performance of Major General Grant. I heard that the main reason Grant stayed in charge of his army was John's favorable report to the president. Anyway, as a reward John was given command of the Fifth Michigan, when its previous commander became ill. He's shown real skill in training his people and he brought over some of his old Sikh warriors from India. The Fifth is solid as a silver dollar, right now. John got ahold of some of the new Spencer seven-shot carbines. Most of his regiment is now armed with them."

Kilpatrick grunted, determined not to show that Custer's story impressed him. "That reminds me. The division recently received a shipment of the new Spencer carbines from the Ordnance Department. I'm giving enough to both brigades to outfit two regiments. Who do you want to have them, besides the Fifth Michigan?"

Custer shrugged his shoulders. "I don't know. What do you recommend?"

"Give them to the First and Sixth Regiments. They're two of the better regiments in your brigade, and both are seasoned units."

Custer nodded. "Will we be getting any more before we start out?"

"No, that's all we get, for a while. Your Third Regiment already has the single-shot Spencer breechloaders, so you're not too bad off. I'll give the other half to Farnsworth's brigade. His First and Ninth New York Regiments still have the old eighteen fifty-six short-barrel muzzle loader."

"We'll put them to good use, I promise you, sir."

"Damned right, Fanny. I plan to attack, attack, attack, at every opportunity. I'm gonna run Stuart right off the battlefield, as soon as we can find him. I've got General Pleasonton's assurances that the Third Cavalry Division is out of the escort business and into the fightin' business."

"By damn, General. It's about time." In spite of Custer's aggravation at Kilpatrick's hazing, Custer welcomed the general's call to battle. "What's our first move?"

Kilpatrick shook his head. "Not yet, Fanny. Be here at seven. I'll brief you and Farnsworth at the same time. I can say we're going to stay on the march until we've caught JEB Stuart, I can promise you that. Meanwhile, return to your brigade. You don't have much time to get to know your staff before we move. I'll send over the new rifles right away."

Kilpatrick looked down at the stack of papers on his desk and then back up at Custer. "Watch that Whyte, Fanny. I'm not sure I like him, even if he is the best regimental commander in the division. I know I don't trust him. He's not really an American. And those soldiers of his with the turbans—ugh!"

"You're wrong, General Kilpatrick. I've worked with John. He's all right. And he definitely knows his business. I'm proud to have him in my brigade. You wait. He'll prove it to you, too."

21

Custer gave a flourishing salute and departed for his headquarters.

Back at HQ, Fifth Michigan Cavalry Regiment, Lieutenant Colonel John Whyte looked up as Quartermaster Sergeant McQuinn stepped into the main tent. "Yes, Sergeant McQuinn?"

"Good news, sir. The division sent over enough of the new seven-shot Spencer carbines to outfit the rest of the regiment."

"Bloody wonderful. And ammunition?"

"Enough to shoot fer a month." McQuinn beamed at John as if he had just wrangled a two-week furlough from him. The new weapon would give the regiment's mounted troopers incredible firepower, compared to the older, single-shot rifle.

John grinned back at his supply sergeant, rubbing his hands together. "Get the troop first sergeants over and the new rifles issued immediately. Pack ammunition in every regimental supply wagon, like before. Move out, now." John returned his salute, then called out. "Khan Singh, Major Horn. Come here, please."

"Yes, Sahib?" Khan Singh snapped to attention as he entered the tent.

"Old friend. All the regiment's getting the new Spencer rifles. The seven-shot repeaters. I want the entire regiment down at the river at four o'clock to receive instruction in the use and maintenance. You have till then to familiarize the troop first sergeants with the new rifle."

"Immediately, Sahib." Khan Singh saluted and hurried out. John smiled. The proud, Sikh warrior had already made himself a new turban from the maroon silk he had given him earlier.

Wil Horn beamed like a schoolboy, as happy as McQuinn at the mention of a new weapon for the troops. His worn face creased in a broad smile, Horn remarked excitedly, "We'll be able to take on a brigade with those rifles, John. Hot damn. I can't wait till we corner ole JEB Stuart and his boys."

"Chances are quite likely we'll find out if you're right, Wil.

You let the brigade staff know about the shooting practice, so they don't think we're under attack. Make certain all the regiment officers are there. I don't want them left out of this." John looked at Wil, secure in the older officer's dependability. "We all ready for the march tomorrow?"

"Yes, sir. Sergeant Vernon is finishing up the horses now. Very few needed shoeing. We'll be all packed by sundown and ready to march. Any idea where yet?"

"It has to be north, after Lee's army I should think. We'll know at seven, tonight, after officer's call. From what I hear, there's a lot of concern in Washington. Everyone expects that a major battle is coming soon. It may decide the war."

Wil Horn nodded. "I wouldn't doubt it. It looks like a nice night tonight. I'm gonna have the men strike their tents and sleep under the stars. That way, we'll be ready that much earlier tomorrow."

John nodded. "As you wish. Make sure the regimental cooks have hot coffee, biscuits and bacon ready by sunup." John stretched, working the kinks out of his shoulders. "I think I'll walk about a bit and see how we're progressing. See you later."

John slowly made his way around the campsite of the regiment. The men were packing their gear, cleaning the grease off their new newly issued Spencer carbines, some writing one last letter home. He walked toward the tents of the horse artillery, where he could see Lee Mansur and his forty men all gathered around their unit's campfire.

John stopped and greeted his friend. "Hello, Lee. What are you up to?"

"Afternoon, Colonel." Lee stood as he recognized John. "Me and the boys are making some grapeshot for the cannons." Lee grabbed what appeared to be a stuffed sock. "These four-inchers we got offa the Rebs don't have any grapeshot canisters. So, we're making some homemade ones."

John nodded in approval. "Could be we'll need some this trip. How are you doing it?"

Lee smiled, proud of his little invention. "Easy. We take an old sock and put 'bout half a cup of sand in the bottom, like so. Then, we add thirty seventy-one-caliber musket balls, a cup of black powder, a handful of nails, an artillery fuse cut to burn for half a second. That means it'll explode at two hundred yards. Then we tie it off at the top and put it on a half-charge of solid shot powder. We fire the cannon, the powder blast lights the time fuse, and at two hundred yards the fuse explodes the powder in the sock, scattering the balls and nails. Voila! We have a grapeshot as good as any the regular artillery boys have. I suspect it'll have about three hundred yards of effective range."

John's eyebrow arched at Lee's clever description. "You mean you haven't tried it yet?"

"Nope. I just come up with the idea while ridin' up here from Washington. We got a keg of nails back in Fredrick and put the men to makin' some to try out."

"Excellent. I'm having the entire regiment test fire their new rifles down at the river at four. Why don't you set up your battery on that hill over there and give everyone a demonstration?" John pointed to the hillock. "It's about two hundred yards from the far side of the river. The bank is ten, twelve feet high. Be a perfect target."

"You betcha, sir. We'll be ready. I'll shoot the entire battery."

"Good. Also don't forget to draw the new carbines for your men. You'll need them as well, I'm afraid."

Lee threw John a hasty salute. "You bet, Colonel. We'll issue them as soon as we finish making our grapeshot. I want at least a hundred made up before we start out again."

"You have enough old socks?"

"Hell, sir. The one thing this regiment has plenty of, is old socks." Lee returned to his labors.

John completed his walking inspection among the troops, and returned to his tent to finish his paperwork before the afternoon live-fire practice with the new carbines. Khan Singh brought him one of the new rifles, freshly cleaned and ready for use. He also delivered two tins holding six each of the thin-walled brass container tubes of bullets that fit into the feed hole bored through the back of the stock. John inserted one of the tubes and pulled down the trigger guard, which reloaded and cocked the weapon at the same time. He aimed and repeated the action, watching the ejected cartridge spin through the air.

"By heavens, old friend. These things are quite easy to use. With these rifles, we'll certainly have the Rebs outgunned man for man."

John was at the river's edge with the rest of the regiment at four. His men quickly mastered the use of the new seven-shot carbine, which was the same size and shape of their old, single-shot carbine. As soon as every man had fired seven rounds, John called for Lee and his light artillery to demonstrate their new grapeshot rounds.

John pulled the troopers back to the side of the small hill where Lee Mansur had the four captured cannon set up. They watched in silence as Lee fired one gun, to adjust the timing of the internal fuse. Then, he fired all four guns at once. The roar of the cannons was heightened by the additional *kerpow* of the black-powder charge, as each round reached the edge of the river. The far bank disappeared in a thunderous explosion of boiling dust and clumps of clay as the countless lead balls and iron nails slammed into the dry soil. The bank was shredded for over a hundred feet of its length. A mighty cheer rose from the onlookers.

"By damn, we hit Johnny Reb with some o' those and he'll wish he never come up agin the Fifth Michigan," one soldier loudly exclaimed. John smiled, and walked over to where Lee and his cannoneers were swabbing out the smoking muzzles of the four cannon.

"Bloody marvelous, Captain Mansur. My compliments to you and your men. I shudder to imagine what it will do to a mounted charge against us. Quite impressive."

Lee grinned like a young schoolboy just released for the summer. "Thanks, Colonel. We're looking forward to showing our stuff to ole JEB and his gray backs." As John rode off, Lee's men gave him a rousing cheer, proudly proclaiming their loyalty to him and the regiment. He acknowledged their support with a broad smile. His horse artillery was clearly prepared for the coming battle.

John returned from the brigade commander's officer's call about eight thirty. His ten troop commanders, along with Wil Horn, Lee Mansur, and Khan Singh, were all gathered around a small fire in front of his tent awaiting the expected operations order. Every man watched anxiously as he strode up.

John wasted no time. "Gentlemen, we march tomorrow for Pennsylvania. Lee's army is threatening Harrisburg. Stuart is somewhere to the north of us. We're to find him and Lee's main body, if possible. When we find them, we fight them. Wil, Sergeant Singh, have every man fed and mounted to ride by six a.m."

Horn nodded. "I'll have biscuits and bacon for three days ready for every man at five."

John nodded. "Good. We'll be starting north toward Hanover, Pennsylvania, along with the First Brigade. General Custer wants the brigade to be in the vanguard and I agree, so we'll be mounted and ready to ride at dawn. Any questions? If not, I want you to rest until tomorrow. We don't come back until we've found and whipped General Lee's troops." John turned to Khan Singh. "Sergeant Major, insure every man has at least three tins of reloads for his carbine. That means every man.

26

Understand?"

Khan Singh nodded. "Every trooper has four tins, Sahib. The teamsters and artillery have two apiece. The scouts have six cylinders of reloads for their Colt rifles as well."

"Excellent. Now, try to rest, old friend. Tomorrow, we'll most likely have a long day."

"And you must rest as well, Sahib." The old Sikh warrior turned from the fire and faded into the darkness.

As the morning sun cleared the eastern horizon the next day, the last day of June, 1863, John sat on his black Morgan horse, Socks, his regiment standing in formation before him, every trooper holding a saddled horse, ready to mount and ride upon his command. He looked at the nearly six hundred men of the Fifth Michigan. He knew some would not return from the coming battle and he silently offered a quick prayer for their souls. Khan Singh sat on his big bay gelding just to John's left and Sean Gallagher, the regimental bugler, just to his right on a sturdy chestnut gelding.

The ten troop guidons flapped in the morning breeze, adding their red and white color to the green foliage, blue-clothed troopers, and dark horses all bathed in the soft golden glow of the new dawn. The experienced cavalry mounts swished their tails and bobbed their heads, eager to begin the march. John nodded, satisfied. He spoke loudly so every man could hear him. "Good fortune to every one of you. Do your job, like your NCOs trained you and keep your head when the bullets fly. You are a fine bunch of soldiers, as the Rebels are about to find out to their extreme discomfort."

As he finished, General Custer came galloping down the lane, wearing the same elaborate black coat with the gaudy, embroidered gold braid on the sleeves. His staff galloped after him, most not nearly the horseman the general was. The wind blew Custer's scarlet-red kerchief against his blond locks, barely held in place by a straw, plantation-style hat. He slid his black horse to a stop in an impressive display of mounted daring-do. Custer returned John's salute with a showy sweep of a gauntlet-covered hand toward his forehead.

"Good morning, Colonel Whyte. Your regiment ready to march?"

"Yes, General. Fully provisioned and ready."

"Damn good. You're the first regiment to so report, so lead off. North, toward Hanover and the Rebels. Keep your scouts well forward. Stuart's out there somewhere. Good hunting. I'll ride with the Sixth Michigan, at least today."

"Yes, sir." John saluted, as Custer thundered off in a flurry of dust, chased by the faithful staff officers. "Sergeant Vernon!"

Sergeant Vernon galloped up to John from his place at the far end of the formation. "Yessir?"

"Take your scouts and ride north, on the Hanover Road. Drop off two men about a quarter mile in front of us. They are to keep the main body in sight. You stay ahead of them, but watch them, so you don't ride too far ahead of the regiment. Keep alert. When you reach Hanover, stop and wait for me to come up. It's about twenty-five miles from here."

Vernon gave a snappy salute. "Yessir." He galloped back to his scouts. They immediately mounted and galloped off. John looked again at his waiting men. He nodded at Khan Singh. "Let's go, old friend."

Khan Singh shouted the commands as John turned Socks north on the dusty road, followed by the color guards carrying the Stars and Stripes and the blue regimental flags unfurled and ruffling in the morning breeze.

Khan Singh's mighty roar thundered over the anxious men. "Prepare to mount! Mount! By troops, column of fours, right turn, march!"

The Fifth Michigan Cavalry Regiment trotted north, toward Gettysburg and destiny.

CHAPTER 4

The road to Hanover was in far better shape than the war-ravaged roads of Virginia. The fields beside which they marched were green, awash in ripples from the light wind. A blue sky, with only a few storm clouds high on the far horizon, created a pastoral scene. The regiment made excellent time, and was at the outskirts of the small, Pennsylvania town before noon.

John held up his hand, motioning a stop at a small hill overlooking the town they were nearing. The clouds seen on the horizon at dawn were now overhead and a light afternoon rain started to fall upon the men. The column stopped while the tired troopers took the opportunity to slip on their ponchos. Most of the men had the Army-issue rubberized cloth, while some had purchased the more expensive sealskin cover, which was warmer, more waterproof, and far more durable. The bulky shapes of the troopers in their dark rain gear dotted the road behind John as far as he could see.

John spotted a tiny dot moving in the distance. A rider was galloping out of the town, toward him. It was Tim Vernon, as usual riding like the wind, a habit from his days in the pony express. The youthful sergeant reined his panting horse to a stop in front of John, and flipped a hasty salute at his commander.

"Beg pardon, Colonel. The town's clear. And Colonel . . ."

"Yes, Tim?"

"The town's done gone and fixed up the damnedest spread

fer us. All the ladies has got together at the Methodist Church and made us beef stew, with fresh vegetables, and biscuits, and cool buttermilk. They're a'waitin' on us right now, ready to serve the entire regiment."

"How'd they know?" Wil Horn asked, catching most of the conversation from his place beside John.

"Telegraph from Jonesboro, after we passed through this morning," Tim answered. "They've been waitin' fer us ever since. The town mayor says JEB Stuart's boys are to the southeast, in large numbers. They got the word from Emmitsburg, before the Rebs cut the telegraph lines."

John nodded. "Very well. Tim, ride back to General Custer and report your findings. He's traveling with the Sixth, so I suspect he's two or three miles behind us right now. I'll insure they save you some of the food."

Tim Vernon smiled. "Hell, Colonel, don't fret. Them ladies done cooked so much food, even the Fifth Michigan couldn't eat it all. I'll be back directly." Tim saluted, and galloped off down the road, his horse throwing muddy clots up behind him.

John grinned at Wil Horn. "Well, Major. Let's take our noon break in the town. If they've gone to all that trouble, we shouldn't disappoint them."

"Absolutely, Colonel. I'll pull the rear guard in and join you at the church. Don't you eat all the food now, you hear?"

John nodded at Khan Singh, and then scanned the gray sky. "Let's enter in a column of fours, Sergeant Major. Everyone looking sharp. Pass the word to remove ponchos. It's almost quit raining anyway."

"Yes, Sahib. We shall give the people a good review."

John led the procession into the town. The boardwalks of the main street were crowded with cheering citizens, many waving small, American flags. The enthusiastic reception infected the spirits of the weary men, filling the dusty soldiers with pride.

A portly man, dressed in a brown suit with silver-streaked mutton-chop whiskers framing his cherubic face, rushed up to John as he dismounted at the town center. "Ah, good day, Colonel. Welcome to Hanover. I'm Joseph Hodgkin, mayor of our fair town. Welcome, welcome to you and your brave men."

"Thank you, Mayor Hodgkin. I'm Lieutenant Colonel John Whyte, Fifth Michigan Volunteer Cavalry. This is Sergeant Major Singh, my senior enlisted soldier."

"Welcome to you and yours, Colonel Whyte." His gaze lingered on Khan Singh, given the Sikh warrior's unusual appearance, but he made no comment. He then turned back to John and gushed proudly, "The ladies of Hanover have prepared a repast for you and your men, over to the church. Will you be able to stay and eat with us?"

"Thank you, sir. Are you aware that I have nearly six hundred men with me?"

"Certainly, Colonel. Nothing's too good for our brave lads in blue. We're ready for you and more. We've been cookin' and preparing for the last three hours, ever since we heard from the folks in Emmitsburg that you were headed our way. Thank God for that, too. The Rebs were in Union Mills last night, 'bout ten miles southeast of here. Tore up the town and burned many a folks' store and home, they did."

John nodded. "Any word where the Rebels went, once they left Union Mills?" He pulled out his map and located the Maryland town.

The mayor shook his head. "We just heard that they left, headed north up the York Road. They could be coming this way, or they might cut east to the Baltimore and Ohio Railroad tracks, about ten miles east of here. That would play hell with both Baltimore, and Washington, if they cut it."

"Umm. Why would they cut the telegraph lines around here if they were going to the east? It had to be their advance scouts that did it. I'm afraid, Mayor Hodgkin, you're in for a visit from Johnny Reb. We know that there were Rebels in York, Pennsylvania, night before last. Stuart must be headed to join up with them."

The town mayor nervously nodded his head. "Will you be staying here to protect us?" He nervously brushed his white mustache with the back of his right hand. "You know Reb scouts were seen west of here three days ago? They rode off to the south. As they left, they bragged to the local farmers that they'd be back with all of JEB Stuart's cavalry in a few days."

"No, sir, I can't stay, I'm afraid. But, I'm the first contingent of six thousand Union cavalrymen, riding toward you from Littlestown. General Kilpatrick's entire division is on the road behind me. The Rebels will stay away from a force that size, I presume. Now, sir, if you will pardon me, I wish to partake of the generous meal your wonderful ladies have prepared for us."

The mayor was not completely satisfied with John's response, but the idea of an entire division headed his way was reassuring, so he nodded his consent.

John rode his horse to the Methodist Church and was soon wolfing down a full plate of hot mutton stew, boiled greens, and cool buttermilk. He had just finished a slab of dried apple pie when General Custer rode into the churchyard. John passed the empty plate to one of the women at the serving line with profuse thanks and hurried over to Custer. "A hot meal for you, General, if you want it. The town ladies have done themselves proud."

Custer fretted a second, then relaxed. "Very well, Colonel Whyte. We've been on the road for six hours now. I suppose it will be all right to enjoy a hot meal. Have your men back into the saddle just as soon as everyone has eaten. Intelligence says Stuart's headed to York, which is fifteen miles up the road. I want to be there before him."

John glanced back at his men, spread all over the church lawn and town square, hastily eating their bounty of hot, freshly prepared food. "I should be under way within ten minutes, General."

"Very good, John. Now, I think I'll try some of that stew. Smells awfully tasty." Custer hurried toward the serving table, trailed by the two captains he used as aide-de-camps and the young private who was his orderly.

"Mount the troops, Sergeant Major Singh," John called to his senior NCO. "We head north on the York Road, troops in columns of fours."

John mounted Socks and trotted to the intersection of Main Street and the road toward York. He waved up Tim Vernon. "Lead out with your scouts, Sergeant, same disposition as before."

"Yessir, Colonel." Tim led his scouts off at a fast trot. The rest of the regiment trotted out of the town, many of the men turning to wave good-bye to the friendly people who had just served them the welcome food. As the Fifth Michigan left the town, the Sixth Michigan began to arrive, already dismounting to receive their serving of the offered food.

Wil Horn trotted up beside John. "By damn, Colonel. That was a refreshing break, wasn't it? Nice of those folks to put themselves out for us like that." He looked up at the sun, finally breaking through the clouds above. "Lordy, but it's gonna be hot and humid before much longer. We'd better water the horses at every stream we pass or they'll be suffering before we reach York." Major Horn worked a finger at a lodged scrap of gristle caught in his teeth. "You want to change formation before we hit York?"

John shook his head. "I don't think so, Wil. Not as long as we're on this road, anyway. Not enough room for anything other than a column of fours, and if we don't stay on the road, we'll move too slowly for General Custer. Just keep after the men to stay alert, so we aren't ambushed by the Rebs." He patted Socks on the animal's sleek, muscular neck. "Ole Socks hasn't sniffed any Reb horses yet, so I suspect we're ahead of them."

John and Wil Horn rode together for a few minutes, discussing how they suspected their new general would react, among other things, the first time he faced the enemy's guns as a brigade commander. Suddenly both men fell silent at the same time. A low, intermittent rumbling had caught their attention.

"Thunder?" Wil questioned, cocking his head to hear better.

"Bloody hell, Wil. That's cannon. Back toward Hanover. The Rebels must be attacking the town."

John halted his regiment. The troopers had turned in their saddles toward the south from which they had just come, listening to the distant cannon fire. John debated whether he should turn back when a rider came galloping over the hill toward him. The young captain was one of Custer's aides. He slid to a stop before John and flashed a hasty salute.

"General Custer's compliments, Lieutenant Colonel Whyte. The general desires that you return toward Hanover and take control of the high ground to the west of the town. He asks if you know what ground he means?"

"Yes, I saw it while there," John answered. "The low ridge of wooded hills just outside the town."

The aide nodded. "Yes, sir. The general wants you to clear them and set up your artillery so that you can support the right flank. General Stuart's cavalry has deployed to the south of Hanover and is preparing to attack the town. The general says hurry. He says to make it perfectly clear what your orders are. You are to hold the hill, no matter what."

John nodded. "My compliments to the general. I will obey."

The aide nodded, and galloped away, his horse throwing up muddy clots of dirt behind him. John turned to Rava, Khan

Singh's oldest son and his personal orderly. "Rava, ride ahead and tell Sergeant Vernon to return with all his scouts. Quickly, man."

"Aye, Sahib, immediately." Rava galloped off in the opposite direction, toward the north, to find Vernon and his scouts. John motioned Sean Gallagher to him. The youthful bugler saluted, as he arrived.

"Sean, ride back and tell all troop commanders and Sergeant Major Singh to meet me at the rear of the column. Then return here and escort Sergeant Vernon to me as soon as he arrives."

"Yessir." Sean galloped off as well.

John turned Socks back toward Hanover. "Come on, Wil. Let's ride to the rear of the regiment. We'll meet with the troop commanders there and simply turn everyone around into the new order of march. Did you notice the hills off to the west of Hanover, the ones Custer means?"

Horn nodded his head. "Yep, I saw 'em. Maybe I oughta ride ahead and secure them early, if I can. If we have to push the Rebs offa 'em, it will be bad work, I reckon."

"Sound thinking, Wil. As soon as Vernon gets here, have him remount the scouts on fresh horses and you take the rear troop. Who is it—A Troop?"

"Yeah, A."

"Take A Troop and ride hard to the hills. Brief your men on the go. I'll follow as fast as I can push the regiment without breaking down the horses. If you're too late, scout the Rebs' positions, so we can plan an attack to drive them off. If you beat the Rebs to the top, decide on a good fighting position and start fortifying it. Leave a scout to guide us to you. We'll meet him at the spot you turn off the road to start up the hill. Clear?"

"Perfectly, sir," Wil answered. "Here comes Vernon, riding like the wind, as usual. I don't know how we keep him in horses, the way he pushes 'em."

Horn quickly briefed Vernon and the scouts as to his plan, and then galloped off with them, to collect A Troop, and hurry back down the road toward Hanover. John briefed the rest of his troop commanders on his plan. Then, he led the regiment at a brisk canter back the way that had come, toward the sound of the guns.

It took them half an hour to return to where Horn had left one of the scouts as a guide. Following the guide, John led the regiment off the road into a field of swaying, green oats. Major Horn had insured that the split-rail fence was knocked over so they could easily enter the field. As they entered the field of ripening wheat, John halted the regiment and let the scout report. The horses took the opportunity to snatch several mouthfuls of the succulent grain.

"We ran into some pickets, Colonel, but run 'em off quick. Kilt one, and captured two. They's at the top, with Major Horn. He says come quick, he can see the Rebs across the fields and they're headed this a'way."

"Lead on, then, Private. And my compliments, for your clear and concise report." John waved his hand and followed the scout, the rest of his men right behind him.

They reached the top of the rather sharp-ridged hill and found Major Horn. A Troop was cutting trees and clearing brush. Wil gave John a hasty salute. "We just did beat the Rebs here, sir. They're over yonder, in those woods to the south, working their way toward us."

John climbed off Socks, giving the reins to Rava, who led the sweating horse to the rear. He could see the smoke of cannon fire, bursting out of the woods, to the south of Hanover and occasionally, the red blink of rifle fire in the field surrounding the town. "Looks like the Rebs are still outside the town."

"Yep, the woods to the south are full of 'em. I saw Custer's flags a while ago. He's there," Horn pointed with a finger. "At that church, at the far end of Hanover. Probably up in the belfry, I reckon, where he can see."

"Your scout said you ran into some pickets?"

"Most likely scouts. Got two, over here. They's from the Seventeeth North Carolina. Fitzhugh Lee's boys."

"General Lee's son?"

Horn shook his head. "Naw, his nephew. Rooney Lee is his son. He's another of Stuart's brigade commanders."

"The Confederate Cavalry Brigade is as large as our division, isn't it?"

"Yep, almost. We have three thousand in a cav division, and the Rebs got twenty-five hunnerd in their brigade. It allows Stuart to command everything, personal-like. Easier fer him to control, I guess. You want to talk to them Rebs we got?"

Horn led John to where two men were crouched down, next to a large tree stump, their hands tied behind them. They were both young and were dressed in the grab-bag style of the Confederate soldier. One had on a fairly new pair of dark pants, with a threadbare homespun butternut-colored shirt, while the other was wearing worn, Confederate-gray pants, stained and dirty, with a businessman's white linen shirt, already sweat-streaked and dingy from the elements and the dirt of many days on the trail. Both were wearing new boots, probably taken from a store they raided since leaving Virginia.

"Boys," Wil spoke to the two sullen prisoners. "This here is Lieutenant Colonel Whyte, the regimental commander."

"You lads part of the Seventeenth Virginia, are you?"

The older of the two rebels looked at John, his face curious. "Yep. What bunch might you boys be from?"

"Fifth Michigan. Where you headed?"

"Don't rightly know, Colonel. Me and Seth was told to check out this here hill, and see iffen any blue bellies was on it. That's what we done, and that's all we knows."

John nodded. "Bad luck you found us here, I guess. I suspect you were headed toward York, right? Your whole command, I mean."

The younger prisoner nodded. "I recollect hearing that place talked about."

"Don't say nuttin' more, Seth. They's trying to find out too much. Just stay quiet." He flared up at John. "We ain't sayin' no more, Colonel."

"Very well," John nodded. "Your people seem to be headed this way. Stay down, and you should be safe, here. Come on, Wil. I want to talk to Captain Mansur and position his cannon." John walked away from the two men, his mind on more pressing matters. In a few minutes, Confederate cavalry would be trying to push him off this hill. He had to be ready for them.

His orders from Custer were clear. "Hold the hill, no matter what."

The phrase rang in his mind as he walked along the top of the ridge, watching his men rapidly making defensive fighting positions out of freshly cut trees and the gray, slate rocks that covered the ground. He tried not to let his imagination get the best of him. He needed a clear head to direct this fight. He concentrated on what needed to be done and not what might be.

Hold the hill, Colonel Whyte, no matter what. Hold the hill.

CHAPTER 5

John stood at the crest of the hill and expressed his approval of the defensive barrier Major Horn had constructed. "Looks good, Wil. Have C Troop deploy to cover our rear and D Troop tie in with us over at that fallen tree. Tell Captain Kennedy to make sure he gives us ample warning if they come that way. I plan to put the rest of the regiment on line, across this front. The Rebs will probably attack across that field in front of us, or perhaps harass us from those woods to the south. Fortunately, they can't mount any concentrated attack from that direction, the woods are too dense. Where's Captain Mansur and the cannons?"

"Over here, sir." Lee Mansur poked his head around a large tree trunk. "I'm deploying to cover the field to our front."

John briskly walked over to where his friend had unlimbered his four cannon. He wanted to move more quickly, but knew he needed to project confidence to the nervous troops watching him. John looked out, over the field of fire Lee had chosen. To the front, a steep, twenty-foot sheer bluff protected the cannon position from a direct assault. When Lee's men finished cutting down a few more trees, he would have an unobstructed field of fire into the field.

"Very good, Lee. Instruct one cannon to be prepared to deploy to the rear, to cover the trail up the hill, if the Rebs try and maneuver behind us."

"Yessir. I'll give the job to my best crew. Anything else?"

"Pick an alternate spot to deploy which will cover the far right side, in case we are attacked from that direction. C Troop is covering our rear, and is stretched awfully thin."

"Will do, Colonel. Oh, by the way . . ."

"Yes?"

"Can I fire a couple of shots now, so I can set my distance fuses for the grapeshot, if the Rebs try a mounted assault right at us?"

John looked over the field, toward Hanover. "No, Lee. Estimate it, to the best of your ability. Let's not let the Rebs know we're packing artillery. I'll send Khan Singh to see you. He has the keenest eyes I ever saw in a man. He'll provide you with the right distance; he has the incredible ability to estimate by eye."

John walked back to the center of his position, and instructed his Sikh NCO to inspect the fighting positions and then provide his keen eyesight for Lee's distance settings. Finally, he sat down on the trunk of a freshly cut tree, pulled out his binoculars and resting his elbows on his knees for stability, looked for enemy activity. Through the field glasses, he had a clear view of the far distant fields and woods. Once again, he blessed his friend and solicitor in London, Woodrow Higgins, for the fine departure gift of Swiss-made binoculars, presented when he left England over a year ago.

As he watched, a long, ragged line of enemy cavalry burst from the tree line, and charged toward Hanover. "There goes the attack against Hanover," he remarked to Wil Horn, standing next to him.

"Here come some, our way," Wil shouted, pointing his arm.

John swung his glasses to the southeast. Sure enough, about two hundred cavalrymen were lining up shoulder to shoulder across the field, pointed directly at him. As the first line of horsemen cleared the woods, another line formed behind them.

John turned to Lee.

"Pass the word. Begin firing as soon as the first horsemen jump that rock fence, out to our front." The fence was about three hundred yards to the front of where John stood. John turned to Rava, kneeling behind him, his rifle in his hands. "Go immediately to Sahib Mansur. Tell him to fire explosive shot until the horses jump the rock fence. Then, to switch to his new grapeshot. Understand?"

"Yes, Sahib. The rock fence. I will tell him."

"Then go to Captain Kennedy, in C Troop, and tell him that the enemy approaches and to stay alert, in case others try and sneak up on us from the rear." John paused to catch his breath, and then continued. "Next, find Sergeant Vernon, with the horses. Tell him that the bullets will soon fly, and watch the horses. I don't want them to stampede away. After that, return immediately to me. Understand?"

"Yes, Sahib. At once." The son of Khan Singh ran off, unconsciously ducking his head, as if running under a low branch of a tree.

John looked over his other shoulder. Sean Gallagher was there, his .44 Colt Revolving Rifle, which John had purchased for him, in his left hand and his bugle in his right. His face was blanched and grim. He'd seen the elephant before today, when his old unit was decimated at Fredericksburg, and dreaded the coming firefight. John smiled, his features tense. "Stay close, Sean. I won't need your bugle, but you may have to run messages for me."

The young man from New York City swallowed, hard. "I'll be here, Colonel. You can count on it."

"I know you will, son. Well, here they come. God help them and us."

The gray line charged, with a second line not far behind. John heard the high-pitched yells of the Rebel soldiers, their infamous war cry that struck fear in many a Union heart. The first line reached and bounded over the low rock fence, a display of horsemanship that John appreciated even under the circumstances. The first shells from Lee's cannons burst among the second row, scattering men and animals. The second line reached and jumped the fence.

"Fire!" John screamed, at the top of his lungs.

The entire line erupted in a frenzy of fire, as John's cavalrymen sent round after round from their new rifles at the charging enemy. Men and horses spilled onto the ground. Several kicked and flopped in their agony of death. Lee's cannon boomed once again. The homemade grapeshot burst among the charging riders, unseating even more screaming riders. John's mind could scarcely comprehend the turmoil. The rapid crackle of rifle fire was relentless and the continuous *boom* of Lee's cannon added to the deafening discourse. The acid tang of burnt gunpowder assaulted John's nostrils. The hideous screams of dying men and horses competed with the thunder of hundreds of horses retreating back to safer ground in the far woods. Through the smoke and confusion, John became aware of Wil Horn, screaming in his ear.

"They're runnin', they're runnin' away. We flushed 'em right back to their nest. Let me take a couple of troops and chase 'em right back to Virginny."

John shook his head, both to deny the request, and to clear his mind. "No, Wil. If their commander is smart, he'll try to work dismounted troops up the ridge now, using all the cover he can find. Those repeating rifles probably got his attention about the futility of a direct charge." He looked at Wil, whose face was flushed with excitement. "Also, check and see to our casualties."

As Wil scooted away, John ran to the furthest end of his defensive line, where he felt most vulnerable because the woods grew almost to the top of the ridge. It was manned by D Troop, commanded by Captain Chuck Ludwigsen, a fair-haired Scandinavian youth from a small town called Bayfield in northern Michigan. John had grown quite fond of the soft-spoken young man, and his solid, trustworthy personality. "Chuck, send two squads as pickets into the woods to our front. I suspect the Rebs will try and work their way up close to us through them. Tell your men to give one volley, then hurry back, if the enemy does come that way. We must have early warning."

"Yessir, Colonel. I'll order them out immediately." He saluted and rushed away, forgetting to wait for John's return. John smiled at the broad back of the young officer, and returned to his spot at the center of the position.

Khan Singh and Wil Horn were waiting for him. He told them of his plans, and sat back down on the same tree trunk. "What's the butcher's bill?" he asked.

Khan Singh answered. "One dead, three wounded. None of the wounded are serious, Sahib. We were lucky."

"Yes," John answered. He looked over the battlefield. At least thirty men were down on this side of the stone fence, and maybe that many more on the far side, as well as numerous horses. He could see a half dozen men staggering painfully toward the tree line where the rebels were hiding.

"Shall I go out and collect those wounded?" Wil asked.

"No, let them go. They'll be more of a burden to the Rebs than if we capture them." John wiped the sweat from his forehead, with the back of his gloved hand. His shirt clung to his body, soaked with sweat.

"Sahib," Khan Singh announced. "Our cavalry is charging the enemy at the edge of town."

John grabbed his glasses, and pressed them to his eyes. Over a thousand yards away and through the dust and gun smoke,

John dimly saw the flamboyantly dressed Custer, leading the charge directly toward the woods where the cannon had fired at the town before the battle. "Custer's leading them. Right straight at the cannon. Captain Mansur," John shouted.

"Yessir," Lee shouted back, from his position down the ridge.

"See those cannon in the trees at the south edge of the town under fire. Custer's charging right at them. You can't reach them from here, can you?"

"Yessir, I may be able to." Lee replied and soon had four-inch solid shot winging at the suspect wood line. It was mostly luck, but one round did hit a Rebel caisson, sending trees, leaves, horses, and rebel cannoneers flying in all directions.

John watched the charge through his field glasses. Custer rode at the front of maybe two hundred men, waving his sword and motioning for the charging cavalrymen to stay up with him. As the long line of riders approached the tree line, a surge of white smoke marked the deadly volley unleashed by the waiting Confederates. Men in blue and their horses went sprawling to the ground.

John's breath caught, as he saw Custer fall, thrown over the top of his collapsing horse. To his relief, Custer leaped to his feet and swung up behind a nearby trooper, who then proceeded to retreat back to the safety of the town, followed by any man still alive and able to ride.

"Lee," John shouted again. "Keep putting fire into that tree line. We have to cover Custer's retreat."

Lee answered in the most expedient way possible. He unleashed another volley of cannon shot at the hidden Rebels. Lee's volley was returned by counterfire from the Rebel cannon, but it hit at the base of the hill, and caused no damage. Lee's rifled four-inch cannon had superior range to the enemy smoothbore cannons.

Nervously, John paced his defensive line, only pausing to

duck as a second volley of enemy cannon fire smashed against the sheer bluff where Lee had placed his cannon. The range was too much for the Rebel guns, so they turned back to fire into Hanover and the barricaded Union troops therein. John headed toward the right flank, where Captain Ludwigsen had his men positioned. He spotted the stocky officer and approached him.

"Hello, Captain. Your pickets out?"

Ludwigsen snapped a quick salute. "Yes, sir. Sergeant Modma Singh has twenty men out, in two-man teams, all along the ridgetop."

"Excellent. I don't think the Rebs will come at us across the field again. But they may try and work their way up close through the woods. Stay alert, Chuck. Don't let them move in close."

"Right you are, Colonel. Sergeant Singh is my best NCO. He'll let us know if they come at us."

"I know he will, Chuck. See you later." John continued his inspection of the line, urging everyone to stay alert. He met Wil Horn as he finished checking the troop holding the reverse slope.

"Hello, Wil."

"Hello, Colonel. I just finished looking over C Troop's position, to the rear. No chance the Rebs can sneak up on us from there."

"Excellent. Come on, then. We may as well go back to the regimental flag."

Horn nodded. "Yessir. By damn, John. Weren't those new Spencer carbines something? The Rebels must have thought they had run into a brigade, instead of just a regiment. It sounded like firecrackers on the Fourth of July."

"It was something, wasn't it? I sure hope we don't run into many Confederate units armed with guns as fast as ours. That reminds me, though. You had better check with the troop commanders and insure the men still have plenty of ammunition. We may have to hold off who knows how many more attacks before the day is done."

"By God, John. Let 'em come. We'll send the entire Reb cavalry off to Hell in a handcart, with guns like we got now." He turned and quickly walked toward A Troop's guidon, just visible through the trees to the right.

John smiled at Wil's retreating back. The ex-staff officer was turning into a regular bloodthirsty field officer. John sat back down on the tree trunk, next to the regimental flags, and scribbled a hasty note to General Custer, telling his commander of their fight, and that they were in position to hold as long as necessary. He finished the note, and drew a quick sketch of his position on the back. He gave it to Sergeant Vernon, and told him to deliver it to Custer, somewhere in Hanover. He watched as Vernon rode back down the ridge, and then made a wide loop to the north, riding into the town well away from the Confederate forces, hidden in the trees to the south.

Just as Vernon entered the town, John heard several bursts of fire to the right, where Ludwigsen had his pickets. "Come on, Sergeant Major, the pickets have spotted something," he called to Khan Singh, running toward the spot where Ludwigsen's troop guidon fluttered in the afternoon breeze.

Ignoring the wizz of minié balls that cut through the air overhead, slicing leaves or thumping into tree trunks, John rushed to the center of D Troop's line, where he found Captain Ludwigsen standing at the barricade, looking intently into the woods to his front, disregarding the whistle of bullets flying past him.

"What's happening, Chuck?" he asked, as he joined his young officer, Khan Singh right behind him.

"So far, no word, Colonel. But listen to that firing. The Rebs are coming up the ridge in strength, it's certain. Oops! Here comes the pickets."

Wil Horn came running up, just as the first of the pickets came tumbling over the logs and rocks. John watched, as sixteen men burst out of the thick woods and rejoined their comrades behind the barricades. He and the others hurried to a bearded corporal, a stocky man well into his thirties who was the closest NCO to them. Ludwigsen spoke to him first. "Corporal Long. What's the situation?"

"Rebs, Captain. A whole bunch, workin' their way toward us. Just like injuns, they was, crawlin' and usin' the trees fer cover."

"Damn, I was afraid of that. Wil," John commanded. "Head down the line, and make sure everyone is ready. The Rebs are attacking us up the ridge. Khan Singh, join C Troop and stay with them. If the Rebs break through here, you and Kennedy will lead C Troop in a counterattack and push them back out of the perimeter. Understand?"

"Yes, Sahib." Khan Singh ran back to the reserve force, leaving John and Ludwigsen standing behind the row of waiting soldiers. Through the dense trees, shadowy figures dodged and wove their way toward him. The puffs of white smoke that came with every firing of an enemy rifle wisped from the tree line and slowly dissipated in the soft breeze. A bullet *pinged* off the rock barricade to his front, and John flinched involuntarily as it passed too close to his head.

"Get down, Chuck. They're getting pretty close with those bullets." He suppressed a sigh of relief as Captain Ludwigsen ducked behind the rock barricade, because that meant that he could as well.

Ludwigsen shouted, "Commence firing!"

The Union cavalrymen opened up on the advancing Confederate soldiers, and a lively firefight ensued between the two lines. The heavy and sustained fire of the barricaded Union troopers and the thickness of the woods prevented the Rebels from charging in mass. Both sides settled in for a long, drawn-out exchange of rifle fire, neither side raking up many casualties on the other because of the good cover for both sides. John could see that Ludwigsen's men were able to hold the line without help, so he shouted in his ear. "I'm going back to the regimental command post, Chuck. If you need help, send word and I'll come with C Troop. Watch your ammunition, these new guns go through a lot in a hurry."

Ludwigsen gave John a quick nod. "Right, sir. We'll be fine. Watch to the right. I think they're trying to slide that way, looking for a softer spot to break through."

John nodded, and started back. He passed Corporal Long-acher, and ducked down beside him. "Corporal, where is Sergeant Singh? He didn't come back with you."

Longacher pointed his rifle at a target, and fired two quick shots. Then, he ducked back down, and opened the slot and inserted a new tube of seven shots. "Dead, Colonel. At least I think so. Hit by a sniper, in the first exchange. He's back out there, 'bout a hundred yards or so."

Longacher reloaded his rifle and rose back up to continue firing, leaving John to dart on back to the regimental flags, his heart heavy. His old friend's brother, now one of the many dead from this damned war. He wondered, as he dodged toward his battle flag, *How many more? Will I be one of them?*

CHAPTER 6

"Spinnnng!" the bullet glanced off the tree trunk and whined off into the sky. Involuntarily, John ducked lower, even though it was too late. "Bloody hell," he muttered. "These damned Rebs just won't back down." He crab walked on toward Captain Ludwigsen's position.

The long-range sniping had continued all afternoon. There was no way the frustrated Rebel soldiers could mass enough men to charge John's hastily built, but impressive, defensive barricade. The rocks and trees provided his soldiers cover from the fire of the Rebel cavalrymen, while the thick trees would not allow the attackers to advance in a force strong enough to break through the line. The Rebels had shifted their probing from one end of the line to the other, without success. John formed a flying wedge of reserves, which went from hot spot to hot spot, adding their fire to the imposing fire of the regular defenders. Due to the crown of the hill, it was relatively safe to move from point to point, as the enemy could not fire over the hilltop at them.

In the end, as the day waned and the sun touched the western horizon, the weary cavalrymen from North Carolina slipped away, defeated and licking their wounds. John's regiment had suffered some casualties, but not nearly the magnitude of the Southern soldiers. Cautiously, he walked beyond his position to where the Rebels had been, Khan Singh nervously at his side, his rifle ready. John had counted over thirty enemy dead, out in the field to the east, with eight more near enough to the rock barricade that their comrades could not drag them away.

Just inside the cover of the trees around John's position, he saw numerous blood trails, as he swept the area. "Khan Singh," he commanded, satisfied the enemy was gone, "send a patrol out to the last position of the pickets. See if they can find Sergeant Singh and the others."

He had just returned to his command post at the top of the hill, when a courier arrived from General Custer. John wearily returned the courier's salute. "The general's compliments, Colonel, sir. You are to join him in Hanover, with all your command, immediately. The division has been ordered to march to Abbottstown, eleven miles to the north."

"By damn, John," Wil complained. "A three-hour road march, after fighting all afternoon. Looks like they could leave us here, at least for the night."

John, irritated as well, returned the courier's exit sighing, and ordered Rava to bring him his horse. "I'll ride to Hanover, Wil and find out what the general has in mind. When the patrol recovers Sergeant Singh's body as well as the other missing pickets, bring them into town with the rest of our dead and wounded. We'll leave them in Hanover." He walked over to where Khan Singh was standing with his brother Basu and his son Rava.

"I'm sorry about Modma, old friend. We'll find him, before we leave this place, I promise."

"Thank you, Sahib. He fell as a warrior. He is content and honored, in the next life." Khan Singh's face was collected and impassive. John knew the Sikh warrior code was harsh, but he also knew his friend was grieving for his youngest brother, inside.

"Khan Singh," John announced.

"Yes, Sahib?"

"You tell your Basu to assume the position of first sergeant of

M Troop, effective immediately."

John saw the pride shine through in the solemn faces of both Rava and Khan Singh at the announcement. "Come on Rava, let's ride down to Hanover." John lithely leaped on Socks's back and trotted down the rear trail, intent on getting to Hanover before it became too dark to see the way. He stopped at the spot where Tim Vernon had the regiment's horses corralled in a hasty rope enclosure.

"Tim, take a few men and round up those horses in the field there. I saw Custer's horse go down in the charge. I mean to present him with that black one out there. That one, see him?" John pointed at a beautiful Morgan, black as night, standing quietly by the body of a Rebel officer.

"Yessir," Vernon replied, and swung up on his horse. Motioning for several of his scouts to follow him, he quickly returned, leading the captured horse. Rava took the reins and followed John, leading the fine animal.

He found Custer and Kilpatrick at the town hall, hunched over a map placed on a table. John quickly saluted and related to the two generals a quick report on his fight at the top of the ridge.

"Killed fifty or more, you say? By God, John, that's just grand. We kicked JEB Stuart's boys pretty good here, ourselves. They've completely withdrawn and swung off to the east." Custer was effusive in his praise of John's regiment. "And by the way, thanks for your artillery support during my charge this afternoon. Your counterfire effectively suppressed the rebel artillery fire. It was becoming a bit sticky there, for a while."

"You must restrain yourself, Fanny." Kilpatrick overemphasized the belittling nickname for Custer. "We don't need a dead hero but instead a live general, leading his men to victory after victory."

Custer was too elated to allow the dour, mean-spirited Kilpatrick to bother him. "Yessir, but wasn't it glorious? We charged them like the knights of old, and would have broken their lines, had they not killed Captain Thompson and my horse. Then we lost the momentum of the attack. The troops paused too long, waiting for a new commander to take charge. But, just wait till next time. By God, I'll trample 'em into dust."

"By the way, General Custer," John broke in, "I saw your misfortune during the charge and beg you to receive a horse the Fifth Michigan captured during our fight. He's just outside. He's a Rebel horse, but a good one, from appearances."

"Well, come on, let's have a look at him." Custer rushed out the door, much to Kilpatrick's displeasure. John and the division commander followed, a bit slower. Custer was rubbing the horse's velvety nose, cooing soft words of reassurance to the nervous animal. "Colonel Whyte, John, thank you. Thank your regiment for me. He's marvelous, a truly magnificent animal. Orderly, come here. Ride out and recover the saddle and tack from my horse. Bring it here, to me. John, thank you again for this fine gift. By the way, I see a rather nice map case tied to the saddle there. Would you like it?"

"Thank you, General." John untied the map case and retied it to his own saddle. "My men are on the way in. What are our orders?"

"Take your regiment to Abbottstown and bivouac there. I'll join you later tonight. General Pleasonton thinks Stuart will circle that way to link up with Bobby Lee, over at Gettysburg, about twenty miles west of here. Buford's boys had a real knockdown fight with 'Baldy' Ewell's First Corps today, and General Meade's got our army converging on the town. It appears that Lee's got all his gray backs headed that way as well. Looks to be a big battle there, tomorrow. We're to cover the left flank, so Stuart don't slip in behind Meade and attack his rear."

"Very good, General. I'll leave my dead and wounded here

and resume the march with my regiment. Someone will take proper care of them, I assume?"

"Of course, don't worry. Oh, yes, tell your men I'm naming my new horse "Fiver," in honor of the Fifth Regiment." Custer returned John's salute and watched him ride away, before following the impatient Kilpatrick back into the building, to continue their planning session.

John met his men at the north end of the town. Major Wil Horn rode up to report. "We took the wounded to the aid station, John. We had eleven in all. Also six men killed. Oh, yes, good news, sir. Sergeant Singh was only wounded. We found him in the woods, unconscious. Khan Singh is delivering him to the surgeons. I put the dead in the barn there." Wil pointed to a nearby building. "I told the senior orderly at the aid station. He said they would take care of them later."

"Jolly good, Wil. Wonderful news about Sergeant Singh. Is he badly hurt?"

"Arm wound. Rather nasty, but if he's lucky, he'll live. He'll be sent back to Washington, on the ambulance train, I imagine."

John nodded and relayed Custer's orders to Wil. "I sent Sergeant Vernon on ahead, with the scouts." Soon, the entire regiment was wearily riding north on the narrow, dirt road, to the small village of Abbottstown.

They arrived two hours after the sun set and bivouacked in a field just outside the village limits. Tim Vernon reported there was no sign of enemy cavalrymen, but John made certain numerous pickets guarded the bivouac area before he and the rest of the regiment grabbed a few hours of much-needed sleep.

They spent the next day in a fruitless search for the elusive Confederate cavalrymen. John reported to Custer about six in the evening, disappointed at his lack of success. All day, the distant rumble of big guns foretold of the vicious fighting going on in the hills around Gettysburg.

"Don't fret, John," the irrepressible Custer consoled him. "Nobody can find ole JEB. That's why he's so damned good, I suppose. He musta rode way to the north, and then swung around to join up with Bobby Lee. Anyhow, we're getting a new assignment, now. Here, look at the map." Custer pointed to the map on his field desk. "See this road? Called Low Dutch Road. Here, where it crosses the Hanover Road. Take your regiment there immediately and secure it. I'll bring the brigade, as soon as I can collect them. We're to cover Meade's left flank. General Meade has stopped Lee for two days now and he plans on defending his position at Gettysburg until the Rebs break off the action and retreat. General Pleasonton thinks Stuart may try and strike our force from the rear, tomorrow. We're blocking the main route into Meade's lines, if ole Pleasonton's right. Put your regiment along this creek, um, what's it called? Oh yeah, Little Run Creek. Face to the north and I'll locate the rest of the brigade to your right. Got it?"

"Yes, sir, General. Any idea where the First and Second Brigades are?"

"Kilpatrick's got them here and here, covering the Baltimore Pike, to our south. Start your regiment movin', John. I want you in place before the sun sets. Have guides at the crossroads, to point the other regiments into their position."

John saluted, and rode back to the Fifth Michigan. Wil Horn and Khan Singh had the men already prepared to march and they were at their assigned location two hours later, just as the sun touched the low mountains to the west. The last mile, they could clearly hear the furious gunfire coming from Gettysburg, about three miles west of the crossroads.

"Sounds like the infantry are catching the devil over to Gettysburg," Wil remarked, as they rode up to the tiny creek, which was the furthest west their area went.

"Poor sods," John remarked. "A hot day and a hot firefight. I

55

certainly hope we are winning, for a change."

"If we ain't, we'll be movin' agin, real soon I'd imagine." Wil shaded his eyes. "How do you want to set up?"

"Put the horses behind us, in that field. It's not that big, so let them roam free and eat their fill. Keep the saddles on the fence rails, by troop, ready to remount in a hurry. I don't think the Rebels will try and come down to the west of the creek, it's too wooded, so send pickets out for two hundred yards, on this side only. Line the regiment by troop, along the road, on the south side. That will give us cover, if the Rebs attack from the north, across the field there." John pointed to the wide field north of the Hanover Road. It was covered in two-foot high oats, waving gently in the wind. John wrinkled his nose. The evening breeze brought the acid smell of burnt gunpowder, and with it the faint but unmistakable never-to-be-forgotten odor of dead flesh. The early casualties at Gettysburg were already getting ripe in the hot July sun.

"Merciful God," John remarked. "It must be nauseous there, if we can smell it clear over here."

Wil looked to the west. "The way those guns are going now, it'll be even worse tomorrow." The dependable Horn turned away, shouting for the troop commanders to deploy their men as John had instructed.

Lee Mansur rode up and threw a hasty salute toward John. "Where do you want the cannons, Colonel?"

"Put your battery on that little knob, back there about two hundred yards, Lee." John pointed back down the road, to the east. "Look to the north and west. If they come at us, it'll be from that direction, most likely. How are you fixed for ammunition?"

"Good, sir. I sent Sergeant McQuinn off to see if he can find an ammo supply wagon among all those wagons we passed on the way here. He'll bring it to us, if he finds one with powder and shot in it."

"Good. Carry on then, Captain."

Lee rode back toward his men, leaving John alone. Khan Singh rode up, and reported the entire regiment had arrived, and was preparing fighting positions next to the road.

"Excellent. Oh, by the by, old friend. I'm grateful Modma was not killed. Did you manage to see him?"

"Yes, Sahib. He is being well cared for. He said to tell you that he is sorry to miss the coming battle."

John nodded at the Sikh warrior. "I'm certain he is, old friend. But his contribution was most honorable. Please convey that to him, in your next letter to your family."

"Thank you, Sahib. I will, most assuredly."

Rava Singh brought John a cup of fresh tea and informed the two men that the regimental cooks were preparing a hot meal. By the time everyone had eaten and attended their horses, the night was complete. An ominous silence descended over the Pennsylvania countryside, broken only by the calls of the summer crickets and an occasional throaty bark of a cannon, somewhere to the west.

John walked his line just before ten o'clock and then returned to his tent, the only one erected within the brigade. His men slept under the stars, blanketed by a warm and sultry night. By the light of a half-consumed candle, John wrote a quick report for General Custer, before turning in for a few hours of much needed sleep. He scratched his head, his fingernails filling with the grime accumulated from long days in the field. He thought for a moment. It had been too long since his last bath.

"Wil," he suddenly asked Major Horn, settling down on a field cot next to John's cot. "What day is it tomorrow? The fourth?"

Wil's voice was muffled, his face covered by his arm, as he tried to shut out the glow of the small candle John used to illuminate his desk. "No, I think it's only the third. Yeah, tomorrow's the third."

John finished his report, and walked outside to give it to Rava Singh, who would carry it down the road to where General Custer had made his camp. As he watched the young Sikh trot off on his horse, he spotted Sean Gallagher sitting with his back against the split-rail fence by the road. He walked over.

"Evening, Corporal Gallagher. Please, don't get up. All settled in for the night?"

"Aye, Colonel. I've got a spot just over there. I sure hope we can sleep the night away. My butt's so sore from riding, I can't even stand up."

John chuckled. Gallagher was notorious as the regiment's worst rider. But, he was brave, dependable, and a talented bugler. John dreaded ever having to replace him.

"You're getting used to it a bit though, aren't you, lad?"

The New York City youth groaned. "I don't know, sir. Everyone says I'll become used to it, but I sure ain't yet."

John remained silent. Sean spoke softly. "You heard the guns over to the west, didn't you sir?"

"Yes, lad. It was something, wasn't it?"

"Reckon we'll get some of it tomorrow?"

"I imagine, Sean. JEB Stuart's around here someplace. Chances are we'll find him tomorrow."

"I'll pray to God we all survive the coming horror, sir."

"We will, Sean, God willing. Now, go to sleep. You'll need it, come the morning."

"I'll be there with you, Colonel, don't you worry."

"I don't, Sean. I know you will."

CHAPTER 7

The low, incessant rumble of cannon fire awoke John just before daybreak. He groaned, and looked at his watch, lying on the field desk next to his cot. It was not yet five a.m., and already another day of killing had commenced. The sound was muffled by distance, so he assumed it was from Gettysburg, but it precluded any further sleep. He rolled upright, pulled on his boots, groaning once for every aching muscle, and stood up, ready to face what the day might bring. And he tried very hard not to think what that might be.

Wil Horn snored softly, in his cot. As John rustled about, he sighed, and started to get up as well. "God almighty, John," he grumbled, his mouth sounding like it was full of mush. "Fightin' already? What time is it?"

"Nearly five. Come on, rise and shine. No telling when our turn will come. Get the regiment awake, and stand them to. I'll troop the line with you and Sergeant Major Singh in fifteen minutes. No fires, everyone eats a cold breakfast."

Wil swung his feet out of bed, into his boots, pulling them on as he yawned mightily. "Five hours sleep ain't enough, after the last three days, dammit."

"You're correct. But consider those poor sods in the infantry, over at Gettysburg. They would trade their misery for ours in a heartbeat."

Wil sniffed. "Serves 'em right for not joinin' the cavalry in the first place. Days like this, I wish I'd stayed in my billet at the War Department."

"Really? Why Major Horn. I thought you liked it here, in the Fifth Michigan. Shall I see about transferring you back to Washington?"

"Hold on there, John. If I go back, who'll take care of you?"

John chuckled. "Come on, then. Let's have a good look at the ground we're going to fight on today, if my guess is right." As John pushed back the flaps of the tent, he mumbled under his breath. "Pray to God, I'm not."

The troops were already stirring. Sergeant Major Singh hurried up to John and Wil, fully dressed as if he had not taken time to sleep at all. "Good morning, Sahibs. Your tea will be ready in a moment, Colonel."

John had converted Wil Horn and Lee Mansur to the bracing pleasure of early morning tea, instead of the bitter coffee that was standard fare in the Army of the Potomac. He looked to the east. A fiery-red sun was just peeking over the horizon, turning the gray sky a blush pink. John looked around. The surrounding countryside was still sheathed in gray dimness, the woods still dark and unfathomable. He modified his earlier order to Wil.

"Wil, let the men have a small fire for their coffee. Lord knows when they'll have another chance for some." He turned to Khan Singh. "Sergeant Major. Have the men fall to their animals, right after they eat. All saddled, and picketed by squad and troop. Two men per troop to care and watch them. Send me Tim Vernon, please."

John was sipping his morning tea, as young Vernon ran up to him. "You want me, Colonel Whyte?"

"Yes, Tim. Take your scouts and ride north, to that high ground up there." John pointed at the ridge to the north, which was called Cress Ridge by the locals. "If the Rebels come at us, it will be from there. I don't think they'll try to approach from west of the creek. It's too wooded. They'll come across these

60

fields, if Stuart stays true to form. You'll be out a mile or so, to our front. Ride like the wind to me, if you see them coming."

"Yessir. You still be here?"

"I think so. If we move, I'll send Rava Singh to alert you."

Tim Vernon ran back to his detachment of scouts and they galloped off, headed for Cress Ridge. As they crested the hill and were lost to John's view, a courier from General Custer galloped up the dusty road. He saluted and informed John that he was wanted at the brigade HQ, immediately.

John rode along with Lieutenant Colonel Gray, the commander of the Sixth Michigan, located along the road to his left. Custer was visibly agitated, as his four regimental commanders reported.

"Gentlemen," Custer started as soon as everyone lowered their hands from their salute. "The Second Brigade is stuck here, while General Kilpatrick takes the rest of the division to join the fighting at Gettysburg. General Gregg, with his Second Cavalry Division, is on the way from Uniontown, and should arrive around noon, when he'll relieve us so we may rejoin Kilpatrick. Until then, we sit here and hope Stuart is headed our way, otherwise we miss all the fightin' today, damn the luck."

Lieutenant Colonel Gray of the Sixth Regiment spoke up. "General, what's happening over at Gettysburg? It sounds like a hell of a fight goin' on."

Custer pointed to the map on his desk. "Apparently so. The Rebs have attacked the Union's north flank this morning. General Meade thinks they'll hit the center of his lines later today. He says to watch for Stuart, as intelligence says he rode out about four hours ago, headed north and east, which is toward us."

John spoke softly. "It makes sense. If he hits Meade from the rear, when Lee attacks at the center, there will be hell to pay."

"If, and that's a big if. He may be off on another raid

somewhere." Custer's fighting blood was boiling and he was anxious he would miss the coming scrap. The young general nervously paced back and forth in the narrow confines of his tent, slapping his gauntlets against his thigh.

John shook his head. "No, General. That's a waste of effort. Lee needs his help to win the coming battle. Stuart's around here somewhere. We'll see him, sooner or later, I'm certain of it."

"By damned, if we don't, we'll be left out of the glory, for a fact." Custer rubbed his drooping, blond mustache with the back of his hand. "Damn the luck. So, just in case, John, your regiment will cover the west approaches. Colonel Town, you cover Low Dutch Road with your First Regiment. The Sixth and Seventh stay in place, along Hanover Road. Everybody ready to ride at a moment's notice. Now, back to your unit. I'll keep you informed. John, I'll ride back with you. I want to look at the ground to the west."

Custer stood with John, next to the cannon of Lee Mansur's battery. It was the highest ground along the road. He trained his glasses, as did John, at Cress Ridge, now clearly visible in the early morning light. The noise from Gettysburg had continued unabated for the last two hours.

"Some doings over there," he grumbled to John. "You have pickets on the ridge, you say?"

"Yessir, General. In place since daybreak."

"Excellent. If Stuart comes, he'll mass behind that ridge and sweep down these fields to our front. If your regiment's over there, along that creek, you'll have a flanking shot at him. Then, I'll charge him head-on and cut him to pieces."

"Be careful, Audie," John warned, using Custer's name to drive home the seriousness of his point. "Don't jump too soon, or you'll be the youngest dead general in the Army."

Custer spoke as if describing a love affair. "By God, John, it's wonderful. Leading a cavalry charge, I mean. Like having sex with a beautiful woman. I love the feeling it gives me."

"Yes, sir. However, remember, be prudent. I saw you at Hanover. You hit the enemy with too light a force. You were lucky you came back. Hit 'em hard, with enough power to drive them from the field."

"I can put two regiments abreast on this field. That satisfy you?"

John nodded. "But, so can Stuart. Let my men cut him up a little, from cover of the creek, and then you attack."

Custer giggled, in his high-pitched, schoolboy way. "Yes, by damn, it'll work. You hit him hard until he crosses that brook out there about a quarter mile and then I'll charge, with the First and Seventh on line and the Sixth in reserve. By gad, we'll have him for certain."

John looked over the pending battlefield. "My men will be isolated, if the Rebs turn on us, General. Make sure they don't." He glanced at Custer to make certain the mercurial general was listening.

Custer simply nodded, studying the fields of half-grown oats. "By the way, tell your men my new horse is a keeper. Thanks again, for him."

"Yes, sir. Shall I deploy my regiment now?"

"No, wait until we either receive word that Stuart's coming or General Gregg relieves us. But be ready."

The morning hours passed and all remained quiet. About ten a.m., John saw General Gregg's party and flag approach the spot where Custer had his command post. He got to his feet, and remarked to Wil Horn, dozing next to him. "Wake up, Wil. There's Gregg and his boys. We'll be moving soon, I suspect, to rejoin Kilpatrick at Gettysburg." He realized that it was suddenly eerily quiet for the first time that morning. No thunderous cannons roared from the direction of Gettysburg, no birds singing in the trees nor animals calling in the fields.

Wil stood and shielded his eyes as he looked toward Cress Ridge. "You already sent for Sergeant Vernon and his boys?"

John turned. "No. Why?"

"Here they come, riding like the Devil was after 'em."

John squinted in the hot, harsh sunlight. Vernon and his scouts were riding hard, leaping over a split-rail fence about five hundred yards from John and Wil.

"They certainly are coming fast," John remarked. "I dare say they've seen something, right enough."

Tim Vernon slid his panting horse to a stop before John, and leaped off its back in a graceful bound. "Rebel cavalry, Colonel. Coming this a'way." The rest of his scouts galloped in behind him.

"How many, Tim?"

"A hell of a bunch, Colonel. I seen Stuart's battle flags and three brigade flags. I'd say everybody he's got."

"How long until they're here?"

Vernon looked back toward Cress Ridge. "They'll be at the ridge yonder in twenty minutes, I reckon. We waited until their scouts were right up on us, afore we skedaddled."

"Very well, Sergeant. Let's inform the generals. They're down the road a bit." John headed for Socks, Vernon right behind him.

Custer and Gregg listened as Vernon delivered his report. Gregg, who was several years older than Custer, ran his fingers through his bushy beard, sucking wind through a gap in his teeth. "All of Stuart's command, you say? George, he's gotta come through us, if he's trying to attack Meade's rear. I'll deploy my division along Low Dutch Road. You stay where you are. I'll accept responsibility for you not rejoining Kilpatrick as ordered. We have to stop Stuart here. Agreed?"

"Yes, sir, General, I concur, absolutely. I'll attack upon your orders."

Gregg nodded his head absently, thinking hard. "We'll not start the dance, George. Let Stuart begin and let's see what his intentions are before we react. Don't let him break through you to the west, no matter what."

Custer agreed. "Understand, General. He'll have to strike us before he turns on Meade, though, or we'll be at his back. I'll go insure my brigade ready, with your permission."

Gregg waved John and Custer off, calling after them as they mounted. "A good job with your scouts, Colonel Whyte. I'll mention it in my report to Meade."

John rode quickly back to his flag, Custer's hasty orders ringing in his ears. He called for Wil Horn, Lee Mansur, and Khan Singh as soon as he arrived. "We're staying to fight. Custer is sending us up along the creek, as dismounted skirmishers. We'll fire on the enemy flank if he attacks across the field, as I expect him to. Lee, you deploy your guns over there, in that grove of trees. I'll make that the center of our line. Wil, you take Ludwigsen's D Troop and Bill Brignon's A Troop as security for the cannons. You take the horses with you. If we are charged by too big a force, you'll have to counterattack them, or we'll be pushed back into those trees, and we'll never get untangled."

John grasped Wil's arm to emphasize his point. "Watch close, Wil. You'll have to decide if and when to attack. Don't let the Rebs seize our cannon, so keep your men alert. Understand?"

"Right. Er, Colonel, there's a small problem."

"What's that?"

"My horse is lame. Got a bad stone bruise. He can't run a lick, right now."

"Take Socks, Wil. He knows you. I'll be on foot, with the rest of the regiment, anyway."

"Thanks, John. I'll take good care of him. Come on, Lee."

The two officers hurried away.

John turned to Khan Singh. "Get the men on their feet, old friend. We'll need all the preparation time we can get, if we're to fight six thousand Confederates on horseback, while we're afoot."

The big Sikh warrior nodded, roaring out the marching orders for the anxious troopers. John instructed Tim Vernon to have his scouts bring their mounts, in case he needed riders, and then he led the way toward the creek, which ran north-south at the western edge of the great expanse of fields. He picked the spot where he wanted to plant his regimental flag and watched as the two hundred men with him spread out along the creek bank. Quickly, they started to prepare fighting positions, using rocks from the creek, and limbs from trees in the heavy woods to the western side of the creek.

He could see Lee Mansur, emplacing his battery of four cannon behind him to the right rear, slightly inside the tree line. "Lee will be shooting right over us," he remarked to Khan Singh. "We'll have to keep our heads down."

"And our ears plugged," the old warrior remarked, dryly.

One by one, the soldiers finished their fighting positions, and quiet settled over the field. John kept his glasses trained on the ridge, now less than half a mile from him. The ridge sloped gently toward him, with a scattering of trees on it, but easily traversed. Just as he was beginning to wonder if the Rebels were even nearby, he saw two batteries of horse artillery race over the top, sliding to a halt in a favorable area to fire toward the intersection of Hanover and Low Dutch Roads.

From the edge of the woods rode a line of riders and several cannon. The mounted men stopped and looked toward the Hanover Road. Battle flags fluttered in the breeze as the enemy commanders looked down the wide field to the road that led to Meade's rear. "There they are," he remarked to Khan Singh, standing silently beside him. "The men all ready?"

"Yes, Sahib."

John looked back at Lee Mansur, hidden from the ridge by the trees. "Ready, Lee?" he half shouted.

Captain Mansur nodded his head emphatically.

John watched as the Confederate artillerymen unlimbered their eight-pounder smoothbore cannon and aimed them at the crossroads. It was a long shot for the small cannon, but still reachable, with a full powder charge. "They'll not have much accuracy, at that range," he remarked to Khan Singh.

"True, Sahib. But, once they know that we are here, their aim will be much more accurate."

John grimaced at the old man's observation. "Right you are, old friend. Slip over to Captain Mansur and make sure he is aware that once the shooting starts, he must drive those cannons off the ridge before engaging enemy soldiers."

Khan Singh slipped away, barely disturbing the tall grass and gave Lee his orders. He swiftly returned, and took his position beside John. Basu was behind them, the regimental flags sheathed in their travel case, awaiting John's command to unfurl them against the enemy. The younger Sikh was busily preparing a place for John to take cover, once the bullets started to fly. John felt secure, surrounded by his Sikh warriors.

Silently, they waited for the gray horsemen of JEB Stuart to burst over the ridge, and sweep down the hill toward them. And waited. And sweated, in silent anticipation and fear.

CHAPTER 8

The minutes ticked by, yet nothing happened. Still the field was quiet. The Rebel cannoneers stood by their guns, waiting for what, John had no idea. Occasionally, he would see Rebel horsemen ride to the top of the ridge and survey the crossroads, then return to the far side of the ridge. Wil Horn slipped up beside John, panting from the exertion of running through the brush along the creek bottom.

"What the hell's going on, John? Them gray backs been up there for a half hour and still ain't charged. Reckon they see us?"

"I'm not certain, but I don't think so, Wil. They seem to be waiting for something. Your men in place and ready?"

"Yessir. I've got Ludwigsen's troop placed in defensive positions around the cannons, and Bill Brignon's troop in a small clearing back in the woods, with their horses, ready to charge."

"Keep your eyes on the Rebs, Wil. They hit us hard with a mounted charge, you'll have to drive them off of us with a countercharge."

"I'll be there, don't worry. I just can't figger why they are waiting. They have to see the troops at the crossroads. They have to hit them before they turn on Meade's rear. Why don't they charge?"

"It's a question I can't answer, Major. Return to your men, and keep them out of sight, but alert."

"Okay, John, but I don't like it. Not one bit." Major Horn

slipped back across the stream and into the woods behind John where his hidden men awaited the coming battle.

The time wore on, while the men of the Fifth Michigan nervously broiled in the hot July sunshine. Just as John had finally decided he was going to send Tim Vernon up to the ridge for a reconnaissance, things changed rapidly. From the west came the incredible roar of hundreds and hundreds of cannon. The ground trembled beneath his feet, as moment by moment the noise increased in a deadly crescendo. Somewhere around Gettysburg, Lee's cannons had cut loose with a fury that belied imagination.

Stuart's cannon suddenly popped their corks, to begin a methodical cannonade of the area surrounding the crossroads. General Gregg's and Custer's cannons answered and for thirty minutes their little roars tried to blot out the blood-chilling maelstrom of thunder from Gettysburg.

"My God," Tim Vernon whispered to John, standing next to him in the muddy soil of the creek bottom. "Listen to that cannonading over to Gettysburg. How on earth could anyone stand against that? Those poor infantrymen with Meade. It must be hell over there."

"Our turn is coming," John soberly answered.

Vernon looked to the west, as if to see the carnage being wrought. "Yessir, Colonel, I suspect you're right 'bout that. You want me to deploy my scouts with Major Horn?"

"No, Tim. Stay here and help defend the regimental flag. We're going to receive a Confederate visit quite soon."

Vernon hurried back to his hole, dug into the side of the three-foot-high embankment, cut by the tiny creek over many years. The young sergeant laid four extra cylinders of primed .44-caliber rifle bullets in front of him. He checked the load in his Colt Revolving Rifle for the twentieth time. He had thirty bullets ready to fire, if the Rebs did come his way. Satisfied he was ready, he settled against the warm earth, and waited, more calm than men twenty years his senior. But then, howling savages, trying to take a young pony-express rider's scalp had never chased his waiting comrades for days at a time, either.

For a long hour the cannons roared, with minimal damage to the troops dug in along the road. Ominously, the thunderous roar from the west ceased and just as quickly, Stuart's cannon stopped.

For a suspenseful moment, all was quiet.

Then, over the ridge rode a thousand men in gray, as neatly aligned as if on parade, their red battle flags whipping in the breeze.

Voicing their trademark cry of battle that John could clearly hear even from this distance, the gray horsemen trotted toward the crossroads. As they approached John's men, still hidden in the creek bottom, they formed a shallow V, with the point aimed directly at the crossroads where the soldiers of Gregg and Custer were dug in.

John patiently waited until the point swept past him before screaming out the command "Fire at will!"

The sudden shock of the volley from John's hidden men caused the right side of the enemy formation to collapse and veer toward the point. Gregg and Custer's men and cannons opened up as well, tearing gaping holes in the dressed line of charging horsemen and covering the field with dust and the gray smoke of burnt gunpowder. No human line could sustain a charge against such a fearsome shelling. The line of bloodied riders slowed, stopped, and milled about for an instant, before breaking for the rear, retreating to the safety of the cover of the ridge.

As the last of the survivors galloped over the top, John shouted, "Cease firing!"

Only then did he realize that Lee Mansur was again locked in a vicious duel with the Rebel cannon, both sides trying to silence the other. Lee won, primarily because his rifled cannon were more accurate and powerful. Stuart's cannoneers pulled off the hill and back over the top after their retreating comrades.

Briefly, John wondered if the enemy was beaten, but the thought was quickly dismissed, as yet another wave of riders burst over the hill, more numerous than the first. Their swords glittered in the afternoon sunshine, while the dust of their horses hid the cannons that pulled up behind them and opened up on the Union forces again.

"Here they come. Get ready. Fire." John looked around. His men were defiantly facing the charging cavalry, their rifles smoking as they fired. "Stuart's Invincibles," were certainly getting it as badly as they had given it so many times before.

"Sahib," Khan Singh called to him, "Custer attacks."

John looked to the south. Sure enough, a rolling, blue wave of riders, their red and white pennants fluttering out behind them, were charging across the scarred field, right at the advancing enemy. John could see Custer at the point with his flag unfurled, leading the attack, waving his sword and riding directly toward the apex of the enemy's line.

John spun on his heel and shouted at Lee Mansur. "Lee. Put some rounds into their front line. Custer's riding right at it."

Lee nodded and pointed where he wanted the cannons aimed. The rounds impacted just moments before Custer and the Union cavalrymen slammed into the enemy's forward rank. The two lines of charging men dissolved into a tangled mass of struggling soldiers, flailing horses and the recently dead, partially obscured by a mighty cloud of dust and gun smoke, which obliterated nearly everything within it.

John looked again toward the ridge. Another line of fresh cavalrymen was forming, pointed directly at him. He shouted the alert and his men shifted their fire from the confused mass in front of them, toward the new threat. The enemy line charged and John turned again to shout at Lee Mansur, but it wasn't necessary. The alert artilleryman already shifted his cannon's aim toward the more pressing danger.

John ducked as the first explosion of enemy artillery hit the creek, fifty yards to his left. Several men went sailing back, knocked off their feet by the impact. John trusted Lee to take the hidden enemy battery under fire and focused his attention toward the thundering line of enemy horsemen bearing down on his position. His men fired as fast as they found targets. Men tumbled from their horses, or both man and horse slammed on to the dusty earth while the rest galloped on, directly at John.

The pitiful remainders of the first rank reached John's position leaping over the embankment and then swinging around to fire at their blue-coated enemy's back. John's men spun around as well, and knocked still more Rebels off their saddles. The second rank was rapidly approaching, when Wil Horn and his mounted troopers burst out of the woods, up the low embankment and into the charging enemy. It was as if an ocean's wave had smashed against rocks. Men and horse scattered everywhere, with slashing sabers and darting riders turning and twisting on all sides.

John quickly reloaded a fresh cylinder of bullets into his pistol. Clambering to the top of the embankment, he waved at his crouching men. "Charge! Come on, men! Charge!" He ran toward the milling masses of mounted soldiers, snapping off a shot at any gray coats he saw through the dim haze.

A rider swept past, slashing down at him with a shining sword, stained red at the tip. John ducked under the blow, feeling a chilling breeze on his cheek from the near miss. Before he could rise and aim his pistol, Khan Singh shot the man from his saddle. John plunged into the dust and confusion of men fighting men on horseback. He saw Tim Vernon leap onto the back of a horse, unseating the rider whom he smashed in the head with the stock of his rifle. From a more familiar seat, Vernon now charged into a knot of the enemy, scattering them like ducks on a pond and was lost to John's sight in the melee.

John fired both his pistols until they were empty and then grabbed a Spencer carbine lying on the ground at his feet. Disregarding the slimy coating of blood on the stock, he shot with it until it emptied. His warrior's blood on fire, he pulled out his sword and ran still deeper into the fray, slashing and stabbing at the mounted enemy. He had not gone but a few steps, when he realized the Rebels were falling back. They had reached the limits of their endurance and had broken. Afoot, John chased after the retreating horsemen, his sword slashing in defiance as they scattered toward the safety of the ridge. He saw Wil Horn gallop past, his sword waving like a silver wand, shouting like a madman, hot on the enemy's heels along with a dozen more men from B Troop.

John slowed and watched as Wil and the riders galloped away from him. His voice was gone, he had shouted and screamed so long and hard. His mouth was cotton-dry and dust gritted against his teeth. Wiping away the sweat from his eyes with the sleeve of his dirty, white shirt, he opened his mouth to shout at Horn to return. Hesitating, as Wil was too far away to hear, he watched uneasily. Wil and his men galloped up the gentle slope toward the top of the rise.

The next few seconds seemed to elongate, as if time were slowing to a standstill. John saw the puff of gray-white smoke shoot from the four Confederate cannon. He gaped in horror as Wil, Socks, and the other men and horses stopped in their tracks, and then flew backward, sprays of red mist showering the ground around them. The enemy cannon had fired a grapeshot shell directly at Wil, with dreadful results.

The savage fury of the sight caused John to gag and stand

stunned, shock and horror paralyzing his system. Among the death of many, the single death of his friend overwhelmed him. A retreating Rebel cavalryman saw a single Union officer standing in front of him and veered toward the easy target, his sword raised for the fatal blow. He did not see Tim Vernon, riding like a man possessed, closing on him from the rear.

John remained frozen, unaware of the approaching danger. Tim Vernon leaned forward in his saddle, like a race jockey, willing his panting horse to even faster effort. As the Confederate soldier raised up in his saddle tensed to strike the killing blow, Tim pointed his rifle with one hand, toward the gray back of the threat to his colonel, and fired his last bullet. The heavy lead missile sliced into the thundering Rebel's back, tearing through his kidney, causing immediate, incredible pain. Unable to complete his swing, he dropped his sword, swayed in his saddle, and fell in a limp heap at John's feet, his dying hand hitting John's boot with enough force to jerk the grief-stricken John out of his momentary immobility.

John looked around, as Tim leaped from his horse, and ran up to him, grabbing his arm. "Colonel. You all right?"

"Yes, yes, thank you, Tim. I'm fine. Just for a moment there." John paused, and looked around. The field was quiet again. Clumps of what had once been men or horses lay sprawled about and Custer was galloping toward him, waving his hat in wide circles as he rode. The moans of the wounded soldiers mixed with the scream of dying horses overwhelmed any sense of satisfaction within John.

Custer reined his horse, shouting like a schoolboy at the races. "Well done, Colonel Whyte! Well done. We certainly twisted JEB Stuart's nose this day. The field is ours. Gather your casualties and return to your position by the road. Stuart's finished here. He'll be no threat to Meade's rear." Custer paused. "Listen to that, will you?"

John slowly regained his senses, and comprehended what Custer was saying. Tens of thousands of rifles and hundreds of cannon were firing as fast and as furiously as men could humanly fire them at one another. "My God, there's a real bloodbath going on at Gettysburg. I'll send a courier to find out if we are winning. If we are, John, do you know what it means?" Custer answered his own question. "It means Lee's whipped. The Union is delivered. And we, by the grace of God, had a part in it." Custer flashed a grin at John, wiped some of the grime from his face with a dirty glove, and galloped away, waving his hat and shouting orders for his staff to deliver.

John was unable to find any solace in Custer's exuberance. A man he called friend had been savagely destroyed in front of him. He spotted Khan Singh and waved him over. He gave the grimy and sweat-stained Sikh warrior a quick check. "You all right?"

"Yes, Sahib."

"Gather the dead and wounded, and prepare the regiment to return to our position on Hanover Road."

"At once, Sahib."

John turned to Tim Vernon, standing next to him. "Tim, I need a horse. I'm afraid mine is finished. Can you find me one?"

"Sure, Colonel. There's a bunch to choose from. I'll be right back, sir." Vernon swung onto his saddle and headed off, looking with careful eye at the many horses milling about, some in shock while others stood faithfully awaiting their masters, who would never ride them again.

Tim spotted a beautifully formed, well-bred, chestnut-colored Arabian with a flaxen mane, not far away. It was the horse of the man who had nearly killed his colonel. He gathered the reins, admiring the animal's fine horseflesh. "You must be worth a thousand dollars or more, hoss. You'll do jus' fine." Whistling tunelessly, he led the animal toward his colonel.

John inspected the animal Vernon delivered. "My word, this is certainly a fine animal. Wonder where he came from?"

Captain Brignon rode up and overheard John's question. "We were up against the Hampton Grays, Colonel Whyte. The whole damned regiment was riding the finest thoroughbreds I ever saw. We're gatherin' the loose horses up now. We'll have fifty or more to distribute. Look at this one I got."

John nodded, suddenly very weary, as he remembered what had to be done. "Khan Singh, send a litter party to me. Major Horn and some of his men fell over at the rise, up there." John pointed with his arm. "I'll be there with him. Tell Captain Mansur, if you see him."

John rode his new horse, accompanied by Tim Vernon and Khan Singh, who were not about to let their colonel out of their sight for the time being. Unsteadily, John climbed off his horse and walked to the crumpled corpses that once were his friend and faithful mount. Grapeshot had killed both, mercifully fast, it was obvious. Wil still had his sword in his hand, his face contorted with a half grin, half grimace. John knelt by Wil, his hand on the dead man's back, as if to reassure its owner. "You saved us, Wil, my friend. Well done. I shall miss you."

John swallowed the lump in his throat, feeling the pain of loss like a knife in his chest. He rose, and walked over to Socks, lying a few feet away. The faithful horse was gone, never again to nuzzle John's hand at daybreak's greeting. For a moment, John stroked the dead animal's neck, before returning to his new mount. He looked at the tack and saddle on the captured horse. It was of the finest quality, even better than what he had on Socks, so he unloaded his gear from his old saddle and put it into his new. He watched sadly, as the casualty detail carefully placed Wil's limp form on the blood-soaked litter, and trotted toward a cluster of army ambulances gathered in the center of the field.

Tim Vernon watched as John slowly climbed on his new horse. "Sir, ain't you gonna take the tack from your old hoss?"

"No, I'll use this one. Why? You want it?"

"Yes, sir. I shore do. It's much better than what I got."

"Take it. I wish I could give away everything. Glorious victory, my aching arse. God forgive us. It was bloody slaughter, for both sides."

CHAPTER 9

With nightfall, stillness settled over the regimental bivouac. A quiet born of exhaustion and terrified awe at the horror they had just endured made the weary soldiers content to look into the fire and try and make sense of the past day. It was an uneasy silence, worsened by the remorse of the survivors. Almost to a man they questioned, *why him, and not me?* The thunderous din from the direction of Gettysburg was also gone, replaced by the night crickets' chirp or an occasional snort from a horse to break the quiet.

When John rolled up in his ground cloth about midnight, he slept more deeply than he expected. Khan Singh, hardened by twenty-five years of military service, toured the sentries every two hours, catnapping in between. He knew John was worn out, and let the man he admired—and loved like his own son—take a much needed rest.

About dawn, a "goose drowner" of a rainstorm hit the area, the impact of the heavy raindrops jolting John awake as the wet trickles inside his cover dampened his face and arms. As every man in the regiment was sleeping under the stars, it was not long before they were up, most cursing the fate that placed them in such wretched conditions. The grumbling soldiers failed to appreciate that the dead men laying scattered on the trampled down oat fields around them would have gladly suffered the indignity of getting wet with their comrades, one more time.

In a short period of time, smoky but serviceable fires were lit and the smell of hot coffee permeated the soggy surroundings. John sipped his tea, reviewing the final casualty list with Khan Singh. The two men looked up, as General Custer rode up, his horse a different one than the one John had given him two days earlier.

"Morning, General," John remarked, as he saluted the flamboyant cavalry general. "You lose Fiver, yesterday? You certainly go through horses."

"Good morning, John. Yep. The first charge. Then I had a second horse killed not a minute later. I grabbed this one from a Rebel officer and think I'll keep him. He's a winner."

John nodded. "I lost mine as well, but found a smashing replacement. We were facing the Hampton Grays, who were mounted on the finest collection of horseflesh I believe I have ever seen in one unit. We captured forty-seven of them, thoroughbreds all. Unfortunately, I had twenty-one men killed and thirty wounded as payment for our new horses. Among the KIAs was my adjutant, Major Horn. He was a fine soldier, and a good friend. I shall miss him."

Custer nodded, not very much concerned by the news. "A pity. I lost eighty-two, myself. Still, we had a glorious victory, and drove JEB Stuart's boys from the field. Saved the Union rear and I understand both Gregg and Kilpatrick are mentioning us in their reports."

John clinched his teeth. Custer was a vain, glory-hungry man-child and John knew it, so there would be nothing gained by lashing out at him good and proper for such a cavalier attitude toward the death of good men. "That's nice of them, General. What have you heard from Gettysburg?"

"A terrific battle there yesterday and complete victory for our cause. Lee attacked the center of Meade's line in the afternoon. That's what all the firing we heard was about, just when Stuart charged us. It was a total victory for our side, and Lee lost thousands of his best soldiers. Right now, the two armies are pulled back to their original lines, and Meade is waiting to see what Lee does next. I suspect we'll be rejoining Kilpatrick shortly, so have your men ready to ride. Our work isn't done yet, I'm afraid. Oh well," he chuckled, "we can rest after ole Bobby Lee surrenders."

Custer turned his boyish grin on John before turning to speak to nearby soldiers who stood waiting and hoping to obtain some idea of what might happen next to them. For a few moments, Custer laughed and joked with the men, cementing their affection for him. John admired the brazen display of grandiose. Custer was a master at making the common soldier like and respect him. He worked the gathering crowd of soggy soldiers to perfection. By the time he leaped on his horse and galloped away, they were all laughing and cheering their new brigade general.

John shook his head, and spoke to Khan Singh. "Sergeant Major, instruct the men to saddle up. And send me Captain Mansur. Tell Sergeant Vernon to distribute the horses we captured. First to the scouts, then the officers, then the NCOs, and finally the men, until all are gone. Leave any animal not fit to march here. We hit the trail as soon as Custer gives the word."

"Yes, Sahib. I have already chosen one of the new animals for myself. Is that satisfactory?"

"Of course, old friend. Give your old horse to Rava. His has a tendency to give out on a long march. It must have bad wind."

"Yes, Sahib. Er, Sahib?"

"Yes?"

"What of the enemy dead? They are still on the field."

John looked over at the field where they had fought the brave Confederate cavalrymen the day before. He could see numerous soldiers scavenging among the bodies, looking for souvenirs. He frowned at the scene.

"Recall those men, immediately. We will leave the dead enemy for the gravediggers. They'll be taken care of soon, I suppose. With all the dead at Gettysburg, it may take a while."

"It distresses me to leave brave men out like that, Sahib. They deserve better."

"You are right, old friend, as usual, but we have no choice. Well, off with you, now."

Khan Singh spun and walked away, his massive bulk even more imposing under the draped outline of his poncho. The old warrior shouted his commands over the falling rain to junior sergeants who in turn shouted at their men, until slowly, the regiment stirred out of its lethargy and prepared for movement. The men were still laggard, as if the intensity of yesterday's fighting had drained all the energy out of them. Khan Singh's bull voice and the prodding of the other NCOs soon put that right, and the Fifth Michigan prepared to continue the war.

Lee Mansur trotted up, his head bare, rain streaming off his hair and drooping mustache. "You wanted me, Colonel?"

"Yes, Lee. Where's your hat?"

Lee looked at John with a funny expression on his face. "You called me here to ask me that?"

"No, of course not, you silly sod. But, where is your hat?"

"Lost it yesterday. Out in those woods somewhere. I got Sergeant Jimmy out looking fer one among those boys still in the field."

"Good. I saw in your report that you had one man killed. You find a replacement for him?"

"Got a good man from M Troop, this morning. He'll be fine. The M-Troop boys were artillery before joinin' up with us."

"Who's your best man?"

"Sergeant Jimmy. Jim LeBlanc, that is. Why?"

"Can he handle the men and the fighting?"

"Sure, he's as good as any school-trained artillery cannoneer.

Had a year of college before he joined up. Understands deflection and powder charges. Studies all he can about trajectory and artillery tactics. Why'd you ask?"

"I'm promoting him to battery commander. You're coming up here to HQ, as my new adjutant. Tell Sergeant LeBlanc to sew on second lieutenant bars right away."

"Whoa, John, I don't want that. I'm happy right there with my battery of horse artillery. Can't you find someone else? Really, I don't want to be the adjutant."

"Sorry Lee. I'm not asking, I'm telling. This regiment has to have an adjutant, and you're it. Dig through poor Wil's kit, and see if you can find some major's leaves. I'm putting you in for immediate promotion and you're now the adjutant of the Fifth Michigan Cavalry Regiment."

Lee Mansur shook his head, sorrowfully. "Sure wish ole Wil had ducked. Not only do I lose a friend, but now, I gotta do his job. Some luck, I'd say."

"Check the readiness of the regiment to march, Mister Adjutant, and report back when everything's ready. Check with Sergeant McQuinn. I want every man resupplied with ammunition and rations for five days' travel."

"Yessir," Lee intoned mournfully, and climbed back on his horse, to reluctantly begin his new duties.

Within the hour, Custer reappeared at John's location, accompanied by his entire command entourage, flag bearers, couriers, aides, and orderlies. "We're to immediately rejoin Kilpatrick, west of Gettysburg, Colonel Whyte. You'll lead the Michigan Brigade, and I'll accompany you, at least until I ride ahead to meet with General Kilpatrick."

"Very good, General." John mounted his new horse. He decided to call the handsome gelding Hampton, in honor of the Virginia home where he was sired. John turned in the saddle to look back at his men, mounted by fours and ready to ride. Lee and Khan Singh had gotten them in their saddles as soon as they saw Custer approaching. John smiled, his heart filled with pride for his men and his command. He shouted, at the top of his lungs, "Fifth Michigan! By column of fours! At the walk, ho!"

Custer led off and John swung in beside him, Basu, Sean Gallagher, and Khan Singh behind the two senior officers and staff riders. Lee was at the rear, pushing the stragglers. The battle-weary men of the regiment fell in behind, following in line.

As they rode, the sun peeked out of the thinning overcast and the day became hot and humid. Every man shed his poncho and tied it behind his saddle. Their scratchy, woolen coats steamed in the hot sun. As the long line of mounted men approached the southern end of a barren hillock, shown on the map as Little Round Top, Custer spoke to John. "John, I'm going to ride on ahead, to find General Kilpatrick. I've left Lieutenant Granger to guide you past the town. I'll rejoin you as soon as I have our orders. You remember him? He was in C Troop of your regiment, until being assigned to brigade staff."

"Very well, General."

Custer pointed to his left, toward a field as trampled as all the others in the surrounding area. "By the way, there's where Kilpatrick sent Elon Farnsworth to his death in a senseless charge against entrenched infantry yesterday afternoon."

"Oh? I hadn't heard. What a waste and pity."

Custer looked almost pleased. John sensed a deep animosity in his young general toward the Third Division's commander. "Yep. A stupid order, unworthy of even Kilpatrick. Called Farnsworth a coward when he protested. Farnsworth told Kilpatrick he would call him out in a duel, as soon as he returned. Ole Elon was a dead shot with a pistol. I'll bet Kilpatrick breathed a sigh of relief when he fell. Lost a hundred men and did not cause the Rebs any discomfort at all. Bad business, I tell you, John."

"Yes, sir." John used the familiar nickname as he spoke, so Custer would know he was speaking as a friend. "Audie, you remember that, when you get your blood boiling to attack. Only use up men when it makes military sense, and these boys will follow you to Hell and back. You're already becoming a legend, leading the charges like you do. Just don't waste good men, General Custer, and your men will make you as famous as you would ever hope to be."

Custer gave John a devil-may-care grin and galloped off, not answering. John watched him go, followed by his flags and staff, the very epitome of the gay cavalier portrayed in the books of his youth. He hoped Custer had listened to him and that the advice had taken, at least a little.

Lieutenant Granger reported to John as Custer rode away. "We'll swing around the hill, Colonel Whyte, and ride parallel to the Union lines until we reach the town. Granger pointed toward a low rise of hills across a mile-wide field of trampled wheat. "That's the Rebels' main line, over there. Called Seminary Ridge. As we approach the center of our defensive line, there by that bunch of trees"—he pointed to John's left—"you can see where the battle was, yesterday."

The sun broke through the clouds, casting golden shafts of sunlight on the trampled field, covered in twisted dead. As John and his column rounded the base of the hill, a vision of unforgettable carnage confronted them. It was as if the heavens had ordained, "Look. See. Remember war in all its infamy."

As far as the eye could see, clumps of dead lay where they had fallen, alone, or in crumpled groups, some bodies horribly twisted and some already hideously swollen, depending on when they died, in day one, two, or three of the battle. John would have stopped in abject horror, had he been afoot, the scene was so monstrous in its impact. He rode on, carefully guiding his skittish horse between the dead, silent and morose, desperately trying to bring some sense of comprehension to the slaughter, but his brain was numb with the horror of it. Behind him, his men who had been riding, talking, and even laughing among themselves, grew quiet, as they realized what lay before them. Row after row of emerging riders looked upon the field of human destruction, swallowed, grew silent, and grimly rode on, grateful to be alive and anxious to get away from the bloody killing ground.

Granger noticed John's grim face. "Real quiet, isn't it, Colonel? Not a sound to break the stillness." He looked at the fields as they rode further north, to where the high-water mark of the Confederacy had dashed itself to bloody pieces the day before. "Must be ten thousand dead out there, maybe more. Real quiet."

"No, Lieutenant Granger, you're wrong. Listen closely. You'll hear the dead crying out in bitter anguish. They didn't want this. They cry, 'Why did this have to happen? What is worth all this?' Listen close, and remember what you see here for the rest of your life."

Granger looked askance at John but said nothing. With the ignorance of youth, he brushed off John's remarks. They really did not pertain to him, anyway. John looked to his right toward a tiny grove of barren trees at the top of the ridge. The leaves had been swept away as if from a late summer hailstorm, only the hail was lead bullets and iron cannonballs. Dead Confederates were stacked up along the ridgetop like fallen leaves. Crouched behind a hastily built rock wall at the center of the Union defensive line, weary infantrymen watched with dulled eyes at the passing riders. They leaned motionless against the wall where they had fought so desperately the day before. The grimy infantrymen seemed to be looking down a long road, their eyes vacuous, and their expressions resigned. These men had certainly seen the elephant and the sight would never leave them for long. John called his command to attention and gave a heartfelt salute to the shell-shocked men as he rode past, locking the scene deep in his memory. He would forever carry the grim image in his memory.

Still in stunned silence, John's column snaked through the narrow streets of Gettysburg, scarred from the previous three days' combat. At the far side of the town, where John Buford had fought so hard the first day and convinced his superiors that Gettysburg was a good place to defend, John met General Custer, impatiently waiting on his latest horse, a CSA brand still visible on its right flank.

"There you are, John. We're to march southwest toward Emmitsburg, just across the Maryland line. If Lee stays put on Seminary Ridge, we'll be in behind him. If he moves back toward Virginny, we'll be in his way."

John pulled out his map, and listened intently, as Custer outlined his route of march, before riding to brief the other three regimental commanders, then explained the plan to Lee, Tim Vernon, and Khan Singh, who had ridden up to join him. "We ride to Emmitsburg, here on the map." He pointed the route out to Tim and then looked hard at the young sergeant. "Sergeant Vernon, lead out. Watch for sign that Rebs are around and don't ride us into an ambush, but otherwise go fast as possible."

Within ten minutes, Custer's entire Michigan Brigade was riding south, on the Emmitsburg road, John's regiment in the lead. As if to punctuate the misery, the rains returned, pouring another soaking, miserable downpour on the heads and shoulders of the riding cavalrymen.

By dark, with no letup from the drenching, the saddle-sore men slogged into the tiny Maryland village of Emmitsburg.

They had not seen or heard even one Rebel soldier. After bivouacking in the fields near the village, John joined Custer for a home-cooked meal, courtesy of the local minister's wife.

They had just finished, when Sergeant Vernon knocked on the front door. He presented a ruddy-faced farmer, of medium height, and sandy hair. "Sir, this here is Mr. Fuhrman, from Monterey Springs. He has some news."

The middle-aged farmer, husky but aging poorly, his face creased with wrinkles from a lifetime outdoors, wearing worn pants and a homespun shirt faded and sweat-stained, entered the room and stopped. He made an awkward sort of half bow and stood in the middle of the room, twisting his hat in his work-hardened hands. "Yes, Mr. Fuhrman," Custer spoke in a friendly tone. "How may we be of service?"

"Mr. General, Pastor Wilkins, Mrs. Wilkins." He nodded toward John. "I come over from Monterey Springs. It's about six miles northwest o' here. Right at the opening of Monterey Pass where Furnace Road crosses into the Virginia tit, beg pardon, ma'am."

Custer pulled out his map, and pushed aside the plates until he could lay it out. He quickly found the spot on the map. "Yes, go on."

Fuhrman continued. " 'Bout two hours ago, a great big wagon train of Rebels passed my farm, headed fer the Furnace Road. Hundreds and hundreds of 'em, filled with men and what looked like spoils of war."

"By the grace of God! Pardon me, Reverend," Custer shouted, slamming his hand down on the table with a resounding whack. "Lee's retreating, and we're right in his way."

CHAPTER 10

John shrugged his shoulders, hoping to adjust his poncho to prevent the rain from trickling down the back of his neck. No matter what he did, after a few minutes riding, the relentless rain found its way down his neck to his soaked shirt. He turned and looked behind him. In the pitch-blackness, he could barely see Sean Gallagher and Rava Singh, riding directly behind him. He could only hope and pray that the rest of his regiment was following, as he rode toward the crossroads where the Furnace Road entered Monterey Gap. Custer's orders had been specific. "Block the pass. Stop all Confederate traffic from entering. We must cut off Lee before he reaches Virginny."

John had his doubts. It was as dark as he had ever seen it, and with the pouring rain obscuring everything, just a few pickets could stop his entire regiment dead in its tracks. Still, Custer had given him an order. And, militarily, it was a sound tactic. Now, if he could just do it. He glanced over at Mr. Fuhrman, riding stoically beside him.

"How much further, Mr. Fuhrman?"

"I ain't quite sure, Colonel. I can't see my hand in front of my face. We ain't come to the Plank Road Bridge yet, and the Gap is past it, a half mile or so."

John's blood chilled beyond the cold rivulets running down his back. A definite choke point to the pass. The Rebs would certainly have it guarded, unless he was very, very lucky. John held up his hand, stopping in the middle of the road. Sean

Gallagher nearly ran into him, before the young bugler halted his horse and so it went, as five hundred men each nearly slammed into the man to their front. The men sat silently, too miserable to even utter a complaint.

"Sean, find Sergeant Vernon. Have him report to me with all his scouts. Rava, ask Captain Kennedy to report to me. His C Troop is the first in line of march."

The two men disappeared into the darkness. More quickly than expected both men were back, with Vernon and his scouts, along with Captain Kennedy. John gathered the men around him and explained what Mr. Fuhrman had told him about the bridge they were approaching. "Tim, take your scouts and find it. This damned rain has masked all landmarks. Mr. Fuhrman is not certain where we are. Luke, you take your troop forward in support of the scouts. If they come under fire from Rebel pickets, you'll have to push them away from the bridge, so the regiment can cross. Use your own judgment as to whether to attack on foot or mounted, but clear that bridge. Understand?"

Kennedy eagerly replied. "Indeed I do, sir. Don't worry, we'll clear the bridge." He snapped a salute, unintentionally throwing water from his wet sleeve in John's face, and galloped back to his troop. He returned with his wet cavalrymen and followed Tim Vernon's scouts up the dark road. At the last minute, John sent the redoubtable Mr. Fuhrman along with them as a guide.

Waiting ten minutes, John started forward again, groping his way along the muddy road toward the bridge. Within a few short minutes, the rattle of musket fire and the clatter of horses across a wooden bridge reached him through the rain and slurping sounds of hooves hitting mud. Kennedy was at the bridge and the Rebels were there, just as John had feared. He thanked his lucky stars he had sent a small force on ahead. Had he led the whole regiment into an ambush in the rainy darkness, it could have been a bloody mess.

The rate of gunfire increased, and then, just as suddenly, it ceased. John pressed on, his heart pumping a little faster, unsure of what he was heading into. Out of the wet blackness, a form appeared on the road, and trotted up to him. It was First Sergeant O'Connor, from Kennedy's troop. He saluted and reported. "The bridge is clear, Colonel. We ran into a dozen Rebs. Come right up on 'em. They was tryin' to git outta the rain, not expectin' us. Caught two and kilt four, the rest lit out. They was as surprised at us as we was at them, I reckon."

"Where's Captain Kennedy?"

"I ain't sure, sir. He led the charge across the bridge and into the woods beyond the bridge, where the Rebs was hiding. I reckon he's over there somewhere."

John nodded. "Good enough. Recall your troop and fall in at the rear of the column, behind the supply wagons. You'll be the rear guard the rest of the way. Do you know where Sergeant Vernon and his men are?"

"He went on, sir. Said he was gonna follow them Rebs. The civilian is at the bridge. Says he ain't gonna go no further."

"Nor do I blame him," John replied. "Very good, Sergeant O'Connor. Rejoin your troop, and well done to them all."

John released Mr. Fuhrman with his profuse thanks and resumed the march across the bridge, the clatter of hooves on the wood planks sounding awfully loud to him. Hopefully, the incessant rain would drown the racket from enemy ears. In half an hour, they started up a gentle slope and abruptly, out of the misty gloom, Tim Vernon appeared right in front of him.

"Rebs, sir. Wagon after wagon of them, just over the hill, behind me."

"The Monterey Gap?"

"Has to be, Colonel."

"Infantry?"

"Just wagons, so far. Some men walkin' along beside 'em,

probably infantrymen actin' as guards, but no cavalry that I could see."

John slowly, painfully, got his regiment aligned into a fighting formation. In the dark and confusing blackness, it took some time, but at last, he had four troops abreast, with another rank of four in reserve.

Satisfied, he rode to the front of the formation and took out his pistol. He nodded at Sean Gallagher. "Now, Sean. Sound the charge."

At that same instant, the lightning flashed and John saw the young musician lick his lips, before putting the bugle to his mouth. The thrilling notes of the cavalry charge sounded through the wet night. John shouted at the top of his lungs, as he spurred Hampton's flanks, *"Chaaarge!"*

His men followed him over the top of the hill, into the flanks of a great wagon train, whose drivers and guards gaped in surprise as four hundred screaming Union cavalrymen thundered into their midst.

The fighting was hardly worthy of the name. The teamsters had no stomach for the battle and the few guards were quickly killed or overwhelmed by the mounted soldiers. John consolidated at the end of the wagon train. The convoy was about one hundred wagons long, mostly ambulances, with six to ten wounded men inside each. Wounded men moaned in the damp interiors, as they suffered the jouncing ride back to safety. He gathered up the sullen prisoners and ordered them and the wagons back over the hill toward Emmitsburg under the guard of Bill Brignon's A Troop.

John set up a defensive position, then sent two of Tim's scouts back to Emmitsburg, with a report to Custer recommending that the whole brigade march to his location immediately to bag the rest of the rebels marching south of the Furnace Road. He then set up a defensive position across the road, and quickly captured two more trains of wagons, filled with wounded or supplies, along with a hundred surprised guards. By daylight, John's command had scooped up nearly three hundred wagons, well over a thousand wounded soldiers, and more than two hundred teamsters, plus six hundred mules.

Just as day broke, the sun timidly lighting the dark, sullen clouds to the east, the couriers returned with written orders to return to Emmitsburg. John thought about sending a rider back to protest the order. He knew he was in a good spot to interrupt the retreating Confederates, when Tim Vernon rode up, sliding his panting horse to a stop in the mud and slop of the roadway. "Lots of infantry coming, Colonel. A division, at least. What do you wanta do?"

John's lightly armed and understrength command could not stand up to a division of infantry, even with the new repeating carbines. "Major Mansur, Sergeant Major Khan Singh," John shouted for his key subordinates.

Both men hurried to him, hearing the urgency in his voice. "We march, immediately. Tim, take your scouts and find a spot where Lieutenant LeBlanc can lob a few shells at those infantry. Maybe he can force them to stop and deploy. That'll give us enough time to get away. And Tim, don't let LeBlanc stay too long. I don't want to lose any of our cannon. Throw a few rounds, hitch up and return to the regiment, understand?"

As John led his mud-spattered command back over the hill, he could hear the harsh cough of LeBlanc's four-inchers, sending death and destruction toward the oncoming enemy.

While the regiment crossed the wooden bridge at the Plank Road, John paused, and waited for Vernon and LeBlanc to rejoin him. He watched as Sergeant O'Connor led a squad of men into the dense brush beside the road and then returned in a few minutes, carrying the still bodies of three troopers, one of which had to be Captain Kennedy. O'Connor looked at the men, and then jogged over to John.

"Captain Kennedy?"

"Yes, sir. Him and his guidon bearer and a trooper. All dead."

"I'm sorry, Sergeant. Kennedy was a fine fellow. Take charge of the troop, until I can assign you another officer."

"Yessir. I'll have Corporal Johnson take the captain and the boys on back to Emmitsburg, if it's all right, Colonel."

"Good. Leave them with the local parson. He'll take care of them."

John watched as the three limp bodies were slung across the backs of their horses, before turning away to watch the road leading away from the Gap. Over the top rode Tim Vernon, leading the four caissons and cannon of the very newly promoted Lieutenant LeBlanc. Vernon galloped to John's side.

"We did it, sir. They had a brigade on line, ready to charge, when we lit out. We got fifteen minutes or more, afore they arrive."

"Bloody good, Tim. Come on, let's get moving, then. I want to be in Emmitsburg within the hour, if possible. Custer needs to know what we have here."

General Custer was sympathetic to John's complaint, but shrugged his shoulders. "Orders, old man. We're to take the entire brigade west to Hagerstown. Pleasonton thinks that's where the main body of Lee's troops are headed. He feels we're just cutting his wounded trains where we are. That is all you saw, over to the Gap, right?"

"That's true, but an entire division was marching up as we left." John shrugged his shoulders in surrender. He wondered if they really had a chance to bag Lee and his war-weary veterans. It would take a lot more than just a division or two of cavalry.

John's fears were correct. For the next ten days, he led his men while the Union cavalry probed and nipped at Lee's flanks, but JEB Stuart's Mounted Invincibles held their own against everything General Pleasonton could throw at them. To President Lincoln's dismay, the Army of Northern Virginia crossed over the Potomac on 15 July, 1863, returning to the relative safety of their home soil. It was a great opportunity wasted, and insured the war would continue to extract its daily ration of blood and misery for many more long months. John, Custer, and Kilpatrick cursed and moaned at the waste of their men and effort, but to no avail.

By the first day of September, the Union army was itself repositioned along the Potomac, regenerating itself from the bloodletting of the summer campaign. John received replacements for the nearly ninety men he had lost over the past three months. He put the regiment through a severe training cycle, determined his men would be even better prepared for the next bloody go-round with the Rebels. He temporarily lost C Troop, which drew the honor assignment of Custer's personal color guard.

Custer now rode into battle with a dozen flags flapping brightly and a brigade band playing "Gary Owen" as loudly as possible, rashly showing to the enemy and his men where he and his headquarters were. The men of the brigade had fallen in love with their dashing, bon vivant cavalier and he could do no wrong in their eyes. He personally led charge after charge, losing men and his horse with regular rapidity, but always emerging unscathed. Custer believed himself a glorious figure of destiny and boldly went where no other general dared go. John rode at his side when it was his duty. Every time, he crossed his mental fingers that the Custer luck would rub off on him.

To date, it had. On the afternoon of the twelfth day of September, the Second Cavalry Division crossed the Rappahannock River, along with the First and Third Cavalry Divisions, entering Northern Virginia once again. General Pleasonton had orders to attack Stuart's cavalry, congregated around Culpepper

Courthouse, fifty miles south of Washington, while General Meade retired the Union army to winter quarters at Centerville, close to Washington. The ambitious Pleasonton took twelve thousand Union cavalrymen and headed cross-country, vowing to destroy Stuart in a week. The Union army thought Stuart might try to cut into Meade's rear, and Pleasonton meant to stop him. It seemed certain the Union and Confederate cavalries would clash, just as they had at Gettysburg three months earlier.

John found himself on the left flank of Custer's command, which was the left flank of the entire Union force. John had but one mission. No Rebel cavalry was to slice into the exposed flank of the main body. He had no doubt that the assignment would be very difficult, if Stuart shifted his forces to attack the flank. Fortunately, Stuart chose to fight the Union cavalry head-on.

John deployed and waited. Save for very minor skirmishing with Rebel scouts around daybreak, the morning of the thirteenth of September was quiet for John and his men. The same could not be said for those cavalrymen at the point of the Union attack. They smashed head-on into Stuart's men outside Winchester. By mid-afternoon, the Union cavalrymen had won the day and the Rebel cavalry slunk away, willing to wait for a better day.

Lee Mansur galloped up to John. He had taken M and L Troops to cover a seldom-used road approaching John's area of interest. "John, we grabbed us a Reb patrol in force, coming up that road."

"Excellent, Lee. I didn't even hear you firing."

"Hell, it was over in just about a minute. It was the advance for a whole regiment, the Twenty-second Virginia. We got the commander, and his flag. What shall I do with 'em?"

"Bring him along and the flag. Custer will want the flag for his display around the HQ camp, and we might obtain some worthwhile intelligence from the officer. Well done, Lee. I'll let you make the presentation to the general."

John watched, as Lee proudly motioned for the men with him to approach. The Confederate officer in command of the Twenty-second Virginia was slightly dazed, a bloody rag wrapped around his head.

John gave him a quick salute. "Good afternoon, Colonel. Are you well?"

"I'll survive, suh. What of my men?"

"Some routed, Colonel. Some captured. You are the prisoner of the Fifth Michigan Cavalry, Lieutenant Colonel Whyte at your service."

"Whose command?"

"General Custer's brigade of General Kilpatrick's Second Division."

"That damned Custer. You boys are causing us enough aggravation fer a fact." He glared at John. "Damn Custer and all you blue bellies who ride with him."

"I suspect, sir, that you'll have plenty of time to think about that while cooling your heels in Fortress Monroe Prison Camp."

CHAPTER 11

The Second Cavalry Division camped that evening on the outskirts of Culpepper Courthouse, the former base of operations for JEB Stuart's Cavalry. The Rebels had abandoned their camp in such a hurry that John's cavalrymen captured JEB's supper, a pot of roast chicken, and seized two young ladies of questionable virtue accompanying the Gray Cavalier's entourage. The two doxies were sent packing and the chicken quickly consumed.

John took Lee Mansur and the captured enemy battle flag to find their brigade commander. Custer was at Pleasonton's HQ, his left foot being wrapped by a medical orderly. He took John's hand salute without rising, a boyish grin on his face. "Look at this, will you? I got three weeks convalescent leave for this scratch, John old boy." Custer was fairly bubbling with excitement. "What a wonderful break for me. I aim to be married or at worst, engaged to my Libby when I return from Monroe."

John smiled. "I'm happy you are not seriously injured, sir. May I wish for you the very best of luck. Now, may I present my new adjutant, Major Lee Mansur. His gallant charge this afternoon resulted in the capture of this battle flag of the Twenty-second Virginia Cavalry, along with their commander, twenty-three men and two of his senior staff officers."

Custer leaped to his feet, elated. He forgot to favor the wound in his foot and nearly fell on his face. "By God, Major Mansur. Well done. That's what I want. We'll string JEB's guts around his neck any day now, with men like you against him." Custer grinned again as he carefully reseated himself. "You will wait until I return from Michigan, before you do it, I hope. I'd hate to miss the fun."

By the time Lee and John left Custer, Lee had become a fervent admirer of the cocky, boy general. "I'd follow you and Old Curly to Hell and back," Lee proclaimed. "I'm the luckiest fellow in the army, by gad. You for a colonel and Custer for my general."

"Just wait till Audie tells you to charge an entrenched infantry brigade, Lee. You'll be pulling buck and ball from your backside for a month of Sundays. And he just might. Custer thinks that he's invincible and that every man that rides with him is too. You know better. He thirsts for glory and if it's at the expense of your blood, so be it."

Lee laughed. "That's why I have you, John, Colonel, sir. You can stay between me and him, when he's in a glory mood."

And John vowed right then to himself, that that was exactly what he would do. Custer was both essential and dangerous to the Union cavalrymen he commanded. He would lead them to victory, and John would work to insure that the casualties be held to a minimum.

General Custer did return to Michigan, became engaged to his beloved Libby, and then rejoined the Michigan Brigade, his ardor for fighting diminished not one iota. Late autumn slowly brushed its painted magic across the land, as if nature could somehow transform the ugliness of the war with broad swaths of shimmering red, gold, and yellow colors that marched up the slopes of the Blue Ridge Mountains.

Within the shimmering foliage however, determined men, deadly hunters of their blue-coated enemy, waited with loaded rifles for the unwary rider. The official reports talked of light operations, scattered contacts, and static lines, as the two armies, like punch-drunk fighters, paused to rest after a protracted fight, then finally settled down into their winter positions. Even so, every week, John had one, two, three or more lamentable letters to write to a disconsolate mother or wife, that attempted to explain the loss of their loved one. John always related a story of bravery and self-sacrifice exhibited by every lost trooper, no matter the circumstances of his death.

While Lee offered to take some of this burden from him, John refused to abdicate the painful responsibility, believing it reminded him to be constantly vigilant in the expenditure of the men under him. "What do you want to torture yourself for, like that?" Lee asked more than once as John sat at his tiny desk, working under the glow of a candle's flickering light.

"Wait until you're responsible for a regiment, Lee. Then you'll know."

"Not me," Lee emphatically replied. "I ain't never gonna have that burden on my shoulders."

John gave Lee a bemused look at his friend, sitting on John's cot in the small headquarters tent of the regiment. "It is going to be a long war, my friend. Don't bet against it."

As winter settled in, John and Khan Singh drilled the regiment endlessly on offensive and defensive tactics, mounted maneuvers, and marksmanship. Several of his fellow regimental commanders derided John's insistence on rifle marksmanship, proclaiming it was unnecessary.

"Give the Rebs a taste of cold steel from your saber, and you will win the day. Nothing more is needed," Colonel Gray of the Sixth Michigan would loudly proclaim, when the four commanders discussed their training plans with Custer.

John said nothing. He was the youngest lieutenant colonel by many years, and chose not to enter into a verbal dispute with his older peers. Custer left the training decisions up to the commanders of his four regiments. All he wanted was men ready to charge the enemy with him, when the time came.

On December fifth, John received an invitation to have supper with President Lincoln and Mrs. Lincoln, during the Christmas holidays. He rode back to Washington, leaving a slightly envious Custer and a very jealous Kilpatrick behind, who were forced to share the season with their men in the bleak confines of the winter camp. Kilpatrick did have a camp doxie to brighten his nights, if not his days. Named Annie Jones, she was supposedly a nurse, but in reality was just a bed warmer for the division commander, sharing a bed in the mansion Kilpatrick had commandeered from an absent planter serving with General Lee. John had met her one afternoon, when the commanding general had ridden over to inspect his training.

She flashed him a simpering smile. "So you're the gallant Colonel Whyte I been hearing so much about," the vivacious vamp greeted John.

"I assure you, madam," John answered civilly, "it is my men who are the gallants."

"Ooh, modest, too. I like that in a soldier." She looked around. The two of them were temporarily out of earshot of the others. "General Kilpatrick has to go into Washington City for a few days next week." She winked conspiratorially at John. "Big conference of strategy, you know. What if I come by your camp and visit you while he's away?" She dropped her eyes, demurely. "Can you think of something we could do to while the time away?"

John scornfully answered her brazen offer. "My apologies, madam. I prefer to confine myself to my duties here. I can play when I visit the bawdy houses back in Washington."

With a huff of indignation, the woman stalked away. In retaliation, John subsequently learned that she took every opportunity to belittle his reputation with Kilpatrick.

Unknown to John until after the war, Kilpatrick blocked his

promotion to permanent rank of lieutenant colonel, thus insuring John would only be offered a commission as a major if he chose to stay in the military after hostilities ceased. Custer's intercession on John's behalf was fruitless and the pettiness of Kilpatrick widened the gap in Custer's feelings for the man. In the end, this only weakened Kilpatrick's position, as Custer was beginning to carry substantial clout within the political circles that ran the war.

Soon thereafter, John eagerly returned to his home in Washington for a ten-day furlough. John greeted Mrs. Richardson, the feisty widow whom he had hired to manage his home in Washington, with an exuberant hug. He had purchased the mansion that had once belonged to Rose Greenhow, whose spy ring John had helped to smash upon his initial arrival in Washington. With his consent, Mrs. Richardson had rented several of the rooms in the large home to officers assigned around Washington City.

"My goodness," the gray-haired widow proclaimed, once he put her feet back on the floor. "I've missed you too, John. How's Lee? And your Sikh friend, Khan Singh?"

John had purchased this old rooming house for his Indian friends as their place to live after they arrived in America.

"They're fine. Lee sends a special hello. I told him he could have some time off, once I get back to camp. He's my adjutant now, so we can't both be gone at the same time. The Sikhs are all fine. I guess you heard about Modma."

"Yes, I saw him just the other day. He's over at my old house, with Khan Singh's wife and the children, recovering from his wound. I guess you knew he lost his arm. We'll go by and see him, if you have time later."

"How bad is his arm?"

Mrs. Richardson shook her silver-haired head. "Gone, clear to the shoulder. It must have been a fearsome wound."

101

"We thought he was dead. Yes, I do want to see them. I'm trying to convince Khan Singh to take a few days off as well, once I get back."

Mrs. Richardson smiled and poured him a cup of her truly awful coffee. John added two heaping spoonfuls of sugar, and sipped the noxious brew with the kindhearted widow. His great affection for her prevented him from uttering even the slightest criticism for her bitter brew.

Mrs. Richardson interrupted his stirring. "I heard from Karina Block the other day."

John looked up. Karina was Lee's sister and had married Lee's friend, Craig Block, who had served under John as well. He had been severely wounded the previous May, in the fight at Hanover Station. "Lee reads me some of what she writes him, now and then. How are they?"

"Doing about as you would expect. Craig nearly died from his wound, and is just now beginning to recover to where he can walk about. Karina has worked herself half to death, taking care of him, poor dear."

John nodded his head sympathetically. "However, she's luckier than some. She might have had to bury him. I've lost too many fine young men these last six months."

"Yes. You must be sick of it. Who wouldn't be?"

"Believe it or not, Mrs. Richardson, General Custer isn't, not for a minute. He has as fearsome a warrior's mentality as ever I've seen in a soldier. Fearless to an extreme and utterly contemptuous of danger to himself or the men who follow him."

"Well, bless me, why do the men do it? Ride into danger with him like the papers all say?"

John shook his head. "It's hard to describe, Mrs. Richardson. It's just that when George rides out in front, laughs like a maniac at the Rebels vainly trying to kill him, and says, "Follow me," charging the enemy like a madman, his sword pointed at their throat, it's impossible not to follow, screaming like a demented, wild man yourself."

Mrs. Richardson busied herself with her knitting, a furrow on her forehead and confusion in her voice. "Lordy sakes, I wouldn't, for a fact."

John grinned. "That's why I've always said women had more common sense than men, ma'am."

"And for that, you get my special fried chicken and whipped potatoes with white gravy for supper. And"—she smiled in her own sweet way at him—"I'll throw in some apple pie, if you'll bring in some more wood for the stove."

John hurriedly finished his chore. He eagerly attacked the good home cooking of Mrs. Richardson, eating his fill, drank two cups of strong coffee heavily sweetened with sugar, then slept sounder than he had in six months.

John spent the next day shopping, restocking his trunk with the shirts, pants and toiletries he had worn out or used up during the last six months in the field. As he returned to the house, Mrs. Richardson handed him a letter. "Just got delivered by the postman, dear."

John took the letter and read the return address. "It's from my solicitor, Mr. Noah Silverman, in New York." He tore the envelope open and read the contents of the letter.

Dear John,

It is my pleasure to provide you with an accounting of your assets with me for the past year. Our investments have been more fruitful than even I anticipated.

Shalom,
N. Silverman

John read on, quickly realizing that his account had nearly doubled in the past year. The wretched war was enriching him beyond his wildest dreams. He considered the irony of it all. As he had done countless times, he blessed Khan Singh for hiding those jewels in his trunk when he left India in disgrace nearly two years ago. He folded the letter and after assuring Mrs. Richardson that the news was good, excused himself to prepare for dinner.

The next evening, John dressed in his finest uniform and rode a small hansom cab to the White House. He arrived as the receiving line was forming and presented the uniformed guard his invitation. He stood in the line, behind a pompous general from army headquarters and his overfed, complaining wife awaiting their turn to greet the president. As the social aide murmured his name to the president, Lincoln's eyes widened and a broad grin spread across his homely features, transforming the man's solemn countenance. "By gads, Mother. Here's our young English import. John, my boy, so good to see you again. I've been following your career with interest. You've done some wonderful things for the Union. Well done, well done. Please, have yourself a drink and enjoy the party. I'll speak with you before the night's over, I promise."

"My pleasure, sir. At your convenience," John whispered his acknowledgment, and moved on to greet Mrs. Lincoln. She responded to his felicitations with the same pinched expression that she habitually wore throughout her daily life. As John walked away, he felt warmed by the president's statement. He was pleasantly surprised that the president had followed his career.

John ambled into the main ballroom, his boots tapping softly on the polished, wood parquet floor, where most of the guests were assembling. A huge Christmas tree stood at the far end, with hundreds of tiny candles burning on its green branches and the sparkle of uncountable numbers of glass balls reflecting their tiny glows. He spotted two husky Army privates standing just behind the tree, next to several buckets of water. They rarely took their gaze from the sparkling tree.

John chuckled aloud.

"See something amusing, Colonel Whyte?" a man spoke beside him.

John turned. It was Edwin Stanton, the secretary of war, whom John had met during his stint as a counterspy for Alan Pinkerton and the president.

"Oh, good evening, Mr. Secretary. I didn't notice you come up. Yes, I was just thinking about those two privates hidden behind the Christmas tree. I'll bet some hard-nosed sergeant let them know in no uncertain terms that if anything other than the Christmas tree catches fire, they might as well just throw their asses right on the blaze with it."

Stanton grunted softly, as close to a laugh as he would allow himself, and turned to the two officers with him, one a corpulent general, the other a young lieutenant, obviously his son. The older general looked suspiciously at the young lieutenant colonel. In his opinion, the young officer was far too junior to be included in the White House guest list. Secretary Stanton made the introductions. "General Meigs, may I present Lieutenant Colonel John Whyte, currently with General Custer, in the Second Cavalry Division. Isn't that right Colonel Whyte?"

John was amazed again. The war secretary certainly knew more about him than he expected. "Yes, sir, Mr. Secretary, I'm part of Custer's Wolverines."

Stanton nodded. "General Meigs is the Army quartermaster general. And this is his son, Second Lieutenant John Meigs. Graduated first in his class at West Point last June. Now the chief engineer in General Scheck's division, serving in the Shenandoah Valley."

"My pleasure, General, Lieutenant. A merry Christmas holiday to you both."

John briefly discussed the war from the point of view of one serving in Custer's command with the two Meigs and Secretary Stanton. Meigs quizzed John on the cavalry's opinion for the current Army-issued equipment.

"We certainly like the new repeating Spencer carbines, General. It gives the cavalryman a decided firepower advantage against the enemy."

"Maybe," General Meigs rumbled, his deep voice matching his ample girth, his gray, Burnside-style whiskers marched upward into the gray of his hair. General Meigs was definitely a deskbound soldier. "But, you still can't take on an equal number of entrenched infantrymen, with buck and ball, can you?"

"No, sir, not in a slugging match. But that's not the way to use cavalry. We should be used to slash and ride, penetrate and get behind the enemy. Hit the flanks, circle the entrenchments with our mobility and smash into him from the rear." John smiled. "General Custer and Pleasonton are beginning to do just that. I believe you will see that our success against the Rebels should multiply as time goes on."

Stanton shook his head, a bit irritated by John's audacity. "I forgot to tell you, Montgomery, this young man says exactly what he thinks and damn the consequences."

Meigs nodded, as he measured John's words. "Yes, Edwin, but he's been out there, don't forget. Very well, young man, I'll consider pushing an increase in the issuance of the new repeaters. You use them to best advantage."

"Count on it, General."

John bid the three a good evening, as the head butler gave the command to take their seats at the tables. Young Meigs flashed John a wide grin, behind the backs of his two elders, as he followed them toward their seats near the president's table. "I hope to meet you again, Colonel Whyte. I plan to obtain an assignment in the cavalry, just as soon as my current one is complete."

Lieutenant Meigs was destined to die in action shortly thereafter and his father, in a pique of revenge, had him buried in General Lee's front yard at Arlington Estate, just across the river from Washington. Soon the Lee estate was filled with graves of Union dead and would never again be home to the Rebel general.

John found his card far removed from the seat of power. His table companions, two Senators, from Kansas and Missouri, and a high-ranking member of the State Department, along with their wives, peppered him with questions throughout the meal, along with observations of their home states' contribution to the war effort.

John listened to the brief holiday speech from the president and then settled back to enjoy the rendering of several Mozart and Haydn sonatas by a string ensemble from the Washington Symphony. He was enjoying a particularly fine rendition of the Mozart String Quintet No. 5, when he felt a tap on his shoulder.

A civilian aide whispered into his ear. "Follow me, Colonel Whyte. The president wishes to speak with you, in the upstairs parlor."

John slipped from the room, following the aide. Those who knew what the appearance of the aide meant, raised their eyebrows and cast curious glances his way. Whispered questions followed John's exit from the ballroom. "Who's that? Why is that young officer leaving to meet with the president?"

"Ah, John, here you are. Come in, come in. Have a seat. Drink?"

"Thank you, sir. A small brandy, if you please."

Lincoln nodded to the aide, who quickly furnished the drink and then left the room. John noticed that Lincoln had changed into his tattered house slippers, the same ones he had seen him wear the first time they met. Lincoln noticed John's glance, and grinned sheepishly. "My feet were aching like I'd been walking barefoot under an oak tree shedding acorns. Hope you don't mind if I get comfortable."

"Not at all, Mr. President." John was embarrassed that Lincoln had seen him stare.

"Loosen your blouse, if you want, John. Make yourself comfortable. I want to talk about your impressions on the conduct of the war." Lincoln's voice was pleasant and friendly.

John politely declined to shed his jacket, and waited for Lincoln to ask his questions. He knew the great man wanted straight answers and John prepared himself to supply them.

Lincoln's eyes leveled with John's. "I saw you were at Gettysburg. What a tragic but essential victory for the Union. I went there myself last month, at the dedication of the new military cemetery."

"Yes, sir. I read your speech in *Harper's Weekly*. It was a stunning example of oration. It was incredibly stirring—a speech that will last the ages."

"Thank you, my boy." A small smile creased his worn, weary face. "It didn't seem to hit it off with the folks there, but the papers have begun to treat it a bit more generously these last few weeks. Thank you for your praise." Lincoln paused, and collected his thoughts. "We should have finished them off there, John. We let Lee retreat back across the Potomac, and now, he's building up again, for next year's campaigns. We had him, didn't we?"

John paused. He could faintly hear the music from below. "Yes, sir. I don't have the complete facts to judge by, but it seems to me that we should have at least tried to finish him as he retreated back toward Virginia."

Lincoln nodded. "And since then, Meade has twice taken the army across the Rapidan River, and twice that magnificent devil, Robert E Lee, has maneuvered him back to where he started." Lincoln's face was strained and angry. "Why won't my generals take care of Lee, once and finally? If our army doesn't achieve some success here in the East very soon, I'll never win next fall's election. It is my belief that the Union may very well fall if a Peace Democrat wins the presidency."

"Sir, my answer is the same as it was to you last March. You need a general like our Wellington, in eighteen fifteen at Waterloo. An English bulldog, who'll grab Lee by the arse and not let go till he's whipped."

"You mean Grant, or a man like him, don't you?"

"Exactly, Mr. President. General Ulysses S. Grant."

CHAPTER 12

Major Lee Mansur looked expectantly at John as he entered the headquarters tent. Outside, the cold, February north winds off Chesapeake Bay whipped the canvas sides of the tent in a monotonous thrumming. It was as cold as any day of the winter and the near-gale-like winds made it feel worse. Nobody wanted to draw picket duty on a day like this. The unlucky souls which drew the thankless duty offered plenty of complaining as they headed for the damp, miserable, frigid fighting positions along the edge of the Rapidan River, where the Fifth Michigan Regiment was bivouacked.

"So, John, tell me. Is the general's new wife as pretty as everyone says? Lee hunched over as close to the tiny Franklin stove as he could without scorching his wool pants, vigorously rubbing his cold hands together.

"Lee," John answered enthusiastically, "she's delightful. Lovely as a warm, spring day, full of life, and perky as a fresh colt. She glows with the joys of marriage and her new husband. He's a lucky man, believe me."

"And is Custer gonna keep her at his HQ, for the winter?"

"So he says. And she echoes his sentiment completely. She's some woman, I assure you."

"They mention the silver tea set you sent them for a wedding gift? Did it arrive on time?"

"Yes," John smiled at his friend. "Mrs. Custer was most appreciative. Said it was admired by all who saw it."

Lee nodded his head in satisfaction. "She should have. If she had seen the snowstorm we rode through to order it, she'd be doubly grateful."

John rubbed his hands against the back of his thighs at the warmth of the stove. "If it weren't for the fact that we'll be going out on a spring campaign, I'd wish away these miserably cold days. Even the north of India wasn't this bitter in winter."

"Things are gonna get hotter, real quick," Lee replied. "I heard a rumor over to headquarters this morning. Gen'l Kilpatrick is in Washington plannin' a big raid on Richmond. He wants to cut the railroads leadin' into the town, hopin' it'll discomfort the Rebs. Then, he'll free the prisoners in Libby and Belle Isle prisons before headin' back to here."

John shook his head. "Sounds rather ambitious to me. Hopefully, the War Department won't go for it."

"Don't count on it, Colonel. Kilpatrick's got the president interested. Told his aide that Lincoln wants to spank the Rebs some during this down time, just to let 'em know we're a'comin' as soon as the weather allows."

John frowned, perturbed at the thought of the coming battles and their inevitable casualties. "Now, I wish the winter would last forever, damn it."

Kilpatrick soon returned to his division with permission to make his grand raid on the capital of the Confederacy. Thanks to the luck of the draw, John's regiment was tasked to be the security detail for Kilpatrick's command headquarters, so his men missed the worst of the fighting. The ambitious General Kilpatrick somehow seemed to misunderstand the bitter struggles that his subordinate commands faced every day of the ill-conceived misadventure. The two brigades involved in the most bitter fighting suffered heavily. John's men traded serious shots with the aroused Confederate cavalry only once, as they covered the Union soldiers' inglorious retreat back across the

Rapidan to the safety of their winter camps. Even so, the four, sad letters of condolence that John had to write to brokenhearted families put him in a deep funk for several days afterwards.

The only good drawn from the entire sorry episode was the removal of General Kilpatrick as commander of the Second Division, much to the relief of every man in the unit. However, as Custer was senior to the new commander, General Wilson, the entire Michigan Brigade was transferred on paper to the First Division, under General Tolbert, a welcome move in John's opinion. Meanwhile, the winter day passed uneventfully. John and Khan Singh devoted themselves to training the fresh recruits levied in to replace the losses from the previous summer's hard fighting.

John sat on a campstool while Rava Singh shaved him on a snowy Saturday afternoon, when Lee Mansur entered the rear half of the HQ tent, John's private area. John grunted a mangled greeting at his friend and senior assistant.

"You going over to the general's again, John?" Lee sniffed his runny nose. "You spend more time over there than any other officer in the Michigan Brigade, I reckon."

"I suspect you're right, old chap. Can I help it if Libby Custer has taken a shine to me? In a friendly way, of course. She's solid in love with Georgie, I assure you. I think she's intrigued with my English accent. And, she's mad about the stories I tell her of England, Europe, and India. She has a fertile mind. She should travel, see some of the world, once this damned fighting is done. I might mention that to Custer, if I find him in a mellow mood this evening."

"The general out of sorts, lately?" Lee quizzed.

John nodded. "He's upset about Wilson getting the First Division, now that General Buford has died, and now that Grant has chosen Sheridan to be the new head of the Cavalry Corps, Custer's afraid he's on the outside looking in, as far as influence is concerned."

Lee grunted. "Could be somethin' to that, I suppose. How 'bout you? You told me you rode with Sheridan, when you were with Grant before Vicksburg. He like you?"

John shrugged, as Rava Singh wiped the last of the white, fluffy lather from his face. "Well enough, I suppose. Sheridan is his own man and has no patience for those with whom he finds disfavor. Custer had better not trip over his big mouth, at least until little Phil gets to see our boy general in action. Then, I imagine Custer and he will get along just fine. As for me, I suppose I'll receive a brigade, when one comes available. You ready to take over the Fifth Michigan?"

Lee vigorously shook his head, swishing his long, brown hair across his nose. "No sirree, bob, I ain't. I'm plenty happy just being the regimental major. I don't want nothin' to do with commandin' it."

John chuckled. "Get used to the idea, my friend. Even if I don't obtain a brigade soon, some Rebel minié ball might puncture my brisket, and you'll be commander by default."

"Lordy, John," Lee complained. "Don't even talk that way in jest. Ya don't want to jinx yurself, do ya?"

John smiled as he adjusted his greatcoat. "I'll be over at General Custer's place until quite late, if this little dinner party goes as the last. Check C Troop's pickets, before you turn in. They went out last week without a full complement of ammunition, if you remember. The troop's first sergeant's face was beet-red, when Khan Singh and I inspected them on the line and discovered they had failed to draw fresh ammo."

"Yes, sir, Colonel, sir. You go on over to the general's place. Have a good, hot meal and socialize with his pretty new wife. Ol' Lee Mansur will take care of the mundane details of the regiment."

"Don't you see why I chose you, Major? I'll try and bring

113

you a piece of cake, if they have one. See you later." John stepped out of the back flap of the tent and mounted his new horse, a broad-chested bay with two white socks on his forelegs, just arrived from the remount depot. His new mount was a big animal, standing nearly seventeen hands high and was highly spirited. John had great hopes for him, but of course would not know until the first battle if the animal was indeed a suitable war horse. John's last horse, Hampton, named after the home of the Rebel regiment he had defeated at Gettysburg, had suffered a minié ball in the flank during the retreat across the Rappahannock River. It was the sad aftermath of Kilcavalry's, as the men derogatorily named him, senseless raid against Richmond. He was recovering slowly, but was not yet able to carry a rider without effort.

For now, the faithful animal was stabled on a farm outside Washington. John had purchased him as a war prize and was paying a local veterinarian to treat the wounded horse. John was grateful that the Fifth Michigan's only responsibility during Kilpatrick's grand adventure had been to guard Kilpatrick's worthless arse. The Rebs had cut the main body of cavalry to pieces, killing and capturing many Union cavalrymen.

General Custer and his new bride were spending the winter as guests of a pro-Union plantation owner about two miles from where John and his Michigan regiment had taken up winter bivouac. He rode quickly in the cold afternoon air, trotting into the front drive of Custer's HQ just as the sun, its rays softened by low, gray clouds, settled behind the Allegheny Mountains.

John was admitted upon his knock by Lieutenant Havens, one of Custer's aides. He shrugged away his greatcoat and handed the young officer his hat and gauntlets. "Evening, Edwin. Who's here?"

"Just you and Lieutenant Colonel Darling of the Seventh

Michigan, Colonel Whyte. Mrs. Custer is in the mood for another game of whist."

"Very good. She's really taken to the game, hasn't she?"

"Oh, yes, sir. In fact, I doubt there's much she can't do well, if she puts her mind to it." Lieutenant Havens gave John an odd sort of glance, as if seeking John's input as to what he thought of Mrs. Custer.

He's as smitten by the new woman in our midst as everyone else, John surmised to himself. John also had to be honest with himself. He felt a most pleasurable attraction, when she was near or when he caught her unaware with his glance. He was human, as vulnerable as any lonely man and it had been far too long since he'd dropped in on the working girls at the Little White House, Washington's most exclusive refuge of ill repute. Lee had taken him there the second night he had been in Washington, two years earlier, and he had returned from time to time, when his loneliness for female companionship demanded.

"Ah, here's our good Colonel Whyte." Custer stepped out of the main library, a cigar and a brandy snifter in his hand. "Care for a smoke or before-dinner brandy, John?"

"No thank you, General. I'll wait until after the meal. If your wife and her cook, Miz Eliza, serve a feast as fine as my last visit, I wouldn't want to diminish my taste buds one little bit."

Custer smiled, and looked down at the crystal brandy glass in his hand. "Since I promised Libby I'd forgo spirits of any kind, I'm about to give this one to Colonel Darling. Join us in the library. Libby is still fixin' herself up to dazzle us with the beauty of her feminine presence and Eliza is preparin' the best-lookin' smoked ham you ever saw. It was sent to me by an admirer back in Monroe."

John followed Custer into the library. The lanky, brown-haired Dan Darling, his light-brown beard reaching to the second button of his blue cavalry jacket, stood and nodded politely toward John.

"Evenin', John. How are things with the Fifth Michigan?"

"Splendid, Dan. How are you? Enjoy your trip back to Detroit?"

"It was great. Got one hundred sixty-nine new recruits and saw my folks and sister in the bargain. I'm up to seven-hundred effectives."

Custer broke in. "How 'bout you, John. Refresh my memory. What's your strength, now?"

"With the new levy that came in from Vermont, I'm at six twenty, General."

Custer nodded. "Any more coming your way?"

"I was promised close to a hundred, sometime next week. They are from two additional Detroit companies just finishing their recruit training. That will give me fully manned companies, plus a complete headquarters contingent."

"It will do. I just received a message from General Grant. We're to start preparations for a major operation, sometime around May first. The cavalry will be heavily committed to the operation. That gives you the better part of two months to whip your men into tip-top fighting shape. I assure you, gentlemen, the Michigan Brigade will garner all the honors and glory imaginable if I have to ride them clear to Richmond and back."

Any response was muted by the arrival of Libby Bacon Custer. She entered the room encased in a sky-blue, taffeta dress that hugged her petite figure and swished with every step.

John relished her beauty. Her curly, light-brown hair dropped in ordered ringlets about her bare shoulders, in much the same manner as her husband's golden locks. Her blue eyes were alert, intelligent, filled with a lively spirit that endeared her to every man she met. "Hello, everyone. John, Dan, so nice to see you both. I hope you both are well? How was your furlough, Colonel Darling?"

By the time Darling had replied to Mrs. Custer's question, Eliza had entered the room with the announcement that dinner was served. Libby placed her dainty hand on her husband's arm and together they led the hungry soldiers to the table, where smoked ham, fried potatoes, buttered peas, and a delicious crumb cake were efficiently and enthusiastically consumed. The polite dinner conversation continued while everyone savored the excellent food. After the table was cleared of dishes by two privates in white coats, Custer pushed back his chair and held his arm out for his wife.

"Gentlemen, you're in for a treat. Will you accompany Mrs. Custer and me to the drawing room?"

There, a young trooper awaited them, seated in front of a harpsichord. He grinned shyly, as Libby Custer introduced him. "Gentlemen, this is Private Jeffery Wert, from Grand Rapids. He is a recent graduate of the Michigan Conservatory of Music. He has graciously agreed to give us a recital this evening. Jeffery, you may begin, if you please."

The young soldier opened with a soft, melodic Bach fugue. He eventually played several compositions before Libby would allow him to quit.

"Wasn't he marvelous?" she asked, as the young trooper finished and took his leave.

"Quite," John replied. "General, I hope you can keep that young man alive. His talent is such that he'll surely be famous, after the war."

Custer guffawed. "He's in the wrong damn unit to be looking out for his skin, by gum. The Michigan Brigade always marches toward the guns, you know that by now, John."

"Yessir, I do. But that lad has genius in his hands. Don't waste him, I mean it, General. Even if you have to transfer him to some other command."

Custer smiled broadly at the earnestness in John's voice. "Just kidding you, John. I've already assigned him to my headquarters as a member of the band. He'll be as safe there as anywhere, I suppose. Now, come on. Dan and I mean to regain our championship at cards from you and Libby. Danged if I know why she always insists on you as her partner, Colonel Whyte."

"Darling Audie," Libby enjoined. "I've told you a dozen times. I don't want to take a chance you and I should ever argue over a silly game of cards." She flashed a quick grin at John and Darling. "I'll save my arguments for something really important, like a new dress."

John held out her chair, silently appreciating her peaches-and-cream complexion. They immersed themselves in the cards, speaking things of little importance and enjoying the respite from the oppression of the war. As usual, Custer bid too aggressively and John and Libby slowly forged ahead in the score. Libby held her own in the good-natured give-and-take around the table. She was delightful company and John savored the feelings she stirred in him.

As they played their cards, Custer happened to remark that he had just received orders to report the next morning to General Tolbert's HQ. "He wants a detailed report on our strength and level of training. I suspect Sheridan's asking for a breakdown of the division's readiness for a spring offensive."

"Oh, Audie," Libby complained. "Tomorrow's my day to ride over to Haymarket for my dress fitting. You promised to go with me."

"Can't do it, Lib, dearest. Duty calls. Colonel Whyte." Custer looked toward John. "Could you accompany Libby to Haymarket tomorrow? I'll have a squad of men from the headquarters detachment as escort so's it won't interfere with your unit's training plans."

John nodded. "Be my pleasure, General."

"Thank you."

John smiled at Libby Custer. "May I substitute for your husband, madam?"

Libby shook her head, smiling coyly at her new husband. "Sorry, Colonel. No man alive can substitute for my Audie. But, you'll do fine as a companion in his absence."

The others laughed, but George Armstrong Custer had to force a grin. Faint stirrings of jealousy crept deep inside his heart. Libby liked the Englishman, perhaps just a little too much.

CHAPTER 13

John stretched in the crisp, cold morning air, lifting his arms high over his head. He grinned as Rava Singh led his horse toward him. The new bay was frisky and prancing sideways in his eagerness to be underway. "By gad, I'll call him Frisky. It fits him well." John took the reins, and stroked the horse's velvety nose. "Yessir, you're christened Frisky. All right with you, big fella?"

Rava Singh nodded in agreement, his maroon turban catching the bright sunlight. "A fine name for this one, Sahib. I hope he is as good as your last horse. What a warrior he was."

John nodded. "Hampton was a fine animal. Hopefully he's recuperating well from his wound. I'd like to have him under me again, someday."

"I am certain of it, Sahib."

Sergeant Major Khan Singh strode toward John and his son, a fierce scowl on his scarred, bearded face. "Sahib, don't you think I should ride with you and the general's memsahib? I do not like it when you are so far from my eyes."

John laughed at his faithful retainer and friend. "Don't worry, old friend. General Custer promised that some of his men would ride with us as escort. You must stay here and supervise the latest batch of recruits training in the use of their Spencer carbines. We go on the springtime offensive soon. I'll be fine. Have Sergeant McQuinn issue the new shipment of ammunition to every company after the target practice. Shoot up all the stuff we've had over the winter. Some of it may have mildewed in the humidity."

John called into the headquarters tent. "Major Mansur, I'm on my way. Should return before dark. If I stay at the Custers' for supper, I'll send you word by messenger."

Major Mansur appeared at the flap of the tent and casually touched his eyebrow with his first two fingers of his right hand. "We'll take care of things, Colonel. Enjoy your ride with Mrs. Custer."

John climbed up on Frisky's back, comfortably settling into the McClellan saddle. He nodded at Khan Singh and Lee Mansur, his two closest friends, then cantered off, enjoying the smooth, easy gait of the muscular horse under him.

When he arrived at General Custer's HQ, he saw a trim-looking mare tied to the front hitching post. She was coal-black, with four white stockings past the fetlocks. A woman's sidesaddle was strapped to her back and she snorted as Frisky stopped beside her. "Looks like Mrs. Custer has found herself a dandy little mount, big fellow. Don't you get fresh with her." He stroked the bay's muscular neck, before he climbed down.

Libby was in the dining room, sipping a steaming cup of coffee, as John was escorted to her by one of the HQ orderlies. "Good morning, Colonel Whyte. It looks like a marvelous day. I'm so grateful that you can take time from your busy schedule to accompany me to town. I'm desperate to get out of the house for a while."

"My pleasure, madam. Where's the general?"

"He was up before the dawn and off to General Tolbert's camp. He said to give you his regards and he'll see you when he returns. Shall we be underway?" She stood, a vision of delicate loveliness. She wore a navy-blue, velvet riding skirt and a tan Zouave jacket over a white silk blouse, buttoned to her chin. She grabbed a straw, flat-brim hat and tied it over her brown locks with a scarlet ribbon, similar to the scarlet kerchief Custer habitually wore around his neck. She cheerily smiled and led him from the room, her step bouncy and full of energy.

As they exited the front door, a half squad of troopers trotted over from the edge of the lawn led by a crusty-looking, bewhiskered sergeant-in-charge. He gave a snappy salute and spoke with a thick Irish accent. "Sergeant Hamlin, sir. I'm in charge of yer escort."

John cast a quick but experienced eye over the six troopers. All mounted and armed with carbines, pistols and swords. They passed his critical inspection. John nodded at the waiting Sergeant Hamlin. "Very good, Sergeant. We'll take it easy, if you please. Mrs. Custer and I will follow the point, you bring up the rear with the rest." John knew this would make Libby eat the least amount of dust while they rode.

The experienced NCO nodded and waited while John offered Libby a cupped hand to carefully hoist her into her saddle. As she threw her leg over the leg pommel, he caught a quick flash of creamy, white bloomer and his blood raced in his veins. She was a damned beautiful and intriguing woman, especially to a man currently restricted in his recent encounters with members of the opposite sex.

Libby Custer turned her horse toward the road in front of the mansion, her animal dancing in anticipation. "Let's be off, Colonel."

John held up his hand in supposition. "Mrs. Custer, you must allow the sergeant to deploy his men first. You wouldn't want to cause him trouble, would you?"

"Oh, John. Call me Libby. We're not at the table with the general now. Isn't it grand? I love this pony Audie found for me. Do you like purple? That's the color of the dress I am having made in Haymarket. I found the most skillful seamstress there." Libby Custer was chattering happily, her lively spirit infecting everyone with her enthusiasm.

John grinned at the likable young woman, then called to the sergeant. "Sergeant Hamlin, do you know the route to Haymarket?"

"Yes, sir. Take the Marshalltown Road to the ford and turn due east on the Front Royal Turnpike."

"That's it. Very well, lead off. Put two men at point, and follow at twenty paces with the rest of your men."

Sergeant Hamlin flipped a quick salute. "Yessir. Carter, you and Jerome lead off. You know the way." He turned his horse to the rear, and joined the trailing quartet, about fifty feet behind. John and Libby were somewhat alone, both horses walking briskly, side by side on the dirt roadway. They rode together, laughing and talking, while the distance passed under their horses' hooves. John was continuously amazed at the depth of Libby Custer's interests and knowledge. She had received a far superior education compared to most women of the time.

They arrived in Haymarket before noon. Libby left her escort to enter a small shop just off the main street. John dismissed the escorts, with a stern admonition to return at three o'clock, completely sober. Sergeant Hamlin assured him that would be the case and hurried away, furiously thinking of a way to sneak a few drops of store-bought whiskey down his parched gullet. John strolled around the small town, enjoying the respite from camp life. He was heartened to see several merchants carrying stocks of goods and engaging in everyday commerce.

He purchased a couple of pairs of socks and stopped in a small café for coffee and rhubarb pie, the only dessert that was available. By two o'clock, he had explored the town and stood by the hitching post outside the dressmaker's shop with Frisky and Libby's horse, anxious to depart. He wanted to return her to General Custer before dark.

She exited the shop, laughing gaily at something the

seamstress had said. She gave John a perky grin and tied a wrapped bundle to the rear of her saddle. "Here I am. Been waiting long?"

"Just arrived," John gallantly lied. "All ready to go?"

"Oh, yes, I am, aren't you relieved? Mrs. Coulter has made the most beautiful dress for me. I can't wait till Audie takes me to some formal function. I'll be the envy of every lady there."

"My dear Mrs. Libby Custer. You don't need a new dress for that to happen."

"La dee dah, Colonel Whyte. You are the gallant one, aren't you? Get along, Suzy, before this rake tries to turn my head from my brave Audie." She tapped her spotted pony with her riding quirt and cantered out of the town, John and escort right behind.

As they settled into the routine of the trip, with the two scouts up ahead and the escort troopers trailing, Libby and John launched into a prolonged discussion about the length of time the South would need to recover from the ravages of the war. Time passed rapidly as John and his beautiful companion thrashed the pros and cons of the Republican reconstruction policies recently outlined by President Lincoln.

It was only a short time before the weak, winter sun touched the azure haze that marked the Blue Ridge Mountains. They had crossed the ford, and were on the Marshalltown Road, when John's sixth sense kicked in. He held up his hand, stopping Libby in mid-sentence. John turned to call for Sergeant Hamlin, when all hell broke loose. Gunfire blazed from the stark grove of leafless trees to their right.

"Rebel raiders," Hamlin shouted, spurring his horse forward. A shot hit him, knocking him from the saddle and he lay sprawled in the middle of the road, blood seeping into the dust. John turned to the two men to the front. They were both down. He felt the tug of a bullet passing through his blue greatcoat.

He shouted at Libby, sitting as if frozen, her mouth open in shock. "Ride left, across the field. Go, woman." He pulled his pistol and emptied six quick shots at the menacing trees. Shoving the empty weapon into his holster, he spurred Frisky after the fleeing Libby.

Frisky responded to the spurs dug into his side and fairly leaped across the frozen ground after the rider in front. They had covered most of the distance to the trees when Libby's horse went down, hard. She went flying over the top of the fallen animal, to lay still and crumpled. John slid to a halt beside her, glancing back as he leaped off Frisky's back. A dozen or more butternut-clad riders were just crossing the road in pursuit. He ran to Libby's side, rolling her over.

"Libby, you hurt? Libby, you all right?"

She looked up at him, tears streaming down her dusty face, leaving tracks in the muddy smear on her delicate face. "Oh, John," she wailed. "They killed Suzy. Her head just exploded. Who are they?"

"Rebel raiders. Hurry, we must go. They're coming for us. Come on, we'll ride double."

"But S-S-Suzy," she cried. "What . . . ?"

John slapped her face, hard enough to snap her head around until she was looking at him, amazed and shocked. But, John had her attention. "Cry later," he ordered. "Come on, we've got to go, now!" He ran to his waiting horse, half carrying, half dragging Libby with him. Throwing her on the saddle, he leaped on behind and gave the big horse a savage dig with his spurs.

The horse responded, snorting in pain and surging away, directly toward a thick forest of dormant trees, their stark limbs mute testimony to the winter winds. John gave his horse free rein, looking back over his shoulder, dreading the inevitable outcome of the race he was in. He could not outrun the mounted pursuers with Frisky carrying double, and he did not have the firepower to hold them off very long in a gun battle. He knew the Rebel soldiers would not hurt Libby, but if they captured her, would use her to their advantage.

He looked ahead, in time to see the heavy branch looming up at them, as Frisky ran under it. He held up his hand, warding off the blow from Libby's body, but was unable to keep her or him from being unseated and dragged off the saddle to flop with a painful *thump* on the hard ground. Frisky kept on, running furiously toward the comfort of his stable back at the regiment.

John struggled to suck wind back into his lungs. "Libby," he gasped, "you all right?"

"Oh, my God, but that hurts," she cried softly. "I think I broke my ankle." She reached down to massage her ankle.

"Come on, we've got to get out of here. The Rebs will be here any second now." John got to his feet and helped her up. "Can you run?"

"I don't know. I'll try. Ouch, that hurts. Here. Give me the support of your arm about my waist and I guess I can."

John steered her toward a dense bramble of shrubs, downed trees, and the bank of a shallow creek. They had barely reached the cover of the brush when the Rebel raiders galloped into the woods. John could hear the enemy soldiers shouting at one another. "One of the prisoners said it were General Custer's new wife. Find her. She'll be worth twenty officers. Where'd they go? Anybody see 'em?"

Someone in charge shouted orders. "Spread out and find her. She's valuable to us."

Someone else shouted. "Over here. Here's their tracks."

John peered over the edge of the embankment. The Rebels had found the tracks Frisky had made and were following them deeper into the dense stand of trees. Now was their chance. He pulled Libby to her feet. "Come on, Libby. We've got to get away from here, while they're still after my horse. Can you walk at all?"

She stood and gingerly put weight on her right foot. "Ouch. It hurts. Only if you help me, John. Can't we stay here?"

"No, we're too easily found if they return. We've got to move, and fast. Put your weight on my arm. Here we go." Supporting her as best he could, John headed away at right angles to the direction his pursuers had taken. They reached the edge of the grove, finding another barren field before them. On the far side stood an even larger stand of forest and John pointed Libby in that direction. They crossed the field as quickly as Libby could limp, supported by John, and into the dormant stand of trees. John pushed on through, Libby gasping and stumbling at his side.

"Wait, John. I can't go on. I can't breathe. My corset . . ."

John pulled her jacket and blouse up at the back. She was strapped into a whalebone corset, tied tightly to accentuate her slender waist. He grumbled and opened his pocketknife. Quickly, he cut the drawstring laced up the rear and pulled the device away from her bare back. Her skin was marked by the tight stays of the corset.

"No damn wonder. I don't see how you could breathe at all with that thing on. Now, hurry, we've got to keep going." He tossed the ruined corset under a log and scattered some dead leaves over it.

Libby tucked her blouse and undershirt back into the waist of her riding skirt and pressed on with her protector. As they thrashed through the heavy brush, she wondered if he had seen her bare breasts, as he stripped the corset from her.

They crossed another field, Libby walking better as the exercise increased the circulation in her injured foot. Night was falling and John looked for a place to hole up until morning. He knew it would be bitterly cold before the morning sun returned.

They entered yet another grove of trees, pressing on in the gathering darkness. Bursting out of the woods into another field, John saw a burned house and a half-burned barn at the far end. Cautiously, John led her to the edge of the gutted house, now only a pile of rocks marking where a fireplace once stood amid the charred rubble.

He placed a fresh cylinder of bullets into his .36-caliber Navy revolver and checked the primer caps to insure they were tightly fixed to the firing nipples, before making his way to the shell of a barn. The fire had burned down more than half of the structure, but the rear portion still had a segment of roof over it and walls to keep out the wind. The place was deserted and had been for some time. He returned for Libby, waiting for him at the fence. He helped her to the far corner of the ruined barn. He gathered some moldy hay and made her as comfortable as he could. He gathered several stones from the ruined fireplace and enough sticks and timbers from the barn to keep a small fire burning the length of the night.

Libby watched his efforts, and asked him, "Dare we have a fire, John?"

"I think so, Libby. It's going to turn damned cold tonight. Those Rebs can't stick around too long, I should think. Too dangerous. I'll keep it small and shielded from the view of anyone outside. We'll take our chances. I'm going for water. Shout if anyone comes before I return." John found a small stream and grateful that he had carried his silver, collapsing cup in his greatcoat, drank his fill before carrying a cup of the cold, clear water to Libby. She drank it quickly and timidly asked for another, which he got, barely able to see in the near darkness of the evening.

He felt in his pockets. He still had two dry biscuits and several strips of dried beef, which Rava Singh had put there that morning, in case he got hungry on the road. He gave half to Libby and they chewed hungrily on the unappetizing fare. John started a tiny fire within the circle of stones gleaned from the fireplace. He gathered more dry hay and made Libby a soft bed, next to the fire.

"How's your foot?" he asked.

"Not too bad, I guess. It hurts some." She tried to wiggle it, but cried out at the movement.

John took her dainty foot and untied her laced bootlet. She lay back as he pulled off her stocking and examined her bare ankle by the light from the fire. A dark bruise was showing on the outside, just under her anklebone. "A sprain, I think. I'm going to massage it for a while, to keep the blood flowing. I'll try not to hurt you." Carefully, he kneaded her foot, gently twisting and working it. Libby sighed, chewing on the dried biscuit, luxuriating in the novel sensations caused by the unexpected caresses. In spite of the discomfort, it was a pleasurable sensation.

She watched with half-closed eyes as her friend and protector earnestly massaged some of the pain away. John finished and smiled up at her as he pulled her stocking back on her foot. "Put on your boot or you won't be able to tomorrow. Now, you should try and get some sleep. You want my greatcoat?"

"What about you? Won't you need it?"

"I'll stay awake and tend the fire." He leaned back against the rough, wooden wall of the barn, placing several pieces of wood within easy reach.

Libby scooted over and tucked herself into his arms, pulling the coat around her. "There, this is much better. We'll both be warmer this way." She settled in under his arm and he protectively placed it around her, conscious of the warmth of her bosom, where it burned against his forearm.

The hours slipped by, and Libby slept encased in his grasp, her breath warm against his cheek. Late in the night, she shifted, and he felt her hand brush against his groin. He was instantly aroused, quickly filling until gorged and stiff. He sucked in his breath and held still, knowing she had touched him accidentally and innocently in her sleep, not in passion. She grasped him tighter and he knew the instant she awakened, with a tiny gasp of surprise. He forced his breath to stay slow and heavy and kept his eyes tightly closed, as if asleep.

Without removing her hand, she slowly raised her face up to his. He faked sleep, still savagely aroused. Libby sighed softly and snuggled her head back onto his chest. Carefully, with gentle movement that was meant not to awaken him, Libby Custer felt the length and breadth of only the second man she had ever touched so brazenly. It was as if she were satisfying her curiosity to know the feel of him. She pulled her hand away, and tucked it under her cheek. John maintained his slow and steady breathing until hers deepened and slowed as she fell back asleep. Then he spent the rest of the night castigating himself for being such an honorable prig. He had but to lower his lips to hers and she would have been his. Her interest was so obvious, he felt like kicking himself around the barnyard. This woman whom he admired and yes, desired. Her beauty and innocent celebration of life was like an aphrodisiac to him, whenever he was around her. He tried to console himself that it was but a reaction to the circumstances, but it did little to cool his raging desire. The rest of the night seemed awfully long.

As the dawn turned the sky pink and gray, Libby stirred in his arms, and yawning, pushed herself away. "Good morning, dear John. Surprisingly, I slept wonderfully. If I had but a tiny amount of breakfast, I would be fine. Did you sleep at all?" She gave him a sideways glance as she asked the seemingly innocent question.

"I didn't intend to, but I did. I guess the fire was a little too comfortable." He changed the subject. "How's your foot?" He watched as she took a few tentative steps.

Libby gave him a cheery grin. "Not too bad. I think I can make it. Would you excuse me for a few moments? I'll call out if I see anyone."

"Let me look around first. You wait here until I check the area." John hurried out and satisfied himself all was quiet, as he relieved himself. Then, he waited while Libby finished her morning rituals, before leading her to the stream where they both drank their fill. An hour's slow walk brought them back to the road, and another hour found them rescued by a flying patrol, one of many sent out by the frantic Custer. John and Libby were back at the house where Custer had his headquarters, before the sun was halfway up the morning sky.

Custer rushed in a few minutes later and gathered Libby up in his arms, as she excitedly recounted their adventures. Custer noted the sudden softness of her upper body and softly asked, "Dear, where's your corset?"

This brought a new round of storytelling by the effusive Libby. By the end of the tale, Custer was glaring daggers at John, standing patiently while Libby talked herself out. Finally, she made her excuses, gave John a chaste kiss on the cheek, calling him her protector, and left to repair the damage. Custer turned to John with ice in his voice.

"Well, mister. Your report?"

John reported the event quickly and dispassionately. Custer stiffly nodded and answered John's query as he finished.

"The dead escorts were found within an hour of the event by some dispatch riders, and a reaction force arrived soon thereafter. If you had just returned to the road, we would have had Libby home last night."

"I wasn't certain where the road was, once it got dark, General, and I didn't want to expose her to those Reb raiders. They wanted her badly."

"Now you've exposed her to vicious gossip, staying out all night alone with her."

"General Custer, let me make this very clear. Mrs. Custer has but one shining star in her heart and mind. That's you. She is a one-man woman and that's the Queen's vow of a fact. If you're unlucky enough to have your fool head blown off in this damned war, she'll spend the rest of her life mourning you. Never doubt her loyalty and love for you, never. If I hear any man speak ill of her, be it a private of the rear rank or the general himself, I'll have him on the field of honor before the sun sets, so help me God."

Custer, whose brow was furrowed as he struggled with a bad case of suppressed anger and jealousy, gradually relaxed. A man he admired had just stroked his monstrous ego. All was forgiven, for the moment. "Very good, Colonel Whyte. I thank you for your protection of my dear wife. Now, why don't you rejoin your command? Orders will be arriving within the week, putting us back in the field again."

With a casual reply to John's proper and formal salute, Custer dismissed John and hurried upstairs. He wanted to claim his wife's favors before she had time to think about the handsome man with whom she had just shared an adventure.

John rode his borrowed horse toward his regiment's bivouac area. Glumly, he considered the stories which were certain to surround his and Libby's adventure. He had too much admiration for her and Audie Custer to suffer the gossip of fools. Still, he wished he had stayed closer to the road when he first ran from the Rebel raiders. He doubted that he had heard the last of this day's work.

CHAPTER 14

Two days later, John received a gracious thank-you note from Libby Custer, but he was never again invited to the general's house for dinner and cards. While slightly disappointed that his rescue was not appreciated, he refused to become embittered by the obvious snub, since he expected nothing more from the vainglorious, juvenile Custer. As it was, he had work enough getting the regiment ready for the spring offensive to divert his attention.

A week later, Custer escorted his new bride to Washington where she would wait for him until the end of the spring and summer's fighting. John wrote a short note to Custer offering the couple a room at his home, where Libby could be watched over and cared for by his housekeeper, the warm and friendly widow, Virginia Richardson. Custer never responded to his offer.

The Fifth Michigan was clearly in excellent shape, thanks to ceaseless training of the new recruits by Khan Singh and the senior NCOs of the regiment. In addition, Sergeant McQuinn and Major Mansur had finagled a complete reissue of clothing, saddles, mounts, and replacement weapons for the regiment. A liberal use of John's vast wealth to grease the palms of greedy, rear-area supply personnel had made the task easier, but it was still an impressive accomplishment. John conveyed his gratitude to his valued subordinates more than once.

On the evening of May 2, 1864, John joined the rest of the

regimental commanders at Custer's HQ, for a commander's meeting where they would receive their marching orders. He and Custer exchanged only polite pleasantries. John was prepared for the cool reception, as he had heard the ugly rumors floating around the campfires about his adventure with Libby. Custer apparently still harbored some residual jealously, prompting John to keep a professional and respectful distance, managing to get through the evening without incident.

As quickly as possible, John returned to the Fifth Michigan's bivouac, excited by the coming campaign, yet torn by the knowledge that some men he knew and liked were certain to fall, leaving him with the pain of their loss and the dreaded task of writing letters of condolence.

"Our orders, Colonel?" Lee Mansur had anticipated his announcement by having the troop commanders and Sergeant Major Khan Singh on hand, awaiting his return.

"Yes, for the entire Army of the Potomac, thank God. We march the morning of the fourth for a place called Spotsylvania Court House, across the Rapidan River, on the road to Richmond. General Grant is taking everyone who can carry a rifle and plans to steal a march on Bob Lee's boys, and move between him and Richmond. We're assigned as rear guard to the Twentieth Division. After we reach Spotsylvania Court House, we'll receive new orders."

Lee Mansur smacked his fist into the palm of his hand. "We're the guards for the division trains? What the hell is the general thinking of?"

John allowed a tired smile to cross his face. "It's his way of sending me a little message. Don't worry, he won't keep us there long."

Lee grumbled, but shut up, since he knew what John was referring to, as did everyone in the tent. The young captains who commanded the ten troops of the regiment waited in silence, loyal to John and trusting him to insure they were involved in any scrap that came along. John gave his orders to prepare for the regiment's move and the first day's assignments, before retiring to his back room in the HQ tent to sleep. He knew sleep would once again be scarce in the coming days and nights.

The First Michigan Brigade marched from their winter camps near Stevensburg, at dawn the fourth of May, never to return. John deployed his regiment around the mile-long convoy of wagons belonging to the Twentieth Division trains and settled in for a long day in the saddle. He was mounted on Frisky, thankfully. The big bay had been found by one of the search parties and returned to him the day after the escape from the Rebel raiders.

The regiment stayed on the march the entire day, stopping shortly after dark just in front of the Rapidan River. Custer rode into John's bivouac, just as the young Englishman was beginning a hasty supper of beans, dried biscuits and fried bacon. The flamboyant Custer arrived amid a flurry of flags, outriders, and snorting horses, spreading a fine layer of dust everywhere.

"Evening, General." John saluted his commander. "Care for a spot of supper, or hot coffee?"

"Just coffee, thank you, Colonel Whyte. How did your day go?"

John quickly briefed Custer on the events of the day, which were minimal and uneventful.

"I want you to stay with the trains tomorrow, until we finish crossing the Rapidan, then bring your regiment forward and find me. We may have work tomorrow afternoon. I'll be somewhere around Chancellorsville Crossroads. You remember that place, I suppose?"

John recalled the debacle there the previous May, when

General Hooker's inept leadership got a lot of men senselessly killed. "Yes, sir. I do indeed."

Custer drained the last of his coffee, and handed the tin cup to Rava Singh with a slight nod of thanks. "Good. Get the wagon train across, then join me. Rest well tonight. I've heard we're out ahead of Lee's cavalry, for a change." Custer leaped on his prancing, charcoal-gray gelding and galloped off, his entourage thundering after his dust.

Lee and Khan Singh hurried to John's side, eager to hear what had transpired at the campfire meeting. John related the gist of Custer's orders, and his instructions for the next day.

"By damn," Lee exclaimed. "I knew ole goldie locks wouldn't forget us, once it came time to trade lead with Johnny Reb."

"Go sleep, fire-eater," John laughed. "You're getting to be as bloodthirsty as Wil Horn." At the mention of his friend's name, killed at Gettysburg, John grew quiet and pensive, remembering Wil's tragic death. Hard times were looming again for the regiment. He silently prayed the casualty lists would be mercifully short.

It took until nearly ten o'clock to escort the entire wagon train across the ford of the Rapidan River and into a secure bivouac. John hurried his men ahead to the crossroad where Custer would be waiting, but found it empty, save a single courier, sitting in the shade of his horse beside the road. Custer had left the rider to give him a written message to go into bivouac about a mile away. The courier was there to guide him to the location. As John followed the guide, he cocked his head. Guns were rumbling faintly, somewhere to the south. Lee Mansur galloped up, his face flushed from the afternoon sun.

"Listen, John. Heavy cannon. Lee and Grant have tied in to it already. Whereabouts, do you think?"

"Just a few miles off that way." John pointed to the southeast. "It appears Grant didn't make it through the heavy wilderness before Lee found him. It'll be the devil, trying to use cavalry in this thick stuff. Meanwhile, we bivouac and wait for further orders. Use the time to have the men check their mounts and gear. We want to be ready, when the orders come."

Lee saluted, and galloped away. John listened to the rumbling thunder and offered a silent prayer for the hapless Union infantrymen suffering under the heavy cannonade. Nervously, he and the rest of the Fifth Michigan waited the rest of the afternoon for orders, but none arrived. At sundown, a mounted courier arrived with the next day's orders. They were to move with the rest of the Michigan Brigade, to a road intersection about two miles ahead. John rested by the tiny fire Rava Singh had built, Khan Singh snoring softly beside him. Tomorrow, they would be before the enemy.

At dawn, John and his men were on the march and in position at the road intersection within an hour. Although the dense growth of trees surrounding the crossroads was interspersed with a cleared field here and there, John knew that his men would do most of their fighting dismounted on this day.

A sergeant courier arrived with orders from Custer to deploy in the tangled woods to the north, toward a nearby clearing where he could protect the right flank of the brigade. They built hasty fighting positions about two hundred yards into the tangle, at the edge of the open field. John deployed one mounted troop as picket, to cover the far side of the cleared field. He sent one of his most dependable troop captains, Edward Longacre, as commander. The tall, shy, ex-theology student nodded as John stressed his orders.

"You have to make the enemy deploy, Ed, so you can withdraw your men across the field there and get to safety on this side. If they roll over you, your entire command will be cut off."

"Understand, Colonel. Hit 'em hard enough to make 'em

deploy, and then skedaddle back over to this side." He saluted, and led his sixty-man troop across the barren field, disappearing into the woods on the far side.

John prowled the defensive positions his men were constructing, listening to the thunder and roar of the guns. The big infantry battle was growing much closer to him. About eleven, John suddenly heard the rattle of carbines and deeper bang of infantry muskets in the far woods where Longacre's men were deployed. The noise drowned out any sound of the battle further down the road. As John watched, a stream of blue-clad riders burst from the far tree line and fled across the open field, the riders crouched low over the backs of their galloping horses. Longacre swung down in front of John and panted.

"Rebs, Colonel. Second Carolina, Rosser's brigade of Wade Hampton's division. I saw their battle flag, clear as day. Tryin' to work their way around the flanks. They've deployed just like you wanted, but will be comin' on soon."

"You certain, Ed?"

Captain Longacre nodded his head. "I saw the flags myself, Colonel. There's a couple thousand men ridin' right at us."

John motioned for Tim Vernon, his most trusted scout and courier. "Tim, find Custer. Tell him Rosser's Second Carolina is at our front. We can hold him, but if he slides to the west, he'll outflank us. Custer had best put men to our right, if he hasn't before now. Tell the general I'll send a rider to inform him if Rosser does slide to the west."

The former pony-express rider nodded, and swung up on his favorite horse, riding as fast as he could through the thick tangle of brush and trees. John watched until Tim was gone from view before turning back to the field to his front. He called for Khan Singh and Lee Mansur. Quickly he outlined his plans.

"The Reb commander can't put more than two regiments abreast on that field. He'll probably try and stack his men hoping to overwhelm us. He probably doesn't know we're just a single regiment, or that we've got repeating carbines. Lee, you take the right, Khan Singh, the left. Count off the men by twos, and fire in volleys. One, two, one, two. He'll never know what hit him." The two men nodded, and trotted away. John stayed at the center of his defensive line, confident that his two trusted subordinates would do his bidding exactly as he desired.

It was as if John had scripted the action. Scores of gray-clad riders filed out of the woods to the far side of the quarter-mile square field and took position on line, ready to charge. A second row filled in behind them and at a command, both ranks started a slow trot toward John and his waiting men. Halfway across, a bugle sounded and the entire line spurred to a fast gallop, directly at John, it seemed.

"By numbers!" he screamed. "Fire row one! Fire row two! Independent fire!" The entire defensive line erupted into a steady rattle of carbine fire, acrid, greasy smoke billowing up to shroud the field. Within moments, the enemy had deserted the field, leaving more than fifty men and as many horses lying on the thirsty soil, which soaked up the red blood of the dead and dying.

The enemy cavalrymen redeployed at the edge of the trees across the field and started a steady, annoying, long range sniping at John's position. Warning his men to stay low and behind cover, he moved along his line, insuring every man was in position to repulse any further attempt to cross the field. As the snap and wizz of passing minié balls whirled past or over his head, he scooted back to the rear until he could reach his small band of scouts, commanded by Tim Vernon. Tim reported Custer's receipt of John's message and Custer's orders to stay where John now was to deny any advance by the enemy troops.

"Tim, take your men to the right and keep watch. If the Rebels try and flank us through the woods, send word and slow them down as best you can until I arrive. Understand?"

Tim nodded his understanding and rode away with his dozen men, determination on his young face. John knew Tim and the brave men who were the regimental scouts would not fail him short of death. John ducked as a lead musket cut a branch over his head. Even after so many close calls, he still could not stop himself from flinching. Custer would sit on his horse and not move a muscle as the pointed lead slug zipped past his ear. It was an air of nonchalance that never ceased to amaze John, no matter how often he saw it.

As if on cue, Custer and his escorts rode up to where John's men had gathered their mounts during the fighting. John saw him approach through the tangled underbrush, and made his way back to him. He spotted the young pianist, Private Jeffery Wert, among Custer's entourage and quickly waved to the lad.

"Yes, sir, General?" His salute was as snappy as any given by Khan Singh.

Custer's voice was several octaves higher. His fighting blood was afire. "John, I want you to drive those Rebs outta their position. I'm sending Colonel Stagg and the Sixth Michigan in a sweep to the west, in hopes of getting around them."

"General Custer," John quickly pointed out. "See those bodies in the field over there? Those were Rosser's men, attacking us. May I assault them on foot, through the trees to the south? I believe it will achieve the same result, with far fewer casualties."

Custer viewed the jumble of bodies in the open field to John's front. "Very well, Colonel Whyte, but go hard at 'em. We must push Rossie's troops into Stagg's regiment quickly, before the Rebs reinforce him."

John nodded, and saluted. "I'll attack immediately, General." Within moments, his entire line was slinking through the heavy woods, bent on turning the enemy flank. The enemy was alert, and as soon as John's men got close, the Confederate cavalry-men filtered away, refusing to stand and battle, with a mounted force bearing down on their rear.

John's men flushed the last defenders from the woods, and fired at the retreating Rebels, dropping a few who had waited too long before galloping off. He met Stagg's men at the edge of the field. The tired men of both regiments caught their breath and waited while John sent word to Custer. He also ordered his horse holders to bring the regiment's mounts closer to their new position.

Custer arrived and looked at the dust of the retreating enemy. "What happened? You arrive too late, Colonel Whyte?"

John suppressed his anger at the unjust accusation. Colonel Stagg spoke up, forcefully defending John's actions. "Not at all, General. The enemy had pickets on the west flank. They ran before we could close on them. Colonel Whyte's men did an admirable job, flushing them out of the woods."

John gratefully nodded at his fellow regimental commander, and kept his mouth shut. Custer pursed his lips and grunted a sort of apology. He turned to inspect the enemy positions on the far line of shallow hills about a half mile away with his telescope. Beaming at what he saw, he turned his gaze back to his two subordinates.

"Peter, John, look yonder. The Rebels are swinging to the west. They're hoping to slip around us. I aim to put a stop to that right now. Peter, you lead. Charge up to that hill there," pointing to the hill in question. "John, you support, bearing to Peter's right. I want us there before Wade Hampton's boys. Peter, I'll ride with you, if you don't mind."

"Be my pleasure, General," Lieutenant Colonel Stagg replied. He motioned for his regiment to advance.

Custer addressed his small group of bandsmen. "Yankee Doodle, boys. Good and loud. Let's let them know the Michigan

Brigade is a'comin' to kill 'em."

Stagg shouted his commands. "By troops. Right wheel! On line, advance! At the gallop, charge!" Lowering his sword at the hill, he galloped away, his regiment and Custer right alongside him.

John quickly mounted his regiment and charged off after Stagg and the Sixth Michigan, angling his direction more to the west of Stagg's advance. He led his men up the hill, smashing into a rebel artillery battery, just setting up their position. The surprised rebels got off a hasty salvo, but it was high and John's men overwhelmed them before they could reload. As John's men gathered up the surviving enemy gunners and secured the four bronze Napoleons, Custer galloped up. His face lit up as John presented him with the captured cannon.

"Well done, Fifth Michigan," he shouted for everyone to hear. "Damn good work." He gave John orders to hold and galloped off, still the consummate cavalier, his escort riding hastily after him.

John and his men stayed on the hill the rest of the day, withdrawing under orders after nightfall to a position about a mile to the southeast, near a ruined forge on the aptly named Furnace Road, dropping the captured cannon off at Custer's artillery location. The Union might have use for good smooth-bore Napoleons and John did not want them. John's horse artillery battery was already better equipped with the rifled four-inchers John had scrounged with Wil Horn's help, the year before.

The next day was deadly similar. Ride to a place. Charge, countercharge, attacking on foot, defending from attacks on foot by the enemy. Only the names of the fallen changed with the changing days. At the end of the second day, John had twenty-one men dead or wounded and taken to hospital. He knew some of the infantry regiments had suffered so grievously as to make his losses seem insignificant, but not to him. He suffered with every dead trooper. And still, he led his men to their assigned spot on the battlefield and led them toward the guns when ordered.

On May eighth, Custer and his brigade led the entire Union cavalry out of the wilderness, on an independent raid against Richmond. It was the grand plan of General Sheridan, to draw JEB Stuart and his gray-coated cavalry into a battle to the finish. The place of honor at the point went to Major Brewer of the First Michigan, with John and his Fifth Michigan soldiers immediately behind. Sean Gallagher and Tim Vernon rode close by John, ready for any orders, while Khan Singh and Lee Mansur brought up the rear of the march to push stragglers forward.

John smiled to himself as the massed columns of blue-clad cavalry trotted down the road. Custer seemed to be over his pique about Libby. Now, if he could command his men through the coming fight without losing too many of them. He did not consider his own mortality as he ruminated, swaying to the pace of his horse, sweating in the warm, late-spring sunshine.

CHAPTER 15

"Lee, what the hell day is it?" John angrily brushed at his mustache, holding his pen in his other hand above the paper on his field desk. "I don't know why I can't remember the date anymore."

Major Lee Mansur groaned, struggling to awaken. "Dammit, John, I was just about asleep. Why don't you wait until we return to the far side of the river to write those letters of condolence?"

John grimaced aloud. "Now, Lee. So the family can get the news about their loss immediately, not weeks from now. Besides, it's only three, thank God. I want them out on the morning dispatch."

Lee rubbed his tired eyes with the heel of each palm. "What was it you asked me?"

John grimaced. What had he asked? He was bone tired, as was everyone in the regiment, after nearly a week of hard riding and harder fighting. He looked again at the blank paper before him. "The date. What day is it?"

Lee yawned and scratched the incessant itch from an aggressive mosquito under his right arm. "Let's see. It's May, er, gotta be the tenth. Yeah, it's May tenth and I'm sure, 'cause I had to write a memo to General Custer's adjutant yesterday, and I asked McQuinn what the date was, and he always knows. It was about taking those twenty men we rescued from that Reb prisoner convoy into the regiment as replacement for the twenty

144

men we lost on the eighth, takin' that bridge near Todd's Tavern."

John tried to place the action in his mind, but he was just too damned tired. He sighed and dated the first letter. It was to the parents of Ed Longacre and he dreaded having to write it. The zealous, dependable, young officer had fallen in a skirmish late yesterday, only minutes before the opposing armies had backed away from each other for the night. John had liked the personable Longacre, believing he was destined to be a great author someday, judging from the reports the young captain had delivered over the course of the past year, while serving under John. John bent to the melancholy task, eager to crawl into the empty cot beside Lee, who was already softly snoring.

As John sealed the last letter, he heard a rider gallop up and Khan Singh soon entered with a dispatch packet. The turbaned, Sikh warrior handed it to John and spoke softly so as not to disturb the sleeping Lee. "Orders for the morrow, Sahib Colonel. The courier says we are to have 'Boots and Saddles' one hour before sunrise and be ready to ride by first sight of the morning sun."

"Very well, old friend. Wait until I read them before you go. Lee, wake up. We have orders for tomorrow."

"Dammit it to high heaven. Can't a fellow get a few hours' sleep around here? What's the plan?" He tried to look over John's shoulder at the written orders.

John scanned the written message from Custer's HQ. "We continue on south, toward a place called Yellow Tavern, about ten miles down the road. The brigade will march in column, with the Sixth Regiment in the van and the Fifth following. The First Regiment will follow us, and the Seventh trails, guarding the division trains. Intelligence says Stuart's boys are stretched pretty thin to the south and Custer hopes we'll prod him into a general engagement."

John quickly wrote his orders for the next day's march. "Lee, get this to all the troop commanders right away. And, drop off these condolence letters to the regimental clerk. Khan Singh, you get some sleep. I worry about you, old friend."

As Lee and Khan Singh exited the tent, the old warrior was sputtering as to who could outlast whom. John wearily sat down on his cot and stretched his long legs. He was bone tired and knew tomorrow's action would be as bad as today's—or worse. He lay back, hoping to rest his eyes for just a minute, until Lee returned. He awoke only when Khan Singh gently shook him, several hours later.

"Sahib, wake up. It's nearly four. The troops will stand to in five minutes. Your orders were passed on and every troop commander has acknowledged them."

John yawned mightily, while he rubbed the grit from his crusted eyelids. He kicked the leg of Lee's cot. "Lee, wake up. It's time to make ready."

Grumbling like a farmer in a hailstorm, Lee rolled out of his bed and pulled on his boots. He stomped out of the tent without a word, grumpy as ever at the intrusion to his deep sleep and pleasant dream. John ignored Lee and finished dressing, knowing from experience to avoid any conversation with the stocky, Indiana schoolteacher until Lee had time to gather himself from the foggy depths of sleep and ingest a cup of hot coffee. Lee Mansur was not an early riser by choice.

John checked the caps on both his pistols, replacing one that showed a trace of green discoloration at the crimp. It was vital that he have no misfires if the weapons were needed later in the day. He tied his blanket into a tight roll, tucked it under his arm, and stepped out of the tent.

Rava Singh, Khan Singh's oldest son and John's orderly, waited outside, holding the reins of John's horse. He saluted and took John's bedroll, which he tied behind John's saddle.

John hurried into the trees to relieve himself and then mounted up, just as the regimental bugler Sean Gallagher blew "Assembly," on his shiny, brass bugle.

The men poured out of the woods and lined up along the road in the dim, predawn light. Four of Quartermaster Sergeant McQuinn's privates attacked the HQ tent, tearing it down prior to packing it in one of the supply wagons.

Rava Singh, Sean, Tim Vernon and the color guard sat on their horses nearby, awaiting John's order to march. As the appointed moment approached, a cluster of riders galloped toward them. It was General Custer and his entire entourage, including the regimental band. The general's golden hair danced about his shoulders, his scarlet kerchief stood out in sharp contrast to the dirty, but same elaborate black velvet jacket with the gold braid up both arms that he had worn at Gettysburg. A wide-brimmed, slouch hat was cocked jauntily on his head. Custer returned John's salute.

"Good morning, Colonel Whyte." Custer's presence filled the battlefield. John's men gave him a mighty roar when they realized who it was. Custer casually waved to the assembled troopers. He was as nonchalant of the coming carnage as if he were off on a playful adventure. "Your fellows all ready? Today, I say we're gonna tie a knot in JEB Stuart's tail, or my name isn't George Armstrong Custer."

"Yes, sir. The Fifth Michigan is ready to go, sir," John answered evenly, more aware of the gravity of their coming adventure.

Custer never noticed. "Excellent. I expect nothing but success and victory today. I plan to ride at the head of the Sixth this morning. Carry on, Colonel. We'll eat tonight in Stuart's camp and let him serve us, personally." With an exuberant "yahoo," Custer galloped off, waving his hat to the men alongside the road, who cheered him at the top of their lungs, paying no attention to the shower of dust thrown up by his minions chasing behind.

John shook his head at the spectacle of the departing general and spoke softly to Khan Singh, who had pulled his horse up beside him. "The men certainly like their boy general, don't they, old friend?"

"It is good, Sahib. The men must believe in their officers if they are to succeed on the battlefield. They believe in you as well, don't you know?"

"I hope to God I don't let them down, my friend."

"Never, Sahib. It is not in your soul. You are a true warrior."

John studied his old friend and senior NCO in the regiment. For about the ten thousandth time, he blessed the day he sent for the towering warrior and friend. "Thank you, Sergeant Major Singh. Well, there goes the last of the Sixth Regiment. Here we go. Tim, put your scouts about one hundred yards behind their trailing unit. We'll follow you by another one hundred."

"Understand, Colonel. Scouts! Out!" Tim trotted off with his band of scouts, rifles at the ready.

John waited until the last scout was a hundred yards ahead. "By column of fours, march!" He spurred his horse gently and proceeded down the road, toward the waiting enemy at a non-descript crossroad stopover called Yellow Tavern.

Custer's brigade rode for three hours, stopping only twice while the lead regiment, the Sixth Michigan, cleared the surrounding woods of scattered enemy pickets. As John led his command down the dirt road past the most recent skirmish, he saw two silent forms lying by the side of the road, awaiting the trailing medical personnel for pickup. The two Union cavalrymen were young, never to see their twentieth birthday, nor to grow any older. Probably scouts from the Sixth Michigan, ambushed by skulkers. One face had the serene look of a boy at rest, while the other's was contorted in a grimace of shock and disbelief. From too many nights of bitter dreams, John had learned to shield himself from the horrific reminders of war. The grisly scene barely penetrated his consciousness. His attention was better focused on signs of an impending attack by Stuart's horsemen, who were somewhere to the front.

As mid-morning passed uneventfully, his scouts suddenly drew up. John stopped the column with a hand signal. Lee and Khan Singh galloped up from the rear, as a rider hurried into view galloping down the road toward them. The courier gave a hasty salute and informed John, "The general's compliments, Colonel Whyte. Will you follow me to his location? We're at the Yellow Tavern Crossroad."

"Lee, come with me. Sergeant Major, dismount the men, but have them ready for immediate action."

John and Major Mansur followed the rider forward, while Khan Singh carried John's orders to the waiting men of the regiment. Custer was still on his horse at the intersection of the road when John and Lee rode up.

"Ah, Colonel Whyte. Here we are, and here before Stuart, it appears." Custer pointed to a wooded area across a wide, grassy field. John, take your regiment across that field and secure those woods beyond. You'll cover the left flank of the brigade. The Sixth will wait here, ready to advance, once Stuart deploys his men. Ole JEB'll have to try and drive us away from this intersection. This road leads directly into Lee's rear. Be ready to advance, once the Sixth charges. You may have to go it afoot. If so, don't delay, as Kidd's boys'll be expectin' you to support his flank. I suspect Stuart'll give it his all here. We may have his fanny in a crack for a fact. I'm sending the First and Seventh around to the right. They'll hit the enemy's flank as soon as Kidd makes the main assault. I'll ride with the Sixth if you need to contact me. Understand?"

"Understand, General. I'll move my men immediately."

"Very good. Carry on." Custer raised his field glasses to his eyes to scan ahead. He spoke without removing them from his eyes. "Courier, take a message to General Tolbert at Division. He's back down the road there, somewhere. The Michigan Brigade is preparing to attack as soon as Stuart arrives on the field."

John and Lee followed the dust of the galloping courier back to where the Fifth awaited them. John called for his troop captains, and gave his orders, before leading his men across the half-mile-wide field to the heavy growth of woods Custer had assigned to him.

By now, his men knew the drill and quickly prepared fighting positions along the tree line, where they had a clear view of any approaching enemy soldiers. The four cannon of his light battery were placed where they had the best field of fire. John stood near the edge of the trees, where he would see the Sixth make their attack, or any arriving courier from higher commanders.

Soon heavy gunfire erupted far to the right. "Sounds like Stuart didn't follow our boy general's plans," Lee remarked laconically, having slipped up to John's side. "The gray bellies are hittin' the right flank afore we get a chance to attack them. Ole Audie must be fit to be tied. Lookie there. He's ridin' off to the right, to see if he can salvage his plans, now."

"Keep your eyes open, Major. Stuart may try sending some of his boys around this way, to see if he can get behind Custer."

Almost simultaneously, Tim Vernon ran up. His scouts were well forward, hidden in the tall weeds of the field, watching the woods across the way. "Colonel, Rebs a'comin'."

John nodded. "How many, Sergeant?"

The young scout brushed sweat from his forehead with his right forearm. "Hard to say fer certain, maybe a half regiment.

Dismounted. Working their way over to the southeast. Mean to come right through here toward the road yonder, it appears."

"Get your men back to the woods, Tim. Good job. Lee, alert the cannons. Enemy troops advancing toward us."

Lee hurried away, delivering the message to the artillerymen personally. Khan Singh appeared at John's side, sensing the coming battle. Rava, Sean Gallagher, and the two men carrying the regimental colors also drew close, ready for any orders. From a knoll, about a half mile to the south, smoke and the booming of enemy cannon heightened the tension. "Rava, tell Major Mansur to engage two cannon against those firing at us. Keep two filled with canister for the troops headed toward us. Move, man!"

Tim Vernon arrived with his scouts, the men panting from their quick dash back to the safety of the woods. "Tim, take your men and watch the far left flank. Let me know if the enemy tries to slip men over that way."

"He can't get too far over, Colonel. There's a big swamp just over that little hill yonder."

"Good. He'll have to come through us, then. Carry on."

Vernon saluted and ran to his men, kneeling behind trees and waiting for their new orders. They scooted away, and John turned his attention to the woods to his front. Enemy soldiers flitted through the heavy brush, working their way toward his position. They would have to exit the trees to get at him, eventually, and he cautioned his waiting troopers to hold their fire until he gave them orders. No need to give away their position prematurely. He sent Sean to the rear, to where every fourth man was holding horses for himself and three of his companions. "Tell the horse holders to be ready to bring the mounts forward at my command. If the Sixth attacks, I want to be right after them." Sean nodded and hurried away. He wanted to be back before the action started. He preferred to fight close to his commander's side.

The two counterbattery cannon coughed their deadly missiles at the enemy cannon deployed on the far hill. Almost immediately, the stench of burnt gunpowder stung John's nostrils and the fog of burnt gunpowder dimmed his vision. Khan Singh touched John's arm, and pointed at the edge of the far woods. A line of butternut-clad men were moving out onto the field and dressing their lines, preparatory to making their assault. To the right, John could see the first rank of men of the Sixth Regiment, who were still on their mounts, waiting for the command to charge.

The deadly buzz of minié ball whizzing past brought John's attention back to the soldiers to his front. They had fired a volley and were now advancing, the line wavering and straightening, as the NCOs struggled to keep the men aligned. The enemy fire crashed through the brush and limbs of the woods, snapping off branches and leaves. As the enemy came within two hundred yards, John shouted the command. "Fire!"

Along the tree line, the twinkle of four hundred seven-shot carbines sent death and destruction into the enemy ranks. The line dissolved and a broken, staggering, pitifully few men retreated toward the safety of the trees. For the next hour, the game was one of sniping and harassing fire into one another's woods, hurting few, but still unnerving.

Khan Singh ran up to where John was assessing the enemy positions through his binoculars. "Sahib, the Sixth is aligning their ranks. They are preparing to charge."

John motioned to Rava. "Tell Sean Gallagher to bring the horses up, quickly."

Rava ran off and John shouted out his instructions to Khan Singh over the roar of cannons. "We'll charge into the trees, then dismount and clear them on foot. I ride with C Troop. You follow to push stragglers."

"Yes, Sahib. Shall I inform Major Mansur?"

"Yes. Tell him to put fire into the woods over there until we're in his way, then return to counterbattery on those guns on the hill."

"They have displaced, Sahib. Our fire was too intense for them."

"Oh, so they have. Very well. The cannons will cover our charge and then be ready to advance on my orders."

Sean Gallagher arrived with John's mount, followed by Rava Singh and the color sergeants. "Ready the flags, Sergeant Singh," John ordered, swinging into his saddle. Around him, his men did the same. John pulled one of his .36-caliber Navy Colt revolvers from its holster and settled himself for the charge.

He took a deep breath, and stood in the stirrups. "At the gallop, *chaaarge!*" He spurred his horse and burst out of the woods, aiming at the center of the trees across his front. The first salvo of shells from his four horse-drawn cannon shrieked overhead, exploding in a shower of leaves and trees in the enemy wood line. A bullet cut the air beside his face and he sensed the cry and fall of someone directly behind him. He dared not stop or even look to see who it might be. His entire regiment was thundering after him, directly on his heels.

Chapter 16

As the line of Union cavalry slammed into the first rank of Rebel soldiers, John realized they had already beaten the enemy. The Rebel firing was delusory and quickly faded to scattered sniping as the beaten enemy ran away from John's mounted warriors. The routed Confederate soldiers beat a hasty retreat toward the far side of the road, disappearing into another heavy growth of brush and trees.

John remained mounted, as the men with him leaped from their horses and flushed out the few remaining Confederates from their individual hiding places among the brush and trees. Khan Singh rode up and saluted John with the British-style, open-palm salute that he was prone to use when he was excited or harried. "A complete victory, Sahib. We had nine prisoners, and only three casualties of our own. Unfortunately, one was Sergeant Hightower, our color sergeant."

John nodded. "I sensed that someone close behind me was hit. Who has the colors now?"

"I gave them to Rava. Does that meet with your approval, Sahib?"

"Of course, old friend. But you know how dangerous it is to carry the colors. The enemy naturally fires at them first."

Khan Singh smiled fiercely, his warrior's face warm with pride and satisfaction. "My son asked for the privilege. He is a true Sikh, worthy of dying a warrior's death. I am without concern."

"As you wish, Sergeant Major. I concur with your decision. Have the troop captains, the colors, and Sean Gallagher meet me at the edge of the woods, back there." John pointed to the wooded area behind them.

"As you wish, Sahib. Be alert. There may still be skulkers about."

"Mind your own skin, you Sikh rascal." Laughing, John headed back to the edge of the woods, where he waited while Sean Gallagher, Rava Singh (proudly carrying the Stars and Stripes), his troop commanders, and the rest of the headquarters contingent slowly gathered around him. John adjusted the direction of their advance, to push more toward where the Sixth Michigan was still fighting the remnants of the Confederate soldiers they had also pushed back from the road. He watched while his soldiers swung more to the west and slowly drove a thin line of stubborn Confederate defenders toward their comrades heavily engaged by the Sixth Michigan.

The fighting was sputtering out, albeit slowly, and the enemy fire was decreasing with every passing minute. John had reached the edge of the road, when he noticed a mounted group of Confederates riding furiously in his direction.

"Bloody hell," he murmured to himself. "If they hit the flank of the Sixth, they might turn the tide of the battle against us." He looked around, spotting Sean and the color guards, Tim Vernon and half a dozen other mounted men, as well as Lee and Khan Singh, about fifty yards off. Pulling his hat from his head, he shouted at the top of his lungs.

"To me, quickly. Enemy cavalry approaching." Instantly, every mounted man in sight was racing to his side. Tim Vernon galloped up, sliding his sweaty horse to a spectacular stop at his side, as was his normal procedure. John pointed toward the oncoming enemy troops. He still did not have enough to guarantee victory. "Khan Singh," he shouted at the veteran

NCO. "Gather as many men as you can, quickly. Come to our support. The rest of you, follow me. Sean, sound the charge."

To the stirring trills of the bugle, John spurred his horse directly down the road, toward the middle of the oncoming enemy riders. He sensed the rest of his small band behind him, each man shouting his own personal battle cry. Rava Singh was right beside him, the battle flag streamed out to full presentation by the wind from their dashing horses. A thundering wall of determined cavalrymen slammed into the enemy cavalrymen, scattering them like wind-blown chaff. Blue and gray swirled about, guns firing and swords flashing. John felt the hot blast of a weapon against his cheek and looked to his left. A rebel horseman, scarcely more than a boy, with a frightened look on his face, had shot at him and missed. John's answer didn't. His pistol ball hit the young rebel between the eyes, spilling him into the dirt at the edge of the road.

John's horse continued its charge and he found himself at the rear of the enemy column. Swiftly, he fired the rest of the bullets in his pistol, dropping four of the enemy horsemen. As John drew his second pistol, he spun his mount about, just in time to see Rava Singh and Tim Vernon in the middle of a swirl of gray backs trying to capture the Union flag. Rava was whirling his horse in circles, slashing furiously, determined not to yield the prize to the circling enemy. Tim Vernon shot a man from the saddle and plunged back into the melee, shouting incoherently as his battle rage drove him.

Rava's face was bleeding from a sabre's slash and as John spurred his horse toward the embattled Sikh, he saw a Confederate general officer approach Rava and thrust his bloody sword directly into Rava's side. Rava Singh shrieked in agony and reeled in the saddle, but still clutched the precious emblem by its wooden staff. The enemy officer reached for the flag, and John fired a hasty shot at the man, missing him, but hitting an enemy rider just behind the rebel officer.

"Leave him be, you son of a bitch," John shouted, as his horse slammed into the Rebel's, knocking man and animal several feet off to the side.

The Rebel soldier wore the ranking insignia of a major general, and was a tall, imposing rider with a dark-brown, luxurious beard that covered his entire face. He grimaced and viciously swiped at John with his bloody sword. "The same to you, my Yankee friend."

John ducked and held up his left arm in an involuntary gesture of defense. The heavy blade hit John's forearm at an angle, cutting deep into the flesh, and breaking the bone. John did not feel the wound, so intense was his anger at the man that had slain his young friend. As the two horses slid past each other, John fired his last bullet across his body at the enemy rider. He saw the puff of dust and blood as the pistol ball entered the side of the Confederate officer, just above the gold sash wrapped around the man's waist. John glimpsed the gout of black blood that poured from the wound, and heard the moan of pain that escaped from the man's lips.

The enemy officer swayed in the saddle like a drunken soldier on leave, but grasping the pommel of his saddle, slowly moved to the rear. John slashed at another Rebel with the barrel of his empty pistol and then Khan Singh was there beside him, reins gripped in his teeth, slashing with his mighty sword and firing a pistol at the remaining enemy soldiers. Along with about thirty men, he quickly swept the surviving enemy from the road, slashing the arm completely off of the man holding the enemy colors. The severed arm held tightly to the staff of the enemy flag for a few long seconds then dropped onto the dusty road beside its owner, who thrashed about in agony while he bled to death.

John looked back toward the man he had just shot. He was still reeling in his saddle, being led away by several men.

John heard someone shout, "They shot General Stuart. They got ole JEB. God almighty, they got Stuart. Retreat, retreat! Git away afore they kill us all."

John glared at the enemy riders retreating down the road. He had no time for them at the moment. He leaped from his horse and hurried to Rava Singh still holding the blood-splattered flag in his hands. Khan Singh was there before him, leaping from his horse and running to where Rava swayed in his saddle. With a leonine look of pride and determination on his young face, Rava passed the colors to his father, who immediately thrust them into another soldier's hand. The old Sikh warrior tenderly held up his beefy arms and took his collapsing son out of the saddle. Carefully, he lay him on the ground, gently cradling Rava's turbaned head in his lap.

John knelt down beside Khan Singh and put his hand on Rava's shoulder. "Well done, Color Sergeant Singh. You saved our colors. Well done. Rest easy, now. The medical staff is on the way." Looking up at the mounted men gathered around, he shouted, "Get the surgeon, immediately." Tim Vernon galloped away, without a moment's hesitation.

Rava looked up at his father, still cradling his head on his huge lap. Coughing softly, he tried to smile, as a bloody froth gushed out of his mouth. "Father, I . . . I . . ."

Rava Singh's gaze turned inward and without another sound, he journeyed to the far shore of the great river, never again to walk this side of life. Hot tears coursed down John's cheeks and he tried to say something to Khan Singh. All that came out was a shuttering croak.

The old warrior looked up at John, a misty glaze over his brown eyes, but with immense pride in his voice. "My son joins his ancestors in Paradise. He will be honored for the great warrior we all hope to be. Sahib, you must help me to tell his mother of his brave and proud death."

Without another word, Khan Singh picked up the limp form of his son and carrying him in his mighty arms like the baby he once was, walked the two hundred yards to where Sergeant Hightower lay, in the first field of battle. Gently, Khan Singh lay Rava beside the dead Sergeant Hightower and then covered both men with the Union flag, which they had died defending. The outline of their bodies under the flag gave solemn evidence of what lay beneath.

Only then did John notice the fiery ache in his arm. It was a dull, throbbing thump that grew worse with every heartbeat. He looked dumbly at the bloody mess and swayed, perhaps being saved from falling only by the quick grasp of Tim Vernon, who shouted out, "Colonel! You're hit. Help me, Sean. We got to stop the bleeding. Someone get one of the surgeons from the road yonder."

John allowed Tim to tie a bandage around his left arm and then be led by the helpful young sergeant to the shade of one of the nearby trees. He sweated in agony while one of the regimental surgeons sewed up the fearsome gash and wrapped the arm with flat boards after setting the broken bone.

A frantic Lee Mansur rode up to John, near panic evident on his face. "Colonel, I heard you're hurt? Are you all right?"

"I'll be fine, Lee. You'll have to take over the regiment for a while. Recall the men and tie into the Sixth Michigan's left flank. Send word to Custer that we await his orders, and about me. Find out what our casualties were. Tell McQuinn to come forward, in case Khan Singh needs help. Rava was just killed."

Lee, shocked at the news, bit his lip before saluting and hurried away to carry out the orders. John saw Khan Singh, still sitting beside the flag-covered form of his son, and started to call out to him. However, he refrained, and without realizing it, fell sound asleep, a reaction to the shock of the wound, loss of blood, and utter weariness.

John was awakened by the clatter of horses' hooves pounding down the hard-packed dirt of the country road. He struggled to focus, seeing Custer and the entire brigade staff rapidly riding toward him. He glanced over at the place where Rava Singh lay. The old warrior Khan Singh still sat beside the flag-covered bodies of Rava and Hightower. John forced himself to sit up straighter as Custer slid his horse to a stop directly in front of him.

"Colonel Whyte, I just heard. Are you badly injured?" Custer's horse pranced in a circle, eager to be off and running again. Custer sawed on the reins, trying to quiet the sweat-lathered animal.

"I'm fairly well, General. I think Stuart broke my arm with his sword and I have a nasty slice as well, but my surgeon has repaired it rather nicely. Thank you for your concern."

"Stuart, huh? Well, we drove him and his entire command from the field, thanks in good measure to you and your men. A well done to the Fifth Michigan."

"Thank you, General. The men will be happy to hear your commendation. We did more than just drive Stuart from the field, this day."

Custer sawed the reins of his horse once again. "Oh?"

"General Custer, I have the pleasure of reporting that we captured his battle flag, and that I shot him, inflicting what I am certain is a mortal wound."

Custer's face lit up. "Killed JEB Stuart? Are you certain?"

"Quite certain, General. They led him from the field, still mounted, but he was a dead man riding. I hit him square in the liver. I saw the bile pouring from the wound. He'll be dead before the sun rises. Khan Singh, my regimental sergeant major captured his flag, in a fierce struggle with Stuart's color bearer. He lost his oldest son in the fight. His son is over there, under the flag. That's Khan Singh, sitting beside him."

160

Custer glanced at the still form of Khan Singh, still holding his son's limp hand extended from under the flag. "My condolences to your sergeant major, Colonel." He looked back at John. "Assemble your men at the tavern, about half a mile down the road, there." He suddenly had a crafty look in his eyes. "General Grant and Sheridan are to be at Tolbert's headquarters tomorrow morning. Bring the captured flags with you and report there at nine sharp. Can you make it?"

John nodded. "Yes, sir."

"Good. I want you to present Grant with Stuart's colors, and the news of his impending demise. It will be a great boost to the morale of the Cavalry Corps."

"And to you, General," John thought silently to himself.

"I should like for Khan Singh to present the colors, General Custer. He captured them. It's only fair."

"Very well. Both of you be there. I must go now. I'm sliding the Seventh Michigan on south, toward Richmond. They'll pass your position during the hours of darkness. Alert your sentries. See you tomorrow at nine. I'm very relieved that you're not badly hurt. We need you in our fight." Custer saluted with a sweeping wave of his plumed hat and galloped off, headed for more action.

John struggled to his feet, and signaled for Lee Mansur, who had watched the exchange from a distance. He passed on the orders, and then slowly, painfully, walked over to where his friend sat with the body of his firstborn son. He gave Khan Singh the order for their visit on the morrow, and stood close to his dear friend, his hand on the other's shoulder.

"Come, old friend. The ambulance drivers will arrive soon to take Rava back. I'll leave a man here, to insure Rava's body is shipped to Washington. We must send a message to Madam Singh. And I order you to take a week's furlough, so you may properly place him at rest."

The older man looked up, his eyes misty, but clear of grief. "Thank you, Sahib. It is my hope that you will be able to join my family and me as we bid our farewells to my son."

"As is mine, old friend. I should be able, since I cannot ride a horse in battle for some time now, I'm afraid."

"I am sorry I failed to arrive in time to prevent your injury, Sahib. It is my shame."

"Nonsense, old friend. You moved as fast as any man alive. You saved every man with me, as it was. You have nothing to apologize for. Come, old friend. The soldiers need your guidance now. Rava will be well cared for."

John stood next to Khan Singh as the older man stood and whispered a last good-bye in Hindu and then the two walked over to Lee, still waiting for orders. John dared not look back, for fear that his eyes would overflow with tears, but Khan Singh was all business as John gave the necessary orders to move the unit south.

The next morning, John awoke with a pounding hammer of pain in his arm. Gingerly, he rode back to General Tolbert's HQ in one of the ambulances, Khan Singh riding on horseback beside him. Generals Grant and Sheridan both greeted him warmly, and listened with great interest along with Tolbert and Custer, as John described the previous day's fight with JEB Stuart's cavalrymen. John motioned to Khan Singh to come forward, as he described the fight at the crossroads.

"General Grant, on behalf of the Fifth Michigan Volunteer Cavalry Regiment, I present you with Stuart's personal battle standard. This is my regimental sergeant major, Khan Singh, who captured the flag in a hand-to-hand fight with the Rebel color sergeant. His pride in the action is tempered by the fact that he lost his oldest son, who carried our flag during the battle and surrendered his life rather than yield our colors to the enemy."

Grant and Sheridan both stood and shook Khan Singh's hand, murmuring their condolences. Grant unfolded the flag, fingering the silk fringe around the outside border. "Killed JEB Stuart and took his flag. I'm putting the two of you in for the Medal of Honor. It was a damn fine job. And Stuart has died, just after midnight. We got the news about an hour ago."

Sheridan spoke up. "One less Rebel bastard to hang, by God."

Grant nodded his head, his voice pensive. "Perhaps, but a brave and resourceful soldier and enemy. And, an American who has strayed from the path but still an American, if we are to believe our president. God rest him in peace. And, have pity on those of us who must carry on this bloody work."

"Amen," General Tolbert seconded.

Grant remained silent for a moment, as did the other men around him. A bird sang its song of joy in the treetops above them. John shifted his feet, carefully. His arm was throbbing badly. Then, Grant looked at John, or more specifically at his bandaged arm.

"Well, Colonel, you're no good here for a while, I take it?"

"A few weeks before I can ride a horse, the surgeon said."

"A month's convalescence leave in Washington seem agreeable?"

"Very much so, General."

"Then, you can do a service for me, Colonel Whyte."

"Whatever I can, General."

"I've been tasked by the War Department to replace a West Virginia regiment that has been reassigned to Sherman's command, out in Tennessee. I think I'll send you and your regiment to replace them. Your job is to secure a region that is heavily pro-Union from harassment by Mosby's Rebel partisans. It will give you a chance to recuperate, and still make a valuable contribution to our war effort."

"I am at your command, General. But, please, sir. Don't

forget about us. The Fifth Michigan wants to be with you, when you close the ring around Bobby Lee."

"Don't worry." Grant stroked his beard. "Lee is a long way from being whipped yet. I'll have you back with my dashing young General Custer in a few weeks, I promise."

"That, sir, is all I can ask."

Grant smiled. "I'll have your orders delivered this afternoon. Pull your men out of the line and wait with them where you are now bivouacked."

Grant stood. "If you'll pardon me, I've got some business with Richard Ewell's boys to the north of here. Good fortune, John. I'll see you before too long." He returned John's salute and left.

As Grant rode away, he turned and waved at John. John would have been surprised had he known how long it was to be before he was to see the frumpy, unassuming Grant again.

CHAPTER 17

John awoke early, after a fitful night. His arm had throbbed continuously and he had not rested well. Khan Singh immediately slipped inside John's tent as if he had been standing outside, monitoring John's sleep. The tall soldier brushed raindrops from his curled mustache and stepped close to John's bed.

"Sahib, you are awake? How is your arm?"

"Yes and terrible, in that order. My arm hurts like the very dickens. How are you, my friend?"

"I am at peace, Sahib. My son rests among his warrior ancestors. Sahib, it is beginning to rain. Will you be riding your horse or do you want me to call you an ambulance?"

John glanced at his bandaged arm. "Best obtain me an ambulance, I'm afraid. I don't think I could stay on a horse very long today. And if it rains, I don't want to get this bandage wet. Has Major Mansur got the regiment ready to go?"

"Yes, Sahib. The men are fed, packed, and mounted. All that we have left is your tent. May I help you with your boots?"

"Yes, thank you. But, I want you to find me a new orderly and assign him to me immediately. It is not your worry to help me with my dressing."

Khan Singh smiled. "It is my pleasure, Sahib. There. Now, put your coat over your shoulders, and step outside so the men can take down the tent and we'll be away. Listen. The guns are already firing to the north. The short Sahib general is continu-

165

ing his attack against the enemy positions."

"Grant, Khan Singh. Grant. He'll have your hide if he catches you calling him the short general."

Khan Singh merely nodded and opened the tent flap for his wounded commander. Heavy drops were hitting the ground and stirring up tiny puffs of dust. Slate-gray clouds blocked the sun, threatening much more rain any moment. Several of Sergeant McQuinn's quartermaster privates were waiting to strike the tent. Mounted men sat glumly in the rain, awaiting John's order to departure. He watched Lee Mansur riding toward him, his rain slicker shiny from the raindrops. Lee saluted without dismounting from his horse.

"We've got our orders, Colonel. Back to the cavalry encampment at Washington, two weeks furlough for everyone and then assigned to the Shenandoah District. A place called Romney, in Virginny. We're to replace the Twenty-third West Virginia Volunteer Cavalry as security for the northwest West Virginia region. The men already know and are eager to be on our way, before someone changes their mind about us."

"Very well, Lee. You take command of the march. I'm afraid I'm going to have to ride in an ambulance. My arm's still very sore."

Lee snapped a salute. "Yes, sir. Ride easy, Colonel. I'll make certain we git back to Washington City."

"I'm certain you will, Lee, if for no other reason than to sneak in a quick visit to the other White House with its complement of ladies."

"Colonel Whyte, you wound me," Lee protested.

The heavens suddenly opened with an intense downpour. John gratefully climbed up on the seat of the small, two-horse wagon used as an ambulance by the cavalry corps. It carried the regiment's food and grain into battle and afterwards carried the wounded and dying out.

The regiment wheeled out of the bivouac area in a column of fours, under Lee's shouted command. The ambulance carrying John fell in at the rear of the long column, just ahead of the supply wagons of Sergeant McQuinn. The winding ribbon of blue-clad soldiers on horseback trotted up the road, away from the roar of the cannon. Khan Singh rode up beside the ambulance, his massive body hidden under a dark slicker, as usual ignoring the discomforts of the day. He walked his horse so the two men could talk as they traveled.

As the regiment proceeded along the muddy road, they passed the area where the two mighty armies had fought the previous week. In every field, swollen forms still lay, crumpled in the posture in which they fell. Occasionally, John saw the colored contract workers of the Graves Department placing the dead men into silent rows, before burying them in hastily dug, shallow graves.

"Thank goodness for the rain," he remarked to Khan Singh. "Otherwise, those poor souls would be working in a ghastly stench."

"I suspect they have become accustomed to it, Sahib. They have been around so many dead, these last few months. It is good to put the dead under the ground quickly. Pity the ones left unattended, for the wild animals to feast upon."

The column passed a patch of heavy woods, still smoldering with tendrils of wispy smoke rising up against the rain. Even with the masking effect of the rain, the cloying, sickly stench of burnt human flesh penetrated their senses.

"Merciful heavens, old friend, these woods must have caught fire during the fighting." He placed his handkerchief to his nose to block the stench. "May God have pity on the unfortunate ones who burned to death in there. Lord, what a tragedy this war has become."

John paused, then asked the question that popped into his

mind. "Your son, Rava. Where is he, do you know?"

"Yes, Sahib. He rides in an ambulance behind the column, in one of the pine boxes the Army sends along for that purpose, along with the other men of the regiment killed in the fight at the crossroads. I will take him to Washington so that his mother and family can honor him. I am not sure what I will do then. I cannot build a cremation fire I suppose?"

"If not, my friend, we shall bury him with full honors in the new cemetery across the river from Washington. The one they have created from the estate of Robert E. Lee. I think it is being called Arlington Cemetery."

Khan Singh's voice cracked as he spoke of his dead son. "It will be a fitting place to put Rava, among his comrades in death. In the next world, my son has joined ranks with honored warriors with others from our family that lived before. It matters not how the vessel that held his soul here in this world is honored. Whether it be the cremation fires of India or the burial in the earth of this new land that you and I have chosen, both are fitting."

"On this you may trust me, old friend. Now, return to your duties. I will be fine here." John squirmed to find a comfortable position on the wooded plank that served as a seat on the ambulance. He glanced at the bewhiskered teamster driving the wagon. The old man chewed his tobacco and spit every few feet, but said nothing. That suited John just fine.

By the time the regiment crossed the pontoon bridge at Alexandria and entered the outskirts of Washington, John was thoroughly miserable and nearly exhausted. The wound had drained him of his natural strength and resiliency. He scarcely knew that the ambulance had arrived at his home, until Mrs. Richardson opened the door at Khan Singh's insistent knocking. Seeing John, supported by two orderlies, she took charge and swiftly had him deposited in his bed, covered by a down-filled cover.

As she tiptoed out of the room, she gave orders like a sergeant, not subject to dispute. "You! Corporal. Ride to the second corner that way and turn left. Two houses down on the right you will find the office of Doctor Turner. Tell him to come with you immediately. Tell him Colonel Whyte has a high fever and is almost delirious. Off with you now, hurry!"

John was asleep before the doctor arrived, and slept soundly for the next twenty-four hours. He awoke to find himself in a clean nightshirt, under clean sheets, with sunshine streaming through a break in the closed curtains. His arm was freshly wrapped in clean bandages and supported by a sling around his neck. He relieved himself at the chamber pot and had just settled back into his bed when Mrs. Richardson walked in, carrying a tray with a bowl of steaming soup on it.

"Morning, John. I thought I heard you, so I brought you some hot chicken broth. How are you feeling? How is your arm?"

"I think it's fine, Mrs. Richardson. Good to see you. I wasn't sure if I was dreaming or not when I arrived. The last few hours were a bit of a blur, I'm afraid."

"The doctor said you were just on the verge of developing a serious infection in your wound. He cleaned it again, put in new stitches, and reset your arm. I've been instructed to keep you in bed until your fever has completely gone and the wound has healed together, so don't even think of leaving your bed."

"Thank you, ma'am. But what about my regiment?"

"Lee Mansur said he'd insure the men got settled and arrange furloughs for them. He said not to worry, he'd take care of everything. Your sergeant Singh came by this morning, and said he had made arrangements to bury his son and the other three dead men in Arlington day after tomorrow. I told him you would be there, your injuries permitting." She sat the tray on John's lap.

"Now, eat your broth. It will help your poor bones to mend. Oh yes, President Lincoln sent over word that he would like to drop in and pay his respects as soon as you feel up to it. I sent him word to come by tomorrow evening. Is that all right with you?"

"The president? Anytime he wants to see me, I would be available."

"Not in the shape you are, my boy. You got hurt fighting his war, so he can wait until you're feelin' better before he comes around. Until you're able to walk out of here under your own power, I'm the boss. So, unless you plan to fire me, eat your broth, and rest. Doctor Turner is coming by this evening to check in on you." She gave him a cheery smile and left him, purposely shutting the door behind her.

John sipped his soup and to his surprise, fell asleep again, awakening only once to drink a glass of water and then to fall asleep yet again, not to wake until the sun was setting. He had just finished another bowl of hot broth and a helping of mutton stew, when Lee Mansur stopped by. The two soldiers visited and discussed regimental business for a few minutes, when Khan Singh and Madam Singh arrived. John extended his condolences to the mother of Rava, but she was as much a Sikh as her warrior husband and ended up consoling John, who was brokenhearted at the loss of his friend and orderly. He promised to be at the funeral the next morning.

With Mrs. Richardson's patient help, John dressed in his best uniform the next morning and rode in a carriage across the Arlington Bridge to the new cemetery located on General Lee's old plantation. More than one hundred men from the Fifth Michigan attended the solemn, dignified ceremony, as Rava Singh, Sergeant Hightower and two privates were laid to rest, side by side.

John returned to his carriage after Sean Gallagher played the haunting melody of "Taps," the new military bugle call that bid a solemn farewell to the dead. Lee Mansur stood with one foot on the wheel, watching the men of the regiment file past the four caskets in their graves, dropping a handful of soil on each.

Lee nodded at the graves. "A fine funeral, Colonel. I was moved to tears by the chaplain's remarks. I'd guess nearly every man in the regiment not in route to his home was here."

"That's marvelous, Lee. Convey my gratitude to the men at retreat formation tonight. Now, how about you? Why don't you take a few days off?"

"Would it be all right? I'd sort of like to go visit my sister Karina and her husband Craig, up to Chicago. I'd only stay a few days."

"Certainly, Lee. We may not have another chance for quite some time, once we transfer out to West Virginia. By all means, go. Give my regards to the both of them. Tell Craig that he can have M Troop again, if he wants it."

Lee grinned. "I imagine I'd have to hide from Karina and her broom, if I even mention anything to him about coming back on active duty. After she finished with me, she'd come down here and whop up on you."

John laughed, and turned to Mrs. Richardson, who had just arrived from giving her final condolences to Madam Singh, who had become a very dear friend to the old widow. "Are you ready to return home, Mrs. Richardson?"

"Yes indeed."

"How is Madam Singh?"

"She's an amazing woman. I think she spent more time consoling the men of your regiment than the other way around."

John nodded. "It's their belief. The Sikh warriors have spent the last thousand years glorifying their fighting men. Be grateful they do, else how could she stand such a loss?"

"Well, it's not for me, John Whyte. Let's get you home. I want you to take a nap before the president arrives, do you hear?"

"Yes, ma'am," John meekly surrendered to her iron will.

He slept most of the afternoon, and discovered that he had a ravenous appetite at suppertime. Mrs. Richardson served him thick slices of roast beef and her honest attempt at Yorkshire bread pudding. While it did not quite meet English standards, he appreciated her efforts, thanking her profusely. He grudgingly allowed her to help him change into a clean nightshirt in anticipation of the president's visit.

Lincoln arrived around seven, with Mrs. Lincoln and his oldest son, Robert Todd, in tow. They crowded around John's bed for a while, making small talk and wishing John a speedy recovery. John mentioned how Mrs. Richardson was constantly feeding him a broth made from bone marrow. "I think she's determined to turn me into a cow with horns."

The president laughed and looked at his humorless wife, who had scarcely said a word the entire evening. Lincoln or Todd had done the majority of the conversation, Lincoln about insignificant tidbits concerning the government, and Todd wanting to know all about the battle going on in the wilderness of northern Virginia.

"Mother, why don't you take Mrs. Richardson down to her kitchen and give her your recipe for the pig's feet stew?" He smiled at John. "When Tad broke his arm, Mrs. Lincoln fed that to him nearly every night, until the bone was properly healed. It seemed to do wonders." The homely president flashed a smile at his son, once again, transforming his face into something wonderful. "Robert, my boy, would you tell the captain of the security detail that we are about ready to leave? Have him bring 'round the carriage."

As soon as John and President Lincoln were alone, Lincoln drew his chair up close to John's bed. Placing his large, bony hand on John's blanketed leg, he spoke softly. "Colonel Whyte, tell me of the battle across the river? How does it seem to be going in your opinion?"

"I'm not certain, Mr. President. I think we were doing all right, but Lee's troops were not really beaten, just stalemated."

"The casualties have been horrific. Members of my cabinet are alarmed. Grant has moved on south, toward Richmond, and news has been sporadic. Every dispatch says he is continuing the fight."

"That is General Grant, Mr. President. I heard he made the vow to fight along the line he now marches all summer if need be. He's like our English bulldog. He'll grab General Lee by the pants and not let go, until he's whipped him, I'm certain of it."

Lincoln shook his head. "I don't know if the Union can stand the losses it will take."

"The Union must, Mr. President, 'else the Union won't stand.' Those are your words I believe, sir."

Lincoln smiled weakly. "So you say I should go the distance with General Grant?"

"If you do, Mr. President, he'll whip Lee soon and end this damnable carnage, I'm certain of it."

"I pray you are right, my boy. Now, I must go. Be well. Mother and I are praying for you."

"And I you, Mr. President."

Lincoln rose, stretching his gangly figure to his full height. He smiled once again, his face transformed, yet still reflecting the care and wear of his demanding job. "Good night, my boy. I hope to see you up on your feet soon."

As Lincoln turned, his face crossed the shadow cast by the small lamp on John's side table. For an instant, it appeared to be an eerie reflection of a death mask, and, then, he passed on into the light and was gone from John's room.

John shivered. "I swear," he whispered to himself. "I just saw death, walking." He fell asleep wondering if he would ever see the president again. It was not a complete shock to him that he never did.

By the end of the second week, John was feeling much better physically and even the concerned Mrs. Richardson agreed that he was ready to rejoin his regiment, as it moved to its new assignment in eastern West Virginia. John bid his faithful housekeeper an emotional good-bye and rode to the assembly area north of Washington, Khan Singh at his side. John alternated riding on his horse and in the ambulance that followed him. He felt reassured as he watched the regiment prepare to deploy. Only three men had failed to return from their furloughs, a sign of a veteran unit with high morale.

The regiment rode easily toward their area of operations, grateful to be out of the death and destruction raging in the woods north of Richmond. They reached the outskirts of the small town of Romney, on the West Virginia border at sundown the third day. John decided to enter the town in daylight, the next morning. After a camp meal, he crawled into the ambulance, where Sergeant McQuinn had fashioned him a surprisingly comfortable bed. He was asleep almost instantly.

Chapter 18

John painfully dismounted from his horse at the front of the city hall of Romney. The night had been long and he had awakened several times with his arm throbbing. The trip west from Washington, while made in easy stages, had taken its toll on his slowly mending wound. He felt relieved that his fever had not returned.

He followed Lee and Khan Singh up the steps and entered first, as they opened the front door and then stood aside. A smooth-faced, very young private was sitting at a desk, alone, his hands locked behind his head as he stared aimlessly out the fly-specked window.

"Attention!" Khan Singh rumbled from deep in his burly chest.

The young man leaped to his feet, knocking his chair backwards. "Yessir, Colonel. May I help you?"

"I'm Lieutenant Colonel Whyte, commander of the Fifth Michigan Cavalry, to see your commander."

"Colonel Hagemann? Yes, sir, Colonel. I'll tell the colonel you are here." The orderly ran up the wooden stairs two at a time. He ducked into an office on the second floor of the building.

In a moment he skipped back down the stairs to inform John, "The colonel will receive you now. He says he's been waitin' fer your arrival fer nearly two weeks."

John nodded, and slowly climbed the wooden stairs, his heavy cavalry boots loudly clicking with each step. The first door to the left had the name "Jacob Hagemann, County Magistrate" written on the beveled glass window in gilt lettering. John knocked and entered without waiting for permission, Khan Singh right behind him. He gauged the heavyset man with gray streaks in his hair and beard to be Colonel Hagemann. The individual who looked up from his desk was in cord pants and a white shirt, with his sleeves rolled up past the elbows with no visible sign of rank or military affiliation.

John stood at attention, as did Khan Singh. "Are you Colonel Hagemann, sir?"

The man glanced up at John before gaping momentarily at the tall, muscular Sikh standing beside him. His voice was hoarse and gravelly. "Ya, that I am. Are you da boys vhat's come to relieve my regiment?"

"Yessir, Colonel. My regiment's bivouacked just outside of town. This is Sergeant Major Singh, my senior NCO."

"Velcome to de both of ya. I'm damned happy to see ya. My regiment has been vaitin' fer damned near a year fer dis day. Ve have had enough of dis damned security duty. Ve now go to join Sherman at Atlanta. Maybe ve see some real action soon, by gar."

"Is it bad?" John's face showed disappointment.

Hagemann shook his burly head. "Oh, it's not so bad, fer a vhile. But a year is too damned long. Git yur men away from it in six months or so and it vill seem like a wacation to all of you."

John nodded, trying to decipher the old German's accent. "Thanks, Colonel, I'll remember that. Now, could you show me a map of the area and explain what the current situation is?"

"Ya. Here, take a look at my county map." Hagemann pulled a large map from his desk and spread it over the top, weighing down one side with an old arrest journal and the other with an inkwell. "Here's de territory in question. It runs from here at Romney, south to Moorefield, east to de state border, near Strasburg, un back. Over six hunnerd square miles. But Mosby's partisans ain't here, 'cept when dey come to raid. Der Rebs stay here, in der back reaches of de Blue Ridge Mountains, on farms and in small towns up in der hills. Dey only come round here vhen dey raid de pro-Union farmers or ride thru on deir vay to a raid around Vashington City."

"Oh? Does that happen often?"

"Vhat? Raids against Vashington City? Sure, all de time. Mosby has a hunnerd raiders and more. He has a few out all de time. Dey jus don't come thru Romney vend day do. But, dere ain't a week goes by, ve don't git at least one visit from him or some of his damned band of cut-troats." Colonel Hagemann angrily brushed the heavy mustache over his lip. "Ve git a few, now and den, and he gits some of my boys. But, so far, I ain't figgered out how to stop him."

John traced his fingers over the map, looking at the numerous roads and trails showing paths into and out of the mountains. "Too many to put a guard on each, I suppose?"

"Ya," Hagemann agreed. "You vould never be able to stop him, unless he only send a few men. Most times he runs tirty to fifty men on a raid." Hagemann paused, before continuing. "And, he rides mostly at night. Ve rarely catch him in der daytime, vhen ve can fight him."

John nodded thoughtfully, digesting the information. "Khan Singh, return to our camp and bring the regiment into town." As soon as Khan Singh left, John turned his gaze to Colonel Hagemann. "May I ask, Colonel? What are your plans, now that we're here?"

The crusty German colonel outlined his orders transferring his command to Atlanta and Sherman's army. He finished, "Ve vill depart for Vashington City, tomorrow. I vill leave my adjutant, Herman Ghorst, behind. He is to recruit another tree troops from folks hereabouts, to be my replacements."

"A wise plan, Colonel. I suspect you'll need them, after a few weeks around Atlanta. I had the same requirement after Gettysburg and Spottsylvania." John paused, collecting his thoughts. "I say, Colonel. Would it be possible to borrow your best men, those most familiar with the area for a day? I would like for them to show my troop officers and NCOs the lay of the land." John explained his thoughts for securing the region. Hagemann listened, and nodded his burly head.

"As you vish, Colonel. I'll have dem available to you by der top o'der hour. Now, come, let me see your fine regiment march into Romney. It vill be a great pleasure."

By the end of the morning, John's commanders had assembled in the town's meeting hall and had been briefed by Colonel Hagemann and some of his troop commanders as to the current situation in the region.

After they finished, John stood and pointed to the map tacked to the wall behind him. "Gentlemen, we're going to try a different tack from our friends in the Twenty-third West Virginia. I will assign each troop a sector, shaped like a pie wedge, radiating out from here, in Romney. Troops L and M will stay at my HQ, as a mobile reserve. The other troops will find a spot in the middle of their sector, set up a permanent camp and be responsible for patrolling their area of interest. And, it will be done mostly at night, when the partisans are most active. Each of you will make a map of your sector, from this one before you leave. Learn the area around you like the back of your hand. Each troop will have a courier standing by at all times. If the Rebels break out, you will alert me, and I'll send the reserve troops to help you track them down and defeat them."

John looked at his officers and NCOs. They were busy writing, or listening intently to his directives. "Colonel Hagemann has men standing by to give each of you guided tours of your area before they leave. Take advantage of their knowledge. After you are settled, work to develop the civilians in your area. Use them as guides, and sources of information. Pay for any and everything you take. Most of the families in this area are pro-Union, so don't antagonize them. Now, report outside and pair up with your guides. I want to hear from each of you tonight, as to where you will be locating your HQ and your plan to watch the mountain roads in your area."

As the men trooped out of the hall, John turned to Hagemann. "Is Romney the best place for my HQ? Is it central enough to support the troops in the field?"

Hagemann thought for a moment, scratching his chin through the stiff hairs of his beard. "To be honest, vhile you might be most comfortable here, in Romney, you vould be better off locating here." He pointed to a spot well outside of the town, toward the mountains.

John nodded. "Then, that's the spot I choose. Any farms there, or is it just wilderness?"

Hagemann shook his head. "Oh, no, it is vell developed, clear to the edge of de Blue Ridge Mountains. Many farms."

John nodded his head. "Any suggestions as to where I should stay?"

Hagemann traced a circle on the map. "De best place is here, at Glorietta Plantation. De only problem is, vell, Miz Gloria, she's the vidow of Sam Cortland and she's an unreconstructed Rebel if ever dere vas one." Hagemann shook his head, sorrowfully. "Once, ve vere good friends, but vhen her man fell at Harpers Ferry under Stonewall Jackson's command, she turned bitter and vindictive to all of us who chose da Union. Ve'd most likely shun her completely, cept she has der best salt mine in this part of da state on her place. As it is, ve do business with her and she don't talk to us, nor ve to her."

John shrugged his broad shoulders. "I don't see that as a problem. We're at war, and she's chosen the wrong side. She should be grateful we don't run her off and seize her property, like we've done to many other Rebs on Union soil. I'll commandeer her place, pay her a fair price for her troubles, and throw her out if she causes me any trouble."

Hagemann smiled. "As ya say, Colonel. I leave her to ya. Vell, do ya feel like looking over der area vit me, or vould ya rather git a hot bath at da hotel?"

John lifted his damaged arm gently. "No, I can go for a while yet. If we can stay on the roads, I'll take my ambulance. I ride much better in it, right now."

"No problem. Ve vill take my carriage. I'll be leaving it behind when I depart, so I velcome one last chance to ride in it. Vhen I leave, I vill leave it fer you to use. Come, I vill order it immediately." Hagemann led the way back down the stairs and spent the rest of the day showing John around the area.

The land was fertile, with numerous fields sprouting corn, wheat and beans. Cows, sheep, and horses grazed in the lush, green fields. Hagemann knew his county well, and gave John a roadside view of most of the region, although very cursory. When John returned for his required briefing from his troop captains, he was tired and welcomed the chance to sleep in the small town hotel with its soft bed and hot water.

The next day, he sent Lee Mansur out to personally inspect the locations of every troop HQ, telling his faithful adjutant to stay out as long as it took to insure the men were where they could best watch their area and defend the local farmers. Around noon, he and Khan Singh accepted the farewell salute from the departing Colonel Hagemann and the troopers of the Twenty-third West Virginia Volunteer Cavalry, as they rode proudly toward the railroad and their trip to Sherman's army, fighting at the siege of Atlanta, Georgia.

The young troopers had the innocent excitement of youth off to war on their faces as they rode off. John silently wished them well, knowing what they did not: once they saw the elephant, they would rue the day they left the comparatively safe job of regional security for one of fighting Rebel soldiers on their home ground.

Khan Singh read John's mind. "They are happy, Sahib. And proud. They were born to fight as warriors. That is why they joined. Those who survive will not regret their choice in the end. Those who do not will join a proud clan of departed warriors."

Both men saluted the colors as they were trotted past and then turned back inside the city hall. The empty building was a lifeless chamber after the departure of Colonel Hagemann and his staff. Khan Singh supervised the removal of the office equipment destined for the new HQ, nearer the Blue Ridge Mountains.

"Take care to get all the maps to our new headquarters undamaged, old friend. We'll be using them often, I imagine."

Khan Singh raised his brows with an expression of resignation. His answer was as smooth as his demeanor. "Of course, Sahib. Everything will be well cared for in route. Shall I send for your carriage?"

True to his word, Colonel Hagemann had left his personal carriage for John to use while he recuperated from his injury. "Thank you, Sergeant Major Singh. I'm ready, I suppose."

Lee Mansur and Tim Vernon waited outside with Tim's scouts, to ride with John as escort during the trip. Sergeant Vernon was determined no Rebel raiders would ambush John on the first day. At the edge of town, L and M Troops, with over a hundred mounted troopers ready to ride, awaited John as well.

"It seems I'm in your capable hands, Lee. You know the way?"

"Yes, Colonel. Sergeant Vernon rode there this morning and will be at the point."

"At your pleasure, Major Mansur."

John surrendered the command of his soldiers with as much grace as he could muster. Lee was in charge and his arm hurt like the very devil. Awkwardly, John climbed into the carriage beside Sean Gallagher, his bugler, who welcomed the chance to drive a team, rather than submit his backside to the pounding of a trotting horse and the uncomfortable McClellan saddle he usually rode upon.

As they rode past M Troop, John returned the salute of the recently promoted Captain Greg Simpson, the new troop commander. The young captain wore a proud grin as he waited at head of his troop. Simpson was recently arrived from the Cavalry Replacement Pool in Washington City and appeared to be a good replacement for the dependable Ed Longacre, killed at Yellow Tavern. "Afternoon, Captain Simpson," John greeted the young man.

"Afternoon, Colonel. Troop M, ready to proceed."

"Lead the way, then, sir. Sergeant Vernon will ride point, to guide you."

"Yessir. Troop M. Column of fours, right turn, ho!"

The road was in good shape, not rutted and worn like the roads in Virginia. John settled back to enjoy the trip. The ravages of war had spared the area for the most part. Only occasionally a burned house or barn, or a ruined fence indicated recent fighting. Several vacant homes stood as mute testimony to those Southern sympathizers who had migrated away from the pro-Union area.

About four, the column turned into a long, straight drive, toward an antebellum mansion, situated among huge elm and maple trees at the far end. On either side, a few cows were grazing in green fields. Two old plow horses hung their heads over the fence and curiously watched their younger, more agile brethren carrying the blue-coated humans. Only after all had passed by did they return to the sweet grass at their feet.

The column of Union cavalrymen circled the curved driveway in front of the house. The house was an impressive structure, but showed signs of serious neglect. It needed paint, and several windows were cracked, with one shuttered by nailed boards. The shrubbery around the great mansion needed trimming and the flower garden to the side was strangled with weeds.

John allowed Sean to help him down from the carriage. He climbed the five steps to the broad veranda, with Lee, Khan Singh, and Captain Simpson right behind him. Lee pounded the heavy, corroded brass knocker against the front door. Presently, a frightened black woman in her middle twenties answered. She wore a worn and faded cotton dress, and her hair was tied up under a ragged scarf. She was barefooted, with soil on her hands and feet.

"Yessar. What's you Yankees want?"

"Is the mistress of the house in? Please inform her that Lieutenant Colonel Whyte of the Union army wishes to speak with her."

"Yessar. Y'all stay right here. I'll fetch Miz Gloria right now."

John pushed his way past the timid black woman. "We'll wait in the parlor, thank you. Please inform your mistress that I wish to talk with her, immediately."

As the black girl hurried away, muttering under her breath about Yankee lack of manners, John and the others stepped into the living room. The room was starkly barren. No pictures hung on the walls, and the furniture was sparse and visibly worn. John suspected the original furnishings might be hidden somewhere, awaiting the end of the war. The candlesticks were pressed glass instead of the silver he would have expected. The floor and walls were scratched and needed new coats of paint or varnish. As he looked around, another woman slipped into the room.

"Who are you?"

John turned. The woman was in her mid-twenties and wearing a work dress of faded cotton, much the same as the black woman's. The dirt was more pronounced on the pale, white skin of her hands. Her cheek was smudged where she had wiped sweat away with the back of a soiled hand. Even in the muddy, thick-soled plow boots she wore, the top of her head barely reached John's chin.

"Miss, I wish to see Mrs. Cortland. Would you please get her now? Tell her Lieutenant Colonel John Whyte of the Union army wishes to talk with her."

The young woman pulled the kerchief off her head, spilling luxurious tangles of curly, auburn hair upon the faded fabric of her dress and suntanned neck. The faintest dusting of light freckles spilled across the bridge of her pert nose, while her straight, white teeth gleamed against her tanned complexion. Her striking, hazel eyes blazed with mortification and anger. The scowl on her face conveyed in no uncertain terms her disdain for the man standing so imperiously before her. She was not much more than five feet tall as she stood there, but she faced him defiantly.

"I'm Gloria Cortland. What the hell do you want, you damned Yankee?"

CHAPTER 19

John's mouth dropped and he paused, speechless. He had not expected the owner of this fine plantation to present herself to him looking or speaking like a peasant girl fresh from slopping swine. He tipped his hat. Politely. "Beg your pardon, ma'am, I . . ."

The feisty sprite of a woman interrupted him, repeating her demand. "Well, dammit all, you Yankee fiend. What the hell are you doing on my property? Cat got your tongue?"

John swallowed his smile at her sharp words. "My apology, madam. I did not expect to meet the owner of such a fine home looking like a field hand and cursing like a mule skinner."

Gloria's hazel eyes narrowed in rage at the insult. "Why . . . why . . . you, you . . ." She sputtered in her frustration to hold in the words she wanted to spit at the hated enemy officer standing so grandly before her. But, Gloria Cortland was not stupid and she knew there was a line she should not cross, even before the enemy, if she wanted to stay in control of her home.

Taking a deep breath and her head held high, she started again. "Colonel. I am Gloria Cortland. What is it you wish?" She briefly glanced down at her muddy clodhoppers, wishing she had at least put on her worn, but clean, slippers before rushing inside to confront these grinning hyenas from the bluecoat army. Only the young colonel was not openly laughing at her. "And as for my, as you say, field-hand appearance, I've been working in my garden with my servant, Hattie. Ever since your army deemed it necessary to kill my husband and steal most of my horses, cows, and pigs, what we can grow is just about all we eat."

"Yes ma'am, I'm very sorry. As I was saying, I am Lieutenant Colonel John Whyte, commander of the Fifth Michigan Cavalry Regiment, assigned to provide security to this region of West Virginia. It is my intention to use your home as my headquarters for the time being. I will require that you and your helper make available to me all rooms in the house, save a bedroom for your personal use, and one for your servant. My troops will camp behind your barn and use all outbuildings as they see fit."

Alarm and then hot rage consumed the young woman's face. "Why, you can't do that. You, you Yankees have taken all that is precious to me and now you want my home as well? I won't have it, I tell you. Stay in Romney, like Adolph Hagemann did. I don't want you here."

"I'm sorry, Mrs. Cortland, but it's not your decision to make. I've decided to stay out here and that's that. I am, however, authorized to pay you two dollars a day in Union currency, as rent compensation. In addition, you may eat from our rations, in return for you and your servant helping to cook for the headquarters staff. I'm afraid you have no choice. If you wish, I will provide you escort to the Rebel lines and pass you through to the other side. You can be among friends there."

A quick glimmer of fear crossed the petite woman's face, before she recovered her composure. "Thank you for nothing, Colonel. My family is now gone save one brother, who fought with General Lee until he was captured at Gettysburg. He's in one of your damned prisons, up north. My old home near Norfolk is destroyed and I have no relatives that I could impose upon, even if I were of such a mind. However, I am not about to leave Glorietta Plantation. You are not welcome here, sir. If you choose to force your way in, against the wishes of two defenseless women, so be it. Once John Mosby finds out what you are doing, he'll take care of you and your cowardly blue bellies. You'll be fertilizing the soil of Virginia before long, I assure you."

John bowed slightly. "Wrong on two counts, madam. One, I'm not that easily killed. And, two, this is now the sovereign state of West Virginia."

"Not to me, it isn't, sir." Gloria glanced at John's bandaged arm, still in its sling. "It seems that our boys in gray have already come close. I hope it's crippled you for the rest of your life, you Yankee butcher." Her anger was building again and every man in the room could sense it.

John cut off the coming explosion by abruptly dismissing her. "You may return to your chores, madam. My troops will start moving in, immediately." He turned his back on the mistress of the house and addressed Lee and Khan Singh. "Inform the men. We'll put the headquarters office in this room; the rest of the staff will use whatever rooms they need. The troops will pitch tents around the barn. Put the scouts and color guard inside the main house, on the ground floor. Assign the officers to the rooms upstairs, leaving one room for the lady and her maid."

Lee nodded. "At once, Colonel." He turned and brushed past the incredulous young woman, headed for the front door.

"Where do you want the orderly room, Sahib?" Khan Singh's deep voice reverberated in the nearly empty room.

"The parlor will do. Put the furniture we don't need wherever mistress Gloria desires. I'm going to walk around the yard and inspect the troop bivouacs." John turned at the doorway and tipped his hat. "Madam."

As John left the room, Gloria spun and turned her glare on Khan Singh. Mad as Gloria was, her curiosity about the huge, dark-skinned NCO was even greater. She stared at him, finally asking in a haughty voice, "Who—that is, what—are you? I mean, are you a Negro? Have the Yanks taken darkies into their army? I heard that, but couldn't believe it."

"I am Sikh, madam. Originally from India, across the great sea. I have fought beside my colonel for many years. You should be grateful you have such a man in charge. He is a gentleman, and will see that nothing bad befalls you while he is here. Now, Memsahib, please excuse me, I have much to do."

Gloria stood helpless in her empty living room, fighting the rage in her heart. Suddenly her eyes narrowed. Maybe she could make something good out of this outrage. "Maybe," she whispered to herself, "I'll be able to overhear something useful for John Mosby." Her eyes misted and her voice cracked in bitter anguish. "Oh, dearest Sam, why, oh why, did you die? I need you now." She turned and rushed from the room, determined not to cry. She had to finish planting the sweet potatoes before the rains came again.

In two weeks, the operation John had envisioned was running smoothly. The night patrols had severely interrupted the movement of guerrillas out of their mountain lairs and forced them to seek safer routes to exit their hideaways. John's men had clashed with Mosby's fighters several times, usually in quick, deadly, little firefights that erupted and ended within seconds. A few unlucky soldiers always paid the butcher's bill, but still, much less than the rest of his cavalry comrades were suffering during the heavy fighting around Richmond. For that, John was grateful.

John released his troop captains after the weekly regimental commander's call and watched them ride off toward where their troops were stationed, within their individual pieces of the "pie" for which they were responsible. Lee stood beside him on the porch, facing the setting sun's golden rays.

"Another good week, John. Four contacts, six Rebs kilt, three captured, and only three losses for us. Not too bad, I'd say. Reports of Mosby's raids are down by nearly a third. I imagine the War Department in Washington City is very pleased with the Fifth Cavalry right now."

The last of his young officers rode down the straight drive toward the road. He gingerly moved his left arm. Finally, it was nearly pain free. Now, he could comfortably ride for more than just a few minutes. "Yes, I quite agree, old boy. However, Mosby is certain to put us to the test very shortly and bring out a large group, one too big for our outposts to handle. Emphasize to everyone, if and when Mosby does come out in strength, they are to alert me immediately and avoid contact, if possible. I want us to hit Mosby's men when they least expect it and as far from their hideout as possible. If we can get on their trail before they ride into Maryland, we'll have the advantage. They'll be fighting us on our ground. I want to hurt him badly, the first time we go up against him in mass. Put the word out, Lee."

Lee nodded, lighting up a thin cigar. "I've told 'em once John, but I'll repeat it again tomorrow, when I visit the troop bivouacs."

"Excellent." John caught sight of Gloria Cortland walking out of the French doors that exited the north side of the house. Slowly, she crossed the lawn toward a tiny, picket-fenced graveyard under an ancient oak tree at the west corner of the main yard. She sat still for a few moments, her head bowed, before cleaning away any debris scattered over the two graves. As the sun settled over the Blue Ridge Mountains, she slowly walked to the house, going directly to the room she shared with her black maid, Hattie, as the dark woman said she was afraid to stay in a room alone with so many Yankees about.

There were two tombstones in the little cemetery. One was inscribed, "My Husband, Sam Cortland, Captain CSA. Born Feb 1, 1830, died Sep 30, 1862."

The other was a smaller grave, with a white, inscribed stone. "William Samuel Cortland, Our baby son. Born July 17, 1862, died Sep 19, 1862. Below the dates, the inscription read, "Together with his father in Heaven." Discolored water stains had begun to streak the slabs of limestone, as if the tears of a brokenhearted mother had marked the stones.

The next day, during a ride out to look over C Troop's deployment, John had spotted a small outcropping of snow-white daisies growing along the dirt roadway. On an impulse, he picked a large handful. That evening, as he saw Gloria start her familiar trip to the graves, he followed with the bouquet of wildflowers, their bright white hue contrasting against his dark-blue uniform.

His shadow on the larger tombstone alerted the kneeling woman to his presence. She looked up, annoyed at the interruption. "What, what do you want? Can't you see I'm . . ." She paused, seeing the bouquet of flowers in his hand.

"I beg your pardon for the intrusion, Mrs. Cortland. I saw these beside the road today and wondered if you might want them for . . ." John paused, awkwardly, groping for words. He held out the flowers.

Briefly, Gloria Cortland sat there, facing her hated enemy, then her eyes softened. "Thank you, Colonel. They are lovely." She took the flowers and divided them in two sprays, carefully placing one on each grave. She looked at the twin stones and sighed softly, before rising to her feet. She stepped back, shutting the gate of the tiny fence that surrounded the two graves. "My husband and child." She looked at John, defiant misery in her eyes. "My little Will, was born too soon. The local doctor didn't have the necessary medicine to save him, thanks to the Union blockade. Then my Sam, killed by Union soldiers at the head of his regiment only two weeks later. So, Colonel, you understand why you are not welcome and will never be welcome at Glorietta."

"You have my deepest sympathies, ma'am. I know it must be painfully hard for you. This area seems to be mostly pro-Union. How is it that you aren't?"

"Sam came up here from Tidewater, Virginia, years ago. I was raised around Norfolk before I married. We were never anything but loyal Southerners. Since Sam's death, I've had very little to do with my neighbors except to sell them my salt, at the most exorbitant price I can extract from them."

Gloria slowly walked away from the little graveyard, John at her side. He was content to simply be in her presence and chose not to argue the merits of the Union cause. "How is your arm?" she suddenly interjected. "You seem to be recovering the use of it."

"Yes, it's much improved, thank you. I suppose I should be grateful I didn't lose it to the surgeon's knife."

Gloria Cortland's reply was neutral in tone. "I suppose that's true. Then, you will have the full use of your arm again, soon?"

"None too soon for me. I'm tired of the inactivity it has forced on me."

She looked up at him. His height seemed to make him tower over her. She noticed his cleanliness, his neatly trimmed hair and mustache. The man was obviously a gentleman, even if a hated enemy. "I'm sorry I said I hoped you would be maimed by your wound. That was most unbecoming of me. Will you be leaving as soon as you are healed?"

"I don't know. We will have to stay until relieved, or until Mosby quits raiding and operating from this part of the state."

Gloria's Southern spirit asserted itself. "You'll never catch him, you know. He's like a gray ghost, flitting about at will. All you'll do is get your men killed, if you try to stop him."

They were almost at the side doors into the house. John desperately wished he could think of some way to prolong the conversation, but could not. Then he had an idea. "Mrs. Cortland, I should like very much to see your salt mine. Would you be so kind as to show me the way?"

Her voice immediately chilled. "And if I don't want to show you?"

"Sorry, I'm afraid you must. Military orders, you know. Is nine o'clock satisfactory?" He was determined that they spend some time together.

"I don't have a horse. All my riding horses have been confiscated." Her voice was bitter and cold.

"I'll take care of that, if you will allow me. We have several that you can ride. Until tomorrow morning, ma'am. Good night." He watched as she slipped inside and closed the doors. Walking around the yard, John considered how he might soften her antagonism toward him. "By the eternal, she must be beautiful when she laughs," he exclaimed to himself.

At the appointed hour the next morning, John stood on the front porch. Tim Vernon led a roan-colored, medium-sized mare toward him. "Morning, Colonel," he greeted John. "I found her saddle in the barn and this here is as gentle a filly as ever I did see. The lady won't have no problem with her, I'm certain."

"Very good, Sergeant. You accompany me with a half squad of men, if you please." He turned to Lee and Khan Singh, standing just inside the door of the house. "I'll return within a couple of hours. If an emergency arises, tell Lee to handle it. The mine is only twenty minutes away, according to Hattie."

"Sahib, don't you think I should ride with you? I do not like it, when you are away from my protection."

"Sorry, old friend. You have much to do, here. I'll be fine, and Vernon's men will watch out for us."

"Go on, Colonel," Lee urged. "You can use the diversion. We'll take good care of things around here for you."

Gloria Cortland appeared at the door, dressed in a somewhat

worn, but comfortable, tan-colored riding habit. Her skirt had a patch along one seam. While her white blouse was clean, it was thin and limp from long use and her boots showed the effect of much wear. Still, she was breathtakingly beautiful. Her auburn hair was piled up under a forest-green riding hat. Her face and hands were scrubbed and clean.

Without benefit of cosmetics or expensive clothing, she was as grand a lady as John had ever seen. "Good morning, Mrs. Cortland. A nice day for a ride, isn't it?" He touched his hand to the brim of his hat while flashing an engaging smile.

Gloria's emotions were in a flux. She expected to resent him for forcing her to accompany him, yet she was flattered at his obvious infatuation with her. She reminded herself that he might be trying to seduce her. He could be just another despicable Yankee cur. She asserted control of the situation as she coolly responded. "Yes, not that it matters, Colonel. I am at your disposal, like it or not. Shall we be off? The quicker we are there, the sooner I can return to my garden."

"Yes, ma'am, whatever you say. I have a very gentle horse for you, compliments of Sergeant Vernon. He and a few of his men will accompany us, as security. You will be quite safe."

Gloria stiffly nodded at the shy, young Nebraska born soldier. "I'm sure of it. Good morning to you, Sergeant."

Tim nearly swallowed his tongue. "Yes, ma'am. Here, ma'am, let me help you up." He gave Gloria a leg up and she slipped onto her sidesaddle as if born to it.

"All set, ma'am?" he shyly asked.

The youth was so sweet and innocent, Gloria could not maintain her stern manner any longer. Her sweet smile melted the young man's heart. "Thank you, Sergeant, I'm all set. Shall we go?" She turned her horse down the drive, leaving John and the others to catch up with her.

As the group trotted away from the main house, Lee Mansur

laughed, and turned to Khan Singh, standing at the door, still watching as the party grew ever smaller.

"Did you see his face?" Lee laughed aloud. "Did you see it?"

"What do you mean, Sahib Lee?"

"John," he laughed again. "He looked like a cat what had his pecker stuck in a knothole. The man's love struck, sure as we're standin' here." Lee laughed even harder. "And to a Rebel hellcat, no less."

CHAPTER 20

Gloria delighted in being on a horse again, riding on her land. "Merciful heavens," Gloria finally said, after riding in silence for some time. "This is a lovely morning. It's good to ride again. It's been a long time since I had a riding horse under me." Her gaze roamed over the rolling fields beside the dirt road. She silently shook her head at the sight of her barren fields, going to weed rather than planted in cotton and soybeans.

The morning sky was cloudless, a bright blue with the golden sun halfway up to its noontime perigee. Birds sang in the trees bordering the road, and the fields were cloaked in a shimmering, green carpet. John spoke for the first time since they left the house. "I must agree, it is a wonderful morning at that. It helps to be away from the desolation of the war. I'd almost forgotten how beautiful your countryside is. And"—he smiled at his companion—"it doesn't hurt to have a beautiful riding companion, either."

Gloria pointedly ignored his bold overture, while subconsciously brushing at her riding skirt. "I've not had new riding clothes since the war started and frankly, my appearance hardly matters to me right now. Survival is my only concern."

"Well, for what it's worth, I must say you look smashing to me, Mrs. Cortland. Gloria. May I call you that?"

"Sir, you are the conqueror and I am your unfortunate captive. You can call me what you want, I can't stop you."

"Still, I beg you not to think of our relationship in that way. I

195

hope you will allow me the privilege, because we are friends."

"Friends, Colonel? You have killed my husband and son. You have invaded my country and destroyed my way of life. You have taken my home from me." She could not contain the bitterness from her voice.

John replied, as emphatically and assertively, "No, I have not, Gloria. I am as much a victim of the war as you. I deeply regret the loss of your loved ones. All I can do is try to make your life, since we have met, better. I beg of you, madam. If we can't be friends, can't we at least be civil toward each other?"

Gloria looked hard at John, struggling to sort out the conflicting emotions that stirred within her. After a long moment, the perfect day and his shy, pleading look decided the issue. "Very well, Colonel Whyte. We shan't be friends, we can't. But we can be civil. My Sam was always a gentleman, even among those whose company he did not especially relish." She rode on, in silence. John looked back at his escort. They were a few yards behind, out of earshot, enjoying the easy duty.

"Tell me, Colonel."

"Please, Gloria. Call me John, I beg you."

She paused for a second, then gave a slight shrug of her shoulders. "Perhaps, we'll see. So, tell me. You haven't been here, in America I mean, very long, have you?"

"No, I arrived less than two years ago."

"Why did you leave England?"

John sketched a hasty outline of the troubles with his brother, the current Duke of Bransworth, and his reasons for leaving the country of his birth. "And since then, I've been in the Union army. You can imagine the rest."

"Well mercy sakes, why did you join the Yankee army? Most Englishmen seem to favor the South in this war. Are you just contrary?"

"No ma'am. At least, I don't think so." John paused. "I think it's because I saw how my countrymen treated the native soldiers in India. I do not agree that a man should be enslaved because of the color of his skin."

"Isn't your turbaned sergeant your servant? He acts like he is."

"No, far from it. Khan Singh is his own man, a warrior and gentleman. He chooses to be my friend and to serve me, to my everlasting gratitude. Much like your Hattie, I should say."

"Oh, Hattie was my slave, when I first came to Glorietta. When West Virginia became a free state, I gave her the papers of manumission, first thing."

"Yet, she stays with you in spite of the fact that you once considered her your property?"

"Well, I always loved Hattie and treated her well." Gloria's face pinched in annoyance. "Besides, this war isn't about that. It's about states' rights and self-determination. If you Yankees would just leave us alone."

"I'm sorry, Gloria, but I'm afraid you don't see it from our side at all. To the North, it's about slavery and preservation of the Union. And it's a question that will be answered on the battlefield, to the eternal horror and pity of it all. We will never allow the Southern states to leave the Union. Never. Just as England will never allow Scotland to leave the British empire. All the blood and destruction notwithstanding, you'll never be allowed to leave."

For the first time, Gloria looked at her riding companion with a touch of sympathy in her sad, brown eyes. "You've had some tragedies because of it as well, haven't you? The war, I mean."

"Yes, I lost some very dear friends, including Khan Singh's son, just a short time ago."

"Oh, I'm so sorry for your man. He's been very kind to me. I must offer him my condolences, as soon as we return."

John shifted the conversation to a lighter subject. "Tell me about yourself. How did you wind up here, all the way from Norfolk, was it?"

Gloria laughed. "It was a case of love, I suppose. My Sam came to town back in fifty-eight, to receive some cargo arriving by ship from Boston. My father, who was a banker, met him and invited him to our house for supper. He literally swept me off my feet, and brought me back here as his wife before the month was out. I had just graduated from Mrs. Lemont's School for Young Ladies, in Richmond." Gloria stopped her horse. "Do you mind if we stretch for a moment? I haven't ridden this much in two years."

"Of course. Forgive me, I didn't know." John held up his hand to stop Vernon and his men, and leaped off his horse, to assist Gloria in dismounting. He put his hands around her slim waist, and lifted her to the ground before one of his men did, savoring the delightful feel of her weight in his arms. As she touched the ground, her bosom brushed against his chest, literally taking his breath away.

She tersely smiled her gratitude. "Thank you. That's better. Do you mind if we walk for a while? I need the exercise."

"Not at all." He grabbed the reins of both horses, and walked beside her, his long stride worth nearly two of hers. "Tell me about your salt mine. I've not seen one before."

"Oh, it's been a godsend. I've been able to keep Glorietta from bankruptcy on the income from it. Sam said we were blessed to have it on our property. It's a pure vein of salt, nearly four feet thick."

"Isn't it filled with dirt and rocks?"

"Certainly. A little, anyway."

"So?"

"What you do is take some salt, put it in a bucket and mix with water until all the salt is dissolved. Then you strain the liquid through cheesecloth into another pot. Finally, you boil the water away and you have salt, pure and as white as snow."

"Interesting." John relished the view as they climbed a high knoll. "I say, but the countryside is lovely up here. This is a pleasant ride, isn't it?"

Gloria followed his gaze, her eyes bright. "Oh, yes. Sam and I loved to ride up here, into the foothills. We've come up quite a bit, already. There's my home, over there." She pointed across the fields to Glorietta, some distance behind them and below where they now stood. Gloria paused pensively for a few moments, looking out, then turned back to John. "Well, if you will help me up, we can continue. I'm feeling much better now, and we've a couple of miles yet to go."

John lifted her up onto her sidesaddle, fitting her tiny foot into the stirrup. He looked back to insure his escort was with them, then followed Gloria as she turned onto a smaller trail, leading higher into the low, heavily wooded foothills of the Blue Ridge Mountains.

The green forest enveloped them. With a soldier's caution, John swiveled his head from side to side, nervously looking for sign of an imminent ambush. As they rode deeper into the forest, he slowly relaxed, especially when he observed how vigilant Tim Vernon and his men were. John's gaze returned to Gloria, riding easily on her horse. The shafts of sunlight filtering through the forest canopy highlighted her light-brown hair in glistening shades of red and ocher. She was radiant, as the ride diverted some of the bitterness and loss from her conscience. She attended only to the birds singing above, and the occasional rabbit or squirrel that crossed their path.

They reached the side of a sheer bluff, where a great cataclysm once sliced through the rock of the earth, pushing it upward like a great, bare shoulder. In the face, a cave, its opening framed in old logs, stared blankly at them.

"Here it is." Gloria stopped her horse and awaited John's assistance to dismount, even though she had done it alone for years and years. He reached up, his hands encircled her slender waist, and he set her down carefully, so lightly she was unsure exactly when her feet first touched the ground. "Thank you," she murmured, inhaling the faintest whiff of masculine musk from his nearness. She reached into the bag tied behind her saddle, and took out several small, burlap sacks. Smiling again at John, she cocked her head toward the bags. "Might as well pick up some salt while we are here. I send Hattie into Romney to trade it for necessities, now and then. We can use the salt just like money."

She led John into the opening of the cave. It did not penetrate more than ten feet into the face of the bluff. On the side of the cave wall, a stained, white stripe appeared in the shadows. Against the wall, a pitchfork and shovel leaned. Gloria placed her bag beside the wall and opened it before taking up the pitchfork.

"Here, let one of my men do that," John insisted. Tim Vernon quickly responded to John's request for a volunteer. He easily drove the pointed barb into the white seam, and a large chunk of muddy salt fell at his feet. In five minutes, Tim had more than enough for Gloria's bags, which he filled with the shovel. The smitten youngster carried them out of the cave, where he tied one behind the saddle of each of his scouts. "Carry this back to the house for Mrs. Cortland," he instructed.

The other soldiers entered as John and Gloria left the salt cave, eager to see the interior for themselves. None had ever seen one before and besides, it would make good conversation around the campfire that evening. John followed Gloria, as she walked to a small creek a few yards into the woods from the cave opening. She sat on a log and took off her wide-brimmed hat, shaking her soft curls around her shoulders.

"It's so beautiful up here. I used to come all the time with Sam. We'd dig a few bags of salt, and then picnic here, beside the creek. I loved it here then." Her gaze looked back in time, as well as across the glade.

"It is quite peaceful, and beautiful. You are like a picture in *Harper's Weekly*, sitting there on that log, with the sun on your hair, and the flowers and trees fresh and bright around you." He put one booted foot on the log, and leaned his weight on his knee. His face came to within six inches of hers, so close he could smell the freshness of her hair. He hated to move, so pleasant was her nearness.

After a moment, Gloria returned to the present and looked up at John, still staring intently at her with eyes as dark as a raven's wing. She gave a resigned grin and held out her hand. "If you will help me up"—she paused for a fraction of a second—"John. We have to start back, I suppose. Your men will be worried."

John straightened, and helped her across the log. "I hate to leave, it's so quiet and peaceful. If only this damned war would end, so we could return to normal living."

"Things will never again be normal for me."

"They will, Gloria. I promise you. If it is in my power to make it so, I promise you it will."

Gloria gave him a timid smile, and for the first time in two years, felt a spark of warmth in her cold heart. She looked intently at the tall, Union officer escorting her back to the cave's opening where the mounted soldiers patiently awaited them. This man, her enemy, apparently had strong feelings for her. Strangely, it did not enrage her as she would have thought only a few days earlier, although she warned herself to beware of confusing his motives. He might just be in heavy lust, not love. Try as she might to resist the allure of the handsome, Yankee soldier, she felt a softness emerge from the hard facade of her current life. She felt a weakening of her resolve to ignore him, and became more attentive to his conversation.

By the time they arrived back at Glorietta, she had learned considerably more about her uninvited guest, while he had learned of the pain and suffering that she had endured the last two years. She even laughed at times, as he strived valiantly to amuse her with amusing anecdotes of army life, enjoying his obvious attempts to impress and entertain her. As he helped her from her horse, again lightly brushing against him, she consciously reminded herself that he was the enemy. He wore the uniform of those who had taken her Sam from her.

"Enemy or not," she whispered to Hattie, as they mixed the dirty salt in a tub of water, prior to straining it and putting it on the fire to boil away. "He's very nice, and besides, I shouldn't make him angry. Why, he might burn the house down or something, when he leaves. Don't you agree?"

"Yes'm, Miz Gloria. You be xatically right. Why de Yankees might jus' kill us afore they leave. You should be nice to their colonel, yes'm." Hattie kept on stirring the pot, afraid if she looked at Gloria, she would bust out laughing. Any fool could see that Miz Gloria was more than halfway smitten by him. She was talking to convince herself it was all right to like another man. "You needs to be around a nice man again. It's been long enough to mourn Masser Sam, like we done."

"Why," Gloria tried to recover, "it's not like I'm gonna be unfaithful to Sam, Hattie. I just aim to be civil to the man."

"Yes'm." Hattie poured the last of the raw salt into the pot, stirring the boiling brew until it had all dissolved into the water, her dark, muscular arm flexing with each sweep of the pot. Then she and Gloria carefully poured the salty water through the cheesecloth strainer into a second kettle. Discarding the muddy residue, they placed the clear, salt-saturated water on the fire to boil away. "Them soldiers done cut us enough wood to last fer more'n a year, and still be bringin' in more. It's good to has the help, even iffen they be Yankees."

For the next few days, John made it a point to meet Gloria upon her return from her nightly visits to her graves. He would accompany her to the patio doors or around the yard, admiring the flowers or vegetables in the garden. Together, they watched the evening sun settle against the mountains to the west. After a time, their walks grew longer and their conversation easier. John's men, seeing how gratefully she received their gifts, nearly every day had a spray of wildflowers picked for her which they collected while patrolling in the low foothills of the Blue Ridge. Twice, John took her back to the salt mine, taking the opportunity to make a picnic out of the trip.

One Sunday afternoon, after he had returned from another outing with Gloria, he stood on the porch with Lee Mansur, watching Gloria climb the stairs up to her room. "Tell me, Colonel," Lee asked. "You kiss her this time?"

"What? What on earth do you mean *this time*?" John's face reddened in embarrassment.

"Hell, sir. Don't you know the men are watchin' you two lovebirds like a hawk after a chicken. Every man is a'waitin' to see when you and Miz Gloria get right to it."

"I assure, you, Lee . . ."

Lee held up his hand. "Don't worry, Colonel. The men are happy for you. They like you and they like Miz Gloria."

John grinned ruefully. "I tell you, Lee. She's a smashing woman. I feel like I'm sailing into the stars, every time I see her smile. I'm afraid I've got it bad. I'm just not certain how she really feels for me. She's lost a lot, you know."

"Well, John, she's got a lot to give yet. Step up and take your best shot. You know how long we've been here. We may be recalled any day now. Intelligence says Jubal Early and thirty thousand Rebs are in the Shenandoah Valley. Grant'll be gettin' somebody after him shortly and we might be part of it. Don't wait too long. This war ain't gonna last forever."

"You're right, Lee. I should make my move. I'm almost afraid to for fear that I'll offend her, somehow."

"Damn, sir. How can you offend a woman by tellin' her you care about her? Grab her up and plant a kiss on her. She'll melt, I'll wager."

John turned away from Lee and started down the steps. "Easy for you to say, Major. You aren't the one in love."

"Hell," Lee chuckled. "I've been in love a dozen times, I reckon. I know what has to be done."

"Well," John mumbled under his breath. "I sure as hell don't."

CHAPTER 21

"Scout's comin' in, Colonel."

Lieutenant Colonel John S. Mosby, commander of the Forty-third Cavalry Regiment, Confederate States Army, looked up from the report he was drafting to the new commander of the Army of the Shenandoah, General Jubal Early. "Thanks, Lucas. I'll be right there." He sealed the report, and addressed the envelope before stepping out of the barn he was using as his HQ. He walked over to the fire and greeted the waiting scout crouched there by his first name. "Hello, Seth. What'd you find out?"

The young man quickly stood and fashioned a sloppy salute. His sandy hair and lanky frame made him appear even younger than he was. That did not detract from the hard truth that he was an accomplished scout and cavalryman, with numerous bluecoat kills to his credit. "You was plumb right, Colonel Mosby. They's not more'n a couple o'dozen Yanks at Miz Gloria's place. Most are out patrollin' the passes outa the mountains into the valley. They got a few guards about the grounds, but I didn't see none on the road twixt here and the Moorefield turnoff. If we can slip up there without the Yanks seeing us, we should be able to walk right up to their front door."

Mosby flashed his famous, cavalier grin. "Great news, Seth. That's just what we're gonna do. I aim to have the Yankee colonel's hat on my hat rack by sunrise." Mosby turned to his second-in-command, a dour-faced ex-banker, Major Maxwell Lunsford. "Max, have the men in the saddle in ten minutes. We ride to Glorietta Plantation. Seth, here, will guide us."

The Gray Ghost of the Confederacy rubbed his hands together in satisfaction. At last he would strike back at the Yankee commander whose unusual tactics had disrupted his raids against the Union rear for the past few weeks. Mosby had gathered nearly two hundred men from his scattered command and tonight he would surprise and crush the Yankees in their beds. His plan was to ride on into Maryland after the raid, to see what he could find in the way of Union supply trains to ambush. He absentmindedly brushed back the feathers tucked into the brim of his sweat-stained campaign hat.

Looking at the pocket watch given to him by his father, he gave the order to march. It was time to twist the tail of the Union army once again. He climbed on the back of his roan stallion and trotted away from the cheery warmth of the campfire. His mounted warriors, seasoned partisans all, fell in behind him, riding silently through the dense woods of the low mountain foothills toward the Moorefield road, nearly twenty miles to the east. From there, they would turn north, until turning northwest on the dirt trail that would lead them to Gloria Cortland's plantation and their anticipated destruction of the enemy cavalry bivouacked there.

Meanwhile, at Glorietta, John was finally asleep. He had spent another pleasant evening with Gloria, sitting out on the tree bench next to the garden, debating the merits of Chaucer and Shakespeare as literary geniuses or just good storytellers. He enjoyed her wit and admired her breadth of knowledge, gained mostly from reading the books in her husband's library. She had a passion for literature, and read at every opportunity.

John knew he was deeply in love with the young widow, but was not certain how to proceed in his quest to make her part of his life. "I know I've got to do so, Lee, no matter what it takes." He had confessed to Lee that afternoon, while they rode together to inspect farthest unit, A Troop, stationed on a farm west of Moorefield, close to the edge of the Blue Ridge Mountains. "I certainly don't want to push her too hard."

"I done told you, Colonel. You gotta tell the lady, so she can get herself worked up to the idea. Miz Gloria is surely gonna be flattered when she finds out how you feel. Then, she'll start thinkin' what good taste you got, fallin' for her, and before you know it, she'll be crawlin' into your bed."

John's face contorted in sudden embarrassment. "Why, I didn't mean to imply, that is, I say . . ."

"Hell, John, who ya kiddin'? That's what you've been thinkin' about for the last three weeks. It's as plain on your face as your mustache." Lee Mansur chuckled at his own wit. "Every man in the regiment knows what you're thinkin'."

John calmed down slightly, but his voice was stern, as he let Lee know he did not appreciate the flippant tone. "I say, Major, I'm not certain that I want my private life a topic for campfire gossip." John grumpily wiped at his lips with the back of his hands.

"Sorry, sir. You know I shoot off my mouth now and then. But seriously, John, the men love your little campaign. They all respect and like you, while they've grown quite fond of Miz Gloria. They want you to find something good like her, out of the hell of this war. They're rootin' for you to win her over, to a man."

John could not think of an appropriate retort, so he shut up and said no more about it for the rest of the day. Only after they returned and finished supper did he allow his thoughts to return to beautiful Gloria, the woman who had stolen his heart. He waited until she finished her nightly visit to the graves of Sam and Willie, before falling in step with her. Together they walked through the yard behind the main house until it grew dark discussing, arguing, and enjoying one another's company. Then, they continued sitting on the circular bench built around one of the ancient oak trees in the backyard. Only after they separated at the stairs of the house and she had slipped into her bedroom down the hall from his, did he think again of anything but her.

He finished several reports that had to be dispatched by the next day and took them downstairs, after dropping in on Captain Simpson, of M Troop, who was the officer of the guard.

"All quiet, Colonel," the young troop commander had reported. "I sent a mobile patrol down both roads, just like you directed. They'll be back around four this morning, I reckon."

"Very well, Greg. Wake me if you need anything. Good night."

"Good night, sir." The young captain settled into the chair at the duty desk, prepared to spend a long night awake. John went back up the stairs to his room and quickly fell asleep. He was awake as soon as he heard the door to his room open.

"Colonel Whyte, sir, wake up." It was Simpson, whispering urgently. "Wake up, Colonel."

"I'm awake, Captain. What is it?"

"The patrol that rode toward Moorefield is back. They spotted a large group of Rebs on horseback, headed this way."

John threw off his covers and quickly pulled on his pants and boots. "Where are they?" He grabbed his blue blouse and ran down the stairs, Simpson right behind. "Khan Singh," John shouted. "Alarm, alarm." That was enough to roust the Sikh soldier out of his cot in the room behind the kitchen, along with Lee Mansur, who stumbled out of the bedroom next to John's, rubbing the sleep from his eyes. Even Gloria stuck her head out of the room at the far end of the upstairs hall, her auburn-brown hair wrapped in cloth curlers. General bedlam followed, as the men all converged on the front room where the sergeant in charge of the patrol waited, nervously.

"This is Sergeant Middleton, of M Troop, Colonel. He was NCOIC in charge of the patrol."

John returned the sergeant's salute. "Report, Sergeant." He pulled his blouse over his head as he awaited the reply.

"We was about three miles to the south of here, sir. A bunch of Rebs a'comin' this away. We watched 'em fer a good while, then lit out to report."

"How many?" John asked.

"Hard to say fer certain, Colonel, but a bunch. More than a hunnerd anyways."

John nodded. "Riding up the road from the Moorefield cutoff?"

"Yes, sir. Coming slow and easy, like they was certain we didn't know they was there."

"You're certain they don't know you spotted them?" John was furiously making a plan as he spoke with the grizzled NCO.

"Nope, I'm positive they didn't see us." He scratched his chin. "Mighta heerd us ridin' on the road, but they ain't seen us, fer a fact."

Khan Singh spoke up. "The enemy horses would keep them from hearing any riders, Sahib."

John nodded. He looked at his pocket watch, snapping the cover shut forcefully. "It's nearly five. They'll wait until just before dawn, to insure they can see enough to shoot. We've got a few minutes. Lee, you take what's left here from Captain Lowe's L Troop with you. Mount up and deploy behind the barn in the north field. Greg, you deploy M Troop along the positions around the house. We'll have a surprise of our own for our visitors. Lee you hit their flank as soon as we split their charge." John nervously slipped his pistol in and out of its holster. "Thank God L Troop returned from the overnight patrol early."

"Where will you be, Colonel?" Lee inquired.

"I'll fight with M Troop. They'll need all the help they can get to split the Rebel advance. Go, Lee. Hit them hard, with every man on line when you charge."

"Count on it, Colonel." Lee and Captain Simpson ran from the house. John turned to Khan Singh. "Have the headquarters troops deploy and place the troopers from M when they arrive. I'll escort Gloria and Hattie to the root cellar immediately and join you on the front porch as soon as I can."

John ran back inside without waiting for an answer. He spotted Gloria and Hattie, huddled together at her bedroom door. "Put on your coats, quickly, and follow me."

Both women turned into the bedroom and soon returned, putting on their coats over their nightgowns. "What is it, John?" Gloria nearly fell, trying to keep up with John's long stride as he led them down the curving staircase.

"Raiders coming. I want you two to hide in the root cellar. Hurry, we don't have much time." As John ran out the rear doorway, followed by the two women, he spotted Tim Vernon, running toward him, followed by several of his scouts. "Sergeant Vernon, take these women and put them in the root cellar. You and your men guard them."

"Yessir, Colonel," Vernon answered. Vernon grabbed Gloria's arm and hurried her along. "Hurry up now, Miz Gloria."

Gloria looked back over her shoulder as Tim fairly dragged her away, toward the cellar in the backyard. "Be careful, John. Don't worry about us. Be careful," she called out.

John ran back through the empty house to the front porch. He could see his men deploying around the front yard, in holes they had previously dug in the front yard. He could hear others crawling under the porch and positioning themselves along the sides of the house behind the logs his men had cut for firewood. Khan Singh was standing by the front steps, looking out in the moonless night, watching as the men took cover.

"It will be false dawn in a few minutes, Sahib. I suspect they will come then. Where do you fight?"

John pointed to the cotton bales they had confiscated from a nearby Southern sympathizer and placed along the front banister of the porch. "Here, on the porch. The house will be a magnet for the raiders, as they attack. We split their line here and then Lee will smash one wing, before they can regroup."

"I shall fight beside you, Sahib."

John nodded. He spotted Greg Simpson, running toward him. "Yes, Captain?"

"We're in place, Colonel. My men are all along the fence, both sides of the house, and in the barnyard. We turned over the supply wagons for cover."

"Excellent, Captain. They'll be along shortly. Rejoin your men. Good luck."

"Same to you, sir." Simpson saluted, and ran around the side of the house.

Silence settled over the waiting men, save for the sounds of the night insects singing their last melodic trills before sunrise. John listened intently, waiting for the thunder of attacking horses hooves, glaring at a trooper who slapped a bug crawling on his neck with a loud *smack*! John checked the caps on his two pistols and spun the chambers in the weapons. He held one in each hand and waited, trying to keep his breathing normal like the towering figure of Khan Singh standing beside him. The old warrior had placed four extra, loaded and capped cylinders for their pistols on top of the cotton bale they shared. He also held a pistol in each of his meaty fists.

The minutes dragged by. Slowly, imperceptibly, the dark sky grew lighter in the east. Khan Singh cocked his turbaned head. "They come, Sahib."

Knowing how acute his friend's senses were, John immediately called out in a loud whisper. "Here they come. Fire on my command." He could hear the sergeants echoing his command around the yard. As everyone grew silent, John listened to the faint rumble of galloping hooves striking the hard dirt. It grew louder, as the sky grew lighter.

"There they are, Sahib," Khan Singh announced.

John strained to see. A mighty wave of men on horseback thundered into his view, appearing out of the morning dawn like the wrath of doom. So far, no man had made a sound. The line of approaching riders stretched into blackness on either side. John hoped his men were enough to bear the brunt of their attack. John crouched behind the bale of cotton, its massive bulk a reassurance to his galloping nerves.

The first wave of riders was only thirty yards from him. He aimed his pistols. *"Fire!"* he screamed at the top of his lungs. "Open *fire!*" His first shot spun a rider from his horse, to be swallowed up in the churning dust of the others. His men sent volley after volley of deadly fire at the approaching cavalrymen with their repeating carbines, dropping numerous gray-clad horsemen before them. Others jumped the front fence in a daring display of horsemanship, riding past the house and its defenders, while trading shot for shot with the men hidden along its length.

John heard the mournful wail of wounded men and animals and inhaled the acrid odor of gunpowder mixed with dust and the brassy, pungent smell of fresh blood. As suddenly as they approached, the files of galloping men split around the house and were gone, leaving only the lumps of bodies to mark their passage. John leaped off the porch and ran around the side of the house. Lee's command had attacked the enemy rank closest to him, causing a jumble of slashing riders, whirling horses, and falling men. The group that had split to the left of the house had run into the fire from the men in the barnyard, and had peeled away to the south.

In the early dawn light, John could see the main body of riders galloping away, followed by small groups that had broken away from the fight with Lee's force. John and the rest of his men ran toward the mixed-up cluster of blue and gray riders, adding strength to the Union side. With the added numbers of men John had brought, the Confederate raiders fighting Lee's mounted force were quickly killed, wounded, or captured, except for a small number who spurred out of the melee and thundered after their retreating comrades.

John found Lee, his hat gone, his sword dripping claret-red blood. The Hoosier breathlessly reported to John. "We surprised 'em good, sir. We hit 'em before they even knew we were among them."

"Excellent, Major. Now, reform your command and chase them back to the mountains. Don't go in after them, but make sure they leave the valley. Understand?"

"Yes, sir. Come on, L Troop, follow me. After them. Charge!"

John watched as fifty or so men and Lee galloped out of the yard in pursuit of the raiders. He turned his attention to the milling mass of men and riderless horses. He gave instructions to Khan Singh and Greg Simpson on collecting any reb prisoners, before running to the root cellar, where he saw Tim Vernon standing, his rifle jauntily resting on his hip.

"The women?"

"Fine, Colonel. We had to drop a couple of them, tryin' to see what was down here, I reckon." Vernon pointed at two still lumps, not far from the opening. "But, they didn't get far."

"Good job, Tim. Now, order your scouts to saddle up and join Major Mansur, chasing those raiders. See if you can grab any before they hit the mountains." Vernon saluted and hurried off, while John opened the wooden door of the cellar. He saw

Gloria and Hattie crouched in the dank gloom, clutching each other.

"Ladies, you can come out now. It's over." John held his hand out for Gloria. As the two women exited the cellar, blinking their eyes in the pale morning light, Gloria gasped in horror. "My God, John. Are those men?" Her face blanched at the carnage spilled over her yard.

"Yes, I'm afraid so. I'm sorry. There are many hurt men to take care of now. Would you and Hattie care to help?"

"Of course. Hattie, start water to boiling, as much as you can. John, tell your surgeon that he can use the main dining room as the operating room." Her voice grew suddenly strained and stiff. "May we treat the Confederate as well as the Yankee wounded?"

"Of course, Gloria. As far as I'm concerned, they are both Americans, no matter what color uniform they wear."

Gloria's answer was unexpectedly reserved. "Thank you, sir, for your courtesy." She turned away into the house, while John, perplexed by her coolness, looked for the regimental surgeon. The harried doctor happily received the news about using the main house as the hospital.

"Thank you, Colonel. I'll start operating immediately. Orderly, move the wounded into the house. Worst first and then the others. Hurry boys, now's our turn to work." The chunky, middle-aged doctor from Detroit ran into the back kitchen door, his bloodstained white frock billowing out behind him. The old doctor was reasonably skilled and John appreciated his dedication. Doc Johnston did not have the notorious reputation of a bloody butcher that justly branded some of the Union doctors.

John walked around the yard, Khan Singh falling in beside him. "Our casualties were light, Sahib. Seven dead, twelve wounded, so far. Major Mansur may bring in additional casualties, if he catches up with the enemy."

"He will catch him, I'll bet, old friend. Mosby was stung hard this morning. He'll slink off into the hills and lick his wounds for a while. What did he lose?"

"We have counted twenty-one dead and nine wounded badly enough they could not ride, plus eleven captured. Twenty-four horses killed and nineteen captured." Khan Singh pointed at the main barn. "I have the captured enemy under guard in the barn."

John nodded. "Very good, old friend. You did well, as usual. Not too bad a trade, I suppose, except half our wounded will probably be dead in a fortnight. I'll have some hard letters to write their grieving families. But, not too bad, I guess. Maybe Mosby will avoid us for a time. If so, it might be worth it."

He made the rounds, looking in on the sullen captives in the barn. Most were mere youths, disheveled, lean as fence rails, and shabbily dressed, but still as deadly as mountain rattlesnakes. He wearily climbed the back steps, and made his way past wounded men lying in the hallway to the main dining room. The doctor was hovering over a young man stretched out on the dinner table, Gloria and Hattie nearby, awaiting his directives.

John reviewed the meager amount of intelligence found on the enemy casualties, then wrote a report of the attack for his higher headquarters. The captured horses were mostly private stock of the raiders, so John immediately accepted them into the Union ranks. Lee Mansur trotted into the yard later that day, wearily reporting that they had chased the enemy back into the hills, without inflicting or receiving any further casualties.

John was waiting as Gloria walked out of the back door, as the sun was about to set. "Hello, Gloria. Thank you and Hattie for your splendid help. Doctor Johnston said you were a great service to him."

She looked up at him, wearily brushing her hair from her eyes. As she glanced at the detail, digging fresh graves just outside the fenced-in area of her family plot, her face hardened. "Those are my people you are putting in the ground, sir. I wish to God that you damn Yankees would just leave us in peace. Is that too much to ask?"

"Gloria, I, I'm, that is . . . you know that this is war."

"Yes, damn you, John Whyte. Damn your war. I must remember that we're on opposite sides. For a while I almost forgot that. Now, if you don't mind, I prefer to be alone."

Chapter 22

"Good morning, Sahib." Sergeant Major Singh gave John his customary crisp, military salute. The troopers in John's command rarely executed such precise honors. A quick swipe and a grin were more the order of things among the casual Americans.

John nodded, pulling on his gauntlets. He gave his senior NCO a wan smile. "Good morning, my friend. How are you this morning?"

"Very well, thank you, sir. Your mount and escort are ready. I have decided to join you, if you don't mind. I want to see how the men in C Troop are faring since my last visit."

"Happy to have you, old friend. Shall we be off?" John eagerly climbed on the back of his bay, eager to be out of the stuffy confinement of his HQ office. The late June heat made working inside oppressive. "It's good to be on horseback again, old friend. How are the men handling this hot weather?"

Khan Singh smiled. "They are coping, Sahib. The question on every man's mind, is how are you getting along with the memsahib?"

"Not too well, I'm afraid. The raid has put a severe strain on our friendship. She feels guilty that she almost forgot that she's a Rebel. Damn bit of bad luck. Just a few more days and I would have had the courage to tell her how deeply I feel about her."

"Most odd, your courtship, Sahib. Madam Singh and I never set eyes on one another before the day we wed, yet we are happy

217

and content now. You Anglos make such a difficult thing of it."

"I envy the ease of your courtship, old friend. Unfortunately, it doesn't work that way for us. I must start over, establishing her trust, little by little. Assure the men I haven't surrendered yet."

"The men carefully watch your campaign, Sahib. They won't need me to tell them. Ah, I see some bluebells growing over by the brook. On the way back, we will gather a large bouquet for you. Tonight, take them to her when she goes to the shrine for her dead." Khan Singh gave John an amused grin, the white of his teeth framed by his fierce warrior's mustache that he had curled upward at the tips. "Start from the beginning. You will prevail. I believe in your determination."

John's grunt was noncommittal, but he heard the old warrior. After a day of inspecting troops and hot riding along the dusty road, John did exactly as he was counseled. He washed the dust and sweat from his face and chest, combed his dark hair, and put on a clean blouse before taking the large handful of fresh flowers outside, just as the sun started to dip behind the Blue Ridge range. Gloria was picking up the remnants of a dried bouquet, turning as she heard his footsteps come up behind her. She shaded her eyes and looked up at him.

"Oh, hello, Colonel Whyte. I didn't hear you coming." She took the offered flowers. "These are beautiful. Thank you. I . . ." Her voice trailed away, while she carefully arranged the flowers on the two graves. On the other side of the ancient oak, the long, fresh, dirt-covered trench that held the dead Confederates and the individual graves of his unit's dead stood stark and accusingly raw.

John's voice was gentle. "I've missed our time together, Gloria. May I see you back to the house?"

"I suppose so. Thank you." She started to slowly walk the graveled path, John at her side. "I saw you ride out today. Going off to inspect your men?"

"Yes, I inspected my unit stationed at the James place, near Moorefield."

"I know the Moores. They have a son with General Lee, wherever he is."

John nodded. "Lee's moved his army now, as has General Grant. They are across from each other at a place called Petersburg. About thirty miles southeast of Richmond."

"Oh, my. Is the capital threatened?"

"If you mean Richmond, yes, I think that's Grant's objective. He'll probably tighten the noose, much like he did at Vicksburg. Lee can stop him for a while, but eventually the Union's superior resources will carry the day. Then, thank God, the war will most likely end." John took Gloria's arm in his, as they slowly walked toward the tree bench where they had spent so many enjoyable hours together. She hesitated, but did not jerk away. "When that happens, my dear Gloria, I'll have something important to ask of you."

Gloria stopped, and then moved on to the bench, where she sat down, as did John, as close to her as he could. She looked up into his eyes, and he allowed himself to fall into their deep, giddy warmth. "Oh, John," her voice tinged with despair. "What am I to do? I'm not a fool, nor are you. We both know what is happening to us. How can it be? I detest what you represent, yet I care for you. How can I love someone whose very uniform causes me such distress and hatred?"

"I'll be out of uniform, when I ask you, Gloria. I'll come to you a civilian, with no ties to anything, if that's what it takes. As long as we put the past behind us then and look forward."

Gloria looked at him, her eyes reflecting a soft, vulnerable longing. "Maybe we can. I hope so. I do." She tilted back her head even more, and John's lips fell on to her soft, warm mouth. Their kiss seemed to stop time. When they parted, both were gasping in passion and desire. She put her hand against his chest as he tried to pull her close again. "Enough, please. I beg of you, John. Go slowly. I must resolve this conflict within my soul. Please, John, walk me back to the house."

Resisting the urge to take her into his arms and carry her directly to his bed, John did as he was asked. He kissed the palm of her hand at the patio doors and remained outside, as she ascended the stairs to her room. As he lit one of the slender cigars he favored, he grumbled to himself. "Slowly, you say, woman. If you only knew how difficult that is going to be for me." Glancing around to insure no one had overheard his proclamation, he chuckled and walked to the front gate guard.

The younger of a pair of sentries who had been watching the two lovers from the darkness of the lawn whispered to the other. "Looks like the colonel's back in the lady's good graces, don't it, Ray?"

The older man merely grunted. "Yep, so it do."

John was as good as his word and slowly, carefully the two people distanced themselves from the hurt of the Confederate raid and began to rebuild their damaged feelings for one another. John's days were content, waiting for the evening and the evenings were joyous, because he could see Gloria, talk to her, and usually kiss her at least once, sometimes more. However, she kept a tight rein on her passion, and kisses were all she permitted. As frustrating as that was, John was happier than he could remember, and his men enjoyed the affair right along with the two of them. Always, one trooper or another, just back from patrol, presented flowers to John for Gloria. Gloria's graves were covered in colorful blooms and she usually had enough left over to place some on the fresh, dark earth of the new graves as well.

If his schedule allowed it, John ate his meals with Gloria and Hattie, in the small dining room, after the headquarters staff had finished. John's men had restocked the larder and filled the smokehouse with hams, slabs of bacon and dried beef, as well as sacks of potatoes, beans, and tinned fruit from the Union coffers. John put on a few pounds that the previous year's riding and fighting had robbed from him. Gloria softened and fleshed out, as did Hattie, looking more like women than field hands.

John continued to direct his soldiers against the never-ceasing probes of Mosby and his slippery raiders. The Rebels had been stung badly, once, and were now more careful, but still they had plenty of fight in them and kept the Fifth Michigan on their collective toes. Those troopers who relaxed their vigilance stood a good chance of ending up dead or captured.

On the Fourth of July, John held a review of the regiment, in the town of Romney, culminating in a dance where his men got the opportunity to hold a female in their arms if just for a few minutes. Gloria attended, her bright smile and charm making her popular with the men of the regiment. She would dance but twice with John, preferring to accept an invitation from among the many soldiers who admired her. She did allow him the last waltz and while they tried to keep their mutual feelings suppressed, numerous townspeople chuckled and nodded as they saw through the deception.

They chattered together as they rode back to Glorietta in the carriage that once belonged to Magistrate Hagemann, now fighting with his regiment in Georgia. John told Gloria about Gettysburg, just a year past, and his friend, Wil Horn, lost with so many others of his command. She spoke of the last dance before the South seceded and the colossal fireworks display she and Sam had watched together in Richmond, just before he joined his regiment in July of 1861.

Their kiss that night was especially sweet and for a moment, John thought she would not leave him, but once again, to his disappointment and frustration, she slipped out of his arms and retired alone to her room. He walked the grounds for two additional hours checking the guards, before he felt like he could sleep.

July marched past, as happy a time as John had experienced since he came to America. If the war had been over, it would have been the very best, but the occasional letter to a grieving wife or mother prevented that. By the end of the month, John and Gloria were talking about their life together, after the war. Gloria held firm to her resolve to not marry John, no matter how hard he pleaded, until he was out of uniform and men in blue and gray were no longer killing one another.

"I'm sorry, darling," she said, as he held her tightly to him as they sat on their favorite bench, under the big elm tree, on the way back from the graves. "I can't marry you until I know this war won't take you from me forever, like it did Sam. Be patient with me, I beg of you."

"I am, Gloria. But I swear, it's been damn difficult, living so close, seeing you every day and not being able to advance beyond acting like a schoolboy. I love you, Gloria, and quite naturally, I want you. Now, tomorrow, forever." John smiled ruefully, his boyish, handsome face causing her heart to skip a beat. "You have to be patient with me as well."

Their kiss gave promise to the passion and desire they both fought to keep in check. She slipped from his arms and hurried away, while he sat and cursed fate, his luck, and the war in general. The next day started off as any other, until noon, when a courier from Washington rode up and dismounted, slapping dust from his blue uniform. John was in his office, finishing a report to HQ, when Lee Mansur escorted the courier inside. Lee fidgeted at his desk, as John read the message. The burly, Indiana schoolteacher was curious about the high-level dispatch to a mere regimental commander.

John opened the sealed envelope inside the leather pouch. He glanced at the return address. It was from the office of General Halleck, the Army chief of staff. He scanned the writing inside and looked up at the courier. "Tell the general that I will be there." The corporal saluted and departed the office.

"Well," Lee complained. "Don't keep me in the dark. What does it say? We bein' recalled already?"

John gave Lee the message. "I would guess so, seeing who wrote it. I'll have to wait until I see Grant, Sherman, and Custer on the sixth, I suppose."

Lee read aloud.

"To General Grant, with copies to Generals Sheridan and Custer, and Lieutenant Colonel Whyte, Fifth Michigan Cavalry. You are to proceed by quickest route to Monocacy Station, Maryland, by 5 August, this year, where you will meet the next day with addressees above, to discuss future operations. Signed, William Halleck, Major General, US Army, Chief of Staff, Washington, DC."

Lee looked at John, the message in his hand. "Damn, John. It's a move for certain. They wouldn't call for you otherwise. I knew this soft duty was too good to last. Who you gonna take with you?"

"You'll stay here, in command. I'll take Khan Singh, and some of Sergeant Vernon's lads."

Gloria clutched John's arm that evening, when he told her of his upcoming trip. "Oh, John. Does that mean you will be transferred away from here?"

"I honestly don't know, Gloria. All I can do is show up, and wait for my instructions. I suspect that will be the case." He placed his hands on her shoulders, turning her to face him squarely, looking deeply into her eyes. "Would that help me convince you to marry me right now?"

Gloria buried her face in his shoulder. "Damn, damn, damn," she murmured softly. "I pray it is for something else, entirely. Now, let's talk about more pleasant things. Aren't the new vegetables coming along nicely?" Her mood was spoiled however, and before much longer, she excused herself, leaving John at the bench, his question unanswered.

John spent the next few days inspecting the men, insuring nothing was overlooked in preparation for returning to the war. The day of his departure arrived and John stood on the front porch with Lee and Gloria, watching Khan Singh and Tim Vernon finish their final inspection of his escort. "The regiment's yours, Lee. I'll be back on the seventh or eighth I imagine. Take care, my friend."

"And you, Colonel. I'll check with Khan Singh and see if he's ready to depart. Lee stepped off the porch, allowing John and Gloria some small measure of privacy.

John took her hand in his and softly kissed her palm. "I'll be back shortly, my dear."

Disregarding the gaze of the onlooking soldiers, Gloria drew his head down and kissed him hard on the mouth. "Take care, my darling. Hurry back." She spun and rushed into the house, leaving John to manfully stride down the steps and climb on his horse, studiously avoiding his men's faces.

Looking back over his shoulder at the waiting troopers, he nodded, and trotted down the curving driveway toward the road, his mind whirling with passion and confusion. He was not much of a conversationalist with Khan Singh, who rode at his side. The old warrior was content to hold his tongue and enjoy the quiet time beside the man he loved like an elder son.

Their arrival at the tiny hamlet of Monocacy, just across the Potomac River in Maryland, was barely noticed. Around the surrounding countryside, nearly thirty thousand soldiers of what was to become the Army of the Shenandoah were encamped. White tents sprang up in all directions, as far as the eye could see. Blue-coated soldiers were drilling, marching, milling about, as was to be expected. John found the headquarters tent, a monstrous structure of taut, white canvas. He reported to a prim and proper major sitting at a small field desk outside the tent. The staff officer looked at a paper in front of him. "Ah yes, Lieutenant Colonel Whyte. You and your sergeant major are to report here at eleven o'clock, tomorrow morning. I'll have an orderly show you where your party can stay tonight." He looked at John's dusty uniform and sniffed haughtily. "Please wear your best to meet the commanding general, if you please."

John weighed the pleasure of knocking the man off his seat into the dust against the aggravation of explaining why he did it, and then merely nodded. "Of course." He followed the orderly to a series of empty tents and allowed his men to take his pants and boots for careful cleaning, even though he was tempted to show up the next day looking exactly as he had just arrived.

He and Khan Singh appeared in their best uniforms, with shined boots and polished brass, at the appointed hour the next morning. They were shown into the huge tent, where Grant, wearing a private's blouse with three stars on his epaulets and faded infantry pants stuffed into muddy boots, rose from his chair and heartily greeted John. Generals Sheridan and Custer stood as well, shaking John's hand as they warmly greeted him.

Grant slapped John's arm. "Good to see you again, John. How's the arm?"

"I'm quite fit, thank you. The arm's nearly as strong as ever, and I'm as rested and well as before the war."

"Good, good," Grant murmured. "I spoke with the president yesterday, and he said to give you his warmest regards."

John ducked his head, modestly. "How kind of him. Please return the thought, the next time you see him."

Grant beamed at John. "The president has told me how you lobbied for my appointment, here in the East. I suppose I have to thank you for that, although, I think I would rather be anywhere but up against Bobby Lee's boys in front of Richmond."

"I simply gave the president my evaluation of the one man I thought could take on Lee and win, General. He made the decision, I assure you."

"Hear, hear," George Custer chimed in, eager to butter up his senior commander.

Grant smiled, the circles under his dark eyes showing the strain of his responsibility as senior commander of the Union army. "Well, whatever, my thanks, John. Now, it is my pleasure to award you this medal, for your gallantry at Yellow Station." With that, Grant pinned the Medal of Honor on John's blouse. Turning to Khan Singh, he repeated the award, shaking the hand of the gigantic, but suddenly overwhelmed Sikh warrior.

After Custer and Sheridan added their congratulations to the two surprised soldiers, Grant dismissed Khan Singh. He was rewarded with a ramrod stiff military salute that shook the tent, so crisply was it rendered. The big Sikh warrior spun on his heel and departed, pride bursting open on his bronzed face like sunshine after a thunderstorm.

Grant's face beamed at Khan Singh's response. "That is some soldier, Colonel Whyte. If you ever grow tired of him, send him around to me."

"Not to happen, sir. He's my friend, senior NCO, and regimental father figure, all rolled into one."

Grant nodded. So it seems. Well, down to business. You ready to return to the work at hand? How about your regiment? The men all rested and reequipped?"

"Yessir, we're all ready. At your command, General."

"A major operation is in the works, John. I'm sending Phil here." He pointed at Sheridan with his ever-present cigar. "Into the Shenandoah Valley to drive it clear of Rebels, once and for all."

Sheridan's, short, thick body seemed to grow ramrod straight as Grant spoke. "He has my utmost confidence."

Grant looked to Custer. "General Sheridan has asked for you to be given the Second Division. *Major General* Custer and I have agreed."

Custer's face was ablaze with pride and happiness at the news of his promotion and new assignment.

Grant's face twinkled at his pleasure in rewarding his subordinates. "And you'll take over the First Brigade, Colonel Whyte, effective as soon as I can assign another regiment to relieve you in West Virginia. I plan on sending the newly activated Twenty-first Vermont your way. They'll begin arriving in a week or so. Insure they are acclimated to your area of operations and then report to your new division commander immediately thereafter." Grant then pinned twin stars on Custer, whose beaming face was aglow, and the silver eagle of a full colonel on a somber-faced John.

As Custer and John listened to the initial orders for the coming campaign, both men appreciated how encompassing the mission would be. The valley would be wiped of any means of supporting the Confederate army. The families there would suffer as much, as their fields and barns would be destroyed and their livestock taken from them. Grant saw John and Custer glance at each other.

"I know," he rumbled, blowing a billowing stream of cigar smoke at the roof of the tent. "It's a tough order. But the sooner we clear the valley and stop the people there from supportin' the Rebel army, the sooner the war ends."

That statement made sense to John. The sooner the war was over, the sooner Gloria would be his wife. At the end of the day, after a meal, with toasts of congratulation for the newly promoted soldiers, John and Custer walked back to their tents. Custer was practically hopping in suppressed glee.

"By God, John. We'll kick old Jubal Early's ass from one end of the valley to the other. Glory and honors have only begun to fall on us. Here's my tent, so I must say good night. I must write Mrs. Custer and tell her of my promotion."

John saluted. "Good night, General. My congratulations and my respects to Mrs. Custer." He walked on to his tent, where his men were asleep. He would have to wait until the next day for them to see him with his new rank. He tossed in his bed, thinking about leaving Gloria. He hated to leave her, but knew the sooner he returned with the war over the sooner they would wed. It would have to do. His sleep was late but peaceful.

CHAPTER 23

As John walked out of his tent the next morning, Khan Singh saluted as usual, until spotting the new shoulder boards with the silver eagle centered therein. His pointed mustache twitched as for an instant a curl pulled his lips upward, then he was all business again. "My sincere congratulations, Sahib Colonel. Do we leave the regiment?"

John grinned at his friend. "Yes, old friend. I've been given command of the First Brigade. General Custer takes over the division."

Khan Singh nodded, his uniform perfect, his dark-maroon turban expertly wound on his great head, silver and black hairs peeking from around his ears. His heavy mustache and beard were as black as powdered coal, lightly sprinkled with silver dust, and his raven eyes were shining in pride. "I will, of course, accompany you, as your sergeant major?"

"Of course, of course. I'm taking Tim Vernon and a few of his scouts, as well as Sean Gallagher as my brigade bugler. I wish I could take more, but Major Mansur will need them. I plan to make him commander of the Fifth Regiment."

Khan Singh chuckled. "The major will not like that, Sahib. He is always saying how happy he is right where he is, as adjutant."

"Nobody's asking him where he's happiest. Orders are orders. I think you should bring Sergeant Miles up from C Troop as regimental sergeant major, don't you agree?"

"Most assuredly, Sahib. And Sergeant Hewlett should take over as chief scout of the regiment. Sahib, if you can, take Sergeant McQuinn as commissary NCO of the brigade. He'll do fine work for you there."

"A good point, Sergeant Major. Do it. We are due to be relieved in a week, so let's hurry back to Glorietta and start preparations. I want everyone to be freshly equipped and remounted, before we rejoin Custer and the division on the second."

Sergeant Vernon's eyed widened as John walked toward him and the rest of the waiting escort. "Attention!" he shouted. "Good morning, Colonel Whyte, sir." Giving John a snappy salute, he grinned in pride for his commander. "I see the big brass finally spotted a good officer. Congratulations, sir."

"Thanks, Tim. You'll be coming with me to the brigade, as senior NCO in charge of scouts, headquarters staff, and the color guard."

Tim's face lit up at the news of the promotion. "Thank you, sir. Escort, fall in behind the colonel. At the walk, ho!"

John's return to Glorietta Plantation was filled with the triumph of the day. The guards spotted his new rank, and the word passed through the camp faster than John would have imagined. Lee Mansur spotted the new rank as soon as John dismounted and hooted a mighty yelp.

"Eeehaw! By dogs, sir, full colonel. Way to go. Congratulations. We'll have to have a party tonight. Corporal Pate, tell Miz Gloria that we'll be havin' a blowout tonight. I'll send men out to buy a couple of chickens and fresh vegetables. And tell her to make some dried apple pies. We're gonna have us a real, old-fashioned promotion party."

John smiled at Lee's exuberance. "Include the enlisted men on this list, Lee. They're getting a promotion as well." He handed Lee the list of men that he planned to take with him.

He waited to see if Lee caught on as to what the promotions meant, but the young Hoosier major was too excited about the coming party to think through the implications.

John walked out to the garden and greeted Gloria, sitting in the shade of a big elm, peeling potatoes from a large tub. Hattie was vigorously chopping weeds in the garden, a big straw hat covering her head. He decided that his news could wait until after the party. He embraced Gloria, kissed her in greeting. "I'm back, my dear. Just like a runaway pony, returning to his stable."

"John," Gloria chided gently, not really trying to move away from his warm embrace. "Your men will see you. Mind your manners, sir." She favored him with a smile and returned to her potatoes. "Is everything all right? At your headquarters, I mean."

"Yes, I suppose so. I'll tell you about it after dinner tonight. Major Mansur will be here shortly, to explain that he wants to throw a party for a dozen or so of us. I suppose I'd best get out of your way. See you later, my dear."

He reluctantly returned to the piles of paperwork that had stacked up in the three days he had been away, his mind continuously refocusing on a beautiful, Rebel widow instead.

At the big table, with the men seated around, Lee raised his glass, a toothy grin spread across his face. "Here's a toast to the best colonel in the Union cavalry, our very own Colonel John Whyte."

"Hear, hear," echoed around the table in the main dining room. John sat at the end, with Gloria on his left and Khan Singh on his right. Lee was at the far end, with Tim Vernon, Sean Gallagher, and Amos McQuinn sitting nearby, all somewhat uncomfortable in the presence of their regimental officers and the lady of the house. The captains and lieutenants of M and L Troops sat in between.

John stood to applause, looking at first at his men and then at Gloria. "Thank you for your sentiments." He focused his attention toward Lee, who sat unconcerned and relaxed, unsuspecting. "One of the nice things about promotions, is that it allows others to be promoted as well. As you may have heard, I will assume command of the First Michigan Brigade when we rejoin Custer. That will be soon. I expect our replacement regiment to arrive within the week." John paused as he overheard Gloria's soft gasp, one that she could not completely stifle.

"I will take my friend Khan Singh as brigade sergeant major, Sergeant Vernon as chief scout, Sean Gallagher as brigade bugler, and Sergeant McQuinn as brigade commissary NCO. He smiled at Khan Singh and Sergeant Miles, sitting stiff and formal as if on parade. "Miles will become the regimental sergeant major. And the new commander of the Fifth Michigan will be Brevet Lieutenant Colonel Lee Mansur. Lieutenant Colonel Mansur will promote others to take over the newly vacated places within the regiment."

Lee nearly choked on the mouthful of apple pie. He jumped to his feet, sputtering and hacking. "Now wait a minute, sir. I don't want to be the commander. Can't you find someone else?" His voice faded out as John continued to grin at him, slowly shaking his head from side to side.

"Sorry, Lee. Those are your orders, so no complaints. Gentlemen . . . and madam"—John gave Gloria a small bow—"I suggest we return to our duties. My thanks to all of you for your company at this occasion, and my special thanks to Mrs. Cortland and Hattie for the wonderful meal they prepared for us. I bid you all good night."

The men filed out of the house, thanking Gloria and paying individual respects to their commander. John stepped out with Lee and lit a cigar, listening with amusement as Lee protested his promotion.

"I sure wish there was some other way to work around this,

John. Damn, but I hate having the burden on my shoulders that you've carried this past year."

"Don't kid yourself, Lee. You're ready, or I bloody well wouldn't have given it to you. You'll be fine. Utilize the experience of your senior NCOs and officers. Think the problem through, and then act decisively."

"Well, I'd just as soon gone with you, up to Brigade. Who'll be your adjutant there?"

"I'll find someone, Lee. He'll not be as good as you, but I'll find someone. Good night."

Lee moved off the porch, intent on making the rounds of guards before turning in. John stood smoking, thinking of what was coming. He sensed Gloria slipping out of the front door and coming up behind him.

"John, I'm so proud of you. But do you have to leave so soon?"

"I'm afraid so. Just as soon as the replacement regiment arrives. I hated to spring the news on you so unexpectedly, but I didn't want to spoil our little celebration."

Gloria sighed softly. "Oh, John. I hate this. I have so much I want to say, yet what good will it do? You'll be gone and I'll soon be forgotten. Damn this war." Her voice broke.

"You are wrong, my dearest, you'll not be forgotten. I want you for my wife. As soon as the war is over, I aim to marry you, Gloria, my dearest. That is something you can go to the bank with. I hoped to find a more romantic time to speak to you of this, but circumstance forces me to push ahead. I hope you will marry me before I leave."

"Oh, John. Marry you now? I had hoped that you would stay at Glorietta longer, that is, I knew, but . . ." She paused. "You know what I mean. I need to think this through. You have my head spinning. Can I answer you later?"

"Certainly, my dear. Like I say, I know this wasn't the most appropriate time for this."

Gloria stood on her tiptoes and pulled his head down to hers, pressing her warm lips hard against his mouth. She slipped away from his embrace, to hurry inside and up the stairs to her room. John picked up his cigar from the porch deck, where he had dropped it, and ground out the fiery end against the stone walkway.

He inhaled deeply, then returned to his desk, determined to finish the report on current activities he wanted to pass on to the commander of the regiment coming to replace him. Finally, satisfied that he had covered the salient points adequately, he slowly climbed the stairs to his room, undressing in the dark, lying down on top of the bedcover, naked, thinking about Gloria and her reaction to his blurted proposal.

As he was drifting into sleep, he faintly heard a soft squeaking of a hinge from the direction of his closet. He raised up on one elbow and turned his head to look, just as the closet door opened and a willowy figure in billowing white floated toward him. "What the . . ." was all he could utter before Gloria's hand clamped over his mouth, to be followed by her lips.

"Hush, darling. Sam and I put doors that open into the dressing room between our bedrooms on both our closets, so we could visit one another without walking down the hallway. I wondered if you would ever notice it."

John tried to rise up, flustered at her sudden and sensuous arrival. "Um, Gloria, I'm not properly dressed, that is to say . . ." He paused, confused. What was there to say?

Gloria pushed him back with her hand and looked down at him, her eyes lingering on the very visible sign of his rapidly rising passion. In the dim light of the crescent moon, she lovingly smiled down at him. "You're just like I hoped you would be. Wait." She raised her arms, pulling the filmy negligee over her head, then lowered herself against him, the heat of her bare skin making him hiss in pleasure and desire.

Her kiss was fire and hope, promise and yielding, and his tongue met no resistance as he probed into her warm mouth, drinking of her as deeply and intensely as he had dreamed of. She raised her head, looking down at him, her hair tickling his chest, planting tiny kisses around the corner of his mouth between words. "I've come to give you my answer, dearest John." They kissed again, harder and deeper than before. "And to seal the bargain as well. Do you mind?"

"My God, no," John gasped. He wondered if he could keep from exploding as they talked, even before he took her to himself. He struggled to roll her over, to enter her and fuse themselves together, forever.

"Wait, wait," she panted, trailing down his cheek, jaw and throat with her lips, giving tiny kisses and nips every inch of the way. "It's been so long for me. Sam taught me well, my darling, and I want to savor this moment." Her next moves had John gasping and shuddering in pleasure and he fought to hold back the rush of pleasure that was threatening to burst out.

John lay there for a few more seconds and then, unable to wait any longer, rolled her over and hooking her heels on his broad shoulders, drove into her with such force and desire that both of them grunted in pleasure. While their frenzied lovemaking was brief, the rippling wave of sensation as both achieved satisfaction left two quivering, limp souls in its wake. John continued to kiss Gloria, all over her face and neck, and bosom, taking her again and again. Gloria held his head in her hands as she encouraged him with words and moans, until they both were sated and exhausted.

The second night exceeded the first. The two of them kissed, touched, tasted, and worshipped each other's body until the sky showed the first tint of pink and gray against the blackness. Gloria roused herself, lifting her head from its cradle in John's arm and shoulder, kissing awake a thoroughly sated John from his slumber.

"John, darling, I must go. It's almost time for Hattie to wake and start the breakfast fire. Let go, honey."

"Umm, don't go, stay just a little longer. Did I tell you how good you make me feel?"

She smiled, and bit the soft underside of his arm. "A time or two, I think. By the way, Colonel, John Whyte, my answer is yes. Yes, as soon as the war is over, I'll marry you."

"What?" he said, letting her go and rubbing the bite mark with his hand.

"Yes, you silly goose. Yes, I'll marry you, just as soon as this damned war is over. If you will have me then, I accept."

"I'll make certain you are never sorry, my darling." He kissed her, savoring the mouth that had given him so much pleasure the previous hours. "Will I see you, tonight?" He paused, afraid she might say no. "I want to, you know."

Gloria brushed his lips with hers, and pulled on her nightgown. "Of course. Every night, for all the nights we are together, if you want."

"Do I?" John sat up, to watch her as she departed. "No more than a starving man wants food, I do."

Gloria smiled, her teeth gleaming in the morning gloom, and blew him a kiss as she slipped into the closet disappearing from his sight.

John flopped back down on his bed, grinning at the darkness. He was in love, and did not care who knew it. "And," he mumbled to himself, "it's damned wonderful."

Not a man in the headquarters section failed to notice the happy colonel who came downstairs a few hours later. His demeanor was as exhilarated as a newly discharged soldier's and his infectious grin warmed the disposition of everyone John met the entire day. Lee did not take long to inquire why his colonel was in such a good mood.

"What's going on, John? You find a gold coin in your pocket or something?"

John could not hide the joy in his heart. "Something like that, I suppose. Gloria has agreed to become my wife, as soon as the war is over."

"And that's makin' you grin like a dog treein' a possum? Hell, we all knew that, a long time ago. Didn't you?"

John chuckled at his irascible friend. "Well, now I do, thank you. If I had known you were so well informed, I would have asked you long ago, and bypassed Gloria."

Lee smirked. "You may as well. Hell, Colonel. The way you two look at each other, not a man in the regiment figgered it would be any different. Do you mind if I sort of pass it around?"

"I suppose that would be acceptable. Why don't you run it past Gloria, to make sure she is in agreement?"

Lee nodded, his face aglow with a plan. "That gives us an excuse for another party. Some more of Gloria's good pie fer dissert."

It did not take terribly long for every Union soldier at the farm to hear the news, and John spent the rest of the day accepting congratulations from his men, as did Gloria, accepting their shy, hesitant offers of good will with grace and compassion. She knew most of the men by name and many had some sort of crush on her.

The ensuing days and nights rolled past quickly, John sleeping less than if he were on campaign, but rising every morning after a night of incredible passion, as rested as if he had slept eight hours straight. Gloria had learned the needs and desires of a man well, and John silently blessed Sam Cortland more than once, as he lay in aroused passion while she lavished him with her special brand of love. Every night, his love for Gloria grew and every day his need for her increased.

As if to say farewell, Mosby's raiders intensified their probes on his scattered patrols, keeping John's command busy responding and patrolling to counter the next effort by the pesky Confederate guerrillas.

The last night, John held Gloria in his arms, the sweat from their impassioned love making cooling their flushed skin. "I'll write you as often as I can, my darling, and come as often as I can obtain leave. I pray you will be all right while I'm gone. Since Colonel Stahl insists on making Romney his headquarters, you will only have a half troop here as protection."

"I'll be fine, John. I've done nothing to make either side mad at me. I'll have enough food, thanks to your men, to last for a year and hopefully, you'll be back long before then. You will be careful, and come back to me, won't you darling? I do love you so."

Their kiss was answer enough for the present. They drifted off in exhausted sleep, desperately clutching one another.

John stood with her the next morning, his men mounted in marching order, awaiting his command to move out. Gloria clung to his arm, tears spilling from her sad eyes. He looked down at the woman he loved and in front of the cheering men, gave her a long, intense kiss, before mounting and marching them away from the house. At the turn onto the road, he stopped and looked back. Taking his campaign hat in hand, he gave her a sweeping wave of good-bye.

His ride into Romney was one of melancholy.

CHAPTER 24

John ducked under the heavy canvas tent flap. The battle flag of the First Cavalry Division snapped on the flagpole from the stiff, westerly breeze. In the shakeup following the debacle of the Richmond raid, General Kilpatrick had been transferred to the Army of the Tennessee, and the Michigan Brigade had joined the First Division. General Wesley Merritt, the new division commander, was standing at his field table along with two other full colonels. General Merritt looked up. "Ah, Colonel Whyte. Welcome to the First Division. You know Colonels Powell and Lowell don't you?"

At John's nod, Merritt continued, "Please, join us at the map, John. Gentlemen, as you know, Colonel Whyte's joining us as commander of the First Michigan Brigade. John, we were discussing the first phase of General Sheridan's operation in the Shenandoah Valley. He has been ordered by General Grant to first, defeat Jubal Early's army and second, deprive Bobby Lee's army of any sustenance derived from the valley farmers. That means"—Merritt looked at each of his brigade commanders in turn—"that we take what we can and burn the rest. Nothing, I repeat, nothing is to be left to send to the Rebs in the trenches around Petersburg."

"Jesus, General," Colonel Lowell exclaimed, "we surely aren't planning on starving the valley's inhabitants, are we?"

Merritt's face was grim. "No, but the next thing to it. We leave only enough food to suffice them through the winter. No livestock, no grains, either cut or still in the fields. We burn the barns, storage sheds, and haystacks. We will leave them their houses, but that's all. We will do this if and when we retreat back down the valley, but as long as we are advancing south, up the valley toward Staunton, we'll not bother." Merritt pointed on a map at the objective, over a hundred miles to the south of them. "Any questions?"

John considered a moment then spoke gravely of what he had been thinking about the orders. "You know, General, those folks will never forgive us." The other two colonels nodded their heads in support.

"Tough for them. It has the president's approval. He and General Grant agreed on the strategy, and Grant gave us our orders." Merritt flashed a weary grin. "If it ends the war a day earlier, it will be worth it, wouldn't you agree?"

At that, the three men had to agree.

Merritt rubbed his nose. "Let's just do it and not spend time worrying about the consequences. We march day after tomorrow. John, will you have control of your brigade by then?"

John looked up from the map. "Absolutely, General. I am fully confident that the brigade is ready to fight. We await your command."

Merritt bobbed his head in satisfaction. He pointed to the map again, and the men drew close, each with a pencil and paper at hand for notes. "Very well, here's our first objective . . ."

Later, in his own tent, John spread his map so his four regimental commanders could see it. His brigade tent was smaller than Merritt's divisional tent, so they crowded closely around his little field desk. Khan Singh and Lee Mansur stood at his right, with Lieutenant Colonels Kidd, Stagg, and Brewer, of the First, Sixth, and Seventh Michigan Regiments on his left. John pointed at the route Sheridan's army was to take in two days on their advance into the Shenandoah Valley.

"This is Sulfur Springs Brook, gentlemen, and here's the ford across it that we must take at first light on Wednesday. The Rebels are reported to have a reinforced company of infantry strung out along its south bank. General Merritt is taking the entire division across at eight o'clock, and we must have secured it before then. Lee, I want you and Colonel Kidd to reconnoiter it tomorrow and report back with your ideas on how to best accomplish it. I plan to let your regiments secure the ford, while Colonel Stagg's Sixth and Colonel Brewer's Seventh cross after you and take the high ground to the west, here, and here."

John pointed on his map to two small hill masses that dominated the area of the ford. "Colonel Stagg and Colonel Brewer, you will ride up as close as possible tomorrow without crossing the creek and reconnoiter those hills. If Johnny Reb has any artillery on them, he could smash the entire division on Wednesday morning. I have to return to Merritt's HQ in the morning, to listen to Sheridan outline his vision of the coming campaign or I would accompany you."

Lee Mansur smiled. "Not such fun as you thought, being brigade commander, is it? You have to put up with the hot air of the big shots, instead of riding about in the clean, fresh air."

John grunted, his eyes still on the map. This was the first engagement for the brigade with him as commander. It was a lonely, isolated feeling and he hoped he had not overlooked anything. "That's all for now, gentlemen. I'll meet with you tomorrow at six, and hear your operational plans." He nodded to each man in turn as they trooped out of the tent, to their individual bivouac areas. The three light colonels he had inherited seemed competent, professional, and tough. Lieutenant Colonel Charles Mount, his new brigade adjutant, entered as the others left.

Charles Mount, left over from Custer's days as commander

of the brigade, was almost as tall as John. A face of brown whiskers almost hid his mouth, while intense, deep-set eyes that seemed to never rest looked for anything not as it should be. Mount had a nervous habit of brushing the heavy mustache on his upper lip. John wondered if Mount was upset that Custer had not given the brigade to him. But, so far, the thirty-year-old ex-newspaperman from Faris, Michigan, had given no indication that he was unhappy with his situation.

Mount spoke, his voice as clipped as his manner. "I'll ride with Colonel Mansur tomorrow, Colonel Whyte, and Sergeant Major Singh can accompany Colonel Stagg. That way, everyone can provide input to the final plan."

"Good idea, Charles." John gave his new adjutant a nod of encouragement. "I hope to return in time to look over the ford, at least. You take Sergeant Vernon with you. His men will be the guides for the rest of the division as they cross."

Mount looked at John. "Please, Colonel, call me Charlie or better yet, Chuck. My father is the only Charles Mount I know."

John nodded, almost absentmindedly, his thoughts on the coming mission. "Sergeant Major Singh, have every man in the brigade test fire his weapon tomorrow. It's been some time since they were last used." John tapped the map for a second, then looked at his two immediate assistants. "That will do, I suppose. Check in as soon as I return from Division tomorrow. Now, let's all get some rest. Our days will soon be much longer."

"Yes, Sahib, as you wish." Khan Singh saluted in the British manner, as he sprang to stiff, military attention.

At the unusual acknowledgment, the heavily bearded Charlie Mount laconically looked up at the impressive countenance of the Indian Sikh warrior, a tart remark forming on his lips. At the last instant, he wisely held his tongue. Every man in the Michigan Brigade knew of the fierce warriors who had accompanied the Englishman into the Union army. He wasn't about to utter any remark that might upset the turbaned giant. Charlie Mount was infamous within the brigade for his biting wit and the practical jokes he liked to play on an unsuspecting acquaintance. Until he knew Whyte and Sergeant Singh better, he would delay their initiation into his web of surprises.

As the senior sergeant departed the tent, John waved Mount back into his chair. "A sip of brandy, Chuck?"

Mount licked his lips. "Absolutely, Colonel Whyte. Thank you."

John poured two small drinks into the tiny, silver cups that were part of a small, leather valise containing twin bottles of French brandy.

John gestured at the bag. "Picked this up on my last trip to Washington City. Makes a handy carrying case for liquor and doesn't take up much room."

Mount sipped his drink and smacked his lips. "Mighty fine brandy, Colonel."

He drained the last of the drink. "I'll look forward to the next. His gaze lingered longingly on the bottle."

John sipped his drink, ignoring the hint, his eyes hooded as he looked at his next in command. "You all right with my appointment as commander, Chuck? I suppose you had hoped you would command the brigade?"

Mount raised his eyebrows at the question. "Actually, Colonel Whyte, I'm delighted you are the new CO. I've been in the Army less than two years and been promoted from sergeant to lieutenant colonel. I'm a damn good newspaperman, Colonel, and can handle myself with a pen and paper. But, I find that leading men to their death is more than my stomach can take. Custer scared me, to be honest. He was rash and reckless and I never figured he would live as long as he has. You have a good reputation among the men in the Fifth Regiment. They say you are deliberate when it comes to a fight and don't expose them to needless risk, just for vainglory."

Mount paused, his eyes again caressing the case with the bottles of brandy, to no avail, so he continued. "You run the brigade and I'll keep the paperwork off your back. I'm satisfied and the brigade is better off. That answer your question, sir?"

"Completely, Colonel Mount. I bid you good night, then." John watched as the intense adjutant left the tent. Satisfied that he had received an honest answer, he went to sleep. His dreams were of a slight, brown-haired beauty. He ached for her comfort and love. As the bugle call of "Boots and Saddles" cut through the gray morning air, he groaned in disappointment at leaving his dream.

The next morning, as the faintest smudge of light pushed against the dark horizon to the east, John watched as Lee Mansur and the dismounted troopers of the Fifth Regiment silently waded across the chest-deep waters of Sulfur Springs. His old unit was going into battle without him at its head. He could only watch in glum silence as they waded across the rippling waters toward the hidden enemy pickets on the far side. His gut churned with bile. He physically fought to keep from shivering, although it was far from cold. He wanted to lead his men into battle, not impotently watch from a safe distance.

As the last of the Fifth troopers slipped into the rushing water, John turned and quietly rode back into the woods, well away from the river before turning south, along with the brigade color guard. He intended to observe as Lieutenant Colonel Kidd's First Michigan slammed across the bridge in a mounted charge a half mile to the south, once Lee's men had swept down on the flank of the Rebel security guard at the ford.

He joined the waiting Kidd about one hundred yards above the bridge, the Detroit ex-lawyer sitting on his horse, his saber already in his hand. Kidd saluted as soon as he recognized John in the early-morning dimness.

"Your men ready, Colonel Kidd?" He looked intently at the young officer, whose heavy, Walrus-type mustache and beard hid the bottom half of his face.

"Yes sir, Colonel Whyte. We'll take that bridge, don't worry. I got a good look at their trenches yesterday. They don't expect us to hit here and haven't done a very thorough job of preparing them. We'll sweep them from the field, I'm certain."

"We have to." John softly smacked his gloved fist into his other palm. "We must take those cannon on the hilltops beyond."

"We will, sir. Peter Stagg told me he only saw a few infantrymen up there besides the cannon crews. They expect the forces down here at the bridge to provide security for them." Kidd shifted in his saddle, looking back at his mounted command. "As soon as Colonel Mansur's boys open up the fray, I'll attack."

"Hit 'em hard, Jim. We must clear the cannons from those hills. If we fail, they'll cut our troops to pieces when they try to cross."

As if to punctuate his remark, the rattle of rifle fire broke out on the far side of the creek. Lee's men had engaged the enemy flank. Kidd raised up in his stirrups, waved the sword in his right hand, and shouted at the top of his voice. "First Michigan, *chaaarge!*" He spurred his horse and galloped into the darkness, followed by several hundred men, shouting and screaming as they charged across the wooden planks of the bridge before fanning out along the far bank, shooting and slashing with their sabers at the entrenched enemy, shaken and still half asleep.

As the last of the First Michigan clattered across the bridge, John galloped across, followed by Tim Vernon and the brigade flags, billowing in the easy, morning breeze. A few red-orange flashes burst from the Rebel riflemen on the wooded hillside, but already, the intensity had dropped dramatically. He spotted

Lee Mansur, running toward him, a raw scratch on his right cheek oozing blood. From a bullet or a branch, John could not tell. Lee stopped by John's stirrup, flashing a hasty salute with his smoking pistol still in his hand.

"They're on the run, sir. Colonel Stagg is sweeping the area, gathering prisoners. I'll deploy along the bank, in case of counterattack."

"Well done, Lee." He turned to Tim Vernon, waiting beside him for any orders. "Tim, send a courier back to the Sixth and Seventh commanders. My compliments and they are to attack the hills immediately. The bridge is secure."

"Yessir," Vernon turned and galloped off.

Within minutes John's two remaining regiments were streaming across the arched bridge, the clatter from their horses' hoofs hammering on the heavy, wooden planking. They thundered toward the twin hills, disappearing in the dim light. John could hear the rattling ripple of their carbines, answered by the heavier thunder of the enemy soldiers ripping the morning air. As John mounted his horse, preparing to ride toward the hills, Lieutenant Colonel Kidd trotted up and reported.

"Sixteen enemy killed, at least that many captured, and maybe more. Colonel Mansur's men have taken up positions around the bridge. Shall I take my regiment toward the hills to support Stagg or Brewer?"

"Sound idea, James. I'll accompany you." John looked down at Lee Mansur, still standing beside John's horse, holding his pistol in his hand. "Lee, clean up around here, and send word to General Custer with my compliments. The bridge and surrounding hills are secured."

"Yes, sir." Lee beamed, his facial features sharpening as the morning sun lightened the eastern sky. "Be my pleasure."

John grinned back. "Wipe the blood off your cheek. Mustn't have our general thinking you are unkempt." John turned to

Lieutenant Colonel Kidd. "Lead on, Colonel. It's our turn to capture some Rebel cannon."

They stopped at the base of the higher hill, now able to see clearly. John's soldiers were steadily pushing the Confederate gunners off the hill. He pointed to the south base of the far hill. "Colonel Kidd, the Rebels will head that way once they retreat off the top. Let's ride down there and see if we can cut some of them off."

After a hard gallop, John held up his hand to stop the regiment. They had reached the edge of a road leading down from the top of the two hills. Coming toward them were over three dozen butternut-clad men. "There they are, James. Sweep them up. I'll accompany you on the charge, with your permission."

"Be my pleasure, Colonel." Kidd turned to his bugler, riding close by. "Phillip, sound the charge, if you please."

To the stirring strain of the cavalry charge, John and the three hundred men of the First Michigan fell upon the retreating Confederate soldiers. John's horse leaped the split-rail fence at the side of the road and slammed into a group of men trying to pull a cannon away from the hill with only a single horse. He shot down a burly Rebel who tried to bayonet him and slashed another from the back of the horse with his sword. The rest fled or threw up their hands, as several of his men joined him around the enemy cannon. Some of the retreating soldiers fired a dilatory and ragged volley at the charging horsemen, but most simply threw down their arms and fled into the woods along the road or held up their hands in surrender.

John and the First Michigan captured three cannon and killed or captured twenty dispirited rebel soldiers in five minutes. He slowly walked his panting horse along the road, congratulating his victorious troopers and then followed the road up to the top of the hill. He met Lieutenant Colonel Brewer at the top, who reported. "We have both hills, Colonel Whyte. I just heard from

Peter Stagg. He has two cannon and nine enemy captured. I have two cannon and eleven captured." Brewer wiped the sweat from his forehead with the back of his leather gauntlet. "A damn good day's work and it's not yet seven o'clock in the morn."

John agreed. "And, I have three more cannon down at the bottom of the hill, plus several captured soldiers. Jolly good show, Colonel Brewer. You and Colonel Stagg stay up here on the hilltops in case they try to counterattack, which I doubt. I'll report to General Merritt as he leads the division across the bridge and then contact you with any new orders."

John spied Charlie Mount riding across the field and motioned him over. He knew that Mount had fought with Brewer's regiment, in spite of his professed lack of skill in combat.

"You all right, Chuck?"

"Tip-top, Colonel. I think I even got me a Reb or two."

Together, they rode back across the saddle to the smaller hill where they congratulated Lieutenant Colonel Stagg and his men, picked up Khan Singh and then returned to the bridge, where Lee Mansur's Fifth Regiment had set up security.

Promptly at eight, General Merritt led the remainder of his division across the bridge, his colors streaming, out in the early morning breeze as the men slowly trotted behind.

John was waiting at the side of the road. Merritt trotted his horse over, his face flushed in the glow of coming battle lust. He took John's report, slapping his gauntlets against his thigh. "By God, Colonel Whyte. Damned good job. Seven cannon and thirty captured plus that many more killed. Well done, to the brigade. I expected nothing less from them." He flashed a rakish grin at John, standing by the bridge, looking up at him on his black Tennessee trotter. "Or from you. Sheridan will hear of it, I promise you."

Merritt turned, to watch as a seemingly unending column of

blue-clad troopers trotted past. The boy general had a mighty weapon under his command and he could not take his eyes off it. When the last man had crossed the bridge, Merritt sighed, almost expectantly. "Well, I must be off. Wait here until the commissary wagons and ambulances cross, then take up rear guard. We have much more to do this day, and I'll have need of you and the brigade again, never fear."

John grinned at his new general, not yet thirty years old. "General Merritt, my brigade and I stand ready to answer any order you choose to give us. The Michigan brigade delivers. We think with good reason that we are the best brigade in the whole bloody Union army."

Giving a whoop of laughter, Merritt spurred his horse and galloped away, already grateful that the Michigan Brigade had been assigned to his division.

John followed his departure until the general was out of sight, then turned to Khan Singh, at his side. John knew what he was about to receive. "Well, old friend. Give me the bad news. What was the butcher's bill for our glorious victory?"

CHAPTER 25

John sniffed the air in his tent, his nose wrinkling at the residual odor. He stank. Or, more specifically, his clothes stank, from the pungent mixture of horse sweat, human sweat, trail dust, and gunpowder. "Damn, gentlemen," he remarked. "I stink, you stink, we all stink. Let's have this meeting outside. Lee, bring the lantern to the campfire. We can conduct our business there, as well as in this airless tent."

"Good idea, Colonel," Lee answered. "However, I feel compelled to inform the rest of you that I fell into that creek we fought over this afternoon when my horse slipped. I'm much the cleaner of you boys, at least in comparison."

"I resent your implication, Mansur," James Kidd humorously chimed in. "I never smell, even after seven days of riding and sleeping in wherever we happen to stop for the night."

Peter Stagg added his reply. "That's just 'cause your mustache is so full of dirt and bread crumbs, Jim, that your nose hasn't a chance of smelling anything else. Believe me, you stink. You're just as ripe as the rest of us." Stagg gave a snort of derision before looking at John. "Lead on, Colonel. The air out there can't be as full of horse drops as in here. Right, Lewis?"

Lewis Brewer, the oldest of John's commanders, merely nodded his sandy-haired head, his light-brown beard brushing against his sweaty shirt. "It's not a wonder. A solid week of dawn-till-dark fighting and chasing Rebs. My butt's so sore, I hate to think of getting into McClellan's torture saddle tomorrow morning." He stood and stretched, arching the kinks out of his back. "Colonel, any chance we'll have some time to recover tomorrow? We've been at it hard all week."

John shook his head, as he carried his campstool to the fire and the four junior lieutenant colonels gathered around him. He pointed to the map he carried in his hand. "We're part of the attack of this hill tomorrow. Fisher's Hill, it's called. General Merritt wants the First Brigade to assault the right flank while the Second Brigade charges head-on against the Confederate defenses."

"Mounted, or afoot?" Lee asked, straining to see the spot on the map from his place at the fire.

"Mounted. General Merritt will accompany us in the initial charge. Once we take the top, he plans on sending the Third Brigade down the road toward Front Royal for a couple of miles. He wants to push the Rebel soldiers clear to the city, if he can."

"Where's Hampton's gray backs?" Stagg inquired. He was speaking of the Confederate cavalry, who supported Early's Second Army Corps against the incursion by Sheridan and his Union Army of the Shenandoah.

"The plan is for Custer's division to harass him down by Front Royal. If Custer can keep him busy, we should only have Dodson Ramsuer's division to our front, and it's not even at brigade strength now. Intelligence says they've been up on that damned hill for two days. So he's most likely got them well entrenched." John traced the outline of the path he wanted to take. If we can roll up his flank, the Rebels will have to fall back to Front Royal before they can defend again. After tomorrow, I'll try and get us a few days off. We could use it." John traced his plan on the map with a grimy finger. "Lee, you and James will attack abreast, right here. Use this draw as the divider between your regiments. Peter, you and Lewis follow five minutes later in the second wave. Ride hard to the top and keep your regiments in formation, otherwise, we'll be all tangled together, and loose our momentum." He tapped the map with his fingertip. "Any questions?"

At their murmurs of understanding, John turned to his adjutant, Lieutenant Colonel Mount. "Chuck, you stay with the artillery. I want the top of that hill covered in iron and don't stop until you see our brigade flag reach the trenches."

"Understand, Colonel. What time do you want to start the bombardment?" Mount's face was serious and tight. He just would not relax and kid around like the other officers in John's immediate command family. He was another Khan Singh, without the turban, as John thought of him and just as necessary to the brigade. The past week had proven his value, as he kept the First Brigade resupplied and supported from the wagon trains carrying the new issues from the Army Quartermaster Depot back in Winchester.

"Start them thirty minutes before the attack, Chuck. Make sure you have plenty of ammunition on hand. I don't want a single Reb on the top of that hill to feel like he can stick his head out of his trench to look around. I want to be on the top of the hill before they ever fire a shot at us."

Mount called for his horse and rode off to coordinate with Captain Peterson, the artillery commander. John sighed and got his bedroll from the tent. He decided to sleep in the open, beside the fire. The tent was stuffy and confining in the heat of the late summer night. First, he hurriedly wrote a few lines to Gloria, reread her last letter yet again by the flickering firelight, then drifted off into a restless slumber.

"Sahib, it is four o'clock. Wake up, sir." Khan Singh's insistent monotone voice drove the sleep from John's mind. Sitting up and reaching for his boots, he stretched and yawned mightily.

"All right, Sergeant Major, I'm awake." He could hear the

stirrings of the rest of the brigade, as the men prepared for another day of war. Coughing, hacking, snorting, subdued talking, all sounds of tired men forcing themselves awake. Several horses whinnied, eager for their morning rations of oats.

John had just finished drinking a vile concoction of camp coffee, while forcing down a rock-hard biscuit, when General Merritt arrived with the thirty-odd men of his entourage. Everywhere the general rode, he was accompanied by the guards, flag bearers, messengers, aides, and orderlies. The ensuing commotion would have raised the dead, had any been listening. John saluted, and climbed into the saddle of his newest horse, a black Morgan gelding, captured during Mosby's raid at Gloria's farm. The spirited animal was well over sixteen hands high and was possessed with an abundance of stamina and strength. Most importantly, the handsome animal was not spooked by the noise of battle, as so many horses were.

Merritt looked up at the slowly lightening, eastern sky. "Looks like a good day for a fight, Colonel Whyte. With your concurrence, I'll accompany you to the attack assembly area?"

"By all means, General." As they rode, John described his plan for the attack, while Merritt listened intently. The only sign of nervousness from the general was that he continuously fidgeted with his saber.

"A good plan, John. We'll blast the gray backs off the hill in short order and run them all the way to Front Royal." Merritt's voice was almost ecstatic.

John shook his head. The man was quite daft, he was certain, since John had no stomach for what was coming. A charge like Merritt was ordering meant empty saddles and sad letters to be written later, in the silence of the night.

The group of cavalrymen reached the road that was to be the start point for the charge up the hill, just as it became relatively easy for a man to see farther than the front of his horse. The men in the first wave were slowly filling into ranks, facing the hill about two hundred yards ahead, still only a black mass in the predawn light. John strained to read the time on his pocket watch, just as the first volley of his cannon barked their throaty thunder of death and destruction.

"Good," he spoke over the roar to Merritt. "We attack in exactly thirty minutes." Without waiting for a reply, he trotted down the road to check on Lee Mansur and the men of the Fifth Michigan.

As the minutes ticked by, the tension in the air grew thicker. John rejoined General Merritt, impatiently squirming on his horse, his saber already in his right hand. John noticed that a yellow kerchief was tied around Merritt's neck, where it would flow behind him like a beacon as he galloped forward. John checked his watch. The bombardment had been on for twenty-nine minutes. It was time to go. He took out the extra pistol from his saddlebag and put it in his waistband. He grabbed his holstered pistol and raised his hand, turning left and then right, to insure both regimental commanders were watching, and slashed his hand forward, not bothering to try and shout over the noise of the cannon fire.

Beside him, rode Khan Singh, followed by Tim Vernon and the brigade flags, slowly waving in the breeze. As they reached the point where the ground tilted upward, Merritt suddenly flashed past, screaming "Charge!" at the top of his lungs, while the trumpeter broke out into the cavalry bugle call, "Charge!"

John added his scream of "Charge!" and thundered up the hill after Merritt, his troopers galloping after him. As they reached the top of the denuded hill, the first shots from the enemy whizzed past. John glimpsed a man falling to his left. A ragged-looking man stood up in a trench to his front, drawing a bead with his rifle at Merritt, who still rode recklessly ahead of John. John spurred his horse harder, and fired two quick shots at the grizzled, bearded head of the enemy soldier. A red spray splashed out from the rear of the enemy soldier's head and he slipped back into the gaping cut in the earth. With a bound, John's horse leaped across the gap cut in the dark soil and into the rear of the enemy lines.

The cannonade's fury was evident, with ruined wagons, broken trees, and sprawled bodies lying about the hilltop. Merritt was engaged in a saber duel with a Rebel officer on a dun horse off to John's right. John shifted in that direction, as Khan Singh thundered up and blasted down a bareheaded youth in ragged pants who was aiming an old, muzzle-loading shotgun at John's head. John nodded his gratitude to the old warrior and shouted over the din. "Thanks, old friend."

He sawed the reins of his horse, causing the animal to spin in its tracks. "I'll worry about Merritt, you worry about me. Come on, he needs help." John saw Merritt's horse fall, blood streaming from a wound in its side. Several ragged enemy soldiers ran toward the general, intent on capturing the prize of prizes. "It's a blue coat Gen'l. Git 'em fellas. Grab him!"

John and Khan Singh slammed into the bunch with their animals, scattering them in all directions, while the rest of John's men roared past, slashing with their sabers and firing their carbines like pistols.

John leaped from his horse and shot a bald-headed man who was about to bayonet Merritt in the back. He felt the breath of near miss by a musket ball and turned to his left. A wide-eyed Rebel was aiming his pistol at him. John dropped to one knee and fired, hitting the man in the belly. The enemy soldier staggered back, screaming in agony, while the shot he fired at John cut the air over his head.

Merritt slashed the last man standing of those who had attacked him, then turned to John. "Good job, Colonel. They're on the run. I need your horse, if you please. I'm diverting the

Second Brigade's attack to the left, to see if we can cut them off from retreating. Continue your attack down the hill to the south and reform at the base of the hill. I'll send word what your next objective is there."

"Yessir, General. Here's my horse." John handed Merritt the reins.

Merritt immediately leaped into the saddle, galloping off the hill toward the attacking Second Brigade, his entourage streaming off the hill after him. John fired his pistol at a retreating rebel, ran after his men, still pushing the defeated enemy down, off the top of the hill. He found a riderless horse and leaped into the saddle, shouting for everyone to continue the attack. It was an unnecessary command. The First Michigan Brigade was going about the work they did so well and the enemy soldiers were running or dying as they chose, in front of the screaming Wolverines.

And so it went for the next three weeks. Front Royal, Crooked Run, Berryville, Leaders Crossroads. The brigade fought south, almost every day another nasty battle with Early's soldiers or Hampton's cavalrymen. Just as they reached the outskirts of Staunton, one hundred miles south of the Potomac, they were given orders to retreat north. As soon as he read the orders, John hurried to Merritt's temporary HQ, in a half-burned house down the road about a mile from where John had bivouacked the First Brigade.

The youthful general grimaced at John's adamant condemnation of the move. "I know it means giving up all the hard-earned ground we've captured, John, but just listen a minute." Merritt looked around, to make certain none of the enlisted men could hear him. "Sheridan told me personally what's going on. There's a rumor that Longstreet is bringing his First Corps from Petersburg to reinforce Early. We've smacked Jubal and his boys pretty hard. Grant's orders to Sheridan are not only to whip

Early, but not get beat by him in a major engagement. We're coming up on the presidential elections, and Grant's afraid that if the Army loses a major engagement anywhere, it might swing votes to the "peace at any cost" faction. McClellan's talking about a negotiated peace with the Rebs. That'd be a disaster for the Union."

Merritt smoothed his golden locks. "So, my boy, we go back. Burning and destroying everything we can't take with us. Probably all the way to Harper's Ferry. I want you to take your brigade west and find the Orange Line railroad tracks to New Market. Destroy it, as well as all food stocks, animals, and horses along the way. I'll meet you in Strausberg in four days. That's sixty miles, so you'll have to ride hard. Understand?"

John's lips tightened. "I hate the idea of depriving so many families of the hard-earned bounty from their farms."

Merritt shrugged. "It's war and they chose the wrong side. Those are your orders. Can you carry them out?"

"Of course, General. I'll see you in four days at Strausberg."

John led his men to the west until they reached the iron rails of the enemy's railroad. They turned north, destroying the rails by heating them red-hot and bending them around trees, ripping ties from the roadbed, and burning bridges as they rode. The men rounded up any cattle or sheep they came across, grabbed all the pigs and chickens they could carry and burned crops and barns filled with grain and corn. The land they rode out of was blackened and barren and the bitterness left behind them was so virulent that a person could feel it in the looks the Union men received.

"It's a bloody miserable war," John remarked to Chuck Mount, as they watched another barn going up in smoke, the farm's womenfolk crying, the old man of the house nearly apoplectic in rage and frustration.

"You'll notice there are no young men about, Colonel.

They're all over in Bobby Lee's army, killing men in blue, like us." Mount was matter-of-fact, and unconcerned by the devastation John's troopers were inflicting on the unfortunate population.

"You have a point, my dour friend. Well, let's start going. I want to be in Strausberg when Merritt arrives."

The Army of the Shenandoah retreated all the way back across the Potomac River, where the men got a week's rest and John received two hundred replacements for the casualties his unit had suffered during the past two months of campaigning. Merritt went off to report to General Sheridan, while John wrote Gloria every day, growing more convinced with each letter that she was the woman with whom he would spend the rest of his life.

On the sixth day of October, John opened the flap and stepped into his tent, where the four regimental commanders, Lieutenant Colonel Mount and Brigade Sergeant Major Khan Singh awaited his return from Merritt's evening staff meeting.

"Gentlemen, like all good things, our down time is at an end. On Friday, we cross the Potomac, heading back to engage the Rebels, located somewhere around Cedar Creek." He waited while the others groused and cursed fate, before continuing. "Merritt says we're going in to finish the job on the Confederate troops in the valley. Here's the order of march."

So, back the brigade went, as did the Army of the Shenandoah, fighting over the same ground they had fought over the previous month. Only the names of the dead and maimed changed. By the morning of October 19, they were deployed across the valley, facing Early's soldiers in the hills outside the tiny hamlet of Cedar Creek. They had relentlessly been driving the stubborn Confederate defenders out of their entrenchments, toward the more open terrain at the south end of the valley.

John was in camp that fateful morning, just completing his

coffee, when he heard the faint but continuous roar of cannons to the west. He cocked his head to listen. Khan Singh walked up as John threw the vile brew into the smoky campfire.

"I believe those are Rebel guns, Sahib. A large attack is occurring against the west flank."

John listened. He was on the far eastward side of the army, protecting that flank against reinforcements from the interior of Virginia. "Sheridan's away, too," he answered. "He went to Winchester yesterday to confer with Grant."

A courier from Merritt's HQ galloped up. He saluted and gave John a written message. John scanned the writing and then turned and spoke softly. "Khan Singh, send for the regimental commanders and Colonel Mount. We march in ten minutes."

John peered through his field glasses at the smoking ruin of Cedar Creek. Per his orders, he had led his brigade around to the south and cut back across the fields that surrounded the town. His orders from Merritt were explicit. He was to attack the rear of the enemy at Cedar Creek, causing as much confusion as possible, while the main units of the army recovered from the initial shellacking they were taking from the surprise enemy assault that morning.

"Chuck, you take the right flank, Khan Singh, the left. We attack, the brigade in line, all regiments abreast. Cut through the town and then hit the enemy headquarters on the far side." He looked at his two principal subordinates. "Good luck to you both."

Khan Singh looked intently at John, almost oddly, as if something was troubling him. But he was a soldier and had his orders. "As you say, Sahib."

John watched as the two men rode down the line, passing on his final instructions. As the brigade lined up, it stretched over a half mile across, a shimmering mass of mounted blue warriors, weapons at the ready. He waited for a moment, then held up his hand and motioned toward the town. "At the trot, ho!" Nearly two thousand men trotted forward in a line, waving and weaving like a winding, blue, snake. As they got closer, John raised up in his stirrups and shouted again. "At the gallop, *Chaaarge!*" Sean Gallagher's bugle accented the command and the men thundered into the town, firing at the surprised, rear-area soldiers of the Rebel army.

The charge was too massive to contain and the Confederate soldiers quickly broke and ran. John led his shouting and firing troopers through the town and into the tents of the Rebel leadership emplaced in a field at the far side. Confusion reigned supreme. Men running, guns firing, sweating horses rearing in the dust and smoke, both falling, rolling into twisted forms, tortured shrieks of agony cutting through the noise of battle.

Slashing or shooting at anyone who was in front of him, John fought his way through the encampment and then turned his men around and led them back into the melee. He flinched as a soldier fired his rifle at him and felt the bullet tug at his sleeve. He rode past, slamming his pistol barrel down on the bare head of the enemy soldier, dropping him like a limp sack of potatoes. John saw a cluster of men trying to protect a man dressed in grey, with lots of gold braid. A high-ranking officer. He spurred his horse at the men, shouting for his men to join him.

The guards saw him coming and several knelt and aimed their weapons at him. John's voice was hardly more than a hoarse croak. He desperately attempted to bring his pistol to bear on the enemy soldiers. A blinding cloud of gun smoke and red fire enveloped him. A blaze of pain shot across his head and he felt himself falling, a blanket of darkness descending down upon him. He did not feel the ground when he smashed into it, nor did he feel the enemy soldiers gather him up and carry him off the battlefield as a prize of war.

John woke, slowly. It was dark outside. He was in a wagon,

rocking and jostling along, every bounce like a firecracker going off inside his head.

"What happened? Where am I?" he groaned.

A hand brushed a rag soaked in cool water against his lips. "Easy, sir," a discombobulated voice floated down to him. "You've been captured by the Rebs, same as me. We're in a wagon, headed toward Richmond, if I calculate right. It's Charlie Mount. Can you focus on me? A bullet hit your head. I don't think it busted your skull, but you got yourself a good concussion."

"Chuck? Captured? My God. What about the brigade?"

"Gone, Colonel. I don't know where. My horse got hit and I was pinned under it. The Rebs grabbed me and threw me in this here wagon with you. I think they retreated out of Cedar Creek, so the brigade did its job, but I'm not certain."

A voice cut through the darkness. It was low and slurred, with a heavy Southern drawl. "Y'all shut up in thar."

John's spirits collapsed. "My God," he whispered. "We're prisoners."

"Damn right you air, Colonel Whyte." The driver hissed in triumph. "You're on your way to Libby Prison, with the rest a'you Yanks what we done captured."

"You know my name?" John blurted out.

"Your officer thar told us."

"Sorry, Colonel Whyte," Mount apologized. "I let your name slip out."

John tentatively put his hand to his head. "That's all right, Chuck. They will know soon enough anyway." He touched the bandage wrapped around his head. "Oh, my aching head. It feels like it's about to bust open."

The voice from the unseen soldier spoke again. "You the Colonel Whyte what done kilt JEB Stuart over to Yella Tavern?"

"I suppose I am," John murmured to the unseen voice. "It's

nothing I take any pride in, I assure you."

"Well, iffen ya air," the voice came back, "Don't worry 'bout your head. Worry 'bout your ass, you goddamned Yankee murderer."

CHAPTER 26

The trip was an endless nightmare. John slipped in and out of consciousness for the four days he and his fellow prisoners rode in the bouncing, swaying wagon. The nights were almost as bad, sleeping roped together, unable to move or turn without disturbing the solicitous Charlie Mount, who had appointed himself John's nurse.

Charlie fed the often-incoherent John, bathed his feverish head with water whenever the wagon crossed a stream, let John sip from the single canteen shared by the six Union POWs in the wagon, whenever John was conscious.

The last day, as the wagon rolled through the inhabited area surrounding Richmond, John started to recover his faculties. Aside from piercing, blinding headaches, he felt somewhat better. He sat up and Charlie introduced him to the other four unfortunate Union officers who shared his captivity. John and Lieutenant Colonel Mount were the only two from the Michigan Brigade. The others were infantry officers captured in the initial phase of the battle at Fisher Hill. One, Major Samuel Thomas, of the Twenty-third New York Infantry, peeked out from under the canvas siding of the wagon as they rolled down a cobblestone street.

"This is my second time as guest of Johnny Reb, gents. We'll be getting to Libby Prison soon. If any of you has any money in your coats or sewed into your boots, best be getting it out now." As a precaution, John had several gold coins in both his boot linings, as did many Union officers, in the event of capture. Gold was the one commodity that might help to make the imprisonment bearable, as tender to bribe guards for better food, blankets, medicine, and favorable treatment.

"Why do you say that?" John inquired.

"The Rebs ain't fools, Colonel. They know that's where most of us stash our gold. They strip away your jacket and boots as soon as you arrive. Sometimes you get 'em back after they've been searched, sometimes not, if a guard takes a shine to 'em."

"Where do you hide them, then?" Charlie Mount ripped the seam of his jacket, as he spoke.

"Iffen they're small enough, swallow 'em. You can recover 'em back when they pass through, iffen you catch my meanin'. If they're too big, stick 'em in your sock or twixt the crack of your ass." The older major was stuffing several gold and silver coins in his socks as he spoke.

John ripped the leather seam of his boot tops and pulled out the ten twenty-dollar gold pieces placed there. He secreted them in the secure places recommended by Major Thomas. He took the five diamonds he always carried in a tiny chamois pouch and swallowed them. He placed four silver dollars from his pocket in the pouch and put it back in his pocket, to insure he had something for the guards to find.

As the men finished hiding the things they wanted to save, the wagon jerked to a stop and the back canvas was swung open, allowing bright sunlight to pour inside the dark interior. A burly soldier, his eyes nearly buried by a heavy growth of reddish-blond eyebrows, growled at the men. His curly mustache and heavy beard were both encrusted with filth, as if soap had never met the mass of red hair covering his face.

"Outa the wagon, you Yankee sons of bitches. Line up in two rows accordin' to rank. Hustle it up, goddamn you."

The six prisoners clambered out the back of the wagon, blinking and squinting in the bright sunlight. Charlie Mount spoke up, annoyance in his tone. "We are Union officers, Sergeant. You address us accordingly, or I shall report you to your superiors."

The burly, redheaded Confederate sergeant whirled and smashed his fist directly into Mount's face, knocking him staggering back against the wagon. Blood spurted from his split lip, while Mount sputtered in amazement and shock.

The Rebel guard leered malevolently at the stunned prisoners and spoke again, as the rest of the captives pulled the bleeding Mount back into place beside them. "You damned Yanks keep your friggin' mouths shut unless spoken to, ya heer? Far as I'm concerned, y'all are nothin' but Northern shit I gotta put up with. Don't be expectin' no airs from me over your so-called rank. Now, follow me inside, and keep yur damned mouths shut."

John examined the outside of the prison soon to swallow him. It was an imposing, ex-warehouse, made of red brick, its windows barred over, standing four stories high, and measuring perhaps one hundred fifty feet by three hundred. A tiny doorway marked the entrance, while the rear seemed to back right up to the James River, which ran through Richmond and spilled into Chesapeake Bay fifty miles to the east. The building had been whitewashed up to the bottom of the second-floor windows, while the top half was dusty red.

A sign over the door, black letters painted on a white background, proclaimed its name. "LIBBY PRISON." Glumly, the six men followed the burly guard inside. They entered the main office of the prison, covering fully a quarter of the first floor. The room contained desks and chairs for guards and administrators. Boxes of what appeared to be records were stacked against one wall and several iron manacles hung from hooks along one wall.

A rack of rifles stood behind a desk where a dapper-looking man sat, his gray uniform clean and creased. A dark, pencil-thin mustache offset his finely chiseled face. He glared up at the intrusion to his routine, as the six new prisoners were marched up to the rail in front of his desk. His black eyes seemed to be too close together, making his face seem pinched and perpetually angry.

"Yes, Sergeant Rose?" His voice was high-pitched, like a boy tenor.

"New arrivals, Captain. Just in from Early's command, in the valley."

The slender captain rose to his feet and glared at the six subdued Union officers. "I am Captain Alexander, CSA Provost Marshal Corps and Libby Prison commandant. You men are assigned to my prison and here are my rules. Do what you are told, and do it immediately. Try to escape and you die. Speak only when spoken to, and start every sentence with sir, no matter what rank addresses you." He glared at his newest captives. "What happened to him?" He pointed at Charlie Mount's bloody lip.

Sergeant Rose smirked. "He fell, getting out of the wagon, Captain."

John's bile surged up. "Captain Alexander, that's not true. This NCO struck him, for no reason."

Alexander said nothing, simply looked blankly at John. "Sergeant Rose, you'd think the damned, black Republicans in Washington City could find men able to avoid fallin' over their own clumsy feet, wouldn't you? The next time he falls, put him in the hole on bread and water for three days. We'll see if that improves his dexterity."

Rose maliciously glared at John, before answering the Confederate jailer. "Yes, sir, Captain. I shore will. Should I discipline this here smart mouth fer lyin' 'bout me?"

"Next time, Sergeant. Next time. Carry on." Rose motioned to one of the clerks. "Rogers, record these men's name, rank, unit and home address. Then send for Sergeant Martin and put them into prison uniform and assign them to a floor."

The meek-looking clerk, wearing corporal stripes of faded yellow on his worn, threadbare, Confederate-gray jacket, over faded blue, ex-Union army pants, motioned the men over to his desk, where they sullenly lined up by rank, as before.

He glanced up at John. "All right, Colonel. What is your name, military unit and home address?"

John answered the question and watched as the clerk laboriously wrote his answers down in a thick ledger. "Colonel John Whyte, commander, First Brigade, First Cavalry Division, Army of the Shenandoah. Home address is One-two-five West M Street, Washington City."

The clerk looked up, his eyes wide. He suddenly stood and hurried to Captain Alexander's desk, bent over and whispered into his ear. John watched mystified. The captain rummaged inside one of the drawers of his desk and pulled out a paper. He motioned for John to return, to stand before his desk.

He asked suspiciously, "Are you the same Colonel Whyte of Custer's Command, who kilt JEB Stuart, back at Yellow Tavern, in May?"

"Yes, I suppose I am," John conceded. "As I told your man, I take no pride in the fact."

Alexander nodded, his eyes hooded. "Very well. Rejoin the others."

As soon as everyone had been questioned, they were turned over to another Confederate soldier, who called himself Commissary Sergeant Martin. An old man, with watery, shifty eyes, and a scruffy, gray-streaked beard, marched them into a huge storeroom behind the main office. He appeared to be one of life's perpetual losers, a man who had found a niche in the military system of the South. Scruffy, devious, far from honest, he ordered the men to take off their boots, giving them worn replacements from a box filled with used footwear. He also took their coats, before issuing them each one thin, cotton blanket, a tin plate, cup and spoon. He quickly checked each man's person, by patting his hands up and down their body, completely missing John's sack with the silver dollars in his haste, as well as the gold coins John had stuffed in his socks and other places.

John spoke up, softly. "Sergeant Martin, might I keep my boots? I'd happily give up those coins for them. He slipped the pouch out of his pocket. There might even be more of these for you, later."

Martin glanced around. None of the Confederate guards were watching. His voice lowered and he gave John a conspiratorial wink as he held out a grimy hand. "I suppose so, Colonel. Iffen you ever need anything just let me know. Fer the right price, I can do a lot fer ya."

"Thank you, Sergeant. I shall remember that."

After every man had finished being stripped of any clothing of value, they were marched off under two armed guards up the back stairs and separated, John and Charlie Mount going to the top floor, the rest to the third floor, just below.

The heavily barred door at the top of the stairs was pushed opened and John and Mount were ushered inside. Immediately, the door was slammed shut behind them. Filthy, dispirited men crowded the room, standing, sitting, or lying on their blankets. The interior was dim, the few windows grimy and flyspecked. The center of the room was almost dark, even in the midday sunlight. The wooden plank floor was covered in filth. A rank odor assailed their nostrils. The walls, once painted white, were filthy, with graffiti written all over them.

At their entrance, the room fell silent. All eyes turned to size up the new arrivals. A man limped up on a bad foot, his pale face was creased with wrinkles and his beard was gray, while most of the hair had fallen from his head. His clothes hung off his frame as if he had once been much larger. He had a pair of spectacles perched on his button nose. Despite the appearance of physical decline, he still retained a spark of life in his eyes as he addressed John and Chuck.

"Welcome, gentlemen. I'm General Miloy, former commander of the Ninth Indiana Volunteers. You are now residents of what is called the Miloy Floor of Libby Prison. Who might you boys be?"

John and Charlie Mount introduced themselves and were met by the numerous officers gathered around them. Miloy then took each man's arm and escorted him to a corner of the huge room, which covered the entire fourth floor of the old warehouse. "You can meet the rest later. First, tell me and Sidney Greene here, he's the prison newspaper editor, what's happening out there. Those of us that's been in here a long time, are starved for news. We grill all the new arrivals like this, so don't be shy. Anything you know what can improve morale, we want to hear it."

"You have a newspaper?" Charlie Mount blurted out. "I was a newspaperman, back in Michigan."

"Wonderful," Greene replied. "I can use the help. It's only one sheet per floor, writ by hand, but it's important to the boys, believe me."

For the next few hours, John and Charlie related all they could about the battles in the Shenandoah Valley, and what they remembered from recent newspapers they had read. Finally, the two weary men were released. John's head was splitting with pain. He needed to find a place to sleep and relax until the supper meal roll call, which took nearly two hours to complete. All the prisoners on the floor lined up by rank and by alphabet while two guards walked past, checking off the names.

As the roll call was completed, two husky, black men carried a large pot of soup and a few sticks into the room. At a fireplace by the rear wall, the thin, meatless, bean soup, was hung over a small fire until it was lukewarm, then every man shuffled past while a cupful was put on his tin plate. A stale bread slice was added to soak up the juice. There was only water from the communal barrel to drink. Immediately after eating, the pot was removed, and the single door to the great room was slammed shut and locked for the night.

"Don't look out the windows," the prisoner next to John informed him. "The Reb guards'll shoot you on sight. They killed a boy from Massachusetts on the third floor just last week. All he was doin' was looking at some geese flying past."

John took his hidden gold coins from his sock, and began gouging out some of the grime that filled a crack in the wooden floor, next to where he had placed his blanket. Charlie Mount lay beside him. Fortunately, the guards had missed Charlie's tiny pocketknife when they patted him down.

As soon as he and Mount had hidden their gold coins, brushing dirt and filth over the crack until it was hidden again, they both tried to sleep. It was hard, as over six hundred men were crammed into a space where half that many would have been crowded. The noise and smell prevented any peaceful sleep and morning seemed a long time coming. John prayed that Gloria was well, and that she loved him as he did her. He vowed he would survive to see her again. Knowing the mortality rates of Confederate prisons, he knew it was a gamble. But then, he had a lot to live for.

The next week crawled by, while John tried to adjust to his captivity. The food was terrible, in insufficient amount, and not very nutritious. By the end of the first week, John had carefully approached and purchased a scrawny chicken from Sergeant Martin for a five-dollar gold coin gleaned from their hoard. The pitifully small bird was put in the evening's stew and every man on the floor got to savor the welcome flavor, if not the meat of bird.

On Sunday, a guard summoned John to the door. "Visitor to see ya, Colonel," the guard announced.

Mystified as to who it could be, John followed the guard down the back stairs, and into a small room that was cut in half by inch-thick, iron bars from floor to ceiling. A chair was on his side and another faced him across the bars. A woman in a billowing, green dress, cut low in front and lined with lace, a fancy white hat upon her head, was seated in the chair, face down as she searched for something in her purse. For an instant, John's heart skipped a beat. Gloria had found out about his capture, and had come to visit him. He sat down, carefully eyeing the bored guard, who stood next to the door, watching them in silence.

John started to say Gloria's name, when the woman looked up. John's mouth parted, and confusion washed over him as he recognized the face glaring at him in unrestrained hatred.

"LaDonna, LaDonna Chambers. I say, wh—what on earth are you doing here?" It was the woman he had seduced from Rose Greenhow's spy ring. The very woman he had made love to in order to obtain the information needed to break the case wide open. He had played a major part in the entire ring's exposure, arrest, and ultimately being expelled across the lines into the Confederacy.

The woman seated across from him raised her head, her eyes bright with triumph and a sneer on her lips. "John Whyte, you son of a bitch. I've got you now."

CHAPTER 27

The prisoners clustered around John like ragged scarecrows as he related the strange encounter with the fiery LaDonna Chambers. Thirsty for news of any kind, the men hung on John's every word.

"Can she really make trouble for you?" Chuck Mount asked. "I mean even more than you have already?"

John shrugged his shoulders. "I honestly don't know. She ranted and raved about her connections with high-ranking Confederate officials, but the guard told me while escorting me back up here that she's just one of many whores in a bawdy house over on Beacon Avenue. I guess I'll just have to wait and see."

"How did she find you, Colonel Whyte?" one of the other prisoners piped up.

"Apparently, she has been watching the paper for two years checking every man with the name of Whyte who has the misfortune to end up in Libby Prison." John ruefully grinned at his listeners. "It's just my misfortune that the lady, if I may stretch the term a bit, has a long and vengeful memory."

The answer to the question of her making good on her threat was not long in coming. He was detailed to clean-up duties on the first floor the following morning. As he swept the supply room, he spotted a pile of canvas-covered shapes stacked near the rear cargo door. A cloying, heavy stench emanated from the stacked bundles. The other prisoners stayed as far away from the pile as possible. John only needed one look to know what was there. Bodies of dead men, stacked up like cordwood, awaiting transportation to the cemetery.

John wiped his sweaty forehead with the back of his hand. The scab covering his wound on his head was rapidly receding. Although he had not seen a mirror since his capture, Chuck Mount said the bullet groove was healing.

"Sort of gives you a buccaneer look," was how Mount described the scar. "It sort of disappears into your hairline. Funny," he said, "I just noticed. Your hair around the cut is coming back in solid white. You're liable to have a white streak in among the black." John returned to his sweeping, not eager to attract the unwanted attention of a guard by loafing.

John waited until the crafty Confederate supply sergeant walked past him. "Sergeant Martin," John asked softly, not wanting to cause any of the other guards to see that he was cultivating the friendship of the older soldier. "Why are those bodies stacked up like that? Why don't you take them out and bury them? They stink. Are you waiting for something?"

"Xactly, Colonel. It's this week's dead, ready fer plantin'. Whenever a prisoner dies, they sew him up in one of them canvas sacks and stores him over thar, until they's enough to take over to the cemetery on Belle Island fer burial."

John shuddered and continued to sweep. It was a futile chore considering the years of accumulated filth on the wood floor. As he worked, another shrouded body was carried down the back stairs and placed on the pile.

"Looks like a wagonload. I'll tell the darkies to plan on takin' the burial wagon over to Belle Isle tomorrey. It's a sad business, Colonel. Say, by the way. You needin' another chicken, yet?"

"Sergeant Martin," John whispered back, "that last poor thing which cost me a five-dollar gold piece was more like a pigeon than a chicken."

Martin cackled in mirth. "It were at that, weren't it? Well, I'll keep my eyeballs peeled fer a bit more plumper 'un this time. I'll let ya know, Colonel."

Captain Alexander entered the storeroom and shouted loudly, "Prisoner John Whyte, get yur sorry ass over here."

John walked as slowly as he dared to the impatient Alexander. "You call me, Captain?"

"You know damn well I did, you smart-aleck, Yankee trash. You're to appear in front of the Confederate States Court-martial Board at ten a.m. tomorrow. Tell Sergeant Martin to give you a coat and clean shirt, if he has any. Be down here at eight, I'll have material available for you to shave and clean up. You Yankees seem to enjoy being stinky dirty, but I want you lookin' good before the board. We wouldn't want them to have to condemn a dirty slob to the gallows, now would we?"

"I don't know what you mean, Captain, but I'll be ready."

Alexander did not bother to answer, but simply spun on his heel and left the storeroom. Cursing the man, John returned to Sergeant Martin and told him what had occurred.

"Yeah, I heard him, Colonel. You look in that barrel yonder. I think that's where I put your jacket when you got here. Ya already got your boots. I'll have a clean, white shirt fer ya tomorrey. Ya'd better head back on upstairs and git yur pants and boots as clean as ya can."

Mystified as to what to make of the orders, John did as he was told. Chuck Mount and some of the other prisoners helped him prepare himself as best he could. One prisoner even trimmed his hair with a tiny straight-edge razor he had smuggled into captivity. The next morning, John washed and shaved, luxuriating in the tiny sliver of soap furnished by his captors. It was the cleanest he had been since his capture. The shirt was old, but clean, while his uniform and boots were almost passable, although the pants were still a trifle malodorous.

Shackles were placed on John's hands and feet. He shuffled to a waiting wagon outside, where he was driven to the building where his court-martial was to take place. Apparently LaDonna did have enough clout to cause him trouble, although John could not imagine how a common prostitute could have such influence. His guards would not speak to him, so he was forced to wait in silent, nervous anticipation.

A guard hustled him into a building, past several curious onlookers. The interior was simply furnished, and the windows were painted over with whitewash. Oil lamps gave the room a dingy illumination. The furnishings included a long table with six chairs behind it, facing a small desk with two chairs and a prisoner's dock. Several chairs for onlookers lined the rear of the room. The guards chained John to the dock and stepped back, taking up positions by the doorway. Two Confederate officers entered the room, one carrying a large folder of papers. One a major, the other a lieutenant, both wearing staff officer sashes around their waists. Neither of their uniforms showed any sign of field campaigning or wear. Their officious demeanor as they shuffled papers and glared at him proclaimed them to be lawyers. John presumed they were the military prosecution.

Moments later, six senior officers entered the room. The first was a brigadier, white-haired, short in stature, and well advanced in age. Following were two colonels, two lieutenant colonels, and a major. They lined up behind the chairs at the long table and then sat down. The two lawyers did the same, along with several men in civilian clothes, and two Confederate army officers, wearing the yellow of cavalry officers. LaDonna Chambers and another woman entered with a flurry and sat in the spectators' section, along with two men who pulled out paper and pencil as if they were reporters.

The general looked around, then loudly cleared his throat. "Let the record show this court-martial, convened by the First

Military District of the Confederate States of America, is now in session, Brigadier G. W. Simpson, senior officer and judge advocate. Is the prisoner in attendance?"

The major sitting at the table next to John's small, wooden dock spoke up. "He is, sir. Colonel John Whyte, First Brigade, First Cavalry Division, Union army." He turned to John. "You are John Whyte, are you not?"

John looked at the old general. "Sir, I protest. If I am on trial, what am I charged with? Am I not allowed a counsel to assist in my defense?"

"Hurrump! Read the charges, Major Wilmott."

John listened in disbelief as the chief prosecutor intoned the charges in a bored voice. He was accused of spying against the Confederacy and murder of JEB Stuart.

"How do you plead, sir?" The prosecutor waited for John's answer.

"I'm not guilty of either charge. I say again, will I have a solicitor to assist me?"

"No, Colonel, you will not. Under Confederate law, you are not guaranteed one, as you are a belligerent against the sovereign States of the Confederacy." The Confederate general turned back to the major. "Proceed, Major Wilmott."

The rest of the morning, John defended himself against the charge that he had somehow murdered JEB Stuart. The two witnesses against him, both former subordinates of Stuart, had nothing but the conjecture that no Yankee could kill a soldier as good as the Confederate legend in anything but a devious and skulking manner.

As the noontime break for lunch approached, the senior board member dismissed everyone until two. As the room emptied, John looked at his guards, who were sitting down on the empty chairs and eating their bread and pork sandwiches.

John rattled his chains. "May I have something to eat and drink?"

The older guard sneered at John. "Fer as I care, Yankee, ya can starve to death right where ya stand."

"Get General Simpson, immediately." John was determined not to stand for such an outrage without a fight.

"Get him yerself," the older guard grumbled.

"Very well. General Simpson! Get in here right away. General Simpson, do you hear me?" John's shout could probably be heard outside the building.

"Hey, what the hell?" the guard shouted. He jumped up and ran to John, his rifle swinging like a club at John's head. John ducked and lashed out as best he could with his foot, trying to kick the guard, who was dancing around the docket, trying to land a blow on John without receiving a kick in return.

"Here now!" the old general shouted, stepping through the doorway while wiping a trace of food from his mouth with a white napkin. "What the hell is going on here? Stop that, Corporal. You, sir, Colonel Whyte. Explain yourself."

John ducked a final swing of the rifle butt by his guard and twisted toward General Simpson. "General Simpson, I implore you. I've been chained to this dock since I arrived, without a break, water, or food. Even if I'm the Devil incarnate, doesn't common decency dictate that I be given some measure of dignity? I want food and water and a chance to relieve myself. Is that asking too much of the brave Confederate people?"

General Simpson threw John a frosty glare. "Sir, you were supposed to bring your own food from prison. The court has no requirement to feed you."

"Perhaps, General, but I had no food to bring. Libby Prison does not have enough food to feed the men incarcerated there, much less send any extra with me. May I, at least, eat the scraps from your table and have some water? I would hope our two people have not split so far apart during this damned war that you can't be that civil."

Simpson paused, considering John's statement. "Very well. As soon as we finish and leave the conference room for our midday stroll, you may come in to eat and drink what you will. Meanwhile, guard, escort this man to the privy and be quiet about it for heaven's sake. It's upsetting my digestion."

A short time later, John was taken into the conference room, where the plates of the eight Confederate officers awaited him. He saw that the men had dined on baked chicken, with potatoes and boiled greens. He was able to eat his fill from the scraps and take still more and tie it into his handkerchief, for Chuck and the others back at the prison. For the remainder of the afternoon, John vigorously defended himself against the spurious charge of murder. It seemed to him that he was just spitting into the wind. The bored Confederate officers barely paid any attention to his attempts at explaining what happened at Yellow Tavern.

He was escorted back to Libby Prison as sundown approached. He was immediately taken up to the top floor, where he reported on the day's activities and shared the scraps he had smuggled from the court, although the meager amount did not go far. General Milroy was astounded at the charge and challenged every man on the floor to develop arguments to counter the unfounded accusations.

The next day he was tried on the charge of spying against the Confederacy. LaDonna and two other women who had worked for Rose Greenhow testified against John. Reports of the deceased Rose Greenhow and Bret Redford were read to the court. Redford was the Southern spy who had recruited him to spy for the South on his trip from England. He was currently in Europe attempting to buy munitions for the South. The prosecution blamed the failure of the Greenhow plan on John's infiltration into the ring and the secret information he stole from them and turned over to the Union as the cause of their arrest.

John's explanation that he was simply doing his duty as a Union officer was brushed aside. LaDonna's inflammatory exaggerations conveyed to the court that he was devious and traitorous. Her accusation that he sold out the South for money after swearing an oath of allegiance was the final straw.

The court brushed John's vehement protestation of her lying aside. More than once he was admonished to keep quiet while the vindictive whore branded him as more evil than Judas himself.

At the end of the testimony, the board retired to deliberate John's fate. He turned as LaDonna took a seat behind him, scorn on his face. Her own face was ugly with vengeance.

"I told you I'd make you pay, John Whyte. You'll hang before the week is out."

"And well I might, thanks to you," John replied. "But, my dear, they can hang me higher than the Washington monument, but the facts will not change. You will still be a traitor and a whore."

LaDonna's face purpled in rage, and for a moment John thought she was going to attack him with her painted nails. However, one of the guards stepped in and whispered hoarsely, "Shutup, Colonel. You know you ain't suppose to talk to the spectators. Sit down, ma'am. Don't talk to the prisoner." The burly guard's presence deterred the enraged woman, and she returned to her seat, to sit and glare at John's back while he pointedly ignored her.

The sun's rays lengthened across the wood floor as the day waned. Within an hour, the six officers returned to the room, and reconvened the trial.

John was brought to stand before the table where the six

judges sat, every man impassively looking at their prisoner. General Simpson cleared his throat and rambled on about "closed deliberations," and "majority of members present voting," before he stated the verdict.

"Colonel John Whyte, you are found guilty of crimes against the Confederate States of America and are sentenced to be shot by firing squad on Monday morning, next, at eight o'clock. May God have mercy on your soul. Court is adjourned."

CHAPTER 28

A cluster of Union prisoners surrounded John as soon as he stepped through the door into Milroy's floor at Libby Prison. "How did it go?" the old general queried.

John shook his head, disgustedly. "I've been sentenced to face a firing squad on Monday morning. It was a damned railroad job right from the start. They accepted lying drivel from La-Donna Chambers and another of her whore friends, and some half-baked crap from an aide of JEB Stuart, that I must have killed him using skullduggery, as no mortal could fairly best him in close combat."

"Damn," Milroy muttered. "Monday you say? And today's Thursday, I think. Right?"

A murmur of confirmation rose from the other prisoners. Milroy paused for a minute and then smacked his fist into the palm of his other hand. "We can't let them get away with it. Next thing, they'll be trying us all for fighting as soldiers." Milroy slapped John on his shoulder. "Let me work on it with our escape committee, my boy. We'll have you out of here, if we have to storm the doors with our bare hands."

"No, General, I don't want that. I can't buy my freedom at the expense of your lives."

"Don't worry, son." The older man patted John on his arm. "I won't needlessly waste anyone's life. But, they've thrown down a gauntlet, and I'm gonna make 'em eat it. More's at stake than just your life now." Milroy gathered several younger men around him and whispered instructions. Soon, they were slipping away, headed for the lower floors. The Rebel guards allowed the prisoners to move freely among the upper floors during the day, only keeping them contained to their assigned floor after the evening roll call.

John retreated to his blanket and sat beside Chuck Mount. Chuck was enraged by the pronouncement. "I swear, Colonel, I'll not just sit here and let it happen. There's gotta be some way to stick a ramrod up their collective ass. I'll think on it until I figger it out."

John nodded. "We'll have to see what Milroy comes up with, I guess. Meanwhile, I'm going to write a letter to Gloria. If by chance we do not figure a solution to this whole sticky wicket, I am counting on you to make certain she receives it, just as soon as you can. I can count on you for that, can't I, Chuck?"

"Certainly, Colonel. But don't give up hope, yet. I think I'll go ask General Milroy if there's anything I can do. I'll be back directly." He hurried off. John wrapped his thin blanket around his shoulders and stood looking as close as he dared to gaze out of a nearby window while the setting sun tinted the thin clouds with a scarlet glow. He struggled through several opening phrases to Gloria, finally settling on a straightforward account of his fate. Taking a small sheet of paper which the prison allowed for its captives' letters and using as small a writing script as he could, John poured his heart out to the woman he loved. After evening roll call and the monotonous sludge the Rebels called supper, he continued, to describe what he hoped their life together might have been and the dreams that he held in his heart.

The night was agonizingly long. John slept very little, his mind and spirit both in turmoil. He awoke to his last Saturday at the prison to the shouts of the guards anxious for morning roll call. Then it was another bland, tasteless helping of grits and stale bread for breakfast, delivered by the stoic, silent blacks that worked as manual laborers for the prison guards.

John concentrated on his final message to Gloria. He wrote to comfort and strengthen her to his loss, coming so soon after the death of her child and husband. Around noon, Milroy sent for him from the second floor.

John descended the back steps, passing the numerous prisoners who sat on them, killing time with friends from other floors. He walked into the second-floor bay, an exact replica of the fourth floor. He spotted General Milroy standing with several Union officers none of whom he recognized. Milroy saw him and waved him over.

"Hello, Colonel Whyte. This is Brigadier General Thurman, head of the second floor and this is Major Krammer, head of the prison escape committee."

John shook hands and sat down on the frayed, filthy blanket, next to Milroy. The old general continued. "I've heard something that might be an answer to our problem. Major Krammer has sent for a Major Garnet, who has an unusual plan that General Thurman thinks might be useful. Ah, here he is now."

A slender major, with dark hair rapidly receding from his forehead and fluffy, Burnside whiskers, joined them. He was introduced to John and the two men shook hands. "Sorry to hear about your sentence, Colonel Whyte. I was at the Wilderness when the Rebs killed Major General Sedgwick. We don't think of them as murderers for that."

Milroy broke in. "Tell Colonel Whyte about your little plan, Paul."

Garnet nodded, and sat beside John, quickly scanning the room for unwanted listeners. "I've become friendly with old Mose, the head darkie of the prison's black slaves. They're contracted here by some of the local area slave owners since the growing season is over. Old Mose is the one who takes the burial wagon filled with the latest dead over to Belle Island graveyard for burial every Sunday. So, tomorrow, he'll load up the dead stacked downstairs on a wagon, drive it down to the docks, take the ferry to the island, bury the dead, and then return."

Garnet smiled as John's eyes widened as he began to comprehend the plan. "Right. I planned to take the place of one of the dead men, slip out of the canvas shroud before Mose gets on the ferry and escape downriver to our lines."

John eyes hooded as he thought through the implications. "How do you exchange places with one of the bodies downstairs? And what do you do with it? The body, I mean."

"We don't exchange with one down there, we make the exchange up here. Look, there're over fourteen hundred men in this damned place. One or two will die tonight, or tomorrow. The guards have a routine they use. They hold a mirror to the dead man's nostrils, to check for breath, and prick around his eyes with a knife to make certain he's not faking. Once they certify him dead, we draw a canvas shroud from supply, and sew the dead man into it. Then, we carry him downstairs, add him to the pile of dead, and on Sunday, Mose loads him up, and out the door to the cemetery."

"And if I'm in the shroud, what about the dead man?"

"We put him in your blanket and turn him in the next day, as you, died during the night. During roll call we answer for him. Most of the time, the guards never look up from their tally sheets to see who answers, as long as the count is right. Especially the weekend guards. They're never as careful as the regular weekday guards are."

John paused. "What if nobody dies in the next day?"

Milroy answered. "I'm afraid you won't have to worry about that, my boy. We have three men deathly ill as we speak. I doubt if all three live through the weekend. Sad as it is to say, Libby

Prison never misses a burial party."

Milroy grew very serious. "There are a couple of risks. One, we have no idea what you can do once outside. The burial wagon leaves in the morning, in broad daylight. Two, and most dangerous. The dead bodies are checked one last time, as they are loaded on the wagon. A guard, or Mose, runs a bayonet into each shroud to make certain its occupant is a dead man. If it's Mose, he can make certain he slips the bayonet between your arm and body, but if it's a Rebel guard, he very well may put it smack into your brisket."

John thought for a moment. "Well, I won't be any worse off, I suppose, than what's in store for me on Monday."

Milroy agreed. "No, that's true. If you agree, pack a small amount of food and a container of water. As soon as the next man dies, we exchange him for you. You understand that you'll have to lay very quiet and still the entire time you're at the pile. We'll put you on the far side, on the floor, if possible, but you will still need to be very careful. Rebels go in and out of the supply area all day long."

Garnet spoke up. "Do you have any money? I promised Mose I'd give him a gold coin for his help in this."

"Most certainly. In fact, I'll get two, if you think it will help."

"Can't hurt. Go for them now. I'll take them down and alert Mose that we're going to try it this weekend."

"Good," John replied. "I'm certainly game to give it a go."

Milroy nodded. "Good for you, Colonel Whyte. And good luck. As soon as you give the major the gold for Mose, stand by your space upstairs. I'll send for you the instant one of our unfortunate sick men pass away." He paused, and then patted Garnet on the shoulder. "You owe Major Garnet, Colonel Whyte. He was going out soon, but has willingly given up his chance so you can make your breakout."

John offered Garnet his hand. "I do appreciate it, Major. If you will give me the particulars, I'll contact anybody you want after I'm back to the Army and inform them of your health and status."

"Thank you, Colonel. My wife and two sons are back in Hartford, Connecticut. I'll give you their address and a short message. If you would get it to them, I'd much appreciate it. I'll write it out while you make your preparations. You can memorize it and destroy the paper while you await the time to go."

"I will, I assure you. And thank you for giving up your place."

"That's my pleasure, Colonel. I'll make the next trip."

John hurried up to his floor and laying with his back to the mass of men milling about, quickly dug two twenty-dollar gold pieces from their hiding place in the floorboard crack.

Charles Mount walked over. "What's going on, Colonel? Why you getting the gold? Are you going to make a break for it?"

"It looks like it, Chuck. Stay close. I'll explain it all, as soon as I return." John hurriedly took the money to Garnet, who then headed down to the first floor, in search of the slave, Mose. John returned to the fourth floor and told Mount what he could about the plan. He refused to explain how he was going to use the assistance of the black slave to escape the prison, saying, "The less you know, the less the Rebs can make you tell. Just swear that the dead man is me when they come to check the body."

"You can count on me, Colonel. I know a fellow who has a small canteen. I'll take a ten-dollar gold piece and buy it for your use. You still have that bread from the scraps you brought back yesterday?"

"Yes."

"That's food enough for a day or two. Wrap it in a hankie, and wait here for me. I'll be right back."

Mount soon returned with a tinplated canteen, capable of

carrying about a pint of water. It was already full, so John added it to his stash. He dug up several more gold coins from their hiding place and secreted them in his socks, for use once outside the prison.

The day wore on, John questioning his right to wish for some poor man to die, just so he could exchange places with him in the canvas burial shroud. It was nearly four when a young captain hurried up to John and Chuck, sitting and quietly talking. John had memorized Mount's home address and knew what Chuck wanted him to say should he return to the Union side. He had also committed to memory Major Garnet's message to his family. John swore to himself that he would deliver the two messages, no matter what.

"Colonel Whyte, come quick to the third floor. Lieutenant Colonel Hatcher has just died. They've already sent for the shroud."

John shook hands with Chuck Mount, General Milroy, and several of the other captive officers. "Take care, Chuck. I'll be seeing you shortly, God willing."

"So long, Colonel. Give my best to the guys in the brigade." Mount turned away, his eyes glistening. John was deeply touched.

He followed the captain down to the next floor. Several men were gathered by a still figure at the farthest corner from the door. As John walked up, Garnet announced to several officers around the dead man. "Here's poor Hatcher's replacement. Bob, lay out the shroud." One of the prisoners unfolded the flat widths of canvas. Several of the prisoners fell to sewing a body-sized, sock-like container.

Garnet nodded, satisfied. "Sam, you and the others carry Hatcher up to the fourth floor. Milroy's people will show you where he goes." Garnet looked down at the white, still face of the dead man. "Shave his beard. He's dark, like Whyte here.

He'll look a lot like you with your jacket on, Colonel. Give it to Sam, here. Somebody give the colonel a civilian-looking jacket to wear." John shrugged out of his field jacket, handing it to a ragged-looking major, who hurried off with it. He stood in his shirt, awaiting what would follow.

A young prisoner ran up and gave John the jacket off his back. It was a ragged, deep blue, wool jacket. "I traded my Army boots for it, Colonel. You'll look just like a poor, Rebel civilian from a distance. Good luck, sir."

"Thanks to you all and God bless," John replied. "Well, General Milroy, I'm ready. What next?"

Two men flipped the canvas shroud out to full length. "Wriggle in, Colonel. And, for God's sake, stay quiet. We'll sew you up and carry you downstairs to the dead pile. You have a knife to cut yourself free?"

John nodded his head in affirmation, as he slipped into the canvas shroud. Swiftly, the two prisoners sewed the top closed encasing John in darkness. He would have to struggle just to breathe, much less do it inconspicuously.

John felt himself being lifted and carried by a man at each corner of the shroud. He heard a muffled voice announce, "Lieutenant Colonel Hatcher's body, sentry. We're taking him down to the dead pile."

"Hurry up and do it. Then y'all git right back up here. It's almost time fer the evening roll call."

John mentally followed the route as the men carried him down the back stairs to the malodorous pile of corpses. He was carefully laid on the hard, wooden floor and the sounds of footsteps faded. He was alone. With every breath, the cloying, putrid odor of death and rotting flesh assaulted his senses. He willed himself to take shallow breaths and not dwell on the smell that accompanied it.

Time dragged ever so slowly. He faintly heard the roll called on the second floor, echoed on floors three and four. He waited to hear an outcry of discovery when the guards learned he was gone, but soon it grew quiet. John sensed rather than saw the darkness deepen, as night fell upon the warehouse turned prison.

John tried to sleep, but it would not come. The hard floor, his tension, the confinement in the suffocating bag, and the rancid smell would not permit it. Then he heard the stirrings of morning, and knew that dawn had finally arrived. Sometime later, the morning roll call commenced and shortly thereafter, John heard footsteps. With a grunt, someone added another body to the pile, whispering hoarsely.

"One more, Colonel. Old Mose should be along shortly. Remember, when he sticks the bayonet into you, don't make a sound. Gotta go now. Luck to ya."

John waited. After some time, he heard footsteps approaching the pile. He tensed and lay motionless. He heard the bored voice of one of the guards. "Y'all know the drill, Mose. Stick them corpses and let's see if any squeal."

He waited. Suddenly, he felt a hand grab his arm and pull it away from his body. The ripping sound of the bayonet tearing through the canvas and the stinging pain of the steel blade slicing a nick against his ribs made him clench his teeth in pain. The bayonet was withdrawn and he lay quietly. He was alive. Mose had missed him and gone on without the guard being alerted. Moments later he was lifted and carried by four men. As they left the building, raindrops splattered against the canvas body bag.

For John's benefit, Mose spoke loudly. "Shore be a nasty day. It be rainin' lik' de good Lawd were pourin' piss out a boot. Cum'on, thar, boys. I gots ta catch the ten o'clock ferry ta Belle Isle."

John felt the jerk of the wagon and the jarring of the wheels against the road as they departed down the street. John let a pent-up stream of air escape his lips. The canvas shroud was soaked and the cold rain was trickling through, chilling him. But it did not matter. He was out of Libby Prison. "And," he murmured softly to himself, "by God's Grace, I'll die before I go back inside those walls."

CHAPTER 29

The swaying motion of the wagon acted like a soporific. John felt himself drifting into a twilight sort of sleep. Abruptly, the wagon stopped and a voice pierced into his lethargic consciousness. "Mr. Garnet, Mr. Garnet. Cuts open de canvas. It's time you gets out. Hurry, Mr. Garnet, hurry!"

John opened the tiny penknife, a gift from Chuck Mount, and sliced through the stitches at the top of the shroud. Cautiously, he pulled the cover down, until his head was out of the body bag. The rain beat down on his head in a maddening but cleansing ferocity. He could barely see across the road and did not see another person anywhere, save the man standing at the rear of the death wagon. He looked at the old, gray-headed, black man, who was exhibiting shock at John's appearance.

"You hain't Mr. Garnet. Who is you?"

"It was decided that I go instead of Garnet. Here." He pulled another twenty-dollar gold piece from his shirt pocket and flipped it to the soaking-wet, Negro slave. "Take this, with my compliments. Now, what do you want me to do?"

Old Mose looked around, searching for passersby out in the driving rain. The road and sidewalks were absent of people. "We's almost to de ferry. You can't cross over to Belle Isle wit' me, Masser. Better you gets out here and waits till dark. Canal Street ends just down thar. Lots o' skiffs and such along the bank. Affer dark, you takes one, paddle out to de center of de James River, and let de current take you down to de Yankee ships. 'Bout twenty miles to freedom fer ya."

John wiggled out of his confining sack of canvas, and crawled off the wagon, standing on shaky legs, as he waited for the blood to circulate in his limbs. "Where should I hide until dark, my good man?"

Mose pointed over to his left. "Dey's some stacked cotton bales over thar, sir. You hide out amongst dem, till it's good and dark. Den slip over to da river, thar." He pointed straight ahead. "I gots to go now, afore da ferry leaves. God bless you, Masser. Kill some o' them Reb's fer me, when you gets back to da Yankee army." He chucked the reins leading to a pair of very wet mules. "Haw thar. Gitty up, you dumb mules." He disappeared into the slanting rain, before John could thank him.

John looked around, spotting the store yard filled with stack after stack of cotton bales, most several bales high. Lugging the soaked canvas, he sprinted to the edge of the field of processed cotton, searching for a place to hide, sheltered from the cold, wet weather. John cautiously made his way into the labyrinth of cotton bales, each the standard five hundred pounds of pressed cotton fiber.

Near the far end, he found what he was seeking. One of the stacks had fallen over, and he was able to crawl into a crevasse formed when the pile crashed down. He was reasonably safe from discovery, as long as nobody walked up to his hiding place. He positioned the canvas to shield himself from the driving rain and shivering uncontrollably, huddled in to await the coming night. He spent the rest of the day blowing into his cupped hands, trying to keep his fingers from freezing. He was certain his feet had already succumbed to the numbing damp and cold.

John, miserable and wet, fantasized himself back at Glorietta with Gloria, rebuilding the estate into a profitable, textbook-perfect working farm. He abandoned his reverie as the day dimmed into night and black shadows closed on the rain-swept enemy capital. John forced himself to swallow some of the soggy food he had stuffed in a pocket. He stretched his arms and legs, so he could move when the time was opportune.

As darkness, black and as wet as he had ever seen, masked the town, he took one last look around, slipped out of his hiding place, and jogged toward the river somewhere just ahead. At the end of the storage field, the land dropped several feet and met the dark rolling waters of the James River. John dropped to the edge of the levee to the muddy bank of the river, walking in the slippery slime, looking for one of the boats Mose had assured him were in plentiful supply. He fell, coating his canvas cover and himself in smelly mud. Cursing, he struggled to his feet. Seeing how well the canvas blended in with the darkness around him, he wrapped it about his shoulders.

Once he heard voices in the rainy blackness and he lay quietly as two bored, Confederate soldiers on guard duty walked past, not ten feet above him, without seeing him. They stopped a few feet away, cursing a sergeant who had given them such onerous duty, then walked on. Cautiously, John got to his feet. There, just ahead of him, pulled up above the tide was a small pirogue, muddy, scarred, but entirely acceptable. He found a piece of wood to use as a paddle and pushed away from the river's edge. Covered by the slanting, cold rain, he paddled and drifted along with the sluggish current. "Damn," he muttered to himself. "I can barely function, I'm shivering so badly."

The usually light Sunday evening traffic was nonexistent. Everyone was inside, out of the elements, leaving him the sole traveler in the pelting rain on the murky water. The warm glow of lights in the houses and offices he passed penetrated the deluge, but not once was he seen or hailed from the shore.

As he rounded a slight bend, he came upon an oceangoing sailing ship, tied to the dock. It rocked gently in the current and seemed uninhabited. John started to paddle out, well away from it and then shrugging his shoulders at his stupidity, let the current drift him right up to the great ship's port side. Catching a small rope, he tied his craft and scrambled up until he could look over the railing. "I wonder how the Rebels sneaked past the blockade with a ship this size," he muttered to himself. "And why in God's name am I messing around it when I should be getting as far from here as possible?"

Cautiously, he looked over the railing, his form nearly invisible in the darkness; he was so covered in wet, muddy clothing. He saw the glow of a pipe or cigar up on the foredeck, under a canvas cover flopping in the driving wind, but he could not make out the smoking sailor. Carefully, he slipped onto the decking, then moved quickly to the hatch cover of the nearest hold. He pushed open the cover and slipped inside, closing the cover behind him.

It was black as pitch in the hold, but John did not need light to know what it was that the great ship carried. "Gunpowder," he whispered to himself, recognizing the familiar odor. "Lots of it, too." He felt around the top of the ladder leading down into the hold. Sure enough, a lantern was hanging by a hook. He felt inside the glass case. A nearly burned down candle was stuck therein. Praying that the three sulfur-tips he carried were not soaked, he continued down into the blackness of the hold.

His feet hit the floor of the hold and he opened the small bag made of chamois skin that held his precious matches. At the moment they were more valuable than the five recently expelled diamonds that shared the purse. His hands shaking, he scratched the first against the floor. Nothing. Alternately praying and swearing, he scratched the second. It broke off in his hand. Nearly sobbing in frustration, he took the third match and gingerly dragged its head against the rough wood of the hold. With a blaze of sulfurous smoke, the match flared and settled into a soft, yellow flame. Quickly, he lit the candle, thanking the Almighty for his good fortune.

John looked around. The front half of the hold was empty, but the far side still held many, many barrels of gunpowder, "Made in England, Thos Murdock and Sons, LTD," stenciled in white on every barrel. "Murdock gunpowder," John whispered to himself. "Makers for the Crown and the Confederacy, it seems." He walked slowly toward the stacks of explosive, looking for some manner of firing the whole lot, while still escaping the blast himself.

"Hello," he whispered softly. Atop one barrel, part of a tall stack, he could see where another barrel had broken open during the trip. Although most had been swept up, he was able to gather several handfuls and laid a trail of black powder from the barrels to an open corner. There, he formed a tiny pile of powder, carefully placing the small candle in the middle. It looked as if he had fifteen or twenty minutes to escape. He watched for a second to insure the candle was not going to fall over, then crept back up the ladder, carefully opening the hatch cover and peeking out. Still no sign of sailors, he noted with relief. He slipped back over the side to his tiny craft and slowly paddled away from the munitions ship, trying not to make too much noise or wake in the black water.

Twenty minutes later, a bright flash and a mighty thunderclap illuminated the night. He felt the warm air of the shock wave whisper past him and smelled the stench of burnt gunpowder carried on the hot breeze. Grinning to himself, he paddled even harder, the numbing cold forgotten in the victory of the moment.

He drifted on down the river, growing colder and more disoriented. He was unconscious when the Union gunboat *President Taylor* picked him up just after daybreak, twenty miles south of Richmond.

Hot soup, several cups of hot coffee, and a wrapping of

blankets renewed his strength until he could report to the Navy commander who captained the craft. Within four hours, he was at Grant's headquarters, at City Point, and was telling his story for the third time, to the congenial commander of the Union armies and members of his staff.

As John finished telling about the firing of the ship, Grant guffawed mightily and slapped John on the arm. "What a story, my boy. And verified, too. Commander Pinkham, on the *Taylor*, saw the light from the explosion, and picked up ship's wreckage floating down the James. Well done, John. Well done!"

"Thank you, General. I was lucky, the rain and all, I mean. The Rebels were not expecting anybody to be out in the rainstorm."

"Luck or not, it was some adventure. I'll send word to the president tonight of your miraculous escape. He'll be eager to hear all about it."

Grant peered anxiously at John. "John, my boy, are you all right? John?"

Those were the last words John heard. He folded like a limp rag, his face flushed with fever, and his breath rattling in his chest.

Grant leaped to his feet, shouting for a doctor. The worried general watched anxiously while the staff surgeon poked and listened to the unconscious escapee. Grant's face blanched at the doctor's verdict. "General, this man is desperately ill with inflammation of the lungs. He'll die unless we transport him immediately to the hospital back in Washington, maybe even then."

In John's fevered memory, the trip back up the Potomac to Washington was a blur. He continually slipped in and out of consciousness. Slowly, he awoke, his brain seizing on the annoying squeak of a wheel. His eyes fluttered open. The surroundings swam into focus like looking through a wavy, leaded-glass window. He was inside a room that seemed much different than Grant's headquarters. The walls were painted white, and the ceiling had a parquet pattern on it. He squeezed his eyes shut, his throbbing head ached as if he was coming off a weekend drunk. He smacked his lips, his mouth was dry.

"A drink, Colonel?"

A heavily whiskered face came into focus. The man was dressed in white and was pushing a wooden cart with a wheel that squeaked with every rotation. On it sat a pitcher, some cups, and a pile of clean towels. He poured a cup of water and held it to John's lips.

John gratefully swallowed some of the cool fluid. "I thank you, Mr. er . . . ?"

"Nurse Orderly Walter Whitman, Colonel. You're most welcome, sir."

"May I have some more? My mouth feels like cotton. Where am I?"

"You're in General Military Hospital Seven, in Washington City, Colonel. Excuse me, sir, I must report your awakening to Chief Surgeon Cladis. He's been anxious about you." The tall orderly hurried away, still pushing the cart with the annoying squeak.

John lay back, slowly turning his head. He was in a room with three other beds, but only one was occupied at the moment, by a still figure apparently asleep.

Presently, a slender doctor entered the room. He was very young, with no gray in his hair or beard. He smiled warmly and felt John's forehead. "Umm, your temperature is normal, at last. Very good." He took a listening trumpet from a pocket and put the crown to John's chest and the small end to his ear. "Breathe deeply, Colonel Whyte."

John did as he was told, his deep breaths causing him to cough harshly. The doctor listened and then put the instrument away, apparently satisfied with what he heard.

John caught his breath. His lungs hurt from the coughing. "What happened to me, Doctor? The last I remember, I was with General Grant, at City Point, and then I woke up here."

"You collapsed, Colonel. Lung inflammation. You have been here for a week, and quite frankly, it was touch and go for a while. Are you hungry?"

"Exceedingly, Doctor."

"Good. A Mrs. Richardson had brought you some broth. In fact, she has every day since you arrived. She would take several hours to feed you, a sip at a time, while you slept on. She left about an hour ago, and I think there is still some in the pot that she left in the lounge. I'll send Whitman in with a bowl. Are you up to some fresh bread to eat with it?"

"Yes, I think so. Also, something to drink. My mouth is quite dry."

"Some brandy mixed with water should do nicely," the young doctor declared. "Then go back to sleep, if you can, sir. You are still quite weak. Sleep is good medicine."

Mrs. Richardson showed up the next morning, and was delighted to see John sitting up in his bed. "Oh, John, my boy. I was so worried for you. As was everyone. The president sent a message stating his concern. Madam Singh and her daughter have come nearly every day, bringing food and flowers for you."

She straightened John's pillow and smoothed his covers. "I'll write Colonel Mansur that you are recovering. Your men are very concerned, according to Madam Singh."

"Where are they?" John asked. "Still in the Shenandoah Valley?"

"No." Mrs. Richardson shook her head. "They have joined Grant's forces around Petersburg. The papers say it is the last big hurdle until Richmond is taken."

John lay back, his mind spinning. Would he be here, an

invalid, as the war wound to its climactic finish? "I hope I'll be up and back with my men before the end," he whispered to Mrs. Richardson.

She patted his cheek, motherly concern on her face. "You are going nowhere, young man, until you are well. I promise you that, so just relax and regain your strength. The damned war can wait on you for a while, I declare." Mrs. Richardson crossed her arms defiantly, her chin out pugnaciously. She meant to have John healed, body and spirit before the war reclaimed him, or kick down the doors of Hell trying.

Each day, John got progressively better and by Sunday, he was released to the care of Mrs. Richardson, who beamed at Doctor Cladis's final admonitions to John.

"Ordinarily, I wouldn't let you out of here for another week, Colonel Whyte. However, Mrs. Richardson has assured me she will insure you have plenty of rest and eat properly. Several senior officers are reported sick and in route from Grant's field hospital, and I need your bed. You rest up for another week before you think of resuming a more normal activity. I've gotten you four weeks of convalescence leave before you are to report back for duty. Good luck, sir." He shook John's offered hand and accepted John's offer of gratitude with the usual degree of professional hubris, before hurrying away, other duties demanding his attention.

John dressed, assisted by the helpful orderly Whitman, who was never too busy to lend a helping hand to any of the men under his care. Slowly, like a man twice his years, he followed Mrs. Richardson to her waiting carriage and after a short ride, up to his old room at the house Rose Greenhow sold him two years earlier.

He collapsed into his bed and slept the night away awakening with a voracious hunger, which he sated, then slept some more. After a week of enforced bed rest, supervised by Mrs. Richardson, he began to feel more like his old self. One cold, sunny morning, he took a carriage over to the White House to pay his respects to the president. The same Jeffrey Steward, son of the secretary of state, who had carried a message to the president his first week in Washington, greeted him.

"You just missed him, John. He left last night for Baltimore. He's meeting with some Democratic politicians about their views on Reconstruction after the war. He'll be back in a few days. Make you an appointment then?"

"Thank you, J. W., no. I'm leaving tomorrow for Romney, West Virginia, to see a very special friend. Please give him my best and tell him I'll call on him as soon as I can. Have a wonderful holiday and the same to him." John left the White House, disappointed at missing the president, but anxious to be off. He was going to Gloria with almost three whole weeks of leave to spend by her side.

Chapter 30

It was spitting snow as John rode the B & O Railroad to Cumberland, Maryland. He was able to purchase a horse from the local livery, although for an outrageous sum, before continuing south to Romney. He was bone weary when he turned into the long drive to the main house at Glorietta Plantation, but the thought of seeing his beloved drove him on. As his horse clopped to a stop on the frozen earth, he wearily swung out of the saddle. Like a runaway filly, Gloria flew out the front door and into his arms, nearly knocking him down.

"Oh, John. Oh, darling. You're alive. You're here. I was so worried. I got a letter from Lee Mansur, saying you had been captured. What happened? Are you all right? You're so thin and pale. Are you sick?" She smothered him with kisses, scarcely allowing him time to breathe, much less answer her. He returned her kisses as given, their breaths growing more ragged as their passion grew. Finally, he squeezed her tightly to him, so he could get a word in.

"I'm fine, my dear. I'll tell you all about it. I'm so grateful I could return to you. Come on, let's go inside. Aren't you about frozen out here in the cold?"

"Oh, certainly, my dearest. Here. Let me help you." She held tightly to his arm, as they entered the house. He went to the nearest chair and sat heavily, a whoosh of air escaping from his lungs. "Mercy, that feels good. I was about done in."

"Where did you come from?" Gloria asked.

John told her an abridged version of his adventures since they last saw one another and his recovery leave. Gloria listened raptly, sitting on the floor at his feet, reliving every precarious moment with him. As he finished, she hugged him tightly. "Oh, John. You poor dear. I was frantic with worry for you. If anything had happened." She looked up at him, tears in her eyes.

He dropped his lips to hers, and they kissed, for what seemed an eternity to both. As Gloria opened her eyes, she saw Hattie in the doorway, looking at them. "Oh, Hattie, look. It's Colonel Whyte, come back to us. And for three weeks, until the first of the New Year. Isn't that wonderful?"

"Yes'm it is. Hello, Colonel Whyte, I'm happy to see you again. My Miz Gloria done cried her eyes out, missin' you."

"Now, Hattie. Go on with you." Gloria gave John a misty-eyed grin. "Why would I cry over this rogue?"

"Yes'm, Miz Gloria. Shall I make the guest bed up?"

Gloria looked at John, a touch of red glowing on her cheeks. "No, dear. The colonel will sleep in my bed, with me." She defiantly looked at John, daring him to say anything to try and ease her embarrassment. He was smart enough to remain silent, content with the pronouncement. After a silent pause, Gloria continued. "Now, are you hungry, darling? Hattie, let's cook up something special for our traveling soldier. A welcome home meal."

The following days at Glorietta were a wondrous contrast to the horror of the past few months. The rustling of leafless branches in the cold wind softened by the caress of newly fallen snow accented the calm peacefulness. Gloria eagerly satisfied John's desires with unbridled passion, and John responded lovingly with every technique he had ever learned from brothels all over the world. John and Gloria loved and held one another as if in their union they could eliminate the realities of the world around them. He enfolded her against him through the night.

Gloria slept serene in his arms and awoke every morning with her heart afire in joy. Their days together seemed endless and complete. It was a magical period in their young lives.

As Christmas approached, they rode out together in the carriage to find and cut a little pine Christmas tree. Gloria and Hattie placed tiny candles and lace decorations on the boughs. John rode his horse into Romney and bought out the stores, showering his love and Hattie with yards of bolted cloth for dresses, new boots, winter coats, whatever caught his eye. Gloria acted outraged at his extravagance, but opened her presents with squeals of delight. She made him two shirts, delicately stitched, and handsomely embroidered with his initials. Hattie gave him a new straight razor, purchased with money she had made selling persimmons to local cooks.

John lay in bed the last night of December 1864 recovering his breath from their lovemaking, Gloria tucked into her familiar place on his shoulder. His brow furrowed as he suddenly thought about their coming separation. Gloria raised up, resting her head on her propped arm. Her breast grazed his inner arm, a delightful sensation that he relished, not moving a muscle.

"Darling, why aren't you asleep? Something wrong?"

"No, Gloria. I feel wonderful. It's just that I hate the thought of leaving you tomorrow. If the damned war would only end."

"Soon, my love. The paper from Washington says the spring offensive will be the doom of the Confederacy. For once I hope the damned Yankee press is right. I pray you won't be at risk until it's over. If only you were safe, like my brother, Preston. He's locked away in the Yankee prison in Delaware."

"Those prisons aren't so safe, Gloria. I know from experience."

"Still, they're not being shelled by cannons and such. Poor Pres lost his arm to Yankee cannon fire, you know."

"Yes." John was quiet for a moment, still savoring the sensation of Gloria's nipple rubbing the muscle of his forearm with every breath she took. The sensation was too much. He felt himself firming one more time and clamping his mouth to hers, kissed her deeply, his tongue probing the warm softness of her mouth. As she moaned in passion, he rolled over her, slipping into the familiar yet always wonderful, delightfully warm softness of her. They made love again and again, until both fell into an exhausted sleep, not rising until Hattie discreetly knocked on the door to ask if they wanted any lunch before John departed.

As John rode down the drive, savagely fighting back tears that threatened to spill out with each step his horse took, he vowed to himself, "By the Almighty, I'll never leave her again. I swear it." He waved one last time, memorizing her tear-streaked, beautiful face. He missed her already.

His triumphant return to the First Brigade in camp outside Petersburg suppressed the ache he felt for Gloria. His replacement, Colonel Algers, had taken an indefinite leave of absence for illness. John resumed command as if he had never left. Khan Singh appointed himself John's shadow. He never let John stray far from his sight and nearly drove him mad apologizing for not preventing John's capture three months earlier. John repeatedly reassured the old warrior that he was not to blame, that it had been a misfortune of war. John brought Lee Mansur up from the Fifth Regiment as brigade adjutant and settled in to the burden of running a thousand-man cavalry brigade in extended winter camp.

There were new faces to become accustomed to, including a new color sergeant and chief scout. Lee related to John the story of Tim Vernon's disappearance. "He took three scouts and rode out, about a week after you were captured, John. They came to a crossroads and split up, Tim taking one man and sending the other two the opposite direction. Nobody heard any shooting, they just never returned. We sent out patrols, interrogated prisoners for a month, but nobody saw Tim or the other scout again. It was as if the earth simply swallowed them up."

John sorely missed the competent, brave, former pony-express rider, but war consumed people and John knew he could not stop it by grieving over his loss. He trained the brigade hard, using the time in winter camp to prepare the men for the coming battles. He knew the South would fight with feverish intensity as they saw the inevitable closing in on them. He meant to live and bring back as many of the young men he commanded as possible. He worked hard, wrote Gloria nearly every day, put up with Custer's grand schemes to win glory in the closing days of the war, and counted the minutes until he could return to Glorietta forever.

Merritt sent for him on the fifteenth day of March, a cold dreary day, with wind blowing wisps of snow across the hard earth. The days were steadily growing longer and John knew the time was almost here when Grant would stir his mighty army into action in order to close with Robert E Lee for the last time. John slowly rode to his fiery general's HQ, an antebellum mansion located a mile outside of Petersburg. As usual, Khan Singh and several troopers rode with him, a practice that John had quit trying to break the old Sikh warrior from insisting upon since his return from captivity.

Merritt was in an exuberant mood. "Great news, Colonel. My division is to be the point of Grant's thrust to Richmond. Are your men ready to ride?"

"Yes, General. We await your orders."

Merritt preened his flowing mustache. "I dare say I'll be getting them soon, as soon as the weather breaks. It will be the last hurrah for us, John, I'm certain. Lee is almost whipped and Sherman's on his way north from Savannah. I plan to be the division that captures the most guns, flags and men in the history of the Union army. You'll be the point of my spear, your

Michiganers will be the iron barb that pierces the Confederacy."

John laughed. "Easy, General. We'll be happy to let other units have the privilege of being shot at by those Rebel marksman some of the time. They're damned good, you know."

Merritt grinned. "Don't fret. I'll not waste you now, I promise. But, it will be glorious, I mean simply glorious." Abruptly, he changed the subject. "I hear that that you've found a female conquest among the Rebel ladies."

John nodded shyly, his face blushing. "Yes, sir. It's true. Her husband died with Jackson, back in sixty-two. But she's no traitor, I assure you. I intend to wed her, as soon as the war is over. Rebuild her estate and settle down, like most normal people."

Merritt nodded. "Good for you. It looks like I'm destined to become a civilian as well. Unless, I can convince General Grant otherwise, that is. I'm too junior to receive a command in the peacetime army." Merritt hesitated for a moment, as if contemplating a future without war or glory, then continued. "Grant plans to turn Lee's right flank. We'll ride south, toward Five Forks, see it here, on the map?" Merritt put his finger on the tiny crossroad village. "We'll either pull Lee from his trenches or maneuver behind him. Either way, he's doomed to fight us on our terms."

Then Merritt looked up at John and beamed. "I'm glad you're back with me, John. I want you to know that I've turned in a promotion request for you to be on the next levy of brigadier generals. With any luck, you'll be promoted by the end of April." He waved his hand imperiously as John expressed appreciation. "You earned it, believe me. Now, return to your command and make certain they're ready to ride. As soon as the weather breaks, we saddle up for glory." Merritt watched John leave the room, then turned back to his map. "So little time left, so little time," he grumbled to himself.

A late winter storm delayed Grant's plans, but on the twenty-ninth of March, John led the Michigan Brigade down the road south. Their first day's objective was the crossroad at Five Forks, the gateway to Lee's rear area. Merritt's three thousand cavalry were followed by General Warren's twelve thousand infantrymen of the Fifth Corps, augmented by General Custer's Third division. Grant was deadly serious. He would force Lee from the trenches around Petersburg, or maneuver between Lee and Richmond. A climactic battle was in the offing.

The Seventh Regiment dismounted and lined up in battle formation. At their commander's order, they started across the wooded ground toward the farmhouse sitting at the Five Forks junction. The five roads came together in almost a star, with farm fields and woods between each roadbed. John saw and then heard the ripping pop of muskets and the white smoke of gunpowder drifting out of the woods. He had been right. The Rebels had set up an ambush for his brigade. He motioned to Lieutenant Arthur Graves, his most senior aide.

"Art, my compliments to Major Lyons. Tell him to mount a charge against the south flank of the woods there. He's to stop at the edge and let Colonel Kidd's First Regiment push through the underbrush on foot. Understand?"

The young officer repeated John's orders and galloped off. John watched the mounted attack from his vantage point and then instructed Lieutenant Colonel Stagg's Sixth Regiment to continue up the road toward Dinwiddie Court House. The last three days had seen fierce fighting by the outnumbered Confederate defenders, but Union superiority in men and materials was finally turning the tide. General Warren's Fifth Corps soldiers were pushing the Rebel infantry out of their defensive line and even as John watched, he saw men in tattered gray running north, toward Richmond, throwing guns and equipment aside as they fled.

Galloping to Stagg's position, he joined in a mighty cavalry charge against the retreating enemy soldiers, slashing and firing at the enemy, driving them in mass confusion until the woods and fields beyond were alive with fleeing men. John's brigade captured six battle flags and a dozen cannon that day. Custer rode into the camp that night, shouting his congratulations and cheering the weary cavalrymen, who exuberantly cheered back at their flamboyant general, who once led them to glory.

"We push on tomorrow," he shouted triumphantly. "We must ride ahead of Lee's forces before they can reach their supply train at Appomattox Court House. Well done, Wolverines!" He galloped off, his entourage of bandsmen and couriers riding hard after him.

John sighed, never failing to be both amused and amazed at Custer's delight in combat and his unfailing enthusiasm for war. Shaking his head, he quietly gave orders for the following day's mission, then wearily lay down on the grass for a few hours' sleep. He was so tired that he did not awaken when a light sprinkle began falling, nor when Khan Singh covered him with a waterproof poncho.

The next few days were deadly monotonous. Hard riding, charges against the entrenched enemy, countercharges to beat back, sleep where you stopped, eat in the saddle, and yet another fight just around the next curve in the road. Most of the Confederate soldiers now broke and ran as soon as John deployed for the charge, but always, a few, a grim few, held their ground, firing with deadly accuracy until killed or captured by the tough, aggressive, Michigan cavalrymen. It may have been mopping up, according to the historian, but to the men who rode into the guns and felt the bullet slice into their flesh, it was mortally serious work. At day's end, John had far too many letters to write attempting to explain how bravely did some mother's beloved son fall, his face to the enemy.

John was there, a witness, the morning the guns stopped,

Khan Singh at his side. They watched in awed silence as the great warrior, General Robert E Lee, CSA, rode past on his gray charger Traveler, his gray uniform immaculate, to accept the terms of surrender from the shabbily dressed man who defeated him, General U. S. Grant, USA.

John called his brigade to attention. "Present arms!" He dropped his sword, the tip pointed at his feet, as the revered soldier of the South rode past. Lee glanced at him, tiredly lifting a hand to the brim of his gray-felt campaign hat. Then, the white-haired general rode on, headed to a red-brick house owned by a man who had moved from Manassas Junction to get away from the fighting there, and his fateful meeting with Sam Grant, former saddle salesman.

"Look at that, old friend," John whispered to Khan Singh. "A sight to tell your grandchildren about, someday."

"Yes, Sahib. Truly memorable."

The next morning, John's troop again stood among the guards of honor, as the Confederate battle flags were surrendered, unit by unit. Flag after red flag, carried into battle by units whose name would live in history, were brought forward. John watched in awed silence, as did everyone with him, while ragged, scarecrow men, dirty, some barefoot, reverently rolled a tattered, shell-scarred flag around its staff, then tenderly cased it in its canvas cover.

With tears in their eyes, the broken soldiers tenderly stacked them on the ground, at the feet of General Joshua Chamberlain, of Gettysburg fame and personally designated by Grant to receive the surrender of the Army of Northern Virginia. Afterwards, tears streaming down many of their faces, they returned to their place in formation, members of an army whose name would live in history, the Army of Northern Virginia.

At the end of the ceremony, the starving enemy soldiers dropped their rifles in piles and filed past commissary wagons, where they received rations to fill their empty stomachs. John's horsemen spent several days guarding and paroling the defeated Rebel soldiers, then pushed on, chasing the son of General Lee, Rooney Lee, who was trying to reach General Joe Johnson and the remnants of his Army of Atlanta, retreating just ahead of the pursuing General William Tecumseh Sherman.

The First Michigan Brigade did not come off the battlefield for three more weeks. Hard days just as if the war were still on. Long days, filled with fast riding, late nights, and the occasional flurry of gunfire from hidden ambush. John gave no quarter to those who did not surrender immediately. He overwhelmed them with superior numbers and killed or captured every one. Custer was everywhere, relishing the final days in command of a fighting cavalry division.

With an intense sense of loss, John learned of the assassination of President Lincoln in dispatches from Grant's HQ. He was far from Washington, in North Carolina, still trying to pin down Rooney Lee and his remaining cavalrymen. John berated himself for not making a more determined effort to see the Great Emancipator the last time he was in Washington.

Sorrowfully, John gathered his men around him and told them the grim news, standing down operations for the afternoon, while one of his soldiers, a lay preacher back in Michigan, held religious services in honor of their fallen commander-in-chief.

It was not until the middle of May that he returned with his exhausted men to Washington City. After settling them down in their bivouac area, he reported to Merritt, at his Division HQ.

"Everyone accounted for, John?"

"Yessir, General. What are my orders?"

"The Army of the Republic is to have what the big brass is calling a Grand Review, the twenty-second of this month. The Army of the Potomac will lead, followed by General Sherman's

Army of the West. General Sheridan's Cavalry Corps is to lead everyone and my division is to be the first in line. I want the First Brigade to be the lead unit of the march. Congratulations, Colonel. You will lead the first increment of sixty thousand men in the greatest parade Washington City has ever seen. Insure the men are cleaned up, equip them with new uniforms, remounts, and shined brass. It will be glorious, John, simply glorious."

John was too tired to speak. He simply nodded, and headed back to his tent. "A blasted parade," he grumbled to Khan Singh, as he wearily pulled off his boots. "Sleep is more to my liking, right now. Then, a quick trip to Gloria and a life of my own. Parades be damned."

He was softly snoring as soon as his head hit his pillow. Khan Singh stood looking down at the man he loved like a son, and even more. "Yes, Sahib. A life of your own. May it be so." Carefully, he pulled a thin blanket over the sleeping man and turned down the oil lantern until only a very slight glow pierced the darkness. With a final glance at the silent figure, he slipped out of the tent. "May it be so," he said again, softly, before tiptoeing away, to his own waiting bunk.

CHAPTER 31

John snapped the silver lid of his watch shut. It was precisely five minutes until nine a.m. He turned in his saddle. His brigade was mounted, assembled at the intersection of Pennsylvania Avenue and Independence Road, awaiting his command to begin the march. Up ahead, he could see General Grant on his black charger, Cincinnati, and his Army of the Potomac battle staff, along with numerous mounted flag bearers, all nervously counting the minutes until the start of the Grand Review. Grant would lead the march and after saluting the new president, Andrew Johnson, peel off to join the commander in chief on the reviewing stand.

Custer was up with the big brass, laughing and cutting up, ever cognizant of a chance to impress his superiors. His golden hair was cut short, as his vow to grow it until the war ended had finally come true. He wore a black, velvet coat with gold braid clear past the elbows and his signature scarlet kerchief tied around his neck. A flowing ostrich feather fully two feet long swept back from the brim of his black campaign hat.

General Meade, the nominal commander of the Army of the Potomac, sat dourly on a bay horse, his face in a scowl, alone, as everyone else fawned over Grant and Custer.

John strained to hear any commands shouted over the snorting and stamping of the thousands of horses. Bands assembled in the park across the street from the reviewing stand set up on the grounds of the White House were playing martial music. He had been told over a thousand musicians would be playing as the massed armies marched by. It would take that many to do these men justice, John thought to himself. The estimates were that it would take six hours for the entire Grand Army of the Republic, as the newspapers called it, to march past a single spot.

Lee Mansur trotted up. "The men all ready, Lee?" John asked of his loyal friend and subordinate.

"Yep. They're itchin' to start. Nearly half are scheduled to catch the six-o'clock train to Detroit tonight, me included. We don't want to miss it."

John nodded. He had spoken to them one last time as their commander, just prior to marching from their assembly area to the start point of the parade. He had blushed in fiery red pleasure and humility when the men raised their voices in a rousing cheer for him at the conclusion of his good-bye. It had been a poignant moment for both him and the men of the Michigan Brigade.

John had been gratified to see that every man had a maroon kerchief around his neck, the same deep color as the turbans Khan Singh and his brother Khim wore on their heads. Every other member of the Singh warrior's clan was at home, recovering from minor wounds suffered during the last, bloody days of the war. Unconsciously, John fingered his kerchief, to make certain the ends were free of his collar.

"Should be no problem, Lee. We'll be done before noon, I'll wager. Pity the Commissary Corps drivers. They're not scheduled to even start until two this afternoon."

"Wonder if they'll be as late to this as they usually were when bringing us supplies in the field." Lee looked around. It was a picture-perfect day, warm, sunny, just a touch of breeze. Suddenly, he spoke. "I'll miss you, my wonderful British friend. Three years as close to you as a brother I grew up with. Thanks to you, I got promotions, excitement, glory and honor to last me a lifetime." He held out his hand. "I'll always be there if you need me, John Whyte."

"And go that double for me, my Yankee friend. You helped me, those early days when I first arrived and did not know which way the wind was blowing. Thank you, Lee. Well, there goes Grant and his staff. Sergeant Major Singh."

"Yes, Sahib." Khan Singh gave as snappy a salute as John ever received.

"Unfurl the colors. Give the order. By column of eights by regiment. Forward, march." John gently spurred his black horse and trotted after Merritt, surrounded by his staff and battle flags. He heard Khan Sing shout his commands and sensed the thousand men of the First Michigan Brigade in motion behind him, the noise of thousands of iron horseshoes clacking on the hard macadam and rounded stone surface of Pennsylvania Avenue.

Every man was aligned, the colors were flapping, the pride of a combat tested unit showed in the men as they marched down the avenue, twenty yards behind their famous colonel. The sidewalks and open areas were filled with countless civilian and military spectators. Women waved their lace hankies and men raised their hats as everyone shouted and cheered.

The sounds of military music grew louder and the horses picked up the tempo, pacing in step, their heads bobbing in unison as the seasoned war horses carried their riders forward. John held the reins in his left hand, his right holding his sword, cocked so the flat edge of the blade rested on his right shoulder.

As they passed the huge stands, built up ten feet high so the president and the others would gaze down on the marchers, John shouted, "First Michigan Brigade. Eyes right!" As he did, he dropped his sword point to his right foot, and turned to look toward the new president, a nondescript political hack named

Johnson. He heard the snap of his troopers as they turned, saluted with their swords, and dipped the regimental colors. He saw a young man lean over and whisper into the bearded, bespectacled president's ear. "Probably telling him which unit he's receiving a salute from," John thought to himself.

He saw the president mouth the words, "Well done, First Michigan," and surprisingly, felt a lump in his throat.

As John passed beyond the reviewing stand, he called out, "Ready, front!" and cocked his wrist, replacing his sword against his shoulder. From there, he led the men to the next intersection, where the regiment turned right toward its release point. John swallowed a lump in his throat and dismissed the men to Lee, and then decided to return to the reviewing stand.

He invited Khan Singh. "I just want to watch for a while, old friend. Do you care to join me?"

"Yes, Sahib. I too wish to see this wondrous parade. It's like will not be seen again."

John stood with several senior officers on the grass, next to the stand. He watched as Custer climbed the steps and joined Grant and Sheridan with President Johnson in the rough, wooden reviewing stand. "I wish Lincoln could have lived to see this," he whispered to Khan Singh.

Row after row of cavalry clattered by and then, file after file of infantry, marching in unison, their shining rifles and gleaming bayonets sparkling in the warm sun. "Look at them, old friend. Young and old, veteran and recruit, hero and coward, from Maine to California, all marching past us and into history. Yesterday they saved the country and tomorrow they'll be at their job or farm, reclaiming the life they left behind. Isn't it magnificent?"

John stayed rooted to his position until the last unit marched past, enthralled at the spectacle. Khan Singh stayed at his side, silent, his thoughts unspoken, watching, marveling at the immense power of his new country.

John was pensive as he walked home with the throngs of people at the end of the day. He bid farewell to Lee one last time and sent him off to the train station. He and Khan Singh were themselves leaving the next morning for Romney. The old Sikh insisted on accompanying John, despite his protests.

When the two soldiers rode up to the front of the great house at Glorietta, she was in his arms as soon as he stepped off his horse. Their kisses were so long, so deep, so many, that Khan Singh finally asked if he could take John's horse to the stables before the supper was served.

John and Gloria could barely execute polite conversation at supper, their longing for each other was so urgent. As soon as time would politely allow, John excused himself, and with Gloria, retired up to their bedroom.

Many happy moments later, John rolled over and let a deep breath escape from his lungs. His chest was wet with perspiration. He had just released five months of loneliness, desire, and tension. Gloria was panting as well, as she slipped into her familiar place, nestled tight against him, her head on his muscular shoulder.

She teased his ear with the tip of her tongue, savoring the light flavor of salt from his perspiration. "Darling," she whispered.

"Umph," John was almost asleep, enjoying her ministrations while drifting off. "What, dear?"

Gloria took his hand in hers. "Feel." She placed his hand on her stomach. John lazily rubbed her belly, feeling the taut firmness, like a melon beneath the surface of her stomach. Suddenly, he was wide-awake. "Gloria. Are you? Are you with child?"

Gloria lightly pinched his earlobe. "Yes, you silly goose. From your last visit here. Our baby will be born in September."

John sat up in the bed. "Oh, honey. Did I hurt you just now? Was I too rough? I'm so sorry."

"Don't be silly. I loved it. I'll let you know when you have to be gentle, don't worry. Until then, just love me as you always have, again and again. It is wonderful."

John lay back down, cradling her in his arms. He kissed her, lovingly and tenderly. "I'm so very happy, my dear."

"Are you really, John? I am."

"Very much so."

"I'm glad, darling. I want us to have many children. Lots of sons and maybe a daughter or two running around underfoot. I want this house to ring with their laughter."

John was silent for a moment. "Don't you think we should make our child legitimate?"

"Yes, my dearest, yes. Oh, yes. As soon as possible. I love you so very much, my British Yankee."

"How about tomorrow?"

Gloria shook her head. "No, not tomorrow, but Sunday? We could go into Romney and be married in the church there."

"Excellent. I can't wait."

Gloria giggled, and reaching down grasped him unexpectedly. "You don't need to, my stallion. Have your way now, please dearest John, do it now. Oh, oh, yes."

The next day was filled with wondrous joy for the expectant father. He revealed the secret to Khan Singh, and the old warrior rejoiced at the news. John spent most of the afternoon looking over the estate, deciding what needed immediate attention. As evening approached, he hurried home to Gloria, eager to show her the depth and strength of his love and passion for her.

On Saturday morning, Gloria joined him at the veranda table, both relishing the view of the sun rising across the unplowed fields and forest beyond. "Darling." She smiled at him and squeezed his hand with hers. "Let's go up to the mine today. We'll take lunch and pick up some salt. Do you mind?"

"No, not at all. That sounds smashing. I've missed the tranquility we found there last summer." He smiled back at his love. "I'll take Khan Singh. While we're relaxing, he can try to kill us a deer or two."

The ride was delightful. The clearing was cool and peaceful. He helped Gloria down and gave the reins of their horses to the still-mounted Sikh. "Take the horses over there, old friend." He pointed to a field next to the woods. "They can graze near the water." Khan Singh nodded and swung away, headed for the grassy glade, just out of sight of the mine entrance.

Gloria gave John a hearty kiss and turned away, looking for a place to lay out their picnic in the basket John had carried. He looked so tall and handsome in his army pants with the yellow cavalry stripe down the seam, and his white, linen shirt. She only caught the movement out of the corner of her eye at first. She had to twist her head to see what had caught her attention.

What is was made her heart leap into her throat, effectively shutting off any sound save a slight gasp. A dirty, baby-faced youth, young and so frightened that even from where she stood, it was evident, was aiming a rifle right at John's chest. Time slowed like poured molasses. She watched in horror as the youth's finger squeezed the trigger and the hammer fell on the copper percussion cap. She instinctively threw herself back, between John and the assassin. "Wait" came out in a strangled sort of croak.

John sensed Gloria's sudden movement and turned toward her. The crack of the rifle and her grunt of pain were almost simultaneous. The impact of the bullet hitting her just above her left breast drove her into John arms. He staggered back with her sudden, limp weight. She looked up at him, just for a second seeing him, and then her gaze widened in surprise, as she looked into the beyond, seeing nothing of this world again.

John had looked upon the face of death many times and he
knew what he saw. His Gloria was dead. Unable to hold her, he
let her slip from his grasp, to the ground at his feet. He looked
around. What had happened? In the brush by the mine entrance,
the shocked, grimy face gaped at him and the crumpled Gloria.
John's primordial scream of rage and pain, as he rushed the
shaken youth, hampered the terrified man's desperate attempt
to reload his Enfield musket. Out of the woods Khan Singh galloped, his rifle at the ready.

Unnerved by the charging men, both roaring like mad wolves,
the youth panicked. He could shoot or stab John with the
bayonet on the end of his rifle. He tried to do both. By the time
he finished and swung the muzzle up at John, the enraged man
was upon him. John tore into the youth like a battering ram. He
drove him to the ground with a flurry of blows and then
encircling the skinny neck with his two hands, picked him off
the ground.

Shaking the terrified youth like a chicken he screamed at
him. "Why? Why? What were you thinking of?"

The youth was gasping for air and blubbering like a child at
the same time. "My sergeant. Left me here nearly a month ago.
Said to watch the place. Shoot any Yanks what came around.
He's supposed to come back two weeks ago. He still hain't
come. I'm sorry, mister. I was gonna shoot you, not the pretty
lady."

Shaking the youth like a dog shakes a rabbit John screamed
over and over. "Damn you, damn you! The war's over! Damn
you!"

Khan Singh touched John on the arm. "Sahib, the memsahib?"

John looked through his tears at the concerned face of his old
friend. "Dead, my God, she's dead." He glared at the blubber-

ing boy. "I should kill you like the dog you are, damn you. But, I'm not. I want you to live a long, long time. And every day, I want you to remember that you killed a sweet, wonderful woman and her unborn child. And every day, I want you to try and live a life that makes that senseless waste worthwhile. Now run from here, damn you. I never want to see you again. If I do, I will kill you on the spot."

He dropped the youth and grabbed the dropped rifle. With strength born of rage, he drove the bayonet deep into the exposed root of a tree, where it stood like a monument to the madness. He turned back to Gloria, ignoring the blubbering youth. Khan Singh watched grimly, as the young soldier scurried off, running like the hounds of Hell were after him.

John picked up Gloria and carried her in his arms the entire way back to the house, crying like a child. For her, for all the others that he had seen die. He carried her to their bed and tenderly helped a sobbing Hattie wash the blood from her and dress her in her finest gown, one of pale blue and white lace.

Finished, he drew a chair up beside the bed. Holding his bowed head in his hands, or holding her hand, he sat through the night, and the next day, and the next night. He did not eat, nor leave, but remained on guard of his love, tears of anguish and grief coursing down his face almost without ceasing. On the third day, Khan Singh came into the room and stood beside him.

"Sahib, you must let me take her to her coffin now. We must place her in the earth, as is your custom."

"Never," John snarled, his rage deadly and near insanity. "I'll never seal her in the darkness of the grave. Never."

"Sahib," Khan Singh's voice was soft, gentle, as if talking to a child who had no understanding, but firm in its purpose. "We must. Her soul has flown on, to the next life. Look at her remains, Sahib. Her flesh darkens. Soon she will begin to smell and putrefy. You don't want to remember her like that. Give her to me, my son. I will be gentle with her. Go with Hattie. Eat and drink something. I will call you when I am done."

Sobbing in agony, John walked away, trusting his old friend. He came back later, to kiss her cool lips one last time, and watched in silence as the lid was nailed on the rough wooden coffin. Together with Khan Singh, followed by Hattie, sobbing and prostrate in her grief, they carried the coffin to the graveyard. Khan Singh had dug a fresh grave on the empty side of her son's tiny grave. John stood in mute agony as the grave was covered, his face contorted in grief. Hattie wailed and sobbed beside him, but John's eyes were dry. He had shed all his tears.

For the next three days he sat on the porch during the day, numb with grief. Every evening, he took a fresh bouquet of flowers to the new grave, as she had done, when first they had met. He sent Khan Singh in to Romney and had a stone made. It joined the other two stones, gleaming white against their weathered surface. Every night he lay the flowers against it, and reread the words.

Gloria Hayes Cortland
1839–1865

At peace with those she loved.
Mourned by those she left behind.

On the fourth day, John glumly watched as two men rode up the drive toward him. He did not recognize either. They stopped and dismounted, climbing up the steps to the veranda where John listlessly watched them. The older man mopped his hat brim and shifted his weight from one foot to the other as he spoke. The younger, a one-armed man whose pale face was vaguely familiar, glared at John.

"Howdy, Colonel Whyte, ain't it?" He went on as John did not answer, pausing for a moment while Khan Singh imposed his massive bulk beside John's chair. "I'm County Magistrate Jenkins, from Romney. This here is Mrs. Cortland's brother, Preston Hayes. He done come back from a Yankee, pardon me, Union prison in Delaware. He says he's the heir to this here estate. Colonel, was you and Mrs. Cortland married?"

John looked at the one-armed man. "No, we had not yet taken our vows. Hello, Mr. Hayes. Gloria spoke of you often. I'm glad you returned home safely."

The man's voice was vehement in its hatred. "I can't say the same, Yankee. If you didn't marry Gloria, then I want you gone outa here, now. You hear me, Yankee?"

"You want this place, Mr. Hayes?"

"No, I just want you outta here. Saves me puttin' you next to that whore out there. A damned traitor, even considerin' marrying the likes of you."

John was out of his chair like a shot, startling both men, Khan Singh right behind him. John grabbed the young Hayes by the lapels of his jacket, his eyes aflame, but his voice so soft you had to strain to hear it. "Speak ill of Gloria once again and I'll gut you to your backbone, and feed your liver to the dogs. You hear me?"

The sheriff hastily tried to cool things down with persuasion. The pistol that had magically appeared in Khan Singh's massive hand kept him from doing any more. "Easy, Colonel Whyte. Mr. Hayes didn't mean that to come out that way. However, sir, I'm afraid he has the legal right to ask you to vacate. He done filed as next of kin to Mrs. Cortland's estate back in Romney and this place is his, by law."

John sadly shook his head. "You hate me so, Mr. Hayes?"

"You and all Yankees. You ruined our land and killed us, just to free a bunch of no-good blacks. You ruined our dream of freedom, damn you all."

"Your dream was washed away in the blood of brave men, Mr. Hayes, and your land scoured by the fire of retribution." John shook his head. "I'm weary of killing, Mr. Hayes, so I'll go and be damned to you, sir. However, I am going to place fresh flowers on Gloria's grave at sunset one last time. If you try and stop me, I will kill you where you stand."

The sheriff nodded, anxious to defuse the tense situation. "That'll be jus' fine, Colonel. I'll bring Mr. Hayes out here to-morrey. You take your time about leavin' till then. Fair enough?"

John nodded his head wearily. He was tired of the both of them. "We'll be gone by dark, sir. The place may be yours by law, but, if you damage those graves, or ever speak ill of your sister again, I'll be back, I swear to you. I'll kill you as fast as I'd kill a mad dog. Your sister was a wonderful human being and deserves homage, not scorn from the likes of you."

Preston Hayes backed off the porch, shaken by the rage he had engendered in the man who was almost his brother-in-law. He said nothing, but awkwardly climbed on his horse. He was not eager to try the man any farther. The hate he felt was tempered by the need for caution. He stiffly nodded at John. "So be it, you have my word." Then turned and rode down the drive.

The sun was dipping behind the low clouds over the Blue Ridge Mountains when John carried his flowers to Gloria's grave for the last time. He tried to speak, but a strangled, "Good-bye, my dearest" was all he could force past the bitter lump in his throat.

He stood there for a long time, grieving. Finally, he walked back to where Khan Singh waited, already mounted and holding John's horse by the reins. John climbed into the saddle and silently guided his horse down the drive toward the road. At the turn, he looked back. The white of Gloria's stone was still vis-

323

ible in the descending gloom. He sighed, his heart constricting with pain and grief, then turned back to the road ahead. It was dark, lonely, empty, foreboding. Savagely he dug his spurs into his horse's flanks. With a snort of surprise, the animal bolted straight ahead, into the night.

ABOUT THE AUTHOR

Thom Nicholson was born in Springfield, Missouri, and grew up in Northern Arkansas and Southwest Missouri. He graduated from Missouri School of Mines with a bachelor's degree in nuclear engineering. During the summers he worked out west for the US Forest Service in forest-fire suppression.

After college he briefly worked in a uranium mine in New Mexico before joining the US Army, where his first assignment was to play post football at Fort Knox, Kentucky. He then graduated from the Officer Candidate School at Fort Benning, Georgia, of which he is now in its Hall of Fame. After graduation, he attended parachutist training. Following an initial assignment to the mountain brigade at Fort Carson, Colorado, he joined Special Forces and trained at Fort Bragg, North Carolina.

His initial overseas assignment with Special Forces was with the Fifth Group in South Vietnam, where he was the executive officer of Camp A-224, Phu Tuc, in the highland mountains of II Corps. His camp was actively engaged in interdiction operations against the Viet Cong. Upon his return he was assigned to Fort Leonard Wood, Missouri, training recruits for several months before he returned to Special Forces, first to Panama and then back to Republic of Vietnam, where he was assigned to CCN, MACV-SOG, engaged in behind-the-lines interdiction operations against the North Vietnamese Army. He was the S-3 plans officer, then the S-1 personnel officer, followed by Company B (Hatchet Force) Commander until his return to

Fort Bragg, North Carolina, where he was the chief of Phase IV training to enlisted SF soldiers.

After his discharge from active duty, he joined the Twelfth Special Forces (Reserve) and served in the active Reserves until his retirement in 1996 as a full colonel with over thirty-three years' service. He worked as a professional engineer in his civilian status, obtaining his MBA from Pepperdine University through the GI Bill. He is a registered professional engineer, a graduate of the Industrial College of the Armed Forces, and an Enrolled Agent of the IRS. He has worked for thirty years as a football official, both in high school and college. He is married to Sandra, a public-school speech pathologist, and lives with her in Highland Ranch, Colorado, where they are retired. He writes Western novels while working on his golf game in the summer and skiing in the winter. They have five grown children, scattered from Washington, DC, to Portland, Oregon.